KILLING TIME

K. T. MCCAFFREY

About the Author

A graduate of the National College of Art and Design, K. T. McCaffrey has for the past decade operated a successful graphics practice in Dublin, specialising in corporate and tourist-related design. K. T. is the author and illustrator of eight children's books, based on Irish folklore . His first adult novel, *Revenge*, was published by Marino Books in 1999. A native of Clara, County Offaly, K. T. now lives in Dunshaughlin with spouse, son and five feline friends.

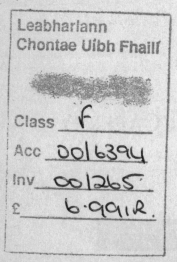

Emma smiled politely at the garda, assumed the role of pathologist, and entered the room. At first nobody noticed her. She watched as two men from the garda forensic unit went about their business, seemingly oblivious to her presence. Flashbulbs lit up the room with all the erratic brilliance of a lightning storm. She moved towards the bed. Alan McCall's body, like some waxwork, lay naked on blood-encrusted sheets, his neck exposed, hacked and clotted with globs of blackened blood, his face distorted into a grimace of terror. Emma's hand shot to her mouth in an effort to stifle the involuntary gasp that came from her throat. It was horrible. Death was never pretty, but this was grotesque.

1

A wash of amber light delineated the clean-cut features of McCall's face as he sat behind the wheel of his parked Volvo 850TDi saloon. Listening to the car radio, waiting for the 6.30 evening news headlines, he lit a cigarette and inhaled deeply. On the street outside, pedestrians hurried past his car, avoiding puddles from an earlier shower, casting great shadows as they moved in and out of the street lamps' radiant spill. With shoulders hunched against the January cold, they appeared anxious to get away from work and into the warmth of their flats, bedsits or whatever shelter they called home. None was aware of the politician sitting inside the dark green car. That such a car, or indeed its occupant, should be parked outside Number 32 Leeson Crescent never gave them a moment's concern. Their thoughts were most probably fixed on a hot meal, a loved one waiting to greet them and the escape, however temporarily, from the demands of the workplace.

If any one of them had bothered to peer through the smoked glass of the Volvo, they would have had difficulty in discerning what lay behind the enigmatic expression on the politician's face. Sitting in the semi-darkness, enjoying his smoke, it was doubtful whether Alan McCall himself could sum up the scatter of emotions running riot in his overcrowded mind. He wanted to listen to the news before going into Number 32, in case there was any mention of the planned government reshuffle.

He was not disappointed. Towards the end of the bulletin, the newsreader referred to the imminent reshuffle, speculating on who would be demoted and hinting at those who might be moved sideways or dropped altogether. Tom Pettit was, according to the newsreader, hot favourite to take over the Agricultural portfolio. This suggestion brought a wry smile to Alan McCall's face. Yes, he thought, even Tom Pettit thinks of himself as the favourite, believing he has the job in the bag. But Pettit was wrong. No one knew that better than McCall. Four hours earlier the Taoiseach, Fionnuala Stafford, had called Alan into her office and confirmed that the agricultural ministry was his if he wanted it. Did he want it? Was the Pope a Catholic? Did Dolly Parton sleep on her back? Yes, of course he bloody-well wanted it. He wanted it more than anything else in the world. Getting one of the top ministries meant he could realistically expect to get the Taoiseach's job one day or at least become party leader. He was a happy man. It was great news, though hardly a surprise to him; he had long believed he was the most suitable candidate for the job. Alan willingly admitted that Pettit had more experience at the cabinet table, having held senior posts in two previous administrations, but at almost sixty, Pettit was twenty-five years older than him, too old for the new party image. These days, age counted.

Although the official announcement would not be made for two or three days, he would celebrate his good fortune tonight. Behind the granite and brick walls of Number 32 Leeson Crescent, Jacqueline Miller was expecting him. For one long night she would help him celebrate his promotion in the most intimate manner possible. Just thinking about her coaxed stirrings in him. Time to get out of the car.

As the weather forecaster was promising snow on hilly ground for the next day, he switched off the car radio and went through the, by now, familiar ritual that preceded his visits to Number 32. First, he donned a Donegal tweed cap, pulled its peak low on his forehead so that it cast a deep shadow across his eyes; second, he wrapped a scarf around his neck, making sure it covered part of his chin; and finally, from the glove compartment he took a pair of horn-rimmed spectacles, not unlike those worn by Woody Allen, and balanced them on his nose. A glance at his image in the rear-view mirror let him know that he was ready. It was a silly, almost childish disguise – he knew that – but if it helped keep his face off the tabloids' front pages, then it was worth the trouble. To date, he had successfully managed to avoid even the merest whisper of impropriety. It was important to him, especially now, that it stayed that way.

Alan McCall's charmed existence was not nearly as secure as he believed it to be. Unknown to him, a camera's shutter clicked busily away, recording his every move as he walked briskly from his car. Press photographer Frankie Kelly remained hidden behind the laurel hedge that marked the boundary between Jacqueline Miller's house and her nearest neighbour, his eye firmly pressed to the camera's viewfinder. Leaves and branches, still wet from an earlier shower, soaked his clothes and prodded his body from every conceivable angle. He would probably end up catching a cold but he considered the risk a small price to pay if the pictures turned out to be good.

For the previous two hours the plain terraced exterior of the Georgian four-storey plus basement had filled the small viewfinder. Initially, as his vigil began, the bricks glowed red in the setting sun but later, neutered by reflected street light, they appeared grey and drab. He had watched distorted shadows from the wrought-iron balconies on the second floor stretch all the way down to the mock-rustic basement wall with little enthusiasm. A glow from the peacock-tail fanlight above the front door picked out the iron lamp standards on either side of the entrance; it was the only architectural feature that Frankie Kelly had concerned himself with. It was important to know whether the politician would choose to climb the steps that led to the main door on the first floor level or enter through the basement door situated directly beneath the steps.

Now, at last, he knew.

McCall choose to descend the three steps that brought him to the ground-floor entrance. This was what Kelly had hoped for. It provided him with a better angle for his pictures. As the side door opened, dim light from the hallway silhouetted a woman's head. The kiss that followed was captured on celluloid; politician and mistress caught forever in a fleeting moment of intimacy, before disappearing into the safety of the building. One last frame of the closed door ended the segment of filming for Kelly. A smile of satisfaction crossed his face briefly as he rolled the film to its end, removed the cartridge and carefully housed it in its container.

It was now time to make some decisions. Should he sneak off to a restaurant, grab a bite to eat or should he wait and see if his subjects left the house later in the evening? They were unlikely to go out, he decided; in all probability they would dine, wine and make love behind the safety of the red–brick walls of Number 32. No point in hanging around all evening freezing his balls off. Decision made: he would go back to base and drop the film into the press-lab boys. After that he would smoke a joint and drop into Cassidy's for a pint.

But the more immediate question on his mind was: what time would the politician emerge from his love nest in the morning? Very early, he suspected. Certainly before eight o'clock. McCall would want to get as far away as possible from Leeson Crescent under the cover of darkness. Well, so be it, the camera would be ready to capture the little scene whenever it happened. A shot of McCall leaving was a vital requirement for the completion of his pictorial exposé. His imagination took flight. Would the mistress, wearing nothing more than a negligee, accompany the politician to the door and kiss him good-morning? A nice thought, but no, it was probably too much to hope for. Still, you never knew with people; they got careless at that hour of the morning, never thinking anybody could possibly be lying in wait for them. Well, he could live in hope but whatever happened he would be there to record the scene. The prize was worth the sacrifice. If everything went according to plan, his pictures would be splashed across page one of the *Dublin Dispatch* the following weekend. Another scoop for him, another step up the greasy ladder of success, an opportunity to get noticed by one of the more respectable broadsheets. A front-page spread would greatly add to the photographic portfolio he had already accumulated and was bound to impress any future employer he might encounter. Working for *Dublin Dispatch* was a pain in the butt, but a necessary evil. At twenty-six years of age the time was right to move his career into a higher gear.

Jacqueline Miller wanted Damien gone before McCall called. She offered him a second cup of tea, hoping he'd refuse it – he had always declined in the past – but on this occasion he accepted. Damien, son of her only sister Regina, had chosen a most awkward time to call on her. He usually did but until now his unannounced visits had never interfered with her secret love life. Damien, a slight young man of twenty-one, stood barely taller than her own five-seven and possessed better than average looks. His hair, true to Miller genes, had the same rich texture and chestnut colour as her own, making the family resemblance unmistakable. In moments of total honesty, she admitted to herself that he represented the son she never had. She had lavished on him more love than one would normally expect from an unmarried aunt. This display of affection had, as often as not, manifested itself in the form of monetary offerings. In recent years she had given substantial amounts of money to set him up in his own graphic design business.

Today she had promised him further funding for a new development he had planned.

'It will all come back to you a hundredfold, Aunt Jac,' he had promised her with total assurance. She knew he meant what he said – he always did – but she doubted whether she would ever see a penny of her money again. It did not bother her to any great extent. It was enough that it helped him to build a business that would one day sustain him. As for the money itself, she could well afford it and, besides, the pleasure it gave her to see the contentment on Damien's face was all the reward she sought.

Damien finished his second cup of tea and wiped biscuit crumbs from the side of his mouth with a paper tissue. 'I'll just wash the cup before I go, Aunt Jac,' he said, getting up from his chair and making his way to the kitchen.

'No, no, leave that to me,' Jacqueline said, relieving him of the cup and saucer, 'I'll put these in the washer with the other stuff . . . I can do it later.'

Damien opened his mouth to speak but stopped

short when the door bell rang. For a split second Jacqueline froze, recovered almost as quickly and then smiled unconvincingly at her nephew. 'That'll be the friend I was expecting . . . downstairs door. Look, Damien, you run on. Let yourself out; I'll go down and let him in. Ring me next week when you've set up the arrangements with your bank . . . I'll make out the cheque then, all right?'

Damien kissed his aunt on the cheek and gave her his usual self-conscious half-embrace, a gesture that never failed to amuse her.

'Thanks again for your help,' he said, 'I don't know what I'd do without you.'

'You know what I always say, Damien, what's the use of having a favourite nephew if I can't spoil him, huh?'

The downstairs door bell chimed again.

'Go ahead, run along,' she said, trying to sound casual as she made her way down the stairs to the side door.

Seeing Alan McCall in his foolish disguise never failed to bring a smile to Jacqueline's face. She planted a quick kiss on his lips and ushered him inside. 'It's good to see you, *Woody*! Come in and take off those ridiculous glasses.'

'That's right, don't spare my feelings, take the pee out of me before I even set foot inside the house. Still and all, 'tis good to see you, Jac; you've no idea how much I need you.'

'Oh, I think I can imagine that bit all right, but listen: I've just had a visit from my nephew, Damien . . . he's leaving by the front door. I'd have introduced you to him except . . . well, it might be a bit awkward . . . you know . . . too many explanations needed.'

'You're right, Jac . . . best not to complicate things, not yet at any rate.'

As Alan and Jacqueline made their way up the stairs that led to the living quarters, they heard the front door close. 'Good, he's gone,' Jacqueline said. 'We have the house all to ourselves.'

'Indeed we have . . . quality time . . . just the two of us together . . . the whole night.' Alan punctuated his words with kisses, his hands already seeking her breasts. Jacqueline responded in kind, her hands reaching for his bottom, pressing him closer to her. 'God, you're on song this evening,' she said, with a chuckle, 'will you be wanting a spot of supper . . . or should we . . . '

'Yes, we should, we should . . . go straight to the bedroom. We just might surface for the nine o'clock news on the box, take a breather, have a bite maybe, then back to the grind – slaves to our passion.'

They had already begun to undress each other before they made it to the door of the bedroom.

Sarah McCall was just about to hang up the telephone when she heard someone speak on the other end of the line. 'Yes,' a breathless voice said, 'this is Greg Mooney, can I help you?'

'Ah, Greg, how are you, this is Sarah McCall here; I was just about to hang up, I thought . . . '

'Yes, I know, Sarah, I was outside my front door when I heard the ringing . . . dashed in, thought it might be someone important . . . '

'Well, sorry to disappoint you, Greg, it's only me, and it's not important at all. I was wondering if Alan was with you. It's just that I wanted a word with him.'

'No, Sarah, Alan is not with me. I was with him about two hours ago down at his department. He left before I did. Did you try the apartment in Clyde Road?'

'Yes I did but the voice-mail was all I got. No, you see, I rang you because Alan said he would stay with you . . . said he wanted to get some notes done for a meeting with the Taoiseach in the morning . . . said something about needing a little help from you on it.'

'Hum, yes, I see. Well, maybe I'm mistaken but I don't recall hearing him say anything of that nature to me. Are you sure? Any chance you might have got your dates wrong?'

'Wrong? No, I don't think so . . . Alan said . . . '

'What I mean is: the house is not in session tomorrow . . . I'd say he's probably heading back to you even as we speak.'

'I'm sure you're right, Greg. I'm sorry to have bothered you. Talk to you again soon. Cheerio.'

'Yeah, right; Cheers, Sarah.'

Sarah replaced the telephone and looked at the instrument in dazed silence. Only the sound of the twins, John and Stephen, could be heard coming from their upstairs bedroom, as they played with their Sony Playstation. Like most nine-year-olds, they were hooked on video and computer games, an enthusiasm their father indulged shamelessly. Alan enjoyed spoiling the boys and they, in turn, saw him as the best person in the whole universe. It was their habit to race down the stairs when they heard him come in the door in the evening, jump into his arms and tell him about their day. He would invariably have some little gifts for them.

Instinctively, she felt that this would not happen this evening. Alan had told her he was staying with Greg Mooney, said he had to have reports ready for an early breakfast meeting the next morning. He had been specific: his meeting was with the Taoiseach and it would be held in the Taoiseach's Leinster House office. It was obvious from the telephone call that Alan was not staying with Greg Mooney, and equally obvious that there was no sitting in the Dáil the following day. So, what was she to think? Alan had always signalled free days from the Dáil well in advance to her. He looked forward to days when they could spend a little more time together. Had something happened to change all that? It appeared something had, but what?

Her mind raced over recent events, trying to see if she could detect anything out of the ordinary that might have happened. But, no, nothing *had* happened, certainly nothing bad, nothing untoward. On the contrary, the reverse was the case; their life together had become better, their time together more precious, their loving more intense, more adventurous. In recent months Alan had found new ways of expressing his sexual prowess and she had responded with a passion she didn't know she possessed. It was like discovering the sensuality of their bodies all over again – a second honeymoon – only this time without the fumbling and awkwardness that was the hallmark of their attempts ten years earlier. It was good back then but now it was terrific.

The clock on her kitchen wall said 8.00 p.m. She tried to dismiss the implications of what Greg Mooney had said to her. Was it possible, she asked herself, that she could be wrong about such things? Yes, she decided, she was wrong; she had been jumping to conclusions, wild conclusions, and they were all the wrong conclusions. The telephone would ring any second now, Alan would put her mind at rest; there would be a perfectly reasonable explanation for the change of plans. Equally, there would be an innocent reason why he was late coming home. He had probably run into an old friend; most likely they had gone for a drink and he was by now on his way home to her and the twins. Yes, that was it. She felt better. For a moment there she had herself going, thinking the unthinkable, working herself into a tizzy over nothing. She smiled at the silliness of it all. She would switch on the television and wait for him. When he came through the door she would, for once, get to him before the twins and tell him how much she loved him. Yes, that's exactly what she would do. All of a sudden she felt so much better.

2

Greg Mooney sat in front of his television, remote control in hand, switching channels but not registering any of the images that flashed across the screen. From the kitchen his wife chatted about her day but he hardly heard her. His thoughts were anchored back on the telephone conversation he had had with Sarah McCall half an hour earlier. The fact that Sarah believed her husband might be with him was a source of curiosity. It could be entirely innocent – probably was – but he was forced to consider whether or not there could be other possibilities? Could Alan be using him as an alibi to cover up some clandestine activity? Perhaps he was jumping to wild conclusions, becoming paranoid, seeing potential scandals around every corner. It was Sarah's reference to Alan's meeting with the Taoiseach in the morning that triggered his disquiet. He would like to know from what source she had got such erroneous information? He knew for a fact that the Taoiseach had flown out on the Government jet from Baldonnel aerodrome only hours earlier for a private meeting with the British Prime Minister and would not be back until late the following day. This would make it impossible for Alan McCall to meet with her in the morning.

Mooney searched for explanations, considered all the possibilities, but came up with no obvious answers. Alan McCall had, on a few previous occasions, stayed over in his house but that was back when they both had worked on the party fund-raising committee. Their term as members on that committee had ended some months previously and he could think of no reason why Alan should lead Sarah to believe it was still necessary to stay overnight with him. So, what sort of game was McCall playing? Was he cheating on Sarah? He was a handsome man – there was no denying that – and he certainly appealed to the ladies, but as far as Mooney could tell, Alan had never shown any signs of straying. Sarah and the twins had appeared with him on the opening day of the Dáil and had cheerfully posed for the photographers outside Leinster House. All in all, McCall did not strike him as the sort of man who would do something stupid to upset the family. So what was he up to now? Most likely nothing . . . but you never knew . . . sometimes it was the so-called steady ones who sprang the biggest surprises.

Greg Mooney's own seat had been secured by the most slender of margins in the last election, less than one hundred votes separating him from the nearest loser. In government, he had been given the position of junior minister at the Department of the Marine – referred to by his colleagues as the *Fish 'n' Ships* – but he was happy there and got on well with his colleagues. There was, however, a cloud on the horizon. The government's majority in the house was balanced on a knife edge. Their strong appeal to the electorate had in recent months been damaged by news headlines that focused on real and perceived scandals.

Greg Mooney continued to ponder Sarah McCall's telephone call. It would not be prudent, he decided, to call her back and check if Alan had turned up; such action could do more harm than good. The best course of action might be to do nothing at all; after all, nothing had happened. But a gut feeling told him that he ought to take some action, do something to check out the situation.

Feeling apprehensive, he picked up the telephone and dialled Francis Xavier Donnelly. Donnelly, as general secretary, was responsible for watching over the elected members and making sure that none of them rocked the party boat. Donnelly answered the phone himself. Greg's preamble included everything from the state of the weather to the traffic chaos on Dublin's main thoroughfare, before getting around to the purpose of his call. Apologising for probably jumping to the wrong conclusions, he told Francis Xavier about his conversation with Sarah McCall. Donnelly listened without comment until he had finished.

'I'm glad you called me, Greg,' Francis Xavier's bass voice boomed over the lines. 'I'm sure there's nothing to worry about. McCall's a crafty one . . . always plays the cards close to his chest . . . not the sort of deputy to be indiscreet; he's way too clever for that. But look, I'll put out a few feelers, talk to one or two party ward bosses, see if I hear any whispers . . . we can't be too careful these days.'

'Thanks, Francis Xavier,' Greg said, 'I'm probably being an old woman about this but as you said yourself: we can't be too careful.'

'Right you are, Greg. If I hear anything I'll let you know. OK?'

'Yes, yes that's fine.'

'By the way, Greg, we didn't have this conversation.'

'We didn't have . . . ? Oh yes, yes, I see. You're right of course, Francis Xavier; we never spoke a word. Bye.'

McCall stared at the ceiling, a flamboyant display of plasterwork showing birds perched on asymmetrical hoops, and took a loving pull on his cigarette. Above him, the rich flight of fancy, created two hundred years earlier, did little to inspire awe in him. He had stared at the same decorative plasterwork too many times in recent months. The cherubs posing in various attitudes among musical instruments, flowers and rococo arabesque could have done without the whorls of cigarette smoke drifting upwards in their direction. As McCall lay on his back, his head resting on the pillow, one hand softly caressing Jacqueline Miller's breasts, the other occupied with the cigarette, he felt a strange unease. He had yet to tell her about his imminent promotion to a ministerial position in the government or talk about the consequences such a change would bring about in their relationship. He wanted to pick the right opportunity to bring the subject up but there was something else he wished to tell her, something even more profound than his forthcoming elevation to minister, something that would, if not handled correctly, cause both of them grief. Inhaling deeply on his cigarette, his thoughts continued to revolve around his relationship with the woman beside him. She looked so peaceful lying there, bathed in a soft glow of light from the twin bedside lamps, her chest rising and falling in gentle rhythm, her face framed by a mass of tangled chestnut hair, its wild strands etched in sharp relief against the pillow cover.

Their extended bout of lovemaking had exhausted both of them. In the two years that he had known Jacqueline Miller he had never ceased to be amazed by her aura of mystery. It was one of life's strange conundrums that he could have such an intimate relationship with someone and yet know so little about that person's life. He looked at her more closely. Half her face still bore the scars from an accident she had been involved in long before he had met her. Evidence of cosmetic surgery, though subtle, remained visible behind the carefully applied make-up; the left eye looked strangely out of line with the right one. These defects, as far as he was concerned, only helped add layers of extra character to what must have once been a truly beautiful face. She disliked talking about the accident and he had never fully succeeded in finding out what exactly had happened. One thing was sure: what happened on that fateful day had changed her life irrevocably.

On occasions, when he allowed his fingers gently to

trace the scar tracks that ran the length of her body, she froze. He had tried to reassure her by telling her how much he loved her and how every little bit of her, including the parts that had once brought her such pain and suffering, were equally beautiful to him. She never fully accepted his reassurances, and after several unsuccessful attempts to bring the subject into the open he had let it drop.

He had seen her for the first time two years earlier at a Department of Education reception. She had been involved in an animated conversation with some academic-looking types as she held a sherry glass in one hand while expertly balancing a paper plate with a *vol-au-vent* in the other. It was at that point that their eyes happened to meet across the room. For no reason that made sense he had raised his eyebrows and smiled in a way that told her he understood her predicament. She smiled back, acknowledging his gesture, excused herself from the people she had been talking to and approached him.

'I hope you don't mind if I talk to you for a second,' she had said, 'but if I don't get away from those bores over there immediately, I will scream. I told them you were an old friend I had to say hello to.'

That was how it had all began.

They introduced themselves and chatted together like old friends. It turned out that she was the author of a series of local study books that the education department had approved. After the reception they lingered on and shared a coffee.

In the weeks and months that followed, he had engineered opportunities to meet with her and soon enough a friendship had developed. For her it was a platonic relationship but from the beginning he had wanted more. It was as though he had been bewitched by the woman. Until his first meeting with her, he had thought of himself as a happily married man, a lucky man; he had a loving wife and two wonderful children. What more could a man want? Nothing, if common sense, morality and wedding vows counted for anything, but a form of madness had addled his brain, an unquenchable desire had ignited inside him. The strange, flawed beauty of Jacqueline Miller became his obsession.

Eighteen months after their initial meeting, they made love for the first time.

He watched now as Jacqueline moved in the bed. How peaceful she looked there, a post-coital glow of contentment on her face, so serene, so utterly changed from the animated lover she had been since his arrival some hours earlier. With wild, sometimes noisy, abandon, their bodies duelled in a vigorous physical exploration of pleasure with an immediacy and force that had left him fulfilled, satisfied but temporarily drained. Looking at her now he could tell that she had withstood the prolonged lovemaking extravaganza better than he had. Her eyes remained closed but her nostrils seemed to twitch. Her voice, when she spoke, was soft, almost a purr. 'Alan, are you ... are you smoking?'

'Sorry, Jac, but it helps to bring me back down to earth after . . . you know . . . '

'I prefer just to drift away. Jesus, God, Alan, but that was so good; we really were good, weren't we?'

McCall smiled and exhaled a plume of smoke. 'Good? Good? I hardly think a pathetic little word like *good* describes what we had. No, no, no, I'd say we were magnificent.'

'Uum, I agree, we were mag-*nif*-icent.'

'And all on an empty stomach!'

Jacqueline opened her eyes and used her elbows to ease her body into a sitting position. 'Oh I see; not content to foul the air with that awful cigarette, now you're telling me you want something to eat as well, is that it?'

Alan stubbed the cigarette out in the ashtray on the bedside table, turned to her and gave her his best boyish smile. 'A cup of tea wouldn't go amiss. We could have a look at the nine o'clock news while we're at it.'

'And after that?'

'We go back to doing what you and I do best again, Jac . . . We make love till we both die of exhaustion.'

'Uum, sounds good to me.'

Francis Xavier Donnelly rocked the telephone back into its cradle, nodded his head in self-satisfaction and allowed his podgy fingers to beat a tattoo on the desk top while pondering his next move. So far, so good, he mused. He had spoken to five of his contacts in the media and each had, in succession, reported nothing out of the ordinary on Alan McCall; indeed his contact at the television centre had declared McCall to be as clean as a whistle.

As general secretary of the government party and chairman of the Personnel Conduct Code Committee, Francis Xavier Donnelly had created a web of contacts in the country's media institutions. But information, he realised, was no different from any other commodity in the market place; you got the all-important tip-off only if you were prepared to respond in kind. Quality goods cost top dollar; in other words, dish the dirt on the opposition in return. Francis Xavier had become a master tactician, trading in half-truths, gossip, innuendo, intrigue and downright lies. He knew the opposition parties employed similar strategies but he prided himself on being more adept than they were at playing the game. Which was just as well, considering that his party was the one in power and therefore more open to scrutiny and more vulnerable to scandal.

Donnelly felt reasonably sure that there was no need to worry in the case of Alan McCall but he was nothing if not thorough; he decided to make a few last calls to put the matter beyond doubt. Flicking through the pages of his notebook he came to the list of names and numbers of contacts he had managed to establish in the 'underground' and gossip journals. Three such disreputable organs existed in Dublin city, all of them dependent on advertisements for sex-call numbers and the classified columns that purported to seek suitable companions for deviants.

From time to time these journals broke scandals that the more respectable papers considered too risky to go after. It was their practice to inveigle government ministers and other senior politicians, wanting to appear 'cool' or seeking to impress an alternative set of potential voters, to write articles. Donnelly made a point of sifting through each issue in the hope of finding some *faux pas* made by any members of the opposition stupid enough to go into print with half-boiled theories on how to right the wrongs of the world. The articles were usually of the pseudo-intellectual variety, full of high-sounding waffle and laced with idealistic aspirations. Donnelly despised these out-pourings of verbal diarrhoea and garbage, as he termed them, and warned all the deputies on his side of the house not to indulge in this practice.

He telephoned his contacts in the three journals and drew a blank in each case. With a sigh of relief he decided he had nothing to worry about. Feeling satisfied, he prepared to leave his den and retire for the night. He was about to switch off the light when the telephone rang. Cursing silently, he lifted the instrument to his ear. The voice speaking to him sounded familiar but he could not place it.

'Is that Francis Xavier Donnelly?'

'Yes. Who is this, please?'

'Jimmy Rabbitte from the *Dublin Dispatch*. You might remember me from . . . '

'Yes, I remember you,' Donnelly cut in abruptly. 'What can I do for you?'

'You were on to this office about twenty minutes ago, right?'

'Was I indeed?'

'You *were*; no point in denying it. You were putting out feelers about one of your charges. I thought I might be able to help you on that matter.'

'Could you hold on for a second while I switch to my private line.' Donnelly put the call on hold – he was already on the private line – but he needed a moment to think about the caller.

Jimmy Rabbitte, known as something of a maverick in journalistic circles, had worked his way through most of the newspapers and journals in the country. After a bright beginning that promised much, his career began a downward trajectory. Currently employed at the *Dublin Dispatch*, a tabloid that specialised in digging the dirt on the wealthy and famous, no story was too outrageous, no gossip too frivolous for him to run with. Infidelities were the stock and trade of the journal. With the recent spate of governmental peccadilloes, the *Dublin Dispatch* fanned the flames of public outrage irrespective of whether the public gave a damn or not. Candid photographs taken in hotels, restaurants or public places contrived to show well-known personalities with members of the opposite sex – or in certain cases, the same sex – but never with their spouses. Most people condemned the *Dublin Dispatch*, calling it the lowest of the low in gutter journalism but if the sales were anything to go by, an awful lot of people liked the weekly diet of sexual shenanigans they served up.

Donnelly released the hold-button and spoke to Rabbitte. 'Sorry about the delay but we can't be too careful these days. Now, my friend, what was it you wanted to say to me.'

'I'm not your friend, F. X. but I do have something for you.'

'Could you be a little more specific?'

'I have the goods on your beauty boy, Alan McCall.'

Donnelly swallowed hard. 'Well, you know how it works, Jimmy: you tell me what's going down. If it turns out to be something significant, I give you first bite on the more unsavoury aspects of our friends on the opposition.'

'Sorry, F. X. No can do – not on this occasion.'

'What do you mean?'

'Okay, I'll lay it on the line for you. We *do* have something significant right now on your precious Alan McCall but I'm not prepared to divulge it for the crumbs of gossip I get from you. We have an exclusive . . . photographs, the lot. It's a big story . . . going to blow McCall and the government right out of the water.'

'You're bluffing.'

'Am I? Fine, if that's what you want to believe, fine. You just wait and see. Goodbye, Francis Xavier.'

'No, no, wait a sec, hold your horses. If you really have something, it might be worth your while talking to me.'

'Are we talking money here?'

'Well now, that depends, doesn't it? If what you have got warrants it, then yes.'

'Warrant it? Hah, that's a good one. Believe me: what I've got warrants bread all right.'

'I see, I see . . . Look, Jimmy, can we meet?'

'Yeah, why not. I'll see you in twenty minutes in the lounge at the Organ Grinder. Is that OK with you?'

'I'll be there.'

'Oh, Francis Xavier, one other thing.'

'What?'

'Bring your chequebook – a very fat chequebook.

3

Francis Xavier Donnelly found it hard to credit that a public house like the Organ Grinder, located in Dunne Lane, the drabbest of drab side streets, less than a hundred yards off Mary Street, could be allowed to exist in such close proximity to the city centre. It was certainly not the sort of hostelry that would normally attract him; the more fashionable Shelbourne bar or the trendy Lower Baggot Street watering-holes such as Doheny and Nesbitt's being much more to his liking.

Barrelling his short, bulky body past leather-clad bikers and young drinkers of indeterminate gender, he squeezed into the only vacant spot at the counter. Compared to the chilly air outside, the atmosphere inside the pub was positively stifling, the heat ensuring that his glasses fogged up. He removed the rimless spectacles and used a tissue to clear the lenses before ordering a drink. His attempts to catch the eye of a bar attendant met with failure. How was it, he wondered, that bar staff all managed to perfect the art of looking right at you while not being able to see you at the same time? It was one of those quirky facts of life that never failed to irritate him. The leather-and-studs brigade milling about him experienced no such difficulties. Body sweat, stale beer, raucous conversation, rock music and the reek of drug-laden smoke invaded all his senses simultaneously. He could not help but notice the extent to which his mode of dress – pinstripe suit, waistcoat and bow tie – differed to the garb all around him and he cursed Jimmy Rabbitte for arranging to meet him in such a place. Equally unsettling for him, he felt that his fifty years exceeded the average age of the pub's regulars by at least two decades.

Just as he caught the attention of a tall barmaid – whom he suspected of being a transsexual male – a hand clasped his shoulder. 'Hey there, F. X.! You got here I see,' a voice behind him said, shouting to be heard above the din. For once Donnelly was glad to see Jimmy Rabbitte.

'Why in the name of all that's sacred did you pick this dive to meet?' he asked, 'I can't hear my ears with all the racket.'

'Pardon?' Rabbitte said.

'I said I can't . . . '

'I know. Just kidding! It's noisy right enough but that's why I picked the place . . . and apart from that they serve a decent pint.' Rabbitte's smile exposed yellowing teeth, his eyes a gleam of crafty intelligence. 'Come, F. X., there's an alcove beside the jacks. It's a bit on the smelly side, I'm afraid, but we'll be able to talk there.'

Being a regular client, Rabbitte got immediate attention and ordered drinks. He let Donnelly pay for them before moving in the direction of a sign that said 'Toilets'. Compared to Francis Xavier Donnelly's expensive clothes, Rabbitte looked as if he had raided an Oxfam rejects warehouse. He wore a dark-blue blazer that had become shiny with age. Loose threads drew attention to the spot where a silver button had once been and a tear in the breast pocket perfected the overall unkempt appearance. His open-neck shirt revealed a T-shirt that would have benefited considerably from a trip to the launderette. Although he was aware of Donnelly's scrutiny, Rabbitte did not let it bother him. Instead, he got down to business as soon as they were ensconced in the small alcove. 'I've something to show you,' he said, taking a postcard-size black-and-white photograph from his inside breast pocket. 'It's a little dark and the definition is not the best but I think you'll have no difficulty in recognising the subject.'

Donnelly took the photograph in his hand and held it in front of his eyes. The picture, showing a man kissing a woman, appeared to have been taken as the subjects stood in a doorway. 'I can't say that I know either of these people,' he said with exaggerated lack of interest.

'Take away the hat and glasses from the man,' Rabbitte suggested, never taking his eyes off Donnelly's face, 'and I think you'll change your mind.' He saw the almost subliminal flicker of recognition in Donnelly's eyes and knew that Alan McCall had been recognised.

'Could be anyone,' Donnelly said, affecting a dismissive tone as he handed the photograph back to Rabbitte.

'No, Francis Xavier, that's where you're wrong; we both know exactly whose face we're looking at so don't act the bollix with me. The man in that photograph is Alan McCall; it was taken at 6.45 p.m. this very evening. When the lab technicians in the darkroom get to work on definition and contrast there will be no doubt in anyone's mind who it is.'

'Who took the picture?'

'A new kid on the block; his name is Frankie Kelly – handy enough with the camera – gets to the places that other photographers can't reach. He'll be waiting at that same doorway in the morning to record the shagger making his exit from the love nest.'

Donnelly remained silent for a moment, twisting his mouth into a series of grimaces while stroking his chin abstractly with his thumb and forefinger. 'Let me have another look at the photograph,' he said at length. 'I need to think about what I'm going to do.'

'You can think about it till the cows come home, F. X. It won't change a damn thing. The evidence is there in black and white for anyone with an eye in their head to see.'

'OK, OK, all right. How do I spike this story?'

'Can't be done.'

'Of course it can be done; otherwise you wouldn't be here talking to me.'

'Humph, you have a point there right enough, F. X. Yeah, you're right, there might just be a way . . . it's going to cost you a lot of money . . . an awful lot of money.'

'So what else is new?' Donnelly said sarcastically, 'Is there somewhere else besides here where we can discuss this?'

'We can go around to my gaff if you like . . . get down to the nitty-gritty. That suit you F. X.?'

'Anywhere has to be better than here; let's go.'

'Look, look, there's Daddy,' Stephen shouted, pointing to the image on the television screen. Along with his twin brother John, he had been allowed to wait up for the nine o'clock news before going to bed. 'It's just the same old piece that they always show,' John said. 'Hey, Mum, why can't they get new pictures of Dad for the news?'

Sarah McCall forced herself to sound light-hearted. 'What they are showing is from an old file clip; they will only update it if something major happens to your Dad.' Sarah had not expected to see images of Alan flashed across the screen and had not been forewarned that his name would be linked with the impending reshuffle. If she were to believe the political correspondent on the television, Alan had an outside chance of being appointed to the cabinet in the new shake-up. This was news to her. Alan had never said a word about it. She knew how ambitious he was and how he planned to get places in the party but she hadn't expected anything to happen so soon. Perhaps the news had something to do with why he had not come home. Yes, she thought, that had to be the reason. But it did not explain why he had not telephoned her.

After cajoling the twins into their beds, she picked up the telephone and dialled Alan's Dublin apartment. She heard the by now familiar message telling her that nobody was available to take her call and the request to leave a message. 'Damn machines, I hate them,' she said hanging up, knowing that her frustration was aimed at Alan and not the answering machine. Without taking time to consider fully what she was doing, she dialled Greg Mooney's number. She knew Alan would not appreciate her ringing one of his colleagues but it did not bother her now; she needed to know where he had got to. Greg Mooney answered the telephone himself and did not seem all that surprised to hear from her a second time that evening. Skipping the usual pleasantries, she told him that Alan had not yet made contact with her.

"I see,' he said. 'Is there something I can do?'

'Well yes, I was hoping that you might do me a big favour.'

'I'll be delighted to . . . if I can.'

'You're going to think I'm crazy, worrying over nothing, making a mountain out of a molehill, but . . . but, well, the thing is, you live in the city, in Drumcondra, and Alan's apartment is in Clyde Road . . . is it possible that you could go to the apartment? The answering machine might not be ringing out. I'm really sorry about this . . . for bothering you, I know it's an awful imposition but I don't know what else to do.'

There was an ominous silence on the phone for a moment before Greg cleared his throat and spoke.

'It's a bit awkward, Sarah. The wife has friends here at the moment . . . but look, all right, it'll only take me twenty minutes, half an hour at the most, to get across the city this late in the evening. I'll check if Alan is there. I'll contact you then . . . one way or the other.'

'Thanks a million, Greg, I really appreciate it.'

'No problem, Sarah; I'm sure Alan would do the same for me.'

'Yes, yes, of course he would; we both would. Thanks. I'll stay posted by the phone.'

Blood. The blood was everywhere. Jacqueline Miller looked at her hands and screamed again. Her blood-soaked nightdress stuck to her skin; a crimson mist blurred her eyes as her face, like some grotesque sculpture, appeared to be freshly glazed in a coat of red dye.

Madness. The world around her had gone mad. She felt herself drift away, far, far away from the madness all around her. Through a red haze, she watched as the monster entered the room, knife in hand, serrated edge flashing through the air.

Alan lay there, not knowing what was happening. She wanted to scream, warn him, but no sound came from her.

He remained asleep. The knife slashed through his throat. Alan's eyes opened. His body jerked violently before falling still. The black-cloaked monster held the blade inches above the open wound as blood pumped free, down his neck and on to the bed linen.

For Jacqueline, the out-of-body experience continued. Wading through the swirling red mist, she saw herself wrestle with the monster in an attempt to push him away from Alan. Suddenly, all dizziness disappeared. The room stopped spinning. Everything snapped back into sharp focus. For a split second she had hoped her experience had been a dream but the sight of blood could not be denied. There was no monster in the room now, just herself . . . and Alan. She tried to hold his head in her hands. But the lifeless thing in the bed was dead; she could not deny it any longer. Again, she felt dizzy, unable to breath. Was the scream she heard coming from her own throat? She could not be sure. It sounded far away and disembodied. Shocked beyond measure, she attempted to kiss the gaping wound, pressing his head with her hands so that the wound closed. Blood oozed between her fingers, on to her face; she could taste his blood on her tongue. 'Alan, Alan . . . oh, sweet, sweet Mother of Jesus, Alan, my Alan,' she heard herself say through gasps for breath. For a moment she thought she saw his eyes smile at her but no, that was not possible. Awkwardly, she moved her body on top of his and began pounding her fists on his chest, insisting incoherently that he was not dead. In a moment of reality, she lifted herself off his body and looked around the room. A million fragmented questions perforated her brain. Where had the killer gone? Why hadn't she been killed? Killing her would have been better . . . much better. With Alan dead what reason had she to go on living! Oh, Jesus, God,

Alan,' she cried, 'please somebody . . . somebody help me.'

But there was no one to hear her cries. The bedroom door was open; bloody footprints on the carpet . . . leading to the window. Without being conscious of moving, she found herself standing beside the window. It was opened. Cold air rushed in, its icy fingers causing her to shudder. She looked into the darkness of her back garden. There was nothing out there for her to see. The knife-wielding monster had gone, vanished somewhere in the dark of the night. Shivering, she attempted to move back to the bed but her legs gave way beneath her. A last thought surfaced in her brain before passing out: she recognised the face of the killer.

Somewhere a bell was ringing, the sound tunnelling its way into her brain. It sounded familiar but she could not pinpoint the its exact whereabouts nor decide whether the resonance was merely a creation inside her own head. She just wanted it to stop. Coming out of the dream, Jacqueline realised the ringing sound was real. Someone was pressing her front-door bell. Disorientated and weak, she opened her eyes and realised she was lying on the floor beside the bed. The clock on the bedside table showed the time at half an hour past midnight. A splash of blood on the face of the clock brought back the terrible events that had taken place an hour earlier. She gasped. It was real, not a nightmare; it had happened. Panic whipped through her, a desperate fear churning up from her stomach and spilling into her mind.

Dring, dring, drrrrrrrrinnnng.

Who could that be at my door? She knew she should go downstairs and answer it. An involuntary moan escaped her throat as she looked towards the bed. Instantly, she looked away. Without rising to her feet, she dragged her body along the carpet towards the door and out on to the landing. Shaking uncontrollably she managed to make it down the stairs using both her hands on the banisters for support. As in a trance, she went through the familiar motions of removing the safety chain and unlocking the front door. A short stout man stood there. She looked at him and through him, as if not really seeing him, her gaze fixed on the middle distance. After a moments stunned silence she broke free from the trance.

'Come in,' she heard herself say to the stranger, 'I expect you're from the police.'

'No, ma'am,' the man said. 'My name is Francis Xavier Donnelly, I'm here to . . . He stopped speaking as soon as Jacqueline moved into the light. Now, he could see her more clearly. His eyes opened wide and his hands reached out to her. 'My God, what has happened here? What the hell is going on? Is that blood? It is! What . . . are you hurt?'

'I'm all right . . . but . . . but . . . ' was all she managed to say.

'Has there been an accident? Christ, all that blood. What's happened?'

Jacqueline tried to focus on the man asking the questions but her eyes were drawn to his hypnotic bow tie instead. She opened her mouth to speak but no words came out.

Francis Xavier stood there, staring at her, desperately trying to fathom what he was seeing. When no answers came, he asked the one question that was pertinent to his visit.

'Could you tell me, ma'am: is Alan McCall in this house?

'Yes, yes,' she said quietly. Her thoughts seeming to be far away, 'Yes, he is upstairs in my room . . . He's dead.'

Nothing could have prepared Donnelly for the sight of Alan McCall's dead body. Yet he surprised himself by the way he confronted the horror so calmly. There were no screams, no histrionics, no pulling at his hair. After the initial shock, he tried to evaluate the scene from a sane and rational point of view. Hardest to take were the open eyes; they appeared to look at him no matter which part of the room he viewed the body from. Never had he seen so much blood; it was everywhere, its smell hanging heavily on the air. He had never thought of blood as having any smell at all but like grass, which only gives off its smell when freshly cut, blood, or at least the volume in front of him, did have its own peculiar odour.

Francis Xavier, feeling a strange detachment from the scene and not a little contempt for McCall's dead body, set about organising what should be done about the situation. Ringing the gardaí was not among the options he considered. First he would have to do something about Jacqueline Miller; the woman was coming apart at the seams. He had tried to get her to tell him what had happened but she was barely capable of stringing a sentence together. He assumed from the few words he could follow that the killer had left by the back window. When he examined the window, he could see traces of blood on the glass and framework. None of what she said made much sense but he felt reasonably sure at least that the killer was no longer in the house.

He telephoned Dr John Morley, a trusted friend of his, apologised for disturbing him at such a late hour, told him about Jacqueline Miller – leaving out the gory details about McCall – and got the address of a private clinic where discreet help would be provided for the distraught woman. Donnelly thanked the doctor, and promised to have the woman delivered to the clinic within the hour. He had by now persuaded Jacqueline Miller to lie down on the couch in her sitting room. Within seconds, her eyes closed and she stopped shaking.

Donnelly began to make what turned out to be a long series of telephone calls. It was after one o'clock in the morning but he needed to contact his two fellow members of the Personnel Conduct Code Committee. Fortunately for him, both men were within reach by telephone. He insisted that they meet him without delay, demanding that they come to 32 Leeson Crescent. It was important to let them know what had happened.

First he would show them McCall's dead body and then he would tell them about his earlier encounter with Jimmy Rabbitte. They would be shocked to discover he had paid £4000 out of party funds to the journalist to keep the story from the news-stands but when they thought about the consequences of McCall's body being discovered in his lover's bed they would understand. With their help he would clean up the mess, sanitise the situation and ensure that what happened in Number 32 Leeson Crescent would never make it into the public arena. He had no doubt that the next three or four hours would be the most crucial of his career. His handling of this crisis would safeguard his party's continuance in power. If he failed to keep the story away from the headlines, the government would fall. The responsibility that now rested on his shoulders was awesome but he felt equal to the challenge. In a strange sort of way, he felt invigorated by the prospect that he had the power in his hands to shape coming events.

4

It was dark, cold, miserable but mercifully dry. White frost covered the ground, its crystal-like particles reflecting the amber spill from the street lamps. Tyre tracks from the sparse early morning traffic created gentle criss-cross patterns on the coated tarmac. It was not the sort of morning that appealed to photographer Frankie Kelly, but on this occasion he braved the elements in pursuit of his 'art'. Huddled as best he could in the laurel bushes, elbows pressed against his sides for warmth, his chin tucked into the collar of his leather coat, he made a brrr sound with his lips. It was the kind of biting cold that his father invariably referred to as brass monkey weather. Frankie had never figured out what exactly his father meant by the expression but one thing was sure: in his present situation, it would help him greatly to have a monkey's agility. Securing a foothold on the slippery boughs of the laurels proved almost impossible. Clumsily, he attempted to balance his body so he could keep his grip on his camera.

Whatever about his discomfort it was imperative that he remain in readiness for Alan McCall when he re-emerged from Number 32 Leeson Crescent. The chalk-like covering of frost did at least have one benefit: it added an extra degree of reflective light to the scene, a factor that would help cut the camera's exposure time and improve the picture's definition. As it was, he was forced to shoot in semi-darkness, relying on the street lamps, the spill of light from the house when the door opened, and the hi-tech power of his Nikon. He used a special film developed for British Secret Service night-time surveillance – a film with eight layers of microscopic filament, each sensitised to different light densities – but even so, perfect results were not always guaranteed. The technicians in the print lab, still coming to terms with the new technology, assured him of their best attention and promised to have prints for him by mid-morning. By that time he hoped to have a new batch of film for them.

At 8.30 a.m. precisely, an hour after taking up his body-numbing position, Frankie Kelly's perseverance looked as though it was about to yield dividends. The ground floor door opened. A bright light illuminated the narrow walkway that led from the door and reflected off the frosted blades of grass in the front garden. A surge of excitement charged through his body, almost knocking him from his precarious perch. In rapid succession, the camera's motor drive began its fast fire rat-tat-tat-tat sounds. His eye, pressed to the viewfinder, watched as a man wearing horn-rimmed glasses and tweed cap emerged from the house. He could hardly believe his luck. This was what he had waited for. But the excitement was short-lived. The person captured in the Nikon's lens was not Alan McCall.

Frankie Kelly's head jerked back from his camera.

He stared directly at the man walking away from the side door. Involuntarily, he inhaled a mouthful of frosted air.

What the . . . what the fuck is happening here?

In a state of agitation, his foot slipped from its hold, causing him to lose balance. One hand darted out to grab a branch but the action was not quick enough to save him from sliding to the ground. The commotion did not go unnoticed by the subject of Kelly's surveillance; the man turned his head, saw the photographer, waved to him and continued on his way. Even in the poor light, Kelly could tell that the man was smiling at him. Recovering his composure as best he could, Kelly attempted to analyse what had just happened.

It made no sense. The person he had just witnessed leaving the house was definitely not the same person he had photographed the previous evening. There were superficial similarities certainly: the glasses, the cap, the overcoat, the man's height, but Kelly had no doubts at all; the bastard who had just smiled and waved at him was not Alan McCall.

The more he tried to convince himself that he was not mistaken, the more his mind began to entertain doubts. Could it really have been Alan McCall he had seen the previous evening? Could a trick of light have fooled him? He stood motionless in the corner of Jacqueline Miller's garden, completely baffled. In the growing daylight the Arctic cold showed no sign of letting up. The numbness he felt, however, had less to do with the chill in the air than with the sinking feeling in the pit of his stomach.

There was nothing for it but to go back to the *Dublin Dispatch* office, think things through. He would check his proofs from the night before, make sure Alan McCall was the person captured on the prints, reassure himself that he was not going crazy and not reduced to shooting rolls of film of some phantom politician.

Sarah McCall pulled the GTi into the schoolyard and let the twins out of the car. The nine-year-olds shouted their goodbyes to her – they never allowed her to kiss them in front of their pals – and joined the other children entering the school building. Although Rathkenny National School was less than a mile from the McCall residence, she disliked the idea of allowing John and Stephen to make the journey on foot, especially on these dark winter mornings. Ever since the twins started school she had insisted on driving them and in the intervening years she had got to know most of the other parents on a nod-and-wave basis. From time to time they exchanged greetings or had brief conversations about one or other of the teachers. Rarely, if ever, did they discuss the progress or lack of progress of their children.

Today, Sarah was in no mood to talk to anyone. Her husband's failure to make contact still bothered her. Greg Mooney had checked Alan's Dublin apartment the night before – a short time before midnight, he had informed her – and confirmed that Alan was not there.

So, where had he got to? It wasn't as if Alan had not stayed away from home before; he had, but up until now she had always known where to contact him. On all such previous occasions he made sure to telephone her. A firm pattern had emerged: he would tell her how much he missed her, how much he loved her, and chat to the twins before they set off for school. It was a ritual she had come to expect and accept. But it didn't happen this morning. That was bad enough but more worrying was the unavoidable conclusion that Alan had lied to her about his plans. Why? She had never known him to deliberately lie to her before. The suspicion that something serious had happened to him was becoming an inescapable conclusion. Until she knew the reason for this sudden change in his behaviour, her mind would not be easy.

As she reversed the Golf out of the school's play yard, a woman approached the car. For a split second, Sarah considered ignoring her or pretending not to see her but instantly reconsidered; such action from a politician's wife would never do. Groaning inwardly, she lowered her window and smiled her best politician's-wife smile. The person smiling back at her was Jane O'Rourke, a waif-like woman in her mid forties with carrot-red hair and freckled skin.

'Ah, Mrs McCall,' the woman said, her smile too good to be true, 'I saw your better-half on the nine o'clock news last night. They were saying he might be promoted to a minister in the government. You must be very proud of him.'

'Yes, Mrs O'Rourke, I am, but it's only speculation; I wouldn't put too much store in what they say on the news.'

'Oh, you're right there; still, it'd be terrific to see him on the front benches; about time they had a bit of glamour up there in the Dáil and wouldn't it be a great feather in all our caps if we had a government minister from the town of Rathkenny.'

'Huuuum, I don't know about that . . . but it's very nice of you to say so,' Sarah said, beginning to wind up her window in the hope that the conversation had run its course.

She was wrong.

'I'll tell you why I stopped you, Mrs McCall,' the ever-smiling face said, the breath coming out like little puffs of smoke against the freezing air, 'next Wednesday evening the committee representing the parents of the pupils have organised a meeting to kick off the fund-raising activities for the new gym-room and, as chairperson, I was wondering if perhaps Alan might be able to attend?'

'I'll certainly tell him about it. It's a pity that it's such short notice; his diary is usually filled out for weeks in advance, but I'll ask him anyway.'

'Good, we'd really appreciate it.'

'No problem. One way or another, I'll be happy to attend the meeting myself; offer what moral support I can,' Sarah said as she gently pressed the car's accelerator and prepared to drive away. The smile remained planted on Mrs O'Rourke's face but the eyes let Sarah know that her offer meant little. Her value to the school committee, she could tell, lay purely in her being the wife of Alan McCall; as an individual, she counted for nothing.

This day can only get better, she thought as she sped away from the school, but she was wrong on that score – very wrong.

'Well, gentlemen, the spaghetti has just hit the fan,' Francis Xavier Donnelly said as he replaced the telephone in its cradle. The clock on the wall above his desk said 10.30, an hour and a half into the working day, but the three men in Donnelly's office had worked throughout the night and all were showing the effects of their lack of sleep. 'A cleaning lady has found McCall's body in his apartment. The gardaí are there already. All hell is about to break loose.' Donnelly's pronouncement was greeted with stunned silence from the two men sitting on the opposite side of his desk.

Tom Pettit, whose dapper man-about-town appearance belied his sixty years under normal circumstances, looked every day his age this morning. As Junior Minister with the Department of Agriculture and a member of the PCCC – Personnel Code Conduct Committee – he had responded to Francis Xavier Donnelly's late-night call, never for one moment envisaging the trauma that lay ahead. Seeing the murdered body of Alan McCall had numbed him into allowing Donnelly to direct operations. Although he had expressed the need to inform a priest, a doctor, McCall's wife, the Taoiseach, and the gardaí, he succumbed to

Donnelly's arguments to contact no one. In the cold light of day, Pettit felt that what they had done under the cover of darkness could be the undoing of them. What would his voters think? They were the ones who had elected him to represent them for thirty consecutive years and considered him a fair-minded man. He doubted they would approve of his current actions. Because voters put their trust in him he joined the PCCC, believing he could help promote decent values among his colleagues in the party. Never in his wildest imaginings could he have expected to come up against the likes of what confronted him now.

The third member of the PCCC, Shay Dunphy, a government backbencher since being elected in the last general election, was the youngest TD in the Dáil. At twenty-four years of age he was fiercely ambitious and loyal to the party. His readiness to serve on committees, some of them decidedly unglamorous and uncool, had as much to do with a desire to enhance his own career as it had to do with serving the party. Coming from a family steeped in politics – his father and grandfather had both been elected to the Dáil – he knew the value of the committee system and how it helped create allies in high places, got you noticed and ultimately brought you to the notice of the leaders. When asked to serve on the PCCC, he accepted willingly. A thrill of excitement had charged through him when Francis Xavier Donnelly telephoned him on the previous night and requested his cooperation on a delicate matter.

Seeing the dead body of McCall had been a shock to

his system but he managed to push the horror to one side with relative ease as he listened to Donnelly's damage limitation plan. He agreed with the general secretary's assessment of the situation and threw himself wholeheartedly into the clean-up operation. In the hours that he had spent 'sanitising' Number 32, one notion took precedence over all the other thoughts crashing about in his brain: *I'm doing this for the good of the party, it will fast-track my career. With what I know, the people at the top will have no choice but to promote me.* The more he allowed such thoughts to take hold in his brain, the more he considered Alan McCall's demise to be a blessing in disguise.

Francis Xavier Donnelly looked hard at Pettit, then at Dunphy, sizing the two men up, assessing them as though they were specimens under a microscope. Except for the muffled sound of traffic in Mount Street, two floors below, the office in party headquarters had gone quiet. Around the walls, stately portraits of former leaders, frozen in time and encased in gilt frames, hung at tilted angles against flock wallpaper. Their unblinking eyes, set forever in time, enforced a feeling in Donnelly that he had a responsibility to keep their memory sacred and not to sully their names or that of the party. When he broke the silence, his words were measured and not without a trace of menace. 'I know you're both tired,' he said, 'but I want you to carry on today as if nothing has happened. I want you to keep whatever appointments you've already made; don't let appearances slip, not even for one second. The future of the government is riding on it; the good of our country is depending on you. When the news about McCall's murder is officially announced, you'll both act shocked, surprised, even stunned; you'll trot out the usual platitudes about a dead colleague and you will condemn the perpetrator of the crime with all the indignation at your command.'

'And what about the *perpetrator* of the crime?' Pettit asked.

'What about him?' Donnelly asked, impatiently.

'Well, what I mean is, the three of us have by our actions last night made it easier for the perpetrator to cover his tracks and get away with his crime.'

'That's as maybe,' Donnelly conceded, 'but we've got to look at the big picture; viewed from an overall perspective it makes very little odds. Our wonderfully inept garda force would probably never get the killer in any event. It could be anyone: some nutcase, a member of the householder's family, a robber who lost his nerve and went berserk – we'll probably never know – and for all our sakes, that's just as well.'

'What about the woman?' Pettit asked. 'How can we be sure she won't say anything?'

'We've been down this road already,' Donnelly said irritably. 'You can leave her to me. As we speak, she is heavily sedated, under the watchful eye of my trusted friend Dr John Morley. Later on in the day I'll talk to her . . . access the situation first-hand.'

Shay Dunphy moved uneasily on his chair, concern etched on his face.

'I have to admit that the woman bothers me; it's important that she keeps her trap shut. One word from her could blow us all out of the water.'

'That, my friend, is very true,' Donnelly said, nodding his head gravely, 'but this woman, Jacqueline Miller, is no common dip-shit floozie, irrespective of how we might view her morals, or lack of them. I doubt if she will present any problem for us. From what little information I have been able to put together in the short time available to me, I have discovered she is a woman of some substance. Apparently she has money – she owns three houses, including the one we were in last night – and writes some sort of school textbooks. Not your average everyday airhead, you'll have to admit.'

'Jesus, I don't know. She's still a loose cannon,' Dunphy suggested.

'The point is, she has as much to lose as anyone if word gets out about her involvement with McCall – *a married man* – so don't fret; she'll not open her mouth. I will personally see to it.'

'I hope you are right.'

'I am right,' Donnelly said emphatically, signalling an end to the subject of Jacqueline Miller.

'What happens now?' Pettit asked.

Francis Xavier Donnelly thought for a second before answering, glancing at the portraits, as though invoking their approval. 'The government press secretary and the public relations people are already in the press office waiting for me. The Taoiseach has flown back from Chequers and is on her way from Baldonnel as we speak. She will in all likelihood call a press conference within an hour or so, tell the world at large about the tragedy. Remember, gentlemen, we must be as shocked as everyone else when the news breaks.'

Frankie Kelly could not believe his eyes. Jean-Pierre Brazin, head technician in the photographic lab, placed a strip of exposed film on the lightbox in front of him for inspection. All the frames were totally black. 'I don't believe this,' Kelly said. 'How the hell can this happen! Not a single image . . . that's not possible.'

'It may not be possible,' Jean-Pierre said sympathetically, 'but it's exactly what has happened. We followed the correct procedure here, as we've done before but the results . . . well, you can see for yourself.'

Frankie Kelly took the black strip of film into his hands, examined both sides and replaced it on the lightbox. There was no doubting the evidence before his eyes. Had something gone wrong with the development procedures in the darkroom? Most unlikely. Jean-Pierre Brazin was someone he trusted, someone he had worked with before. He was a professional.

'It's not your fault, Jean-Pierre,' he said, handing back the film strip to the Frenchman, 'there must have been something wrong with the film itself. One way or another, I've got to accept the fact that I've been freezing the bollix off myself last night and this morning for nothing.'

Dejectedly, Kelly walked away from the lab, wondering if his late father's advice to him to 'get a real job' might not have been such a bad suggestion, after all.

'Umm, breakfast smells as good as ever.' The sound of Damien Conway's voice startled his mother as he walked into the kitchen.

'Where on earth did you appear from?' she asked, giving her dressing gown a quick inspection to make sure it was properly adjusted.

'Sorry, Mum. I meant to phone you yesterday, let you know I'd be staying the night.'

'That's all right, dear,' she said, moving to kiss him on the cheek, 'I never heard you come in; must have been very late.'

'Yes it was a bit late all right; you and Dad were already in bed so I just went up to my room, made as little noise as possible.' Glad that his mother did not pursue the topic any further, Damien watched as she busied herself putting bread in the toaster and placing an extra cup and saucer on the table. Since moving out of the house six months earlier Damien had only been back to stay on two occasions. On both visits he had asked his parents for financial help. This time would be no different. He had waited until he heard his father leave for work before coming down the stairs to the kitchen. What he wanted to say would be difficult but talking to his mother, rather than his father, might make it that little bit easier. Listening to his mother's small talk as he piled home-made marmalade on to his toast, he joined in with mock cheerfulness, waiting for the right opportunity to bring up the subject. Eventually, he was forced to broach the subject himself. 'I popped in to see Aunt Jac yesterday.'

'Oh! And how is my recluse sister? Still locked away in her study, working like someone possessed on her schoolbooks?'

'No, actually, she was all excited about a friend who called to see her.'

'A friend? Huum, do you mean a friend – or a *man* friend?'

'I don't know. I didn't get a chance to meet him. All I can tell you is that Jac practically threw me out of the house when the downstairs bell rang. Bundled me out the front door in case I got a look at whoever it was.'

'Ah now, I'm sure you're mistaken. Jac makes no secret of the fact that you are the apple of her eye. She's been so good to you, helping you with the business and all that. She's quite open about the fact that one day all she has will go to you.'

'The trouble is: I can't wait for *one* day; I need the finance right now ... but, well, that's not what worries me.'

"And what is it that worries you?'

'I've been thinking ... what if she were to meet some man who caught her fancy? I mean she's still a young enough woman; what is she ... thirty-two, thirty-three? She still has her looks. With her money she'd have no difficulty attracting a man. Where would that leave me?'

Regina Conway considered his question for a second before replying. 'Well, that's not going to happen; you can rest assured of that. I know my sister well enough to know she will never get married. No, not Jac, not after the troubles she has had. Anyway, there's no need for you to fret; she'll always give you whatever support you need.'

'Chickenfeed, that's what she gives me: chickenfeed! I needed twenty-five grand from her yesterday, showed her my business plans, showed her my projected profits, the lot. I expected her to give me a cheque there and then but she decided I'd better run the plan before her bank manager first.'

'Well, what's wrong with that? Sounds perfectly sensible to me. If your plan is a good one – which I'm sure it is – I don't see why showing it to her bank manager should bother you.'

'The plan *is* a good one but my problem is time. Going to her bank manager will slow everything down. I hate having to grovel in front of some smug jumped-up moneylender, then wait weeks before he condescends to grant approval. I need some hard cash right now . . . like *today*.'

'I see. Did you explain that to Jac?'

'I was trying to get around to it when this friend of hers appeared on the scene.' Damien paused for a moment and looked straight into his mother's eyes. 'Look, Mum, I know you and Dad have already given me some money, but do you think you could loan me a little more?'

'Oh, Damien, I don't know. We have already gone guarantor for fifty thousand. That's a lot of money. How much did you have in mind?'

'I need ten grand to keep the show on the road, pay the wages, keep the creditors at bay, make the lease repayments . . . '

'I don't know, Damien. I'm not sure we could get our hands on that amount of money straightaway. I'll have to talk to your father when he gets in from work this evening. But listen, take my advice: go back to Jac, explain things to her. I know she won't let you down.'

'Yes, Mum, I might do that . . . but I'd still like you to talk to Dad.'

'Of course I will.'

5

Taoiseach Fionnuala Stafford stood partially hidden behind the cluster of microphones and cleared her throat in readiness for the announcement she intended to make. Television, press and radio correspondents jostled with one another for vantage positions as they waited expectantly. Rumours already abounded that something big was about to break and the assembled media wanted her to get on with it.

Against a backdrop of enormous gold and brown coloured drapes, the government press secretary, Noel Guilfoyle, stood motionless at the Taoiseach's left side. To her right, shifting his weight uneasily from one foot to the other, general secretary Francis Xavier Donnelly, watched the proceedings. His appearance, spruced up, gave no clue to the all-night activity he had indulged in. By sheer willpower he managed to stifle the yawns that begged for expression. Splashing his face with ice-cold water minutes before the press briefing had helped. His night's work, he realised, would all have been for nothing if he were to make any slip-ups in front of the media. His only wish was that the Taoiseach would keep her words to a minimum.

His working relationship with Fionnuala Stafford could not be described as good but he tried hard not to let personal animosity get in the way of his job. She was a professional and as such he respected her; it was the more demanding side to her personality, the side displayed behind closed doors, that he found more difficult to live with. Her handlers made sure that the media never saw this unacceptable side. Television cameras and press photographs invariably showed a handsome woman of forty-six, at the pinnacle of the political heap – the country's first woman prime minister. Dressed and made up with meticulous attention to detail, her petite figure, clad in well-cut 'power' suits, she always managed to come across to the public as a cool and competent leader – a safe, and caring, pair of hands.

Fionnuala Stafford tapped the microphone with her fingertips, heard the resultant metallic sound amplified before speaking. 'At 10.15 this morning,' she began, then paused for a second and looked at her audience, as though having difficulty in finding the right words to say, 'Alan McCall was found dead in his apartment in Clyde Road.'

A collective gasp escaped from the assembled media. The room erupted as everyone attempted to speak at the same time, the deluge of questions overlapping and drowning each other out. Noel Guilfoyle called for calm. 'Please, please, ladies and gentlemen of the press, please allow An Taoiseach to finish her statement. Please, I must insist: order for An Taoiseach.

Calm returned to the room but the atmosphere

remained alive with expectation. Fionnuala Stafford waited for total silence before continuing.

'As soon as I heard the dreadful news, I cut short my visit to the British Prime Minister and flew home. I have already expressed my heartfelt sympathies to Alan's wife and family on my own behalf and on behalf of all his friends and colleagues in the Oireachtas. The death of Alan McCall – a man in the prime of his life at thirty-five years of age – comes as a terrible blow to us all. He will be sadly missed.'

A television journalist at the back of the room interrupted the proceedings. 'How did he die? Can you tell us the cause of death?' His question, like a trigger, set off a second avalanche of questions. Guilfoyle demanded silence, his voice straining to be heard above the din. 'Unless you desist from interrupting the Taoiseach,' he threatened, 'I will bring this briefing to an immediate end.' Francis Xavier Donnelly nodded his head vigorously, knowing the media would take this gesture as his way of showing support for Guilfoyle's threat, but in reality he was attempting to ward off the state of sleepiness crowding his brain.

A reluctant calm returned. Fionnuala Stafford read once more from her notes. 'In the past eight years, since becoming a member of the Dáil, Alan McCall has made significant contributions to parliamentary debate and impressed all who came to know and work with him. He is – *was* – a likeable young man, making friends on all sides of the house. It is no secret that I had been considering Alan for a seat in the cabinet in the near future . . . a future now tragically cut short. As I said, I have spoken to Alan's wife, Sarah, and their two boys to sympathise with them. I am aware of the great love and devotion that existed between Alan, his wife and his children. If there was one thing in Alan's life that mattered more than politics, it was his family. We cannot begin to imagine the pain of their great loss at this time.'

A barrage of questions erupted from the floor and swamped Stafford's delivery. 'Will this affect the government's majority in the house? Was the death self-induced, a lewd act gone wrong? Is there another woman? Another man, perhaps? Do we know if Mr McCall was alone in his apartment when . . . ?'

Fionnuala Stafford cut the reporters' questions in mid-flow by holding her hands up like a schoolmistress chastising a class of errant pupils. 'Stop it, all of you. A man is dead, a member of this house, a good man who gave great service to our country. I expect a degree of decorum. I expect you to show some respect. I am not willing to take questions at this juncture but I will say this much: from the preliminary reports I've had from the gardaí, it appears that his death was not as a result of natural causes.' This revelation brought another onslaught of questions. The media frustration had reached boiling point. Stafford refused to give in to their demands for answers and waited for calm to return. 'My information,' she said at length, departing from her prepared script, 'is that Alan McCall was alone in his apartment, so don't any one of you attempt to sully the name of a good and decent politician. As soon as we have more information, the government press secretary here, Mr Noel Guilfoyle, will release the details to you. In the meantime our thoughts and our prayers are with his wife and children. May his soul rest in peace.' Almost as an afterthought, she remembered to add a final blessing in Gaelic – *Go ndéanfaidh Dia grásta ar a anam.* The few words in the Irish language never hurt with the electorate and would probably be picked up on TG4.

Stafford stood back from the microphones and nodded benevolently to her audience. Questions continued to come from the floor but as the Taoiseach, along with Guilfoyle and Donnelly, retreated through a side door, it was apparent that the press conference had come to an abrupt end.

It took fifteen minutes for the reporters and political correspondents who had attended the press conference in Leinster House to get to McCall's apartment in Clyde Road. On arrival, they were annoyed to discover that they were not first at the scene. A hoard of other reporters, complete with notebooks, cameras, microphones and TV crews, were already pressing against the bright yellow crime-scene tape that cordoned off the apartment block. All traces of the morning's frost had finally disappeared. Midday sun peeked tentatively from behind clouds that hung heavily above the building; a modern five-storey purpose-built redbrick that attempted to blend with the older buildings on the street. The street itself, tree-lined and well-proportioned was one of Dublin's most sought-after addresses, less than ten minutes from the city centre; it had evolved over the past two decades from being the preserve of rich home owners to one of up-market office space and exclusive apartment blocks. It also boasted a sprinkling of embassies. It was here, in the heart of this enclave of wealth, power and influence, that the media came to record the final chapter of Alan McCall's life.

Emma Boylan, investigative journalist with the *Post*, one of the first to arrive at the scene, slipped past the yellow ribbon and walked self-assuredly to the front door of the apartment block. A young garda officer, speaking into his two-way radio, ceased his conversation when he saw her and beckoned her to stop. 'Sorry, Miss, you can't go in there. There's been an incident on the fifth floor, so the whole apartment block is temporarily out of bounds.'

Emma flashed one of her best smiles at the baby-faced garda, pulled out her driver's licence, held it in front of his face, making sure it opened at the page which contained her photograph. 'It's all right, Garda, I live here, fourth floor, apartment 4A.'

'Oh, sorry, Miss, I'm trying to keep busybodies and the press back but as you live here, well that's OK then, you can go on up. Just don't get in the way of any of the investigating officers in the building.'

'No sweat, Garda, all I want is to get into my apartment. 'Bye, thanks.'

Having lied her way past the first line of defence, Emma Boylan walked through the lobby, got into the lift and pressed the number five button. Inside the spacious chrome-panelled cage, Emma's slightly distorted image looked back at her from the multiple angled reflective mirror. It came as a pleasant surprise to note that, in spite of her recent series of late nights, she looked in reasonably good shape. Running her fingers through her abundance of light brown hair, she brushed back some gold-tinged ringlets that had fallen on to her forehead and gave her head a little pleased shake. Except for a trace of lip gloss, she wore no make-up this morning. It didn't matter. She was lucky to have inherited her mother's striking bone structure and large grey-green eyes, and her own even features and fine skin made her seem younger than her thirty-four years. Dressed for the cold weather, she wore combats, sweater, fleece jacket and sensible boots.

Ping. The familiar sound synonymous with lifts the world over let her know she had arrived on the fifth floor. With a whooshing sound the doors opened. Emma stepped into the hallway and saw two uniformed gardaí outside a door to the far end of the landing. *Shit, here goes.* She strode towards them with an assumed air of self-assurance and spoke before they had a chance to open their mouths. 'Good day, gentlemen, my name is Boylan, pathologist's office. Is this the right place?'

'Yes, Miss, er, Doctor, I think you're probably expected,' one of the gardaí said, turning to push the door open for her. 'Detective Inspector Lawlor is inside.

He is in charge of the case and will show you what you need to see.'

Emma smiled politely at the garda, assumed the role of pathologist, and entered the room. At first nobody noticed her. She watched as two men from the garda forensic unit went about their business, seemingly oblivious to her presence. Flashbulbs lit up the room with all the erratic brilliance of a lightning storm. She moved towards the bed. Alan McCall's body, like some waxwork, lay naked on blood-encrusted sheets, his neck exposed, hacked and clotted with globs of blackened blood, his face distorted into a grimace of terror. Emma's hand shot to her mouth in an effort to stifle the involuntary gasp that came from her throat. It was horrible. Death was never pretty, but this was grotesque. She had interviewed Alan McCall on a number of occasions in the past and had been struck by his good looks and pleasant personality. It was hard to believe that the dead thing in the bed had once been the smiling politician that had so willingly talked to her.

Transfixed, Emma found it difficult to break eye contact with the mutilated body. Hearing her name spoken by a familiar voice brought the spell to an end. She had not spotted Detective Inspector Lawlor coming out from the bathroom until his hulking frame loomed large in front of her.

'Boylan,' the detective said, spitting the words out with venom, 'what the hell are you doing here? We're trying to preserve a crime scene here for christsake; what we do not need is some irresponsible female journalist stamping all over the evidence. I'd like to know which of the gobshites outside let you into the building?' Before Emma could attempt to reply, Lawlor grabbed her by the shoulders and pushed her out of the room.

'Get to fuck out of here,' he roared at her, before turning to the garda officers in the hallway. 'You bonehead,' he barked at the bigger of the two officers, 'take this woman out of the building on the double and make bloody sure that she stays out. OK? In future, check out everyone coming up here, then double-check with me; you got that?'

Although Emma Boylan had been forced to leave the building under garda escort, she was pleased with herself; her audacity had paid off. She, alone among the assembled media, had managed to get in to see the crime scene. It did not bother her unduly that Detective Inspector Lawlor had objected to her presence in such strenuous terms; they had crossed swords so often in the past that their relationship had become a game of attrition; a verbal battlefield where the exchange of mutual insults had been accepted as the weapons of engagement.

A ripple of applause and a few good-natured catcalls from the gathered media greeted Emma as her ignominious exit from the building signified the only piece of action in their otherwise uneventful vigil. She decided to wait with them for a while, see if anything developed, then go back and write up her report. Apart from the arrival of the real state pathologist and a number of high-ranking garda officers, nothing of any consequence occurred outside the apartment block. Emma was about to move away from her fellow reporters when she felt a hand on her shoulder. 'Hi, Emma,' Jimmy Rabbitte said, 'long time no see.'

'Jimmy, how are you? God, yes, it's been years,' Emma said, trying not to show her shock at his appearance. '

'Still with the old firm, I see.'

'Yes,' Emma replied, 'I'm still with the *Post*. What are you up to yourself these days?'

He showed her the small tape recorder machine held in one hand. 'Ah you know, a bit of this and a bit of that. Right now I'm slumming it with the *Dublin Dispatch*, a shower of wankers, but it helps pay the bills. You know how it is, keeps the ould wolf from the door.'

Emma nodded sympathetically, but made no audible reply. Five years earlier, she remembered, Rabbitte had been sacked from his job as a senior reporter with the *Post*. He had made something of a reputation for himself with the paper with a fine series of articles on the subject of drug abuse. It was never made clear to the newspaper's other employees why he got the chop but rumours had it that his unorthodox methods of securing scoops, including victim entrapment and payments to underground associates, were more than the management could tolerate. Seeing the deterioration in her ex-colleague's appearance, she wondered how someone could possibly go to seed so quickly. He had lost weight, his face seemed to have collapsed around the bone structure and his hair, which had always been groomed to perfection, looked unwashed and greasy. Even the smile that once served him so well now appeared forced and ugly. If Emma did not know better, she would swear he was a junkie but considering his past work exposing the horrors of drug abuse, that possibility seemed highly unlikely. When he spoke, it was impossible not to notice his lack of attention to his teeth. 'I saw you being chucked out of the building,' he said, attempting one of his old smiles, but failing. 'Tell us, did you get a look at the body?'

'Just about, Jimmy, but before I could really take in the details, my *friend* Detective Inspector Lawlor had me ejected.'

'Yeah, that's Lawlor's style all right, all brawn and bollix, no brains at all; I tell you, Emma, that muscled freak is brimful of shit. Tell us though, did you get a look at McCall's face?'

'Yes, as a matter of fact I did.'

'And is it really him?'

'Yes, no mistake; the dead man I saw up there is definitely Alan McCall.'

'How very interesting,' Rabbitte said, breaking into a parody of what used to be his fetching smile. 'How very interesting indeed.'

Emma watched as Rabbitte turned and walked away from the assembled reporters. There was one thing about him that hadn't changed: the look in his eyes that said – *I'm on to something here.* Emma tried to think what that something might be.

Jacqueline Miller could not be sure whether she was awake or asleep, dreaming or experiencing some strange warped reality. Her equilibrium was in free-fall, tumbling, tumbling, tumbling into the darkest abyss. She was not in her own house, that much she knew, but it did not help much because she had no idea where exactly she was. Subliminal flashes of what had happened to bring her to this state of limbo pierced her brain, never enough detail, nothing substantial to focus on. The man with the colourful bow tie had spoken to her recently; it could have been some hours earlier or it might have been mere moments before, she could not be sure nor had she any idea what he had said to her.

Someone else had visited her, her brother Sean. This, she realised, had been the product of her imagination. Sean had died in his mid-twenties. Yet, somehow he had come back to see her. It had been so real, so very real. He had kissed her on the forehead. She felt his lips and the warmth of his breath. His eyes smiled at her, he spoke her name . . . and then, in the blink of an eye, he had vanished.

Other scenes, fleeting glimpses, fragments in time, jumbled and confused, ricocheted around her brain like strobe lights. Ugly scenes. A knife, its blade dripping in blood, had been held in front of her face. She tasted the drops of blood as they splashed on to her lips. She looked into the face of the person holding the knife. It was a face she knew, a face that had sneered at her before. *Damn that face.* Through a vortex, she heard a voice warp and distort, the words stabbing her like pieces of jagged glass. *McCall was a married man, the voice said, he was wrong, you were wrong, you were nothing more than his slut. It had to be stopped.*

Jacqueline Miller's scream caused the sneering face and the bloody knife to evaporate. They were gone but she could still taste the blood on her mouth. She had bitten her lower lip. Her body shook violently in the bed before sleep, induced by sedatives, overtook her once again.

While Alan McCall's lover tossed and turned in her fretful refuge from reality, his wife Sarah was being comforted by friends. Four hours had elapsed since the local garda sergeant had knocked on her door. After that, everything for her had a surreal feel to it; it was as if she had suddenly found herself out of step with the universe, out of time with her body.

As first she refused to believe what she was hearing. It couldn't be true; this was the sort of thing one read about in the newspaper or saw on the television. It could never happen to her, to Alan, it simply could not be true.

But it *was* true.

A series of telephone calls confirmed the worst. Listening to the Taoiseach express her sorrow left her in no doubt. The woman's expression of sympathy could not be ignored – a series of words demanding attention. Other strange happenings took place around her; none of them set in motion by her or under her control. Her mother had arrived, hugged her, comforted her, told her she would look after things for a few days. The headmaster, Mr McGrath, had brought the twins home from school. His words of shock and sympathy merged and melted into the blur of words coming at her from all quarters.

She screamed, told them all to leave her alone and get out of her house. 'You're wrong; all of you are wrong. This whole thing's some terrible mistake.' But deep down, that awful sinking feeling in the pit of her stomach told her that her world really had been torn apart. Alan *was* dead. Alan, dear sweet beautiful Alan, the man she loved, the man who had become the centre of her universe, the man who . . . oh, God, he was dead. Alan, the best father two boys could ever have, would never come home to them again. Accepting the enormity of what had happened was impossible to grasp.

It was impossible to imagine John and Stephen without their Dad. Quite impossible.

She wept, inconsolably.

Later, her request to go see him was shunted to one side. 'No', someone had said to her in hushed tones, 'you won't be able to see the body until they have examined the apartment.' Hearing Alan referred to as the *body* made her want to scream again. *The body*, they said; she just couldn't take it in.

Somewhere in the back of her mind, an unfocused thought gnawed at her subconscious: hadn't Greg Mooney told her that Alan had not been at the apartment . . . and yet Alan had been found there. She dismissed the thought.

It didn't matter.

Nothing mattered. It would all be made clear to her when she got her head back together again, if she ever got her head back together again. Right now, she doubted it.

Her thoughts returned to the twins – they were upstairs with their grandmother; how would she explain this to them. How? She didn't understand it herself so how could she begin to make sense of it for them? Tears as intense as hot cinders burned the rims of her eyes. *Christ in Heaven*, she thought, *if you really are up there, how can you let this happen?*

6

It was rare enough for a politician to be murdered in Ireland. Not since the killing of Senator Billy Fox in 1974 had the country experienced such an outrage. Back then there had been a groundswell of revulsion that such a thing could actually happen. In the four days since Alan McCall's death, people from all walks of life had reacted with similar dismay. The murder had galvanised the nation into demanding action: something has to be done became the common cry. Television reports and newspaper headlines fanned the fire of outrage. Pictures of Alan McCall's two boys, wiping back tears, made all the front pages and television news. The invasion of the family's anguish was unrelenting. Sarah McCall's grief-stricken face was subjected to close scrutiny from camera and reporter alike. The country as a whole, it appeared, identified with the bereaved family and suffered in unison with them.

Emma Boylan's reports were forthright, thorough, well-researched, and managed to convey the true awfulness of the crime. She had managed successfully to elicit reactions from McCall's neighbours, from the boys' teachers and a number of politicians who had worked closely with the late deputy. By allowing people who had known the McCall family to express how the death affected them, she had managed to create a moving tribute to the man.

However, now that the funeral had taken place, there was little in the way of fresh news to report. Nothing of any consequence had emerged from the garda daily news briefings. They trotted out the, by now, familiar line: we are keeping an open mind on who might have killed McCall. All lines of enquiry are being explored. No, we have no suspects at this point in time. Yes, it could have been politically inspired. No, nothing seems to have been stolen in the break-in.

In other words, Emma concluded, they hadn't a clue.

Re-reading the proof of her latest article before allowing it go to her editor, Bob Crosby, she was interrupted by a telephone call. Frankie Kelly, she was informed, was in the reception area and wished to speak with her. She thought about this for a moment. Frankie Kelly had been responsible for the photograph of her that appeared on the front page of *Dublin Dispatch*. The picture showed her being escorted from Alan McCall's apartment block, accompanied by a garda officer. She would have preferred if the picture had not appeared, but reluctantly accepted that it was a good action study.

'Show Mr Kelly up to my office,' she instructed the receptionist. *Why does Frankie Kelly want to see me*, she wondered. *Maybe he wants to sell me an original print of the photo*. She smiled to herself at such a notion knowing that, whatever else it might be, it wouldn't be that.

'Thank you for seeing me,' Kelly said, holding out

his hand to greet her. 'I'm glad you were able to fit me in without an appointment.'

Emma shook his hand and invited him to sit down. His angular frame moved easily in the chair as he crossed his legs. Dressed in denim and leathers, his appearance put Emma in mind of a leftover hippie from the sixties, with butterscotch blond hair tied in a ponytail and an open face that would not look out of place on a Californian beach. He was, she conceded, almost intimidatingly good looking. She put his age somewhere in the mid to late twenties, involuntarily making the calculation that he was perhaps five or six years younger than herself.

'What was it you wanted to see me about,' Emma asked, forcing herself to stop soaking up his good looks.

'You saw the picture I took of you outside McCall's apartment block, I suppose?'

'Yes I did,' Emma replied, pointedly making no comment on its merits, good, bad or indifferent.

'Well, the thing is, after I shot that picture I saw you talking to Jimmy Rabbitte.'

'Ah, yes, Jimmy Rabbitte; you're right, he had a few words with me.'

'He used to work in the *Post* some years back, I believe.'

'Yes, he did; that was when I first met him.'

'And what do you think of him?'

Emma wondered where the conversation was going. 'Why should it matter to you what I think of him?'

Kelly shifted in the chair and fixed Emma with a penetrating stare. 'I just wondered,' he said, as though challenging her to answer him.

'He told me he works with your lot now – the *Dublin Dispatch* – so you probably know him better than I do.'

'Hm, I thought I knew him but I'm not so sure any more. I think he might be devious.'

'He's a reporter; being devious goes with the territory. What exactly are you trying to get at?'

'I think there's something very shady going on at the *Dublin Dispatch.*'

'Are you being funny?' Emma asked. 'The whole *Dublin Dispatch* operation *is* shady, period. I mean, saying you think there's something shady going on at the *Dublin Dispatch* is a bit like saying there's hot money in offshore accounts'

'Yeah, I know all that,' Kelly said, unsmiling, 'but I was talking about Jimmy Rabbitte in particular.'

'Ah, I see, you suspect Jimmy Rabbitte of being involved in this *shady business,* is that it?'

Kelly nodded his head slowly and affected a boyish grimace before answering her question. 'Yes I do,' he said.

'And how do you make that out?'

'On the night before Alan McCall was murdered, I took photographs of him visiting the house of his lover.'

'Pictures of Rabbitte?'

'No, no, not Rabbitte. I mean Alan McCall; I photographed Alan McCall meeting his mistress.'

'Whoa now! Hold on just a minute,' Emma said, startled. 'What's this about … and why are you telling *me*?'

'I'm telling you because I've handed in my notice to

the *Dublin Dispatch* and you're the only person I can think of who might be able to help me. To be honest, I'm not sure who else I can turn to.'

'Wait, wait, wait, this is all a bit too fast for me; you're not making a whole lot of sense. Look, maybe you'd better tell me exactly how this started and what has happened.'

'How it started was simple enough. On the day before Alan McCall was killed, a caller rang the *Dublin Dispatch* and asked to talk to a reporter. The call was put through to Jimmy Rabbitte. Some time later that day, Rabbitte spoke to me; he said some fellow told him about Alan McCall having an affair with the woman who lived at Number 32 Leeson Crescent. According to the caller, Alan McCall would be visiting her that evening.'

'Did Rabbitte think the call was genuine?'

'Not really; I'd say he put very little store in what he heard. We get messages like that every day about all sorts of people. Rabbitte asked me if I knew what Alan McCall looked like, I told him I did. He then asked if I'd like to stake out Number 32, just in case there was anything to the tip-off. I went there that evening and at about a quarter to seven I saw McCall go to the basement door of the house. It was a bit dark at the time but there was enough light to see what was going on. A woman opened the door, kissed him on the lips, brought him inside and closed the door again.'

'And you captured all this on film?' Emma asked, flabbergasted by what she was hearing.

'Yes, I did,' Kelly said.

'And yet, the *Dublin Dispatch*, famous for dishing the dirt, always ready with its exposé photographs, decided not to print these pictures,' Emma said, sounding sceptical. 'Now why would that be, can you tell me?'

'Well, that's what I want to talk to you about. You see, I don't have all the answers – correction, I don't have *any* of the answers – but if you have the time to listen, I'd like to tell you what I think might have happened.'

'Look, I'll be honest with you; this sounds a bit like a cock-and-bull story but I'd be a liar if I didn't admit to being interested, so I'll tell you what: why don't we go to the canteen in the basement. You can tell me exactly what happened. Then, if I decide there's something to your story, well, we'll take it from there. OK?'

'That's OK with me.'

One hour later Emma and Frankie Kelly returned to her office on the third floor. Kelly took up his position in the chair in front of Emma's desk and waited for her reaction to what he had told her.

'Wheeew, that's some story,' she said at length, 'but you've got *no* film, *no* prints, *no* proof of any sort to support your story.'

'Unfortunately, that's about the size of it.'

'You know something, Frankie, it's such an outrageous story that I think I do believe you. What worries me most though is the bit about the person who emerged from the house the following morning.'

'How do you mean?'

'Well, we know that McCall was lying dead at that time in his apartment in Clyde Road, so why would someone go to the trouble of impersonating him; it doesn't add up,'

'If my theory is correct,' Kelly said, harking back to what he had told her in the canteen, 'they – whoever *they* are – want me to believe that the man emerging from the house in the morning was the same man I photographed entering the house the previous evening.'

'And you are absolutely sure that he wasn't?'

Kelly showed his first signs of annoyance. 'I'm telling you: they were two different men. Christ, if only I had the film to prove it.'

'But you haven't, have you?'

'No, I told you –

' – that someone swapped your film at the lab.'

'Yes, damn it, there's no other explanation; someone in the darkroom is responsible.'

'That narrows it down to a few people. Who do you suspect.'

'The most obvious person is Jean-Pierre Brazin but I'd swear on a stack of Bibles the man is honest. So that leaves me with Jimmy Rabbitte.'

'Rabbitte is a journalist,' Emma said. 'Surely he wouldn't know how to go about doctoring film or prints.'

'I don't think so. As far as I know Rabbitte knows sweet feck all about the darkroom but somehow or other, I'd swear he's behind whatever is going on.'

'What happened to the film you shot that morning;

the shots you took of the man who impersonated McCall.'

'I still have it.'

'Well now, that's something; why don't you give it to me; I'll ask my crowd in the *Post* to develop it. It should be interesting to see if we can find out who the mystery man is.'

'Does that mean you are going to help . . . you believe me?'

'I don't know, I really don't . . . it's all so fantastic.'

'Maybe so but it *is* the truth,' Kelly said, hurt, 'and when we prove it I want you to do me a favour.'

'Oh, yeah? I was wondering when we'd get to *why* you're telling me all this.'

'If this turns out to be a story for you, I want you to put in a good word for me here in the *Post*. I'm a damn good photographer and right now I don't have a job to go to.'

'I'm not sure how much influence I might have in that department but if what you're telling me turns out to be true, I'll certainly try to help you.'

'That's all I ask for.'

Out of time, lost in the wanderings of her mind, Jacqueline Miller revisited episodes from her past, short segments out of sequence being played out with a clarity that duplicated the original action completely.

As teacher and sports coach in the midlands' most prestigious secondary school, Abbeygates, she watches her team – the Abbeygates Babes – qualify for their highest-ever ranking position in the interprovincial college camogie championship. The excitement is infectious. Fellow teachers drop their usual reserve and share in the students' triumph. The players insist that she pose with them for the team photograph. Parents, pupils and teachers alike clap her on the back – well done, Miss Miller, you have done our college proud. Song and laughter fills the air; we are the champions, rah, rah, rah. She blushes; so much adulation, she feels unworthy. All she did was take a team of naturally talented girls and convince them that they had it in them to be as good as the best in the land.

They plead with her to come back to the college this evening and celebrate the victory. She wants to comply, their enthusiasm is infectious, but she has to refuse. Happy faces lose their smiles – oh, please, Miss, please Miss, the party is really for you. But no, she is firm, she cannot go with them on this occasion. She had promised her boyfriend, Larry Carroll, that she will meet him that evening. He had already booked a table in the Hook and Crook, one of Athlone's finest restaurants. She hugs each team member in turn and notes that most of them have tears in their eyes. They love her and she loves them in return.

Driving from County Offaly's capital, Tullamore, she passes through Clara, a picturesque town on the banks of the river Brosna, and heads towards Moate. Bright evening sunshine bathes her head as it streams in through the open-roof of her Honda Civic car. Her thoughts are happy ones. It's good to be alive. The road between Clara and Moate, once notorious for its dangerous bends and uneven surface, has in recent years undergone a dramatic transformation for the better. Funds from the European parliament have turned it into a streamlined motorway. She eases the car past Tober, notes the old village pub with its strange name, The Cat and Bagpipes, and smiles. She drives on.

It is exactly one month since Larry Carroll asked her to marry him and exactly one month since she enthusiastically said yes. Instinctively, she lifts her left hand from the steering wheel and glances at the engagement ring. Sunlight is reflected off the diamond's lustrous brilliance. What the 18-carat gold ring with its solitaire setting cost Larry, she is afraid to think, but she is sure it must have cost an obscene amount of money.

Larry Carroll, son and heir of James C. Carroll, the wealthy industrialist, refused to entertain any talk about the cost of the ring, simply saying – it's a ring fit for a princess, the most beautiful princess in the world. She smiles, her thoughts amused by the romantic side to Larry's otherwise no-nonsense approach to life. I'm so lucky, she thinks, I've found a wonderful man. Larry, handsome and tall, recently returned from Germany where he studied the new developments in agribusiness in preparation for the leading role he expects to play in his father's business. Considered a catch by parents of young ladies throughout the midlands, he has recently been referred to in *Social & Personal* as the midlands' most eligible bachelor. He is going to marry me, she says to herself, me, Jacqueline Miller, soon to become Mrs Carroll. She likes the idea. Already, she has played out her wedding day a thousand times in her head; the march down the isle on Uncle Dan's arm – her father had split with the family when she was fifteen – her older sister Regina matron of honour, the spoken vows; all these things she envisages. Outline seating arrangements for the reception are already being considered in her head, including the delicate decisions of where to place her maiden Aunt Theresa and whether Tim Walshe and Sean Nolan, second cousins on her father's side, should be invited – she has only seen them once in her life and that was when she was a young teenager. Only one cloud overshadows her plans: her mother. She will not invite her own mother, a factor bound to upset her sister Regina and the rest of her relatives. She refuses to dwell on the causes that led to the split between herself and her mother, determined not to let the estrangement spoil the happy day.

She thinks about children. Yes, she would definitely like children. Yes, yes, no doubt about it; two adorable little girls. And what about a boy? Boys are such destructive little devils but yes, she will have to produce a boy; boys are what fathers want. She will give Larry one bouncing baby boy. All this, of course, will not happen straightaway. She will wait a few years before starting a family.

Passing through the main street of Moate, a wide thoroughfare spoiled by locals who treat it as an *ad hoc* parking area, she checks her watch. It's 7.45 p.m.

That gives her time to spare before her date with Larry. Easing her foot back a fraction off the accelerator pedal, she slows down to fifty-five miles per hour. Only five more miles to the town of Athlone. Stealing a glance at her face in the rear-view mirror, she pouts her lips, raises her eyebrows and gives herself a nod of approval. Yes, she tells herself – you're looking good, babe!

Her eyes return to the road. At first she can't believe what she is seeing. Although there is little traffic on the straight stretch of road ahead, she sees an articulated truck approaching her, swerving back and forth across the central white line. Her foot slaps on the brake pedal as her hand jammed the horn. The truck is almost upon her when she swerves to avoid collision. Too late. She is not going to make it. In the split second before impact, she sees the driver's face; he is asleep. Like an avalanche, the huge truck ploughs into her. Noise explodes around her. There is a blinding flash. Instantly, the explosion of light vanishes into a pinpoint and disappears like a television screen being switched off.

She feels no pain at all.

Darkness swallows her.

Later, how much later she has no idea, she regains consciousness. She is in the intensive care unit of the Midland Regional Hospital.

She is alive.

In the days that follow she begins to understand the nature of the terrible injury that has been inflicted on her. Bandages, braces, wires and pulleys appear to be holding her body together. Her mouth is wired and cannot move; tubes protrude from her nose, mouth and wrists. Cuts, bruises and fractured bones are distributed throughout her body but it is her face that has taken the most severe punishment.

Later, days perhaps, weeks maybe – time has little meaning – Larry Carroll sits by her bedside holding her right hand, the only part of her to escape injury, his smile of encouragement to her is not enough, not nearly enough. She wishes she were dead.

Jacqueline Miller forces her mind to return to the present but the reverie of the accident that blighted her life six years earlier still tears at her heart. Remembering events from the past sends shivers through her but she knows there are other events in her past far more painful, events so painful that she cannot bring herself to dredge them up.

She opens her eyes.

Dr John Morley and the 'bow tie' politician are standing by her bedside. Their presence is an unwelcome reminder to her of Alan McCall. The present, like the past, brings her no joy. The doctor and politician try to communicate with her. She watches their mouths open and close, hears the sounds they make but refuses to understand what they are saying. Desperately, she wishes she had enough energy to reply to them but the words won't come. If she could speak she would tell them to go to hell.

Instead, she closes her eyes and allows her mind to float away once more.

7

Emma Boylan stole sidelong glances at her passenger, Frankie Kelly, as she drove along the tree-lined Appian Way on her way to Leeson Crescent. Cramped in the passenger seat, his long legs sprawled apart, one knee pressed against the glove compartment, the other straying as far as the instrument panel, he allowed a coil of smoke from his marijuana joint to drift out the window. Emma had always disliked people smoking in her car but when he had asked if it was all right to light up, she had said yes unhesitatingly, like some schoolgirl with a crush on the classroom heart-throb.

'Want a drag?' he asked, offering the joint to her.

'Not while I'm driving,' she answered, trying to sound nonchalant. Physically, she found him attractive – drop-dead gorgeous best summed-up it up – and caught herself at odd moments thinking about the body beneath the battered denims and leather. She was annoyed with herself for thinking such thoughts and reminded herself that Kelly was five or six years her junior. Besides, she already had a boyfriend, a live-in lover named Vinny Bailey who had asked her to marry him. Vinny, who operated an antique and fine-art business with his father, was in Amsterdam at an antique fair and would remain in Europe trawling for *objets d'art* for the next eight to ten days. She missed him and wished he were back with her. If he were, maybe then she wouldn't be entertaining such ridiculous thoughts about Frankie Kelly.

Frankie was fully aware of the furtive, admiring glances coming his way from Emma. It was something that happened a lot, something he took for granted when in the company of females. However, on this occasion he choose not to allow his thoughts stray in that direction. His preoccupation lay with discovering what or who had messed around with his photographs. Since talking to Emma the previous day, he had endeavoured to dig up more information about the woman who lived in the house on Leeson Crescent. In that task he had drawn a blank. The only thing he knew about her was her name: Jacqueline Miller. That much he had learned from Jimmy Rabbitte, and Rabbitte in turn had been given the name by the mysterious telephone caller. 'What will we say to her when she answers the door?' Frankie asked.

'I'm not sure,' Emma replied, trying to concentrate on the heavy traffic in front of her. 'I'll think of something, I usually do. We'll play it by ear to start with. I might tell her that we're asking people for their reaction in connection with the death of politician, Alan McCall; it should be interesting to see her reaction.'

'A bit obvious, isn't it?'

'Subtlety might not be the most effective strategy in a situation like this,' Emma said with a little chuckle. 'The important thing is that you identify her as the woman you saw opening the side door for McCall . . . if it really was McCall.'

It was Frankie Kelly's turn to smile.

'Doubting Thomas; you're still not convinced about what I told you, are you? But that's OK, it doesn't bother me any more.'

'And why would that be?'

'Because, Emma Boylan, investigative journalist of little faith, I *know* what I saw and I *know* that I'm not mistaken. It's as simple as that.'

'Well, we're soon going to find out . . . one way or another.'

Emma parked her Volvo 360 GLT in a tight space she found about five houses down the street from Number 32 and got out of the car. They remained silent as they mounted the steps that led to Jacqueline Miller's front door. Emma pressed the bell and waited. There was no answer. She pressed the bell again. 'Looks like we're out of luck,' she said.

'Give it one more try,' Frankie suggested.

Emma was about to do as he suggested when they heard movement from inside the hallway. A bolt was drawn. The door swung open. A thin, pale-faced young man stood before them, sizing them up and down from head to toe. A smart dresser, he sported a modern hairstyle and casual clothes that displayed designer labels. Behind small oval-rimmed glasses, quizzical eyes stared out at them. 'Can I help you?' he asked, his Adam's apple rising and falling with his words.

'My name is Emma Boylan – I'm with the *Post* – and

my colleague here is photographer, Frankie Kelly. Could you let Jacqueline Miller know that we are here for the interview.'

'I'm afraid Jac – sorry, I call her Jac, she's my aunt. I'm Damien Conway; my mother is Jac's sister. I was about to say that she's not here at the moment.'

Emma could tell by the few words spoken that Damien Conway was on edge. She needed a strategy to get him to talk to her. 'Could you tell me when she might be back?' was the best she could come up with. 'It's just that I wanted to conduct an interview with her. It's something we'd arranged some time ago.'

'About her books I suppose,' Damien said, a look of concern on his face. 'It's not like her to miss an appointment especially when it's something to do with promoting her books but the truth is, I don't know where she is and, well, to be honest with you, I'm a bit concerned about her.'

'Concerned?' Emma probed.

Damien Conway looked at her for a moment in silence. Emma could see that he was considering whether to talk to her or not. She was about to say something to bridge the awkward hiatus when he offered to shake hands with them. 'Forgive my rudeness,' he said, 'leaving you standing on the doorstep. Come in; come in; we'll talk about it.'

Emma and Frankie followed Jacqueline Miller's nephew into the front living room and sat down on a gold and wine *chaise-longue* when he invited them to. It was a large, well-proportioned room with long elegant windows, elaborate rococo ceilings, genuine period furniture and an overall character that had as much to do with comfort as its undoubted opulence. Damien asked if they would like some refreshments. 'I was just about to make myself a coffee. Would either of you like a cup?'

'I'd love a coffee, thanks,' Frankie said without hesitation.

'Well, seeing as how you're making it anyway, I'll have a cup too,' Emma said. 'No sugar, just a drop of milk, thanks.'

As soon as Damien left the room, Emma stood up and moved to a sideboard covered with ornaments and framed photographs. Until that moment she did not know what Jacqueline Miller looked like but the woman's identity became obvious from the many repeated images of the same person in the photographs. Jacqueline Miller was, she could tell, the teacher posing with the team of schoolgirls. They were holding a banner aloft with the legend: *Abbeygates Babes Are Best*. She showed the picture to Kelly. 'Is this the woman you saw?' Kelly took the picture in his hands and had no hesitation in identifying her. 'Yes, that's the woman all right; that's Jacqueline Miller.'

In other photographs, Emma could see a younger version of the same woman with friends on graduation day, with a handsome man, playing tennis with the same man, shaking hands with the Minister of Education. Just as Emma heard Damien making his way back into the room with a tray of coffee cups her attention was caught by one photograph in particular. It showed a smiling Alan McCall chatting to Jacqueline Miller as they stood among a crowd of people, all with drinks in their hands, at some sort of press reception.

'That's a picture of one of Jac's earlier book launches you're looking at,' Damien informed Emma, 'I think that was the third one to be published, *Tipperary: A Handbook for Local Studies* if I'm not mistaken. Since then she's got through more than half the other counties. My Aunt Jac is a bit of a workaholic I'm afraid.'

Damien waited for Emma to return to her seat before passing the coffee to her and Frankie. He sat down opposite them and spoke about his aunt without preamble. 'It's not like her,' he began, 'to go away from the house without first getting in touch with me.'

'You've contacted her friends?' Emma asked.

'Yes, I have; I've also contacted the people in her other houses; none of them know a thing.'

'Her other houses?' Emma asked.

Damien put down his cup on the coffee table and stared at it meditatively. 'Sorry, I forget that you wouldn't know that,' he said, putting his hands together and interlacing his fingers. 'I keep forgetting that people . . . that people like you only know Jac because of her educational publications.'

Emma knew nothing about Jacqueline Miller's books but she did not intend to let the author's nephew know that. She remained silent, nodded at him with an expression that she hoped conveyed a comprehensive knowledge as she waited for him to continue.

'My aunt had a very serious accident six years ago in which she nearly died. The guy who ran in to her – he was driving a big truck – was clearly at fault, fell asleep at the wheel. Anyway, the case took a few years to get to court but in the end Jac was awarded compensation, the biggest amount ever paid out at the time for a personal injuries claim. She bought three houses with the money as an investment; this one we are sitting in and two others in the city. The books started off as a sort of therapeutic exercise during her long period of convalescence. According to Aunt Jac, there were no textbooks on local history and geography available that excited her pupils enough to grab their attention, so she had a go at filling the need herself. But I'm boring you with all this stuff,' he said with a little nervous laugh. 'You wanted to talk to her about her current activities, I presume.'

'Yes,' Emma lied with ease, 'I wanted to include Jacqueline Miller in a series I'm writing about successful women in Ireland. I want to look at the background to her life, talk to the people who influenced her most; try to discover the driving forces that motivate her – that sort of thing.'

'I know exactly what you mean,' Damien said, never doubting Emma's story for a second, 'and I wish I could help but it's really Aunt Jac you need to talk to. I'm sure she'll get in touch with me sooner or later, it's just that . . . '

'It's just that . . . what?' Emma prompted.

There was a moment's silence while the expression

on his face went through a series of different emotions. When he spoke, his voice took on a more pronounced note of concern. 'I shouldn't be bothering you people with all this but, well, I've the keys to this house and for the last four days I've let myself in only to discover milk on the doorstep and newspapers stuffed through the letterbox. It's not like Aunt Jac to forget to cancel deliveries when she goes away; it's not like her at all. I've looked in her study, looked everywhere, but she has left no messages. I'm not sure what to do about it . . . that's if you think I should do anything at all.'

Frankie Kelly, who had remained silent throughout the conversation, spoke for the first time. 'I think you should at least report it to the gardaí; there's probably nothing amiss but it's better to be sure than sorry.'

'Yeah, I think you might be right,' Damien said, sounding relieved. 'I'll contact them today.'

Emma decided there was nothing further to be discovered by talking to Damien at this point. She nodded to Frankie in a gesture that signalled it was time to go. Thanking Damien for the coffee, Emma and Frankie went off, leaving him a series of telephone numbers where they could be contacted should he receive any news on Jacqueline's whereabouts.

Back in the car, Emma and Frankie discussed their reactions to what they had learned from Damien. Both of them agreed that he appeared overly nervous.

'He was there the evening I took the photographs of Alan McCall,' Frankie said, taking Emma completely by surprise.

'Who? You mean Damien? You're saying that Damien was there when you photographed McCall? But why have you never said anything about this before?'

'It never struck me as being important before. I'd taken the shots of McCall being greeted by Jacqueline and was satisfied that I'd got what I'd come for. After McCall had disappeared inside the house through the side door in the basement, this fellow – Damien, as it turns out – came out of the house through the main door and walked down the street.'

'Most odd,' Emma said. 'I'd like to know what exactly is going on here. Seems to me our friend Damien might know a lot more than he's letting on. I'm now more interested than ever to see whose face is on the photographs you shot on the morning of McCall's murder.'

'Well, I'm fairly sure it's not Damien if that's what you're thinking.'

'Why do you say that?'

'He's a bit small, too thin as well; no I don't think it was him.'

'Hmm, I see. Still, it has to be someone.'

'When will they have the prints for you?'

'I expect them to be sitting on my desk when I get back to my office.'

'Do you mind if I come with you?'

'Well, I suppose it's your picture after all; yes, all right, you can come with me.'

The Hasselblad's zoom lens caught Emma and Frankie as they descended the steps of Number 32 and tracked them as they made it to the Volvo parked some way down the street. Joe Stones, ex garda sergeant, now part-time private investigator, was pleased with himself; he had got perfect shots of the two visitors. For three days he had sat, concealed in the back of his Panda van, observing Jacqueline Miller's house from his vantage point across the street. And for three days nothing much had happened except for the arrival and departure of the slight bespectacled man, whom he knew to be Damien. It was cold and uncomfortable in the cramped conditions of the little van, the boredom was mind-numbing but at least the job paid well.

He recognised Emma Boylan as soon as he had seen her arrive at the house but could not identify the casually dressed man walking by her side. He had met Boylan on numerous occasions in the course of his duties as a garda officer. Like most of his colleagues in the force he considered her a tough cookie and not someone to trifle with. He had seen her on television a few times talking on the subject of crime. She gave a good performance and was vociferous in her condemnation of what she saw as the shortcomings in the organisation of law enforcement. He hadn't agreed with her or liked what she said but, grudgingly, he accepted that, as an investigative journalist, she was good at her job.

In the course of the past three days, Joe Stones wondered why he had been asked to stake out the house but now with the arrival of Emma Boylan and her unidentified friend, he knew there had to be a good reason. Perhaps when he showed the results of his labours to his employer, he might be let in on what was happening.

It was mid-afternoon by the time Emma got back to the *Post* headquarters. The Friday exodus from the city was causing its usual bumper-to-bumper traffic snarl-ups in every street of the capital. Like so many other motorists, she could not fail to notice how Dublin's traffic congestion had gone from bad to worse in recent years. She accepted that it was people like her, young men and women who had come from every corner of the country to find jobs in the city, that were responsible for the growing chaos. Most of them had prospered, bought cars, but couldn't wait to get back to their home towns and villages for the weekends. It was then that she remembered she had promised her mother she would see her this weekend. She cursed silently to herself; as on so many occasions before, she would not be able to make the visit. Observing the drivers all around her as they attempted to leave the city, she resolved to make time to visit her mother and father the following weekend.

It had taken Emma over an hour to travel the short distance from Leeson Crescent to Abbey Street. Frankie Kelly followed her up three flights of stairs and down the long corridors that led to her office. Bemused, he watched as people moved in and out of cubicles; he caught snatches of their conversations, heard telephones ring, keyboards click and in the background the ever-present rumble of the huge printing presses as they spewed out the fourth edition of the evening paper. This was an altogether different world than the one he had experienced in his last place of employment, the more modest premises that housed the *Dublin Dispatch*.

As expected, six black-and-white photographs lay on Emma's desk. She glanced at them, unimpressed, and handed them to Kelly.

'It could be anyone,' she said, with a dismissive flick of her fingers. 'It could be Elvis Costello, Woody Allen, Clark Kent, or anyone you care to mention with a pair of horn-rimmed glasses; the detail is lousy.'

'Who the hell is Clark Kent?'

'Superman, you dummy, Superman in civvies.'

'Well it ain't Superman, that's for sure, but yeah, I agree, they're not the best prints in the world. There's a lot that can be done with them to improve the quality. I've this friend who is a bit of a whizz with computers. He'll be able to scan the original film, select the best exposure, bring it into one of his Photoshop programmes on his Macintosh and work on the quality.

Emma remained unimpressed. 'I can't see that anything is going to improve this lot.'

'There you go again . . . no faith. Look, I've seen what my friend is capable of doing. It's fantastic, honest. He'll work on one of the exposures, remove the glasses and the hat, clone in skin and hair so that we see the complete head, brighten the print, take down the contrast. I tell you, it's amazing what he can achieve with the new technology he uses. If I'm lucky I'll get him to work on this over the weekend.'

'Right,' Emma said, unconvinced, 'call me when you get the results. If we can get a "make" on whoever it is, we'll have our first lead.'

'That's exactly what I intend to do. Can I have your home number . . . so that I can get in touch with you.'

Emma thought about his request for a moment before answering. 'No, I make it a rule never to give out my private number.' She paused for a moment, desperately tempted to make an exception this once. What harm could it do, she asked herself, but then the more sensible side of her brain kicked in. With Vinny away, having a handsome devil like Kelly around would be asking for trouble. What the hell had she been thinking of? 'If you do come up with something it'll have to wait until Monday morning,' she said, hoping he hadn't noticed her hesitation, 'or you could leave a message with my answering service here in the office.'

'Even if I come up with the goods?' he said, a twinkle in his eyes.

'Yes, Frankie, even if you come up with the goods, but I might as well tell you, I won't be holding my breath.'

'Oh, ye of little faith.'

8

Detective Inspector Lawlor would rather have been in the gym on this Saturday morning. His definition of heaven included a room filled with exercise equipment and sweat-drenched men grunting and groaning, testing their bodies' endurance through a series of squats, presses and vertical butterflies. He tried hard not to let his duty as a law officer get in the way of this, the most precious hour of his week, but from time to time a difficult case or a work backlog did intrude. This was one of those times, and his mood, like the weather, was dark and troubled. Heavy rain of earlier morning had abated to a drizzle as he parked his Mondeo LX illegally by the railings of the Busaras building on the Store Street side. Dodging buses that pulled out from the bus station at alarming angles, he ran across the street to the Coroner's office. The old building had undergone a recent facelift so that its façade of blackened bricks had been returned to its original dull red colour, but the sandblasting and the newly painted blue doors failed to remove the gloom hanging over the building on this wet January morning. It was Lawlor's fifth visit in as many days to the building and, once again, his appointment was with Assistant State Pathologist Dr Tara O'Reilly.

Dr O'Reilly, like Lawlor, preferred to be away from the office on Saturdays but had on this occasion given into pressure of work. Results of McCall's DNA profiles had been faxed through from the forensic science laboratory at the garda depot in Phoenix Park. They had rushed the tests through in two days. She had promised to share the results with Lawlor as soon as they became available. She could have put it off until Monday morning – no one would have been any the wiser – but being a conscientious person, duty came before self-interest. She had telephoned him earlier to let him know the DNA profiles had arrived. Office staff did not work on Saturdays in the building so Dr O'Reilly answered the door herself and showed Lawlor into her office. 'I hope you don't mind waiting for a few minutes,' she said to the detective, 'I've got a few things to finish up next door and then I'll be with you.'

'Yeah, Doc, I'll put the kettle on, make myself a brew if you don't mind.'

'Fine, I think there's still a drop of milk in the fridge. You'll need to keep your overcoat on; the heating doesn't come on over the weekends.'

Lawlor set about making himself a cup of coffee as he cursed his luck at being there instead of at his gym. Dr O'Reilly need not have mentioned the lack of heat; it was colder inside the building than it was outside. In spite of that, he realised it could have been worse; at least he was spared the ordeal of having to go into the room where the two dissecting tables stood. In all his years of observing post-mortems he had never got used to the sickly smell of death and the all-prevailing odour of disinfectant that hung in the air and clung to clothes for days afterwards.

As he spooned coffee into a mug his thoughts turned to the developments in the McCall murder. He could never remember a time when so much pressure had been applied to come up with a result. Commissioner Horgan had spoken to him at least twice a day since the body had been discovered. 'I want a result,' became the constant cry. Lawlor felt like telling his boss that this was not like a soccer match and that results in homicide cases did not come from a kick of a ball, but of course he kept such fanciful retorts to himself. He realised that the commissioner was under pressure from all sorts of people; everyone from the Taoiseach and President down to petty county councillors and civic groups throughout the country.

Lawlor would have liked to oblige them all; he would dearly love to collar the perpetrator, hold a press conference and tell the good people of Ireland that they could rest easy in their beds again, but life was never as simple as that. This particular murder hunt was not as straightforward as it appeared to be at first sight. Murder cases were like that; you never knew where the hunt would take you. In this case, the cause of death itself posed no problems. McCall's throat had been cut; a vicious slashing motion had sliced through the trachea and the carotid arteries. Everything else about the case, however, proved more complicated. The murder weapon had yet to be found but he suspected that even if it were found, it would yield no fingerprints. Someone had taken great care to wipe clean all traces of fingerprints in McCall's apartment.

Establishing the time of death proved equally problematic. On the morning of the preliminary autopsy, Dr O'Reilly had put the time of McCall's death at or before midnight of the previous night. Subsequent examinations of the body had confirmed her findings. This information did not fit in with the facts as Lawlor knew them. In his interview with Mrs Sarah McCall, she had told him about her telephone conversations with Greg Mooney and he had followed up on that information. During a subsequent interview, Greg Mooney had confirmed Mrs McCall's story. 'Yes, its true,' Mooney had said. 'I visited McCall's apartment a few minutes before midnight on the night of the murder.'

'And you found nothing?'

'Exactly. I found nothing.'

'How did you manage to get into the apartment?'

'I made contact with the caretaker, Tom Dunne. He's old, maybe getting senile. It seems he lives in a special suite on the basement level of the apartment block.'

On the basis of this conversation, Lawlor had taken the trouble to go back to the apartment and talk to the caretaker. After much prompting, the old man confirmed Mooney's account of the midnight visit. But of far more significance, as far as Lawlor was concerned, was the caretaker's assertion that he had looked in on McCall's apartment about half an hour later – 12.30 p.m. or thereabouts – he claimed. 'And why would you check his apartment at that hour?' Lawlor had asked, wondering if the man was in full possession of all his faculties.

'Because yer man – that TD fellow that was looking for McCall earlier – geb me a phone number and axed me to ring him 'bout half an hour later.'

'You mean Greg Mooney, right? Why did he want you to ring him?'

'He axed me to tell him if McCall cem back to his 'partment or not.' Lawlor had yet to check this information out with Greg Mooney.

As bits and pieces of evidence began to mount, Lawlor's suspicion were confirmed: McCall had been murdered somewhere other than in his apartment. Too many things did not add up. The size of the blood-soaked mattress did not fit the bed-base it was placed on. The sheets and pillowcase did not match the sheets and pillowcases on the other two smaller beds in the apartment. That in itself did not prove anything but Lawlor could tell that the body, along with the mattress, sheets and pillow, had been moved from some other location. The whole operation had been unplanned, probably the work of amateurs.

He had interviewed the people who owned apartments in the block and asked them all the same question: had they heard any peculiar noises during the night of the murder? Responses were not encouraging. Yes, they affirmed, people were always coming and going at all hours of the night, an unending litany of noises. It was something they had learned to live with. But no one recalled hearing anything out of the ordinary on the night in question.

Lawlor was halfway through his mug of coffee by the time Dr O'Reilly re-joined him. It was his first time to see the pathologist in casual clothes; a change for the better, making her look a little less starchy, he thought. She wore fawn coloured woollen trousers, a light greenish tweed jacket and bottle-green sweater with a polo collar that rode half-way up a long slender neck. In her early forties, she sometimes missed being beautiful, but if her crown of black, untidy piled-up hair and total lack of make-up was anything to go by, her appearance came way down on her list of life's priorities.

'I'm sorry to have kept you waiting, Detective Inspector, but there were a few items I had to attend to that couldn't wait.'

'No problem at all, Doc. The main thing is that you've some results for me, right?'

Tara O'Reilly's smile hid the fact that she resented Lawlor's over-familiar use of the word *Doc*. To compensate for this minor irritation, she emphasised his own *Detective Inspector* title.

'Earlier this morning, Detective Inspector, I examined the returned specimens and the reports accompanying them and made copies of the findings for you; they are rather detailed and use medical language but the conclusions are clear enough.'

'Yeah, I know the scene, Doc: pages of waffle to justify the inflated charges they make for their tests.

Your forensic-science colleagues in DNA are no different from anyone else: they milk the system for all it's worth . . . '

'I hardly think, Detective Inspector Lawlor, that *my* colleagues are . . . '

'Yeah, yeah, Doc, whatever. Look, you've had time to look at these reports so perhaps you'd give me a rundown on the main findings.'

'Certainly, Detective Inspector. All items of the victim's clothing were examined, including his vest, underpants, shirt and so forth. Fibres from fabrics not belonging to McCall were found, along with traces of make-up. This would indicate that McCall was with another person shortly before his death. The long chestnut-coloured hairs found tangled in McCall's hair were possibly from the head of a female.'

'A female? But you can't be certain?'

'Well, of course there's always the outside possibility that it came from a long-haired male hippy, but I doubt it.'

'You're sure . . . I mean, sure it wasn't male?'

'Yes. When McCall's penis and lower abdomen were swabbed for foreign skin cells, a partial female DNA-PCR profile emerged, so we can assume he wasn't having sex with a male. In addition, minute amounts of his own semen were discovered on his body and on the sheets but the conclusion is that the full extent of the semen ejaculation is somewhere else. The likelihood is that McCall had sexual intercourse rather than masturbation.'

'So, there's no doubt that McCall was with a woman before he was killed?'

'Yes, Detective Inspector, that would be a reasonable interpretation of the findings. Traces of moisturiser, foundation, lipstick, eyeshadow, mascara, powder and blusher were found on his shirt, underwear and on the swabs taken from his body. There's a full report supplied on all the different types of make-up.'

'So, whoever Alan McCall was having it off with was dolled up to the nines in make-up. You know what, Doc, it's beginning to sound like he was with a prostitute to me.' Lawlor nodded his head in agreement with his own deduction.

'I bow to your superior knowledge on such matters,' O'Reilly said, realising immediately that her intended sarcasm had been lost on Lawlor.

'Right, Doc,' he said, leaving the room, 'I'll take these copy reports and be on my way. Thanks for your help.'

'Just doing my job, Detective Inspector, just doing my job,' she said, wanting to refer to him as Dick but not finding the courage to do so.

For a distance of three miles, the huge truck had drenched her car with grey-brown spray. It was bad enough driving through the unrelenting rain but having her windscreen splashed with filthy sludge made it almost impossible to see the road, even with the wipers going at full blast. Finally, after several attempts, Emma managed to overtake it. Pulling away from the huge truck, she caught a glimpse of the driver in her rear-view mirror. He gave her the increasingly common sexual elbow-jerk, grinning from ear to ear. She grimaced with distaste, hissed the word *creep* at the image in her mirror and pushed her accelerator to the floor. Breaking the speed limit did not bother her; she just wanted to put as much distance between herself and the brute driving the truck.

Since she had set out on the journey for Abbeygates school earlier that morning, rain had poured down relentlessly. Although the Saturday morning traffic was light, driving through the small towns of Enfield, Kinnegad and Tyrrellspass proved painfully slow. Pedestrians, pushing their way along the footpaths, probably making their way to or from the shops, struggling with their umbrellas, were careful to avoid being splashed by the passing traffic. Seeing their plight, Emma realised she should be grateful that she could at least stay dry and warm inside the comfort of her car.

In Kilbeggan she pulled in beside the old Locks distillery building, the scene of the town's once thriving whiskey industry, and ran from the car to a door with a sign above it that read Tea Rooms. A young waitress with carrot-red hair and a welcoming smile took her coat and hung it to dry beside an open fireplace. Burning brightly, the log fire spread its heat throughout the whole room. Emma sat at the table nearest it and ordered a mug of coffee and a hot scone. While waiting to be served she used her mobile phone to call her parents at their home in Slane, County Meath. Her mother Hazel responded with delight to the call and inquired if she was on her way home. Emma let her down as gently as possible. Apologising for breaking her promise to visit them that morning, she explained that something urgent at work had forced her to change plans. Her mother's disappointment, even over a crackly line, was all too evident. Emma tried to make it up to her by promising that she and Vinny Bailey would make it without fail in a fortnight's time. This appeared to cheer her mother up. But even as Emma thought about making the trip, doubts began to form in her mind. She was not even sure if Vinny would be available to travel with her. Both her parents had met her fiancé on several occasions and had taken a great shine to him. They had been thrilled when he asked their permission for their daughter's hand in marriage. They had both agreed unhesitatingly. The only impediment to the couple getting married continued to be Emma's own refusal to name the day. She chatted with her mother until the waitress came with her order before saying goodbye with a promise to be there as soon as she got a break.

Feeling better after her little snack, Emma retrieved her coat from the hook beside the fireplace and prepared to face the elements once more. Twenty minutes later she made her way through Tullamore and pulled up outside the entrance to Abbeygates school, a mile west of the town. Like the complex of buildings in the rain-washed background, the granite pillars that flanked two enormous wrought-iron gates were impressive and not a little intimidating. Emma announced who she was into an intercom and drove forward as soon as the two great gates swung open. A curved gravel driveway wound its way beneath a canopy of oaks that stretched all the way to a small courtyard in front of the private wing of the school. She parked her car as near as it was possible to get to the entrance before making it on foot to the door.

Sr Michele let her in and ushered her into a bright cosy living room. 'You're drenched, you poor dear,' the nun said, helping Emma out of her wet coat. 'It's not too often we get reporters from one of the national papers down here in Abbeygates. You look exactly as I pictured you when you telephoned me yesterday. I just hope I can make your journey worthwhile.'

Emma could sense a genuine warmth in Sr Michele. The face, with its slightly aquiline nose, was unremarkable except for the pale grey eyes that held the unmistakable spark of intelligence. A trim woman in her mid-fifties with salt and pepper hair combed back from the temples and clasped in a bun, she wore a winter-white woollen jumper and a well-cut slate-grey skirt. She insisted that Emma should have a cup of tea and a slice of fruit cake with her while they talked. It soon became apparent that Sr Michele liked to talk. She talked about the weather, the government, the current crop of television programmes and her attitude to all of these items. With an inexhaustible flow of anecdotes, she talked about the midlands and the new-found prosperity of her native town of Tullamore. She talked about her role as director with the local drama group and how well they had performed in recent festivals and she talked about her school's reputation as one of the finest in the country. It was only in the past five years, she informed Emma, that boarders no longer remained in the convent over the weekends. This development received wholehearted approval from Sr Michele.

'Of course we still see some of the girls on odd weekends because of sporting fixtures. Abbeygates has gained quite a reputation for itself in the world of inter-college sport ever since Jacqueline Miller took our camogie team to the Leinster finals six years ago.'

'Were you in charge here when Jacqueline was teaching?' Emma asked.

'Yes, indeed I was. She was a remarkable woman . . . still is, I've no doubt, but back then she breezed through the school like a breath of fresh air. I like to think she was happy here . . . I'm not so sure anymore but one thing is for certain: we all thought very highly of her.'

'So why did she decide to leave teaching.'

'Ah, well now, that's another days work; circumstances have a habit of dictating our lives . . . and so it was with Jac, we used to call her Jac.'

'I know about the accident,' Emma said. 'Was that the reason she left?'

'Yes and no. You see, she did come back after the accident.'

'I didn't know that.'

'Yes, she returned to her teaching job here eighteen

months later but she was a changed woman.'

'Changed? In what way?'

'I don't just mean physically changed, though of course her physical appearance had altered but, no, what I'm talking about is her personality. The bright spark had left her eyes and she was distant with us . . . distant with her students and uncomfortable with herself.'

'Did you ever talk to her about her unhappiness?'

'Oh, you may be sure I tried but she had withdrawn into herself. Her engagement had by this stage been broken off but I think there was more to it than that.'

'Who . . . I mean which of them, do you know, was responsible for breaking off the engagement?'

'Difficult to say really. While Jac was in the various hospitals, Larry Carroll – that's the name of the man she was engaged to – spent hours and days by her bedside. Everyone remarked on his devotion to her at the time. He stuck with her through all the operations and watched as the beautiful face that had been so damaged underwent a series of skin and bone grafts, each operation more painful than the one before. The doctors and surgeons performed miracles but of course they could never recreate God's perfection. By the time she returned to Abbeygates the scars had become less pronounced but, even with generous applications of make-up, her injuries were still noticeable. Rumours abounded at the time that Larry Carroll would not go ahead with the marriage plans because he regarded her, his bride-to-be, as damaged goods.'

'But surely that does not fit with the attention and devotion he lavished on her during her time in hospital?'

'I agree with you, Emma, but that's what the people said at the time.'

'What did Larry Carroll do with himself after that?'

'Three years later he married Muriel Fielding – one of the horsy set – a match created with wealth in mind: Carroll, a son of successful industrialist married to the daughter of Ireland's richest horse trainer.'

'But the marriage took place long after Jac left the school; so why exactly did she quit Abbeygates?'

'Oh dear me, dear me, I still shudder when I think of the day she walked out. It was lunchtime on a Friday as I recall. Jacqueline was in our school library – it's got three rows of back-to-back shelves with aisles running between – she was looking for some book or other when a group of students arrived to look for reference material. The girls were not aware that one of their teachers was present and, as chance would have it, one of them referred to Miss Miller as 'half-face' much to the amusement of her companions. Jacqueline ran from the room sobbing, went to her classroom, collected the few bits and pieces that belonged to her and left the school. She never returned. It is an episode I am profoundly ashamed of, an incident that still, to this day, brings a sadness to my heart. I wish to God it had not happened . . . but what's the use. It did happen, and there's nothing any one of us can do to change that. Even now, now that I know she has made a success of her life, I feel so guilty that this school, Abbeygates, should have hurt her so badly at a time when she was feeling so vulnerable.'

'And her family, what about them? Surely they were around to help?'

'Her family? Hm , yes, one would expect a family to help at a time like that but like everything else in Jac's life, her home was no great shakes. *Dysfunctional*, I think is the word they use nowadays. Her brother Sean was institutionalised – Down's syndrome plus half a dozen side-complications. I think Jac found it difficult to accept his disabilities. He died tragically before her twentieth birthday. This was before she came to teach here, before the accident. Then there was her older sister Regina but she was married and living somewhere up near Dublin, so she wasn't much help.'

'What about her parents?'

'Her parents, yes.' Sr Michele paused uneasily and a frown darkened her face. 'Jac's mother and father split up while she was still in her early teens.'

'Did you ever meet either of her parents?'

'No, I never met them. There was a rift between mother and daughter . . . but Jac never talked about her family. I did *see* her father once. It was several years before Jac came to teach here. I saw him on stage, believe it or not.'

'On stage . . . you mean, as in acting?'

'Yes, I told you already of my involvement in amateur drama and it was in that respect that I saw him. One of the highlights on the drama calendar is the festival held in Athlone each year after Easter. It's a competition to find the top drama group in the country. Myself and a few of the nuns here never miss it. We buy season tickets and go to all the plays for the two weeks. Anyway, one season, let me see now, it must have been ten or eleven years ago, maybe twelve, a local group managed to qualify. Jac's father was playing the lead with them. It was an Alan Ayckbourn play; a very funny one called *A Chorus of Disapproval*. As it was a local group, I wanted it to win – show that we knew our drama in the midlands – but it came nowhere, except for Jac's father, that is. He walked away with the best actor award. And do you know what I'm going to tell you: he well deserved it, as good an actor as I've ever seen. He was a small man but he moved about the stage with elegance and poise, a natural talent; he played the part to perfection.'

Any idea why the marriage split up?'

'No, as I said, Jac never spoke about the situation in the family and I never poked my nose in.'

'So what you're saying is; there was nobody there to help her when she needed it most.'

'That's about the size of it, I'm afraid to say. If we're to believe the gossip doing the rounds at the time – I try not to pay any heed to gossip – Jac suffered some sort of mental breakdown after the incident at the school.'

'But you never found out for sure?'

The nun, hearing the implied criticism behind Emma's question, eased her breath out slowly in what sounded like a sigh.

'Right,' she said, 'I never did find out, but I fancy there was no truth to it. You know how people like to gossip and exaggerate.'

'So you had no further contact with Jacqueline?'

'I'm afraid not, except through her schoolbooks of course. I can't tell you how pleased I was when I heard that she had been successful with her publishing venture. Did I tell you we use her books in the classroom; they are excellent. It's good to see she has put all the misery behind her and is finally enjoying a measure of success.'

It was an hour later when Emma took her leave of Sr Michele and headed back for Dublin. A mental picture of Jacqueline Miller was beginning to emerge in her head. She had heard so much about her, but as yet she had not even met the woman.

It was midday as Emma made her way along Tullamore's long main street. The rain had eased considerably but shoppers, complete with umbrellas, jostled each other as they moved grim-faced along the footpaths.

It would be about 2.30 p.m. by the time she made it back to her apartment. When she got there she intended to make a list of the people she needed to see. Top of that list would be Jacqueline Miller, followed by Larry Carroll and Alan McCall's wife.

9

Droning like a swarm of demented bees, the sound of the vacuum cleaner assailed Francis Xavier's ears as his housekeeper, Mrs McNamee, began her once-weekly task of cleaning his house. Every Saturday, like clockwork, come hail, rain or sunshine, on the dot of 2 o'clock the racket began. Only his private office escaped Mrs McNamee's passion for cleanliness; that room he insisted on vacuuming himself.

Shutting out the sound as best he could, Francis Xavier Donnelly reviewed the plans he had dreamt up to track the government ministers on a twenty-four-hours-a-day basis. Calling on all his editorial skills, he put the finishing touches to the ten-page document he had prepared on the subject, a change of word here and there, a new paragraph break for clarity and several minor alterations to improve the presentation. He was scheduled to deliver his proposal to the Taoiseach at 11.30 on Monday morning. Hopefully, she would see the wisdom of proceeding with his plan to tag electronically the entire pool of cars used by ministers in the cabinet. The rationale had been carefully worded so that the scheme's main objective focused on increasing efficiency while, at the same time, cutting costs. The system envisaged in his blueprint allowed messages to be sent to drivers in regard to re-routing arrangements and could pinpoint more accurately the arrival and departure times of various ministers. He made special mention of cases in the recent past where a car had been sent to Dublin Airport to pick up a government minister when there was already a car there that had just dropped off another minister.

The underlying motive behind his system, that of controlling and monitoring the movements of the ministers themselves, was played down. Radio devices fitted into the car's dashboard would be capable of emitting five signals every minute to a central control unit. This would establish the car's location to within a radius of twenty-five yards and would ensure that certain ministers with a liking for over-long lunches or blaming heavy traffic for non-attendance at meetings would no longer get away with such bad behaviour. More importantly, it would put a stop to ministers taking time out to visit their mistresses, save taxpayers' money and avoid the likelihood of scandals. Francis Xavier sighed. He would need all the tricks in the book to keep the present lot out of trouble.

It annoyed him intensely that so many men in power were incapable of keeping their flies zipped up. A long-time believer in celibacy, he prided himself on the discipline he exercised over his body's baser needs. It never ceased to puzzle him how man, with all his ingenuity in the fields of science, medicine, the arts and industry, could revert to the level of the lowest primates when it came to sex. It wasn't that he believed everyone should follow his celibate lifestyle – procreation was necessary after all, he accepted that – but he felt that the sexual act itself was demeaning and ought to be confined strictly to the privacy of the marriage bed, and even there, strictly as a means of procreation. One day, he hoped, all those he considered sexual deviants – the list included paeodophiles, fornicators, homosexuals and transsexuals – would be subjected to a law that imposed castration or sterilisation as a penalty for their unlawful acts.

Alan McCall, as a fornicator, had earned his place in Francis Xavier's list of wrongdoers. He thought about the murdered politician and the trouble his indiscretion had caused. Newspaper reports had made McCall out to be a regular family man, forced to spend nights away from his wife and children in order to serve his country. It was a source of irritation to Francis Xavier that McCall's lack of discipline should so heavily impinge on his job. As party secretary he was forced to go to extraordinary lengths to maintain McCall's credibility in order to safeguard the future of his party in government.

Earlier that morning he had received photographs from Joe Stones showing Emma Boylan and an unidentified man entering Jacqueline Miller's house. He had no idea how Emma Boylan had connected Number 32 to current activities and that worried him. Yet, he felt confident that her enquiries, if that's what they were, would get her nowhere. There was nothing in the house that could possibly connect Alan McCall to what had happened there. Still, he would feel a lot happier if she had not begun to poke her nose where it wasn't wanted. Being careful, he had asked Joe Stones to continue to monitor the house and to hire a second person if necessary to mount a round-the-clock surveillance operation. If there were any fresh developments, he wanted to be the first to know.

He would tell the Taoiseach the full truth about McCall on Monday and use the episode to bolster his argument for the electronic tracking of the government pool of cars. Fionnuala Stafford would, he imagined, be angry and upset to hear of McCall's despicable behaviour but once she calmed down and thought about the potential scandal he had spared the government, she would see the wisdom of his actions and express her satisfaction with his handling of the situation. In time, he felt sure, she would show her appreciation by appointing him to the Senate. That, he felt, was a prize worth sticking his neck out for. A senator, yes! He liked the idea of being a member of the upper house of legislation and the prestige attached to it. For once in his life, he believed, he could achieve something really worthwhile.

In the past he had harboured lofty dreams and aspirations but something had always intervened to thwart his ambition. As a student at St Ignatius's Seminary in County Galway he had wanted to become the best priest ever to emerge from that college. At eighteen years of age he had pious dreams of going abroad, preaching the message of Christianity to the heathens of the world. He had wanted a mission that would allow him to become a prince of Christ's church on earth and impress his superiors with his zeal and dedication – impress them enough to reward his efforts by elevating him to the top of the hierarchical ladder. As with most of his great aspirations he had been sorely disappointed.

Putting his papers into his briefcase, he noticed that the drone from Mrs McNamee's vacuum cleaner had ceased. The reason for the silence soon became apparent. The familiar sound of Mrs McNamee's three rapid knocks on his door announced her entry into the room.

'There's a gentleman at the door who wishes to see you, Mr Donnelly.'

'Well, I hope you told the gentleman – whoever he is – that I do not see anyone on a Saturday.'

'Indeed I did Mr Donnelly but would he listen? Not this one . . . dead ignorant if you ask me; said you'd want to see him; said to tell you his name was Jimmy Rabbitte; said that . . . '

Jimmy Rabbitte stepped through the door, pushing Mrs McNamee to one side. 'Yes, F. X.,' he said, amused by the shocked look on the housekeeper's face, 'I told this fine lady here that you would make time to see your old friend Jimmy Rabbitte.'

Francis Xavier Donnelly's face turned white with rage. 'How dare you, how dare you push your way into my house. Will you please leave immediately, do you hear me? Immediately!'

'Ah, stop acting the bollix, F. X. No need to get your knickers in a knot; get rid of this ould biddy here and let me and you talk about some unfinished business.'

'I don't believe we have any business to discuss, Mr Rabbitte.'

'Oh, but we *do*, F. X., we do; you were, shall we say, a little economical with the truth when last we talked. Now, will you kindly ask this lady to get to fuck out of here or do I have to speak in front of her?'

'Mrs McNamee, I'm sorry about this, I really am,' Francis Xavier said to his housekeeper, trying to control his fury. 'Could you leave me to sort out this gentleman.'

Mrs McNamee glared at the two men, first her boss, then the intruder, before turning on her heel and slamming the door shut.

There was silence for a moment as the two men eyed each other. Without speaking, Francis Xavier indicated to Rabbitte that he should take a seat. Rabbitte grinned, a cunning grin that did nothing to hide the victory he felt was his, and lowered himself into the chair Donnelly had indicated.

'I almost didn't recognise you, F. X., without your dicky-bow and fancy waistcoat,' Rabbitte said, appraising Donnelly's casual attire.

Donnelly's right hand shot involuntarily to his open-neck shirt and, realising that Rabbitte was making him jumpy, attempted to gain control of the situation.

'Look here, Mr Rabbitte, you have a damn impertinence pushing your way into my house like this, but . . . but now that you *are* here, suppose you tell me what it is you think I can do for you?'

Rabbitte shook his head in a manner that suggested he couldn't believe Francis Xavier should find it necessary to pose the question. He allowed his slight frame to slump back into the leather-studded chair, ran his fingers through his thinning hair and deliberately took his time before speaking.

'The photographs and film I gave you were sold on the basis that Alan McCall was involved in nothing more serious than a little extramarital activity. Right? What you failed to tell me at the time of the exchange was that we were dealing with the heinous crime of murder, not some trifling dalliance.'

'I didn't know anything about the murder when we spoke ... when we concluded our deal. How could I know? McCall was still alive then. I acted in good faith.'

'Good faith, F. X.? Don't make me laugh, you wouldn't know good faith if it leaped off the ground and snapped your balls off. Anyway, it's of little consequence whether you knew or not. The point is this: we now have a totally new situation. With McCall dead, we're talking about a whole new ball game.'

'Look, you got your money, I don't see what the problem is.'

'Oh, come now, F. X. I think you see the problem all right. You're not as green as you're cabbage-looking. But, lest there be any misunderstandings, let me try to make myself clear; you see, to get the roll of film and prints I had to do a deal with one of the lab technicians in our darkroom. Since hearing about McCall's murder, that same technician, a frog as it happens, has begun to panic a little. He's the one I asked to tell Frankie Kelly that his film didn't develop properly and hand him back a blank exposed roll. I paid the frog part of the money you gave me to make the swap and cover for me – which was all very fine and dandy until we discovered that McCall had gone and got himself killed. Now my French friend is shitting himself.'

'Are you saying to me that you want more money to pay some French technician fellow? Is that what this is all about?'

'That's part of it, F. X., just part of it. What I'm really saying is that I want more money – an awful lot more money – to keep the lid on this.'

'But that's madness. I've already given you £4,000 for the prints and the original film. I've since destroyed them so there is no more to be said on the matter.'

'Hardly, F. X.– I've a story that'll create a media feeding frenzy if I divulge what I know.'

'Yes, and in the process you will have to expose yourself to a charge of blackmail.'

'I hardly think so, F. X. I mean to say, I can't exactly see you admitting to paying over money for the film and prints in the first place, can you?'

'Look, Jimmy,' Francis Xavier said, adopting a conciliatory tone, 'what you're saying is not on. We've both got to be sensible about this. You got your money – have you any idea how difficult a problem that was? – but for me now to attempt to get *more* money would be impossible, quite impossible.'

'Then I shall have to proceed with plan B. I'll have to sell my story to the national media. That should bring me a fair penny.'

'No one would believe your story. They would ask why hadn't you run with the story in your own rag, the *Dublin Dispatch*.'

'You're right in some respects, F. X., except for one thing.'

'And what might that be?'

'I held on to one negative frame. I can prove that Alan McCall visited 32 Leeson Crescent on the night he was murdered.'

'What? I don't believe you! You really are the lowest form of life, Rabbitte; you swore you had given me the total contents.'

'Isn't that just life for you,' Rabbitte said through a sneer. 'I've always believed in holding on to a little insurance – watch my back, so to speak. The world is full of sharks . . . sharks ready to gobble up anyone dumb enough to let them. I'll sell the negative to you or the media. The choice, my friend, is yours.'

Francis Xavier thought for a moment before speaking. 'Just suppose, Mr Rabbitte, just suppose for argument's sake that I was fool enough to part with more money, what proof would you give me that you don't have even more negatives . . . you know what they say – once bitten, twice shy.'

'You'll have no proof, F. X., but think about this: selling my story to the media might cause me some pain. It's possible that I might have some awkward questions to answer – I don't deny it. I might even be charged with attempting to pervert the course of justice – who can say? – but I *will* do it if I have to. However, it seems to me I could save us both a lot of grief if you were to buy the negative and my silence. You could come to my house and together we'd burn it. That, I promise you, would be the end of the matter.'

Francis Xavier Donnelly was silent again. The first hint of sweat appeared on his brow. He shifted his bulky weight uneasily in his chair before addressing Rabbitte. 'How much?'

'Quarter of a mil,' Rabbitte replied.

Francis Xavier's intake of breath was audible. His eyes bore belligerently into Rabbitte. 'Are you completely mad? Have you gone stark raving mad? Jesus Christ almighty, man, do you know what you're saying? Quarter of a million – Jesus, I'd laugh my head off except that I think you're serious.'

'You'd better believe it, F. X. I've never been more serious in my life. That's the price, take it or leave it.'

'Look, Jimmy, let's get real here. I could maybe manage to get you . . . six . . . maybe ten grand, even, on top of the four thousand I've already given you. It wouldn't be easy, but I could try. But those telephone numbers you're tossing about . . . two hundred and fifty thousand pounds. Well, that's not realistic at all.'

'In that case, F. X., my old pal, we've got nothing further to say to each other . . . except to tell you to expect to see pictures of Alan McCall and his mistress plastered over the front page of every paper in the country and top feature on every television news bulletin. Need I remind you that the photograph shows McCall kissing Jacqueline Miller in the doorway of her home . . . not the same location where the body was found. When that happens, you and your party cronies will be out on their arses before you can say the word – conspiracy.'

'Look, Jimmy, let's be reasonable about this; can you hold off for a few days? You must know that I'm not in a position to do a deal involving the sort of money you're talking about. I'll need to discuss your demands with the party leaders . . . see what they have to say.'

'Right F. X., that seems reasonable enough, I'll give you until Wednesday – that gives you four days – to come back to me. If you do *not* agree with my terms by then I'll have no choice but to go to the media.'

'I'll be back to you by noon, Wednesday; see if there's some agreement we can come up with.'

'There's only *one* agreement my fat friend, a quarter mil . . . it's not all that much when you come to think about it – the Taoiseach's own house in Ballsbridge is worth nine or ten times that amount – you're getting my silence cheap.'

10

Seeing a stallion mate with a mare was not something Emma had witnessed before. When Larry Carroll had agreed to meet her on Sunday evening at the Eclipse Stud Farm, she had no idea she would be exposed to a display of equine passion. She had driven to Prosperous, a small town in County Kildare, and found the stud farm about a half mile outside the town. She parked next to a Range Rover Vogue and a bright red Ferrari Testarossa that looked like it had just come from a car showroom. Admiring the gleaming car, she made a mental note to have her own more modest vehicle washed next time she visited the filling station. Carroll's wife, Muriel, had met her at the door of their two-storied farmhouse and pointed her in the direction of what she called the 'covering yard'.

'You will find Larry, there,' she said in mellifluous tones and faultless diction. 'Turpin is covering last year's Epsom Derby winner.'

Emma entered the large octagonal building where a group of men were kept busy controlling two horses. The larger of the two animals reared up on its hind legs making loud trumpeting sounds with its mouth while a man attempted to restrain it by holding a leather strap to its bridle. Emma recognised the man overseeing the operation; he was Larry Carroll, the same man whose photograph she had seen in Jacqueline Miller's house. Of medium height, dark, well-built and with better than average looks, he spotted Emma and beckoned her to come closer.

'It's all right,' he said,' there's no need to be afraid; everything is under control. We'll talk when this little performance is completed. I hope you don't mind waiting?'

'Not at all. Thanks for agreeing to see me at such short notice,' Emma said, moving closer to where the horses and their handlers stood. 'What exactly is happening here?'

'You've never seen a mare being covered before?'

'No, I haven't.'

'Well, the big chestnut making all the commotion is Turpin, our most valuable stallion. He's getting ready to cover the mare you see; her name is Eve's Day, you've heard of her I'm sure.'

Emma had never heard of Eve's Day but saw no particular reason to admit it to Larry Carroll. She did not need to be told which animal was the stallion; Turpin's genital organ was swinging wildly, getting gradually stiffer as the huge animal pranced about on two legs. The mare was being held by a man who sought to calm the smaller animal by backing her towards a low wall of poles.

'We use the wall,' Carroll explained to Emma, 'when we have a mare prone to kicking.' As he spoke, the stallion made an ear-piercing sound and plunged on to the back of the mare, its organ now swelled to its full proportions. A man, who Carroll explained was a vet experienced in equine gynaecology, took hold of the great organ and guided it into the mare's vulva. For almost two minutes, Emma watched as Turpin thrust violently while the mare was held relatively still by her handlers.

'Ouch,' Emma said as she saw the stallion bite down on the mare's neck.

'It doesn't hurt,' Carroll told her, 'we've got a padded guard on the mare's neck.'

As soon as Turpin dismounted, the vet pulled the mare quickly away from where the encounter had taken place.

'Mares tend to kick after they have been serviced,' Larry explained to Emma, 'so we've to be careful to protect Turpin – his genitals in particular. A blow on the testicles could render him sterile. When you consider the value in monetary terms of these two thoroughbreds, we've got to be very careful.'

'Why do it on a Sunday?'

'Well, it's not through any choice of ours; you see we monitor the mare's cycle carefully and cover her at the optimum time – which in Eve's Day's case happens to be right now. On top of that, the life of a stallion's sperm is no more than forty-eight hours so we've got to be damn accurate.'

As the animals were led away, Larry Carroll invited Emma to follow him into the house. 'I met your wife earlier,' she said. 'It was she who told me where to find you.'

'It probably never occurred to Muriel that you were not part of the equestrian lot . . . I hope the little mating exercise you saw did not upset you.'

'Not at all, I found it most . . . interesting.'

As they made their way back to the house, Emma pointed to the red Ferrari parked beside her own car. 'I like your wheels,' she said. 'Nice motor!'

'Nice motor all right but I'm afraid the Testarossa was not built for the roads around these parts. Frankly, I just bought it for the Ferrari horse-motif on the badge.'

Emma smiled, thinking about the hundred grand or so that it must have cost him to buy a badge with a black horse on it but said nothing. How did one respond to a remark like that!

Inside the house, Carroll brought Emma into the trophy room, a timber-panelled reception area that served as a gallery for hundreds of framed photographs of horses. Spaced along the walls, a series of glass cases displayed dozens of trophies of all shapes and sizes and a colourful array of rosettes. On a plinth set in the centre of the room, a copper statue of a horse, rearing on its hind quarters, took pride of place. An inscription at the base of the statue read: *Eclipse*, owned by Dennis O'Kelly. Sire to 344 winners including St Simon, 1884 Gold Cup, Ascot.

'Dennis O'Kelly once owned this stud farm,' Carroll informed Emma when he saw her admiring the statue. 'He started it back in the nineteenth century – we try our best to follow in his footsteps.'

'A proud tradition,' Emma said, because she felt that

was the sort of thing you said on occasions such as this.

'Muriel has gone down to the bottom paddocks so I won't offer you tea; perhaps I can get you something a little stronger.'

'No thank you very much, I'm fine,' Emma replied, amused by Carroll's assignment of the tea-making role to his wife, 'I don't want to take up too much of your time, I just want to have a few words with you about Jacqueline Miller.'

'Ah, yes, so you said to me on the telephone. So, what is it you think I can tell you?'

'I'll tell you what I know already, then you can fill in some of the blanks. Does that sound OK to you?'

'Yes, fine, go ahead.'

Emma related most of what she had learned to date about Jacqueline Miller. Carroll nodded his head in agreement with what she had to say, adding slight corrections here and there. When she had finished, Carroll looked at her with a bemused expression on his face. 'You've done your research well,' he said. 'It appears to me there's little more I can tell you.'

'There are one or two further points you could clear up for me. I know this is a bit personal but could you tell me *why* exactly your engagement to Jacqueline Miller broke up.'

'I see,' he said, his brows forming a perplexed frown. 'I'm not sure how to answer that one.'

'Well, could you tell me which of you was responsible for the break.'

'Again, even that's not as simple to answer as you might think. To understand how things fell apart after Jacqueline's accident, you need to know a bit more about her family ... and about her Down's syndrome brother Sean in particular.' Carroll talked at length about the relationship between Jacqueline Miller and her brother. According to Carroll, the siblings experienced a love-hate relationship until Sean's death at the age of twenty-five. As a schoolchild, Jacqueline realised that her brother was different from other boys of his age that she knew. To her he appeared demanding and clinging. Everyone else loved the boy. She imagined that her friends laughed at his oddly shaped head and mongoloid-featured face but she was wrong. Nothing would convince her that her friends accepted Sean, that they really liked him. Because of her perceived notions, she felt ashamed of him. She stopped bringing classmates and friends around to her house thinking they would make fun of him or snigger behind her back. On dates, she made sure to keep her boyfriends well away from her brother. A feeling of guilt developed in her, especially towards the end of Sean's life. She realised that she had been the one blessed with beauty and brains while she saw her brother as being retarded and ugly. She had difficulty in reconciling these two opposite realities. It was not until her own accident that the true extent of this conflict in her brain came home to roost.

'She told you all this while she was in hospital?' Emma enquired.

'Yes,' Carroll replied. 'She would hold my hand and go on and on about him. It was sort of like a stream-of-consciousness thing; all the little incidents of their lives were regurgitated, all except for some disturbing incidents that she found herself unable to talk about. She blamed herself for not understanding the pain and humiliation that her brother must have experienced. On one occasion, she told me that God had deliberately disfigured her face so that she would understand what it must have been like for her brother. To be honest, I worried that she might have been psychologically disturbed. She became obsessed with the idea of God's retribution and consumed with guilt.'

'So, how did it actually end – your engagement, I mean.'

'Slowly and painfully. I continued to see Jac after she left the hospital but by then the phone calls had begun.'

'Phone calls? She began to telephone you?'

'No, no, not Jac . . . She never called. It was a man who claimed to be a mutual friend. He advised me not go through with the marriage.'

'Some man you never met told you this?'

'Yes. I know it sounds daft and of course it was daft – off-the-wall stuff.'

'What sort of things did he say?'

'It's more a question of what didn't he say. Let me see: according to him I was marrying her out of pity and did not really love her. I refused to discuss the matter over the phone. He would ring back and rant and rave about how ugly and disfigured Jac had become and insist that no sane man could possibly look at her without feeling revulsion. This was not true, of course; to me Jac remained beautiful and besides, I loved her.'

'Did you ever discuss the telephone calls with her?'

'Yes I did . . . on several occasions. She said I was making the whole thing up, inventing the caller, using the calls as an excuse to break off the engagement. Nothing I said would make her believe otherwise. In the end the relationship just fizzled out.'

'I see,' Emma said, 'and did you ever find out who the man on the telephone was?'

'Not really; on one occasion he called himself Christy, but I never found out who he was.'

'Christy, no surname?'

'No.'

Emma thought for a second before framing her next question. 'I don't mean to be offensive but, during this stressful period, is there any possibility you could have imagined the phone calls – as Jacqueline suggested – as a way out of . . . ?'

Carroll resented the question. 'No, Ms Boylan, I didn't imagine the man. As a matter of fact he spoke on my answering machine on a number of occasions.'

Emma decided not to push the subject of Christy any further for the present. 'Do you ever see Jacqueline Miller now?'

'No, I haven't seen her for over five years. She disappeared completely for two years after the court case. I believe she suffered some sort of breakdown at the time.'

'You're sure about that?'

'Yes, I contacted her sister Regina at that time to enquire how Jac was doing. She told me that Jac was receiving therapy. According to Regina, Jac responded well to the treatment and was managing to put her problems behind her. She must have been right because about a year later I read a story in our local paper about her success in education. I still read about her occasionally and I'm glad to see she has got on with her life – made a success of things. That's why you are writing your article about her after all, right?'

'Yes, yes, indeed,' Emma lied, having momentarily forgotten that Carroll didn't know the real reason why she was digging into Jacqueline Miller's background. 'Tell me, did you ever meet Jacqueline's mother?'

'Yes, I did. I got to know Mrs Miller around the time of the accident. She stayed in the hospital by the bedside for days during the time Jac remained on the critical list.'

'And how did they get on?'

'It was hard to tell at first. I thought there was a strong mother-daughter bond but I was wrong.'

'How do you mean?'

'I'm not sure I ought to be telling you this, but I suppose it makes no difference now. As soon as Jac regained consciousness and realised her mother was in the room, she demanded that she leave. At the time, I put it down to Jac's state of confusion but later as she gained in strength, she instructed the nurses and the doctors to keep her mother away from her. The whole thing was most upsetting and not a little embarrassing.'

'Did you ask Jacqueline about it?'

'I tried to bring up the subject a few times but she refused to allow any discussion on the matter.'

'What did *you* think of Mrs Miller?'

'I thought she was a fine woman – striking looks, younger than I expected, good personality. I got on well with her and as far as I could tell none of the hostility came from her side. I felt sorry for the way she was treated but there was little I could do to help. I still have no idea why Jac cut her out of her life.'

'I don't suppose you ever met her father?'

'No I didn't. As far as I know he walked out on the family when Jac was fourteen or fifteen. She never ever mentioned his name in all the time I knew her.'

'What? Not even when you asked her to marry you, surely . . . '

'Yes, sorry, you're right of course. Back before the accident, the subject of her father did come up in conversation. I asked her would he be attending the wedding ceremony. She looked at me in the strangest way, a look of dread. She didn't answer me, just shook her head and remained silent.'

'You never broached the subject of her father again?'

'No, I could see it was too painful for her. I hoped that in time she would talk to me about him . . . but she never did.'

Conversation continued for several more minutes before Larry Carroll excused himself, heeding a call from one of the men outside the house.

Emma left Eclipse Stud Farm with more questions than answers about Jacqueline Miller.

As Emma parked her car in front of her apartment she couldn't believe her eyes: Frankie Kelly was waiting for her, wrapped in a sheepskin coat, leaning against the red-brick wall outside the entrance, collar turned up around his neck. It was the glow from the tip of his cigarette that first caught her eye in the encroaching evening darkness. She hoped it was not marijuana. If some of her not-so-friendly neighbours got the whiff of pot there would be hell to pay. How long had he been there waiting for her, she wondered. It had taken her two hours to drive back from the stud farm. She was tired and her mind refused to stop going around in circles. What she did not need right now was a visitor. Her immediate reaction was one of annoyance. She had made it clear to Kelly that she did not want him to contact her outside working hours and especially not at her apartment. After locking her car she approached him with an attitude of hostility but one smile from him melted what would have been a strong rebuke from her.

'For God's sake, Frankie, will you get rid of that reefer before you bring the neighbourhood down on top of me; the smell of dope would knock you down.'

'Sorry, Emma, I didn't think of it like that; to be honest I only lit up to keep myself warm while waiting for you.'

'Why *are* you waiting for me?'

'Got something you'll want to see ... the photograph.'

'Oh, all right, you'd better come in then ... the place is probably freezing. I'll put the heat on; then we can look at the photo.'

Once inside Frankie removed his coat, plonked himself down on Emma's settee, slumped back rakishly and stretched his long legs out to meet the glow from a gas fire that attempted to pass itself off as a real coal fire.

'I don't suppose you've got anything to eat?' he asked Emma. 'I missed lunch today.'

'You suppose right, you cheeky devil. I've better things to be doing with my time than feed the likes of you.'

'Sorry, I only thought that ... '

'Oh shush, will you! I had lunch before I went down to County Kildare but I've a bit of batch loaf and some cheddar cheese in the kitchen if you think that would do you?'

'Yeah, sure, great. Don't suppose you got a can of beer in that kitchen while you're at it?'

'You're some tulip, Frankie Kelly ... what do you think I am? On second thoughts you'd better not answer that. No, I have no beer – the current man in my life has seen to that – but I do have some orange juice.'

'Orange juice? No, it's all right, I'll pass on that.'

'Choosy bugger aren't you. Well, as it happens I think I might have a drop of plonk somewhere in the kitchen.'

Emma sliced the batch loaf, cut a few chunks of cheddar and gave Frankie a bottle of Burgundy to open.

'Okay,' she said, sitting down. 'I'm done playing mumsy for now. So, what have you got to show me?'

Frankie opened the brown envelope he had been carrying with him, took out a photograph and handed it to her. 'We have lift-off,' he said excitedly, 'There's no doubt who the fellow in the picture is.'

'Bloody hell,' Emma said, studying the photograph, 'that's Shay Dunphy,'

'Right first time, it's none other than the country's youngest TD.'

'It's so clear and sharp. Your friend certainly did a smashing job on the photograph.'

'Yeah, he's amazing when he gets in front of his computer.'

'It's the business all right, I just can't understand how he did it. I still cannot work out what someone like Dunphy was doing coming out of Jacqueline Miller's house?'

'Ah now, that as they say is the sixty-four-thousand dollar question!'

'You have to wonder if he stayed there the whole night . . . and if so, what the hell is going on?' Silent for a moment, Emma considered how best to put in words what she wanted to say to Frankie next. 'Look Frankie, I don't mean to offend you but I'm going to ask you the same question I asked you before: are you sure, I mean absolutely, positively, one hundred per cent sure, it wasn't Shay Dunphy you saw entering the house the evening before?'

'Ah, come on now, Emma, give us a break! I told you a thousand times already that the person I saw was Alan McCall.

'All right. But you can't blame me for asking; the whole thing looks so crazy.'

'Yes, it's crazy all right – you're right about that much – but I'll tell you something: I'm going to damn well find out what's going on.'

'How do you propose to do that?'

'First thing Monday morning I'm going to talk to Jean-Pierre Brazin – he's the technician at the photo-graphic lab – and I'm going to find out what he did with my film. I know for sure now that there was nothing wrong with my camera or the film stock. I'm going to make him tell me why he lied to me.'

'What if he doesn't want to tell you?'

'Don't worry. I'll get him to talk.'

As Frankie and Emma ate their batch loaf and cheese, washed down with wine, they discussed every possible scenario that might shed light on why Shay Dunphy should have been at Jacqueline Miller's house. They examined the young politician's career in the Dáil and the various committees he served on. Was there any significance in the fact that Dunphy and McCall were members of the same party? Probably not, they concluded. Still, there had to be a connection and Emma decided she would use all her contacts in government circles to dig up more information on Dunphy.

Emma told Frankie about her meeting with Jacqueline

Miller's former fiancé, Larry Carroll, earlier in the day. She admitted that she was intrigued by Carroll's story about the phone calls he claimed to have received during the latter days of his engagement. Frankie agreed with her that the business about the telephone calls sounded a little odd. 'D'you think the caller could have been Alan McCall? he asked casually, as he rolled a joint and put a match to it.

'Unlikely; we're talking about phone calls made six years ago; I just can't imagine McCall being involved with Jacqueline that far back, but you never know.'

When Larry offered his reefer to Emma, she accepted it and took a drag. It had been years since she had smoked pot and her memory of the experience was one of indifference. At the time she remembered her college friends debating whether marijuana enhanced or diminished the sexual drive. Back then she had never put it to the test but she suspected the latter to be true. Aware that Frankie was looking at her, she inhaled deeply, trying to appear as if smoking marijuana was the most natural thing in the world. She handed him back the joint without comment and continued discussing the McCall murder.

As a journalist, Emma was used to recording events and paying special attention to the twists and turns in a breaking story. Her job demanded it. But if she were asked to be specific in regard to how the meeting in her living room with Frankie Kelly had evolved into a hedonistic encounter, she would have great difficulty. Equally, she would have some difficulty in apportioning blame – if *blame* was the right word – for what developed.

The combination of shared marijuana joints, wine and cheese had something to do with it but, if she were to be really honest, she would have had to admit that it was the vision of Frankie Kelly, six feet of walking testosterone, that had penetrated her usual reserve and got her juices flowing. The first inclination that she was entering uncharted waters was signalled by her fit of giggles. Telling Frankie about Turpin, the stallion she had seen in action earlier in the day, had set off the laughter. Frankie's question made matters worse. 'D'you suppose they named him Turpin after the famous highway man, Dick Turpin?'

'Yes, probably,' Emma replied, '*Dick* seems a most appropriate name. The giggles got worse. 'And d'you know what the mare does to the stallion after she has been serviced?' Emma asked, barely able to string the words together through the laughter.

'No, tell me.'

'The mare tries to kick him in the goolies.'

'Isn't that life for you – no different from human behaviour.' In unison, they both shook with laughter.

Someone had dimmed the lights, it might have been herself – she couldn't be sure. Van Morrison's *Astral Weeks* played on the turntable of her old-fashioned hi-fi as the reflection from the fireplace added a cosy dimension to the living room. As he stretched out his legs, his shoes brushed against hers; she removed her shoes and wriggled her toes in front of the fire. Frankie did likewise. They were now laughing at nothing, hysterical laughter, unstoppable laughter, throwing playful punches at each other when, without any awkwardness or contrivance, they moved into each other's arms and rolled on the floor in front of the fire. Frankie's face, awash with the red glow from the fake flames, looked directly into her eyes. The look spoke the language of passion more eloquently than any words could suggest. At that moment Emma knew she was lost. Through a sweet haze she looked back at him, noted the way his nose jutted out at her, the curves of his upper lip, his even teeth when he smiled, his strong chin and the mop of toffee-blond hair. How could anyone look so incredibly handsome. The kiss that followed provoked a response from every nerve in her body. As their tongues engaged in a subtle dance, a sensuous tango, she felt a hand caress her breast. At the same time, she was aware of her own hand being gently guided to the belt buckle on his trousers. At this point some inner mechanism in her consciousness kicked in. A warning voice coming from the deepest recesses of her being forced her to listen. She would rather not hear what was being said but the voice became insistent; it would not be stilled. *What are you doing, Emma? What on earth do you think you're doing!*

11

The radio next door, Jacqueline Miller discovered, increased in volume during the news bulletins. From the few words that penetrated the dividing walls she could tell it was a Monday. How long then had she been in this place? A week? More? Difficult to say. Impossible to calculate time. Her mind and body had been subjected to a deluge of barbiturate sedatives. Initially, in her first few days of confinement, she welcomed anything that blurred the details surrounding Alan McCall's death but in recent days she had changed her mind. Now, she wanted to regain full awareness and get out of this place. Her waking hours were filled with mental flashbacks that showed a decapitated head of Alan McCall. The horror presented itself again and again, always the same: in a pool of blood, a white death mask, its mouth open in a grin, its eyes twinkling, yet dead, horribly dead. She could no longer tell how exactly Alan had come to be dead in the first place, or who had killed him. Selective amnesia saw to it that she had no memory of the brutal act itself. In moments of full consciousness, she realised she had been there when Alan met his death, so why was it that she had so much difficulty in fixing on the details? For whatever reason, she knew it was for the best. In her present condition she felt unable to revisit the terrible deed itself. The recurring vision insisted on showing her the aftermath of the slaughter, nothing more. She was, she realised, having trouble in distinguishing what was real and what was not.

For some days now, Jacqueline Miller was aware that the sedatives were to blame for her tenuous grip on reality. She had decided to do something about it. In the past twenty-four hours she had fooled the nurses attending her by pretending to swallow the capsules. She took the capsules in her hand, placed them on her tongue but secretly withdrew them when bringing her hand back from her mouth. She drank a mouthful of water and created the impression of washing them down her throat. She continued to appear in a docile state whenever a nurse or doctor appeared in her room. It was important that they should not be aware of her plans to get out of the place. Earlier, on two occasions, while she was half-drugged, fragments of conversations penetrated her consciousness. She recognised the speakers: the stocky man with the bow tie and the doctor in charge. Like echoes coming from some endless vortex, she picked up the gist of what they were saying. Mr Bow Tie, as she had come to call the stocky one, insisted that she be kept under sedation until he advised otherwise. The doctor – she thought she heard a nurse address him as Dr Morley – appeared to disagree with Bow tie, but seemed powerless to do anything about it.

Jacqueline Miller's plan to escape from the clinic –

she did not know the name of the place – was thorough. She had made a mental timetable of the comings and goings of nurses, orderlies, assistants and doctors. Although she had no watch, she had become reasonably good at calculating time. Observing the daylight as it appeared and disappeared on the window of her room helped her plot the hours. Measuring the night-time hours proved more difficult.

Feeling frustrated and dog-tired, she thought about the action she had undertaken some hours earlier. During the night she had ventured from her room and into a short corridor outside her door. On legs weak from lack of exercise and the effect of drugs, she had still managed to move about and get a good idea of the geography of the building. Her room, she discovered, was one of eight similar rooms on the second floor of a three-storey building. At one end of the corridor, a flight of stairs led to the floor above her and another descended to ground level. Barefoot, she had tiptoed down a few steps before halting abruptly. She could see an open area, covered in grey and white chequered tiles, with a counter, a desk and several easy chairs. Two nurses sat on one side of the desk. They were drinking coffee and chatting softly to each other. Jacqueline had quickly withdrawn back to her corridor. On her way to her own room she opened what she hoped might be clothes closets. But she was wrong, the closet contained nothing more than cleaning implements, bed linen, and filing cabinets.

Thinking now about her first tentative attempt at

reconnaissance, she realised how important it would be to find day-wear clothes. Tonight, she intended to make a further foray in search of something suitable to wear. If she found anything that looked reasonable, she would take the next opportunity to make her break. Once outside the place she would find a telephone, contact Damien and get him to collect her. He would take her to his mother, Regina. As in the past, her older sister would look after her. From Regina's house she could set about planning what to do next. She would lie low for a few days and try to regain her strength so that she could attempt to come to terms with the Alan McCall tragedy. She wanted to get her mind straight, try to focus on the killing. There were moments when she believed she knew the killer's identity. She could not be sure; the image that flashed to her brain was fleeting, blurred, but she had little doubt that it was the same person who, six years earlier, had forced Larry Carroll and herself apart. Back then she had buckled under the pressure and given in to the amorphous vision, but this time the situation called for a more serious resolve. This time her lover had been killed; this time the spectre that haunted her had been responsible for murder.

As a nurse entered her room, Jacqueline Miller closed her eyes and assumed the role of slumbering patient.

Fionnuala Stafford was almost speechless with rage. She could not find words strong enough to condemn what Francis Xavier Donnelly had done in the government's name.

Half an hour earlier Donnelly had entered her office to outline his scheme for keeping tabs on the government cars. He had only got past page one of his report when she stopped him. 'The time is not right to put dashboard spies on our ministers,' she said dismissing his plan. 'The Brits tried to introduce a similar idea a few years back; it did not work there and it will not work here . . . so unless there is something else you wish to discuss . . . ?'

Unable to create a soft opening for what he had to say, Donnelly had no choice but to go in cold, tell her the unsavoury, behind-the-scenes truth about Alan McCall's death. Trouble was, he didn't know where, or how, to begin. She was staring at him now, wanting him to say something or get out. The stare unnerved him; it always had. If only he were dealing with a man instead of a woman, he would know what to say, feel more secure, be able to do some straight talking. He cursed inwardly. Since earliest childhood he had always felt ill-at-ease in the company of women. He did not remember his mother; she died when he was four but his father, whom he remembered as being cold and distant, arranged for his unmarried sister Julie to rear him. Aunt Julie, a hard-working woman, did her best to look after him but was not equal to the task. His relationship with her during those early years influenced his attitude towards females for the rest of his life. One memory in particular remained forever in his subconscious. Until his eleventh birthday, Julia had insisted he share her once-weekly bath on a Saturday night. Cost savings on water heating explained Julie's motive, but as a young boy he had been both fascinated and repelled by the sight of her soap-covered pendulous breasts and body hair. This practice only stopped when the onset of his puberty became obvious. As a teenager, girls fascinated him; he idealised and romanticed them but distrusted them and felt threatened by their sexuality.

Looking at Fionnuala Stafford now, he realised he had never fully come to terms with his fear of the opposite sex.

In brief detail, he gave her a sanitised version of what he, Pettit and Dunphy had done on the night of the Alan McCall murder. Fionnuala Stafford appeared stunned by what she was hearing. As his account continued, the colour drained from her face. When he got to the part about Jimmy Rabbitte's latest blackmail demand, she could no longer contain herself.

'I'm hearing this,' she said, 'but I'm having difficulty believing it. Tell me this is some sort of sick joke; tell me that you could not be so stupid; tell me you haven't got shit for brains; tell me that two of my elected members, Dunphy and Pettit, were not dim-witted enough to be inveigled into your mad scheme; tell me anything but tell me this is not happening.'

'What was I supposed to do,' Francis Xavier asked, hurt by her scorn, 'I did what you employ me to do. I saw a potential scandal – one of your ministers about to be exposed as an adulterer – I moved to spike the story like any good party secretary worth his salt would do in a similar situation.'

'Yes, yes, that bit I understand; that bit I follow,' she said with calculated patience, 'but when you found that McCall had been killed, surely to Christ in heaven you could see that everything had changed. Instead of some tittle-tattle indiscretion, the situation had changed to one of murder. Good God, man, do you not realise what your rush of shit to the brain has done?'

'Yes.' Francis Xavier shook his head emphatically. 'I have avoided a scandal, Ma'am.

His riposte took Fionnuala Stafford past breaking point. She pushed her chair back and stood glaring at him with a look of withering proportions. Her five-foot-three stature, slender build, unflinching eyes and angular face framed by a black-dyed, pageboy hairstyle, combined to give her a formidable countenance. Dressed, as was her custom, in black jacket, black skirt and black silk-satin blouse, she looked older than her forty-seven years. It was once said of her, by Jim Carberry, a television reporter known for his caustic wit, that she had the ability to brighten up any room simply by leaving it. His nickname for her, Madame Defarge, was perhaps overstating the case but from where Francis Xavier Donnelly stood, Dickens's famous lady of the guillotine could not have directed a more venomous eye than Fionnuala Stafford now subjected him to.

'You're a thundering idiot,' she said, her voice reaching sub-zero chill factor, her eyes smouldering with fury. 'In trying to save the reputation of one inconsequential member of our party, whose imbecile behaviour might, or might not, have caused a two-day flap in the media, you've jeopardised the very life of this government. If one whisper of what you have done gets out, you are dead . . . Correction, we are all dead . . . do you understand . . . *dead*.

'Only one person can point a finger in our direction,' Francis Xavier said. 'That person is Jimmy Rabbitte. I suggest we take him up on his offer . . . buy his silence.'

'Do you seriously believe that a quarter of a million – assuming we could get our hands on that much by Wednesday – would keep some guttersnipe of a man like Rabbitte silent. Even you can not be naive enough to believe that. He would piss it down the drain or inject it into his arm or whatever the hell it is he does and be back for more in no time at all. And what about this woman that McCall was with? What did you call her . . . Jacqueline Miller . . . how do you propose to keep her quiet, not to mention whoever it was who did the killing in the first place?'

'I know it looks bad, Ma'am, but I believe the situation can be contained if we shut Rabbitte up; the others can be handled easily enough.'

'Shut Rabbitte up?' the Taoiseach asked, sitting back down on her chair, becoming silent for a moment before speaking again. 'Yes, we must shut Rabbitte up but not by paying him money. We must find some other way; buy us time to plan a way out of the mess you've dropped us in.'

Francis Xavier thought about this for a moment, beads of perspiration now visible on his forehead and upper lip. 'I hardly think that's fair, I . . .'

'Shut up for Christ's sake or so help me, I'll . . . Look, here's what I want you to do: get in touch with Shay Dunphy and Tom Pettit. Tell them I've called a special meeting of the PCCC committee for four o'clock today here in my office. We'll try to see if there is some way out of this. Now if you don't mind, I'd like you to get to hell out of my sight.'

Monday dragged on.

It was seven o'clock in the evening by the time Emma Boylan made it to the government buildings. She had hoped to be there by early afternoon but her editor, Bob Crosby, had other ideas; he needed the article she had been doing about bribery and backhanders among county councillors for the next day's edition of the *Post*. She had researched the piece before the Alan McCall murder came along but a few loose ends remained to be tidied up. Crosby insisted she have it on his desk by six o'clock that evening. 'We're having a slow-news week,' he told her, 'and in the absence of any new concrete developments in the McCall story, your exposé on local government sleaze might liven things up. Present it as a breaking story.'

'Jesus, Bob, I don't know; that story is old hat.'

'Yes, damn it, I know,' Crosby said irritably. 'The rumblings about county councillors making dodgy planning decisions on the strength of bribes has been, like the poor, with us for years, but with the creativity I expect from you, Emma, you can dress it up and make it sound fresh.'

Bob Crosby was pleased with the finished piece when she handed it to him – her headline read, 'The Brown Envelope Syndrome' – but pressed her to come through with a break on the McCall story.

'The story will die on its feet if we don't dig up some new angle within the next few days or so,' he said, his eyebrows raised in expectation of a positive response.

Emma gave him a quick résumé of developments to date, outlining brief details of what she had uncovered in regard to Jacqueline Miller. She told him about the work Frankie Kelly had done on the reconstructed photograph. After she showed him the 'before' and 'after' prints, he seemed satisfied. 'Promising,' he said, 'very promising.'

Snowflakes, illuminated in the spill from the street lamps, fluttered down past Emma as she showed her pass to the garda on duty at the Kildare Street entrance to the government buildings. He looked at the pass, looked at Emma's face and winked at her, and allowed her to proceed. The garda's little gesture of flirtation went unrewarded; he had, unluckily for him, picked the wrong day. Today, Emma was in no mood to be humoured by anyone, least of all by a young pimple-faced garda, ten years her junior. Pressing on, her shoulders huddled in an effort to ward off the cold, she thought about Frankie Kelly and the time they had spent together less than twenty-four hours earlier. Even now, it seemed like some out-of-body odyssey into the realms of fantasy, except that it wasn't fantasy; it really had happened. What had got into her? How could she, an engaged woman, have allowed herself to end up in such a compromising position. And what about Vinny Bailey, the man she had promised to marry? What would she tell him? Would she tell him anything at all? These questions, and a lot more besides, flashed through her mind but the most disturbing aspect, as far as she was concerned, was the fact that a tingle of lingering pleasure remained – thoughts of what might have happened if she had not stopped when she did.

Recognising that the marijuana had been the liberating agent that sparked off the romantic encounter, she knew she could not blame the dope entirely. Frankie had sulked when she brought the proceedings to an abrupt ending. Buoyed by his initial success and fully believing he had made all the right moves, it came to him as a body blow to have his advances rejected. This last-minute withdrawal of the 'prize' was, it seemed, a new experience for him. He might not have felt so bad if he knew that she, too, was disappointed with her own action. So why had she stopped just as passions were reaching the point of no return. At the time she couldn't say why but she had thought a lot about it since. She knew the answer now. To have proceeded with Kelly would have been to give in to pure lust. What she felt for Vinny was something different, something far more profound. She loved

Vinny, she had no doubts about that now. Her session with Kelly had been a close call but she had no doubt that she had made the right – if less exciting – decision.

She was still pondering her strange encounter with Frankie Kelly as she entered the Dáil bar. As a frequent visitor, the staff knew her and always had a word of welcome for her. Michael, one of the longest serving barmen there, nodded his high-domed, bald head and smiled at her as soon as she came through the door. Before she reached the counter, Jim Hiney, one-time Minister for Social Welfare, now shadow spokesman for justice on the opposition benches, put his hand out to her in greeting and insisted on buying her a drink. Emma and Hiney enjoyed a self-serving relationship, feeding off each other, shamelessly swapping titbits. Accepting his offer, she ordered a gin and tonic and sat with him at a small table at the back of the bar. The usual pleasantries dispensed with, they pumped each other for the latest gossip before moving the conversation on to the McCall murder and the forthcoming by-election his death had precipitated.

'Although McCall was not a member of my party.' Hiney said, 'I liked the fellow . . . he was a decent chap, had a good word for everyone. I just hope they get the bastard who killed him. You have your ear to the ground, Emma, anything breaking in that direction?'

'No, the gardaí don't appear to be getting anywhere. What's the word in here?'

'Ah sure, everyone has their own version about what might have happened. We hear all the allegations, rumours and hearsay, a lot of over-the-top speculation. The truth is: none of us really know the *real* story but I'll tell you this, the Taoiseach is in a right old flap today about the whole business.'

'Oh?'

'Yes, according to a few of the boys I talked to earlier, she called an unscheduled meeting of the PCCC in her private office. She . . . '

'Sorry Jim, the PCCC? What's that?'

'Ah, come on, Emma, you got to be kidding. The PCCC is the Government's most secret committee – no one is supposed to know of its existence – but of course we all do.'

'Except me, it seems.'

'Indeed, you must be slipping up, Emma. PCCC stands for Personal Conduct Code Committee – a sort of early warning scandal watchdog. The speculation in the house is that there'll be an early by-election and that Fionnuala Stafford is having her secret committee make sure that whoever stands for the government side is squeaky clean. Since losing McCall, their majority in the house has shrunken to nil. So they'll have to get their man in or face an early general election.'

'They'll need a strong candidate, that's for sure,' Emma agreed, 'and you're right, Jim, they'll need to keep their noses clean.'

'Who're you telling . . . one whiff of scandal and this lot are for the high jump . . . and good riddance to the lot of them.'

'So, tell me, Jim, who serves on this secret committee

that nobody knows anything about?'

'Well, there's Francis Xavier Donnelly for a start – the general secretary, then there's Tom Pettit, one of the old guard, and then of course there's the man without whose presence, no committee would be complete; I refer to the greatest arse-licker in Leinster House, Shay-Brownnose-Dunphy.'

'Young Turks,' Emma said, attempting to hide her keen interest at the sound of Dunphy's name, 'trying to impress the Taoiseach, no doubt, but will it get him anywhere?'

'Oh, you may be sure it will; he's a cute hoor that one; mark my words, he's the sort of slithery bollix that'll end up one day as Taoiseach.'

Emma wanted to discover more about Shay Dunphy but a division bell brought their conversation to an end.

'Sorry, Emma,' Jim Hiney said, quickly finishing his drink. 'I've to go through the division lobbies . . . see if I can help defeat the government's bill on welfare restrictions. I'm pissing against the wind, I know, but our side has to go through the motions.'

Emma saw little point in hanging around the bar for what would probably turn out to be a long-winded Order of Business session. The monitor in the visitor's bar showed members of the house filing into the famous raked chamber. She finished her drink, waved cheerio to Michael the barman, and turned to leave the room.

She stopped abruptly.

Fionnuala Stafford and Detective Inspector Lawlor

had just passed along the corridor by the bar door, both of them deep in animated discussion. Emma held back, not wanting to be seen. She could not mistake the look of concern on the Taoiseach's face as she parted from Lawlor and headed towards the sound of the clanging bell. Emma was in two minds as to whether she should catch up with Lawlor as he made an exit from the building but decided against it. Far better, she thought, to stay quiet until she understood exactly what was going on.

But what *was* going on?

In the past few minutes she had learned two things that might have a bearing on the situation. Jim Hiney had told her that Shay Dunphy had been called to the Taoiseach's office earlier in the day and now she had watched with her own eyes as Lawlor talked to the Taoiseach.

A coincidence? She doubted it.

There was something serious afoot and McCall's death was central to whatever it was. But most significant, it went all the way to Fionnuala Stafford, right to the head of government. She thought about Frankie Kelly's prints and decided that the key to whatever was going on lay in those photographs. As soon as she made it back to her apartment, she would telephone him and invite him over.

Twice, Jacqueline Miller almost got caught as she continued her reconnoitre for a second night. On both occasions, the same nurse had unexpectedly come within a few metres of where she was hiding. Some patient, as it turned out, had pressed a night buzzer, probably looking for a drink of water or something. As Monday night turned into Tuesday's dawn, Jacqueline realised she would have to wait until the following night to make her bid for freedom. She had not found any ladies' daywear in her search but something useful had turned up. On the ground floor – she had discovered a way down via a fire escape – she pushed open a door that led to a small kitchen and lounge area and found some garments in a closet there. They were men's clothes. Examining them in partial darkness, she counted four white coats, a suit, a casual jacket, a track suit, several pair of men's trousers, some shirts and a hat. She held a pair of trousers to her waist to judge its length. The legs were a few inches too long but whoever owned them was not much bigger than herself. They were not what she was looking for but they might just about suffice for the plan that she hoped to put into practice the following night.

All she had to do was fool the doctor, the nurse, and Mr Bow Tie if it came to that, for the next twelve hours.

12

It was midday Tuesday by the time Frankie Kelly made it to the office of his old employers, the *Dublin Dispatch*. He had meant to call earlier, had in fact got up before nine o'clock with that intention but seeing a dusting of snow on the ground from the previous night, decided to go back to bed instead. This was his second day in succession to visit the *Dispatch*, the purpose in each case, the same: to talk with Jean-Pierre Brazin. Yesterday, the receptionist, Pam, a nineteen-year-old leggy girl with cascades of blonde corkscrew curls, big eyes and, in Frankie's opinion, a pea-size brain, had told him that Brazin had phoned in sick.

Pam sat behind the reception desk again today, wearing a headset with a slender wire microphone that curved in front of her mouth, and flashed her usual smile at Frankie, Not wanting to hurt her feelings, Frankie played along with her flirting but had no interest in adding her to his current crop of lovers.

'Hi ya, Frankie,' she beamed. 'We're seeing more of you these days than when you worked here.'

'Yeah, right, Pam, it's your smiling face; I miss it so much . . . have to keep coming back for more.'

'Fat lot of good my smile has done for me so far,' she said, blinking eyelashes laden with too much mascara. 'If I've to wait for you to make a move I'll die a virgin.'

Frankie smiled but did not bother to reply.

'Fine,' Pam said, trying not to hide the rejection she felt. 'So, if it's not my body you're after, what is it you want?'

'Can you check and see if Jean-Pierre Brazin is in today. I'd like a few words with him.'

While Pam attempted to locate Jean-Pierre on her telephone console, Frankie thought about what he would say to the Frenchman when they came face to face. There would be little point in beating about the bush; best to come right out with it and accuse him of duplicity in regard to the roll of film. The matter needed to be resolved once and for all. Last night Emma Boylan had telephoned him and asked him to meet in her place to discuss the significance of his photographs. Even on the telephone he could tell that she had upgraded the importance attached to them. Still feeling a little sore that she should have rejected his advances the previous evening, he declined her offer. At the time he was entertaining his 'most regular' girlfriend in his flat – with full sexual satisfaction guaranteed. He promised to get in touch with her today as soon as he had resolved the mystery of the blank film roll.

Pam, her smile gone for once, interrupted his thoughts. 'I'm sorry, Frankie, but Jean-Pierre is not in work today. Maybe you'd like to leave a message or something.'

'Yes, I'll leave a message all right,' Frankie said, getting up from his seat and moving towards the door that led to the interior of the *Dublin Dispatch.*'

'But, but you can't . . . ' Pam started to say.

'It's all right, Pam, you never saw me. OK?' Frankie said as he disappeared into the interior of the building leaving her to stare open-mouthed at the word PRIVATE painted in red capitals on the door.

Taking two steps at a time, Frankie descended a narrow stairs that led to the building's basement. Familiar territory. It was here that he had worked for the past year and a half. Ignoring the 'No Entry' red light, he stepped into the light trap, double cylinder revolving door that would gain him entry to the photographic darkroom.

Jean-Pierre Brazin was in the act of inserting a sheet of Kodak bromide paper into the computer-controlled tray rocker when Frankie walked up behind him and tapped him on the shoulder.

'You and I have some serious talking to do,' he said to the diminutive Frenchman.'

Showing no surprise, Brazin turned and faced Kelly. 'Yes, Frankie, you are right,' he said with an air of resignation, 'I knew there was little point in trying to avoid you.'

'Damn right. I suppose you were here yesterday as well?'

Jean-Pierre had the grace to blush as he nodded yes.

'Hm, I thought so, but *why*? You lied to me. I thought we were mates, I trusted you. What I want to know is *why*?'

'I have done something I'm not proud of, but I can't

live with my deceit any longer,' Jean-Pierre Brazin replied. He suggested that Frankie join him for a coffee in the small corner shop across the street. 'I'll tell you exactly what happened,' he said, 'regardless of the consequences, I'll tell you all that I know.'

Jimmy Rabbitte refused to answer the phone, knowing that after six rings it would automatically switch to the answering machine. In no mood to talk to anyone, he stared blankly at the instrument, clenched his teeth and waited to hear the message. But the caller hung up after the bleep. 'Well, fuck you too,' he said to the now silent telephone before moving to his front door and closing the security bolt from the inside.

The angelus bell rang from the steeple of St Mary's church, situated a block away from Jimmy Rabbitte's house. For good Catholics, the midday chimes reminded them it was time to take a minute out for spiritual reflection but for Jimmy Rabbitte it signalled something entirely different. It was time for his fix. Secure inside his small two-storey terrace house, he opened the medicine cabinet in the bathroom and removed his 'joy toys'. After assembling needle and syringe, he unscrewed the top of the small amber pill bottle and sniffed its contents. The whiff of 'speed' made his nostrils flare in anticipation. It was this moment in his daily ritual that always forced him to question his dependence on drugs, a moment to reflect on his own peculiar spiritual state of being.

More than most people, Jimmy Rabbitte was aware

of the horror of drugs. As a journalist, he had written in-depth articles on the subject. Eight years earlier he had been one of three nominations for best journalist of the year on the strength of his writing. Although he had not won the award, he felt honoured to have been shortlisted for the prestigious honour. Back then, he believed in his job, saw journalism as his mission on earth. He had sought out junkies, lived in their slum dwellings for a time, observed them as they fed their habits, all in the line of research. In one of his more colourful articles, back when he worked for the *Post,* he had described in minute detail how a pathologist cutting a teenage 'speed' victim at autopsy had found the body of an eighty-year-old inside. In the same article he had described acid as 'weed killer for the brain'. But somehow, without understanding how it had happened, he lost his way and got swallowed up in the drug culture himself.

The syringe sucked up the liquid from the small bottle until it was full. He rolled back his sleeve, fixed his trusted strap below the biceps, brought up a vein, jabbed the needle into it and gently pushed the plunger home. As always, at times like this, he tried to avert his eyes from all the old wounds, the black and blue bruises and marks from previous fixes, and the single drop of blood that always appeared after he removed the needle. Clinching his fist, he closed his eyes and waited for peace to embrace him.

It was several minutes before his 'hit' kicked in and just as the world seemed a little brighter, the telephone rang. 'More trouble in our native land,' he said aloud, the same expression he uttered most times when the telephone rang. After four rings he picked it up.

'Can I help you?' he asked.

'Jimmy Rabbitte?'

'Yes, this is Jimmy Rabbitte, who am I speaking to?'

'I think you know who I am,' the voice said, but I'd prefer if you didn't mention my name over the open line.'

By now, Rabbitte had recognised his caller as Francis Xavier Donnelly. 'Well now, my fat friend, what can I do for you?'

'I want to meet you.'

'Hah, I thought you might. No problem, my friend. Where? When?'

'Your house. Tomorrow, Wednesday, twelve o'clock, midday.'

'High-fucking-noon, I like it. I will like it even better if you've the dosh with you.'

'Yes, I'll have it with me. I'll have someone with me to ensure that this time you hand over *all* of the negatives. If you try any funny business this time, the person with me will take pleasure in breaking your neck.'

'Look! I want no further dealings with this business. Just give me the money and you won't see my heels for the dust. I intend getting to hell out of this country and on to the first flight I can book after we have concluded our business.'

'Fine, you do that. See you this time tomorrow.'

Jimmy Rabbitte put the telephone back in its cradle before punching the air several times with a clenched fist. 'Yes, yes, yes,' he shouted.

Back in her office after lunch, Emma had not had time to sit in behind her desk when a call was put through. Hearing the words 'personal call' used by the girl on the switch, she assumed the caller might be Frankie Kelly. Earlier, before her lunch break, she had tried to contact him several times without success. 'Hello,' she said enthusiastically into the telephone.

'Hello, Emma, it's Vinny here; how are you?'

'Oh, Vinny, it's you,' she said.

'Is this a bad time?' Vinny asked. 'You don't sound exactly overjoyed to hear from me.'

'No, no, it's all right, Vinny. It's great to hear from you; it's just that a big story is breaking and I thought this call was in connection with it . . . but it's great to hear you. How are things there?'

The conversation continued along more familiar lines once the rocky start was out of the way. Hearing Vinny's voice brought back a sense of well-being to Emma. She realised that he represented the one constant in her life. Before hanging up, she told him she loved him and asked him to get home as soon as he could.

'Another week only,' he told her, 'then I'll be home . . . ravenous for what I'm missing. I love you, Emma, miss you to bits.'

'I love you too, Vinny. Just get home here as fast as you can.'

Emma stared at the telephone after she had replaced it in its cradle. She thought about Vinny and the love they had declared for each other. There was no point in trying to reconcile the kind of love she felt for Vinny and the more erotic thrill she had experienced when Frankie Kelly was around her. They were as different as chalk and cheese, as different as lust and love.

A summons to Bob Crosby's office put an end to her musing. He wanted to know when he could expect an update on the McCall story. Her answers were less than reassuring. Crosby was having difficulty in hiding his impatience. 'What about McCall's wife? Have you talked to her?'

'No, I've tried to contact her, but she is not . . . '

'Well, find her; discover if she's been asked to stand for election for her late husband's seat. Find out how she is coping without her husband; find out if her children's school arrangements have changed. Christ, Emma, I don't need to tell you your job but get me something. The public want more on this story, go out and . . . ' A telephone call cut Crosby off in mid flow. 'Yes,' he said ungraciously into the telephone, before handing it over to Emma.' 'It's for you; it's important, according to the switch.'

'Emma, this is Frankie,' the voice said. 'I wanted to let you know there has been a development.'

'What sort of development?'

'Jean-Pierre Brazin told me that Jimmy Rabbitte has my original film.'

'Jimmy Rabbitte? But . . . but if he has it, why hasn't he run with the story?'

'Jean-Pierre thinks Rabbitte is after a bigger pay-out than anything the *Dublin Dispatch* could put together. And here's an interesting titbit: according to Jean-Pierre, Rabbitte is hooked on drugs – heavy-duty shit – and is probably trying to sell the negatives.'

'Sell them? You mean to some other newspaper?'

'Could be, but I doubt it, I don't think he'll approach the media.'

'What then?'

'My bet is that Rabbitte will try a little blackmail.'

'You really think so? But who would he blackmail . . . except, yes, Jesus, yes, I think you could be right. Rabbitte knows your pictures could embarrass the government, could even topple them, so he figures maybe he can get them to part with money – a huge sum of money – to buy back the negatives.

'It makes as much sense as anything else we've come up with.'

'Except that it sounds too fanciful even for Rabbitte. I can't see him putting such an elaborate scheme together.'

'I don't know, Emma. When you think about it, he didn't put it together; it sort of fell in his lap, accidental like, all he did was to run with it.'

'You could be right, I suppose . . . especially if he is feeding an expensive drug habit.'

'Well, Emma, it's just speculation at this point but I'm determined to find out one way or another before the day is out.'

'And how do you intend doing that?

'Well, that's why I'm ringing you. Your switchboard didn't want to put me through to you at first but I insisted that what I had to say was relevant to a breaking story. I intend going to Jimmy Rabbitte's house. I'll call you from there if I find anything; get you to come over.'

Yes, Frankie, you do that. As soon as I hear from you I'll get across to the house.'

'Right, Emma, talk to you soon.'

'Bye,'

Emma hung up and looked at her editor, Bob Crosby, whose eyebrows had remained raised for the duration of the call. '

'Well?' he asked.

'Could be the break we're waiting for, but I'm going to have to wait a little longer.'

'How much longer?'

'A couple of hours maybe but I'll know a lot better when Frankie calls back.'

Frankie Kelly watched his one-time colleague enter the Organ Grinder before setting off for the terrace house that Rabbitte called home. Twenty minutes later he pulled his Fiesta alongside the kerb at Barrow Lane cul-de-sac on the city side of Fairview Park. The two-storey dwelling stood out from its adjoining neighbours by virtue of its uncared for exterior.

Eight doors down the street from Rabbitte's house, Frankie found a cobbled passageway, part of a maze of back alleys that intersected the terrace rows and allowed access to the gardens of the houses. A six-foot-high wall of sooty bricks created a border behind each house with individual doors identifying each property.

Counting eight doors down from the alleyway, Frankie came to the rear of Jimmy Rabbitte's house. Unlike the other well-maintained doors Rabbitte's was in need of repair but it still proved sturdy enough to withstand Frankie's best efforts to force it open. He decided to climb over the wall. Using the door's latch as a foothold, he gripped the moss-covered mortar wall-cap and dragged himself awkwardly to the top. It should not have been a particularly difficult movement, the sort of exertion he would have done as a boy without the least bit of bother, but today he had managed to scrape his knee in the process. The pain, stinging at first, abated quickly. It took a moment to catch his breath and regain his equilibrium. Standing for a moment on top of the wall, he examined the back of the house and garden before dropping to the other side. He found himself up to his knees in brambles, briars and weed-covered earth. Neglect stared back at him from every angle. Rust-covered wrought-iron furniture – a circular table, two broken chairs and the frame of a child's swing – stood half buried in a tangle of weeds and dirt, leftover relics from better days, Frankie imagined. Making his way past the derelict furniture to the back wall of the house, he searched for a way to gain entry. He didn't have to look too hard. Missing glass from a narrow toilet window had been replaced by a piece of cardboard, the flimsy structure held in place with nothing more substantial than Scotch tape. With minimal effort, he pushed his arm through to the latch, opened the window frame and climbed inside the house.

A prevailing smell of mustiness and rotting food assailed his nostrils as he made his way to the kitchen. The place was a mess. Scattered books, newspaper supplements and magazines lay higgledy-piggledy on a floor covered with linoleum that had been worn thin by time. Dirty plates, cups, saucers and cutlery were heaped on top of a Formica-topped table that stood in the centre of the floor. All the chairs except one were weighed down with piles of newspapers. But it was the sink's draining board and counter area that finally induced a quiver of revulsion in him. Congealed fried eggs, beans and rasher rind, embedded on grease-coated plates balanced precariously on top of each other, had attracted a multitude of flies. A stack of empty pizza delivery boxes and Chinese take-away containers, covered in fragments of the food they once contained reeked with a sickening stench. It was a mystery to Frankie how any man could live in such filth and squalor.

With an effort, he ignored the mess all around him and concentrated instead on looking for the roll of negatives or whatever was left of the photographs he had taken. He searched the cupboards, shelves, presses and drawers but was not surprised to come up empty-handed.

The living room came next. By this time, Frankie had become slightly more acclimatised to the smell. Marginally tidier than the kitchen and more generously proportioned, the room had built-in floor-to-ceiling shelves, packed with books of all sorts – everything from Jeffrey Archer to Leo Tolstoy. More books and magazines covered the top of the coffee table, the chairs and the television set. A tape recorder, the sort used by reporters, and dozens of cassettes stood in neat stacks, the only items in the room that had any degree of tidiness about them. Frankie lifted one of the cassettes from its stack and examined the label. The word 'Interview', followed by a date, appeared in neat capitals on the small label. A cursory glance at the other cassettes showed similar markings, prompting Frankie to acknowledge that there was at least one thing that Rabbitte cared about.

A computer and printer, set on a bench beneath the window, looked as though they had grown from beneath a pile of papers. This was obviously where Rabbitte worked. A flashing red light to one side of the computer drew Frankie's attention to a telephone and answering machine, half-buried beneath the paper deluge and covered in a mass of yellow Post-It message stickers. Frankie considered listening to the messages stored on the machine but dismissed the idea; he had enough to do to find his roll of film without becoming any further involved in Rabbitte's affairs. His search in the living room, however, yielded nothing of interest.

In the hallway that led from the front door to the stairs, Frankie paused a moment to look at a series of framed newspaper pages that hung on the wall; all of them featured lead articles by Rabbitte. Beside them, six smaller frames contained diplomas, certificates and awards with the name Jimmy Rabbitte displayed prominently. Frankie moved up the stairs, wondering how it was that a journalist like Rabbitte, so full of early promise and talent, could be reduced to living in a dump like this.

Two upstairs bedrooms, untidy and neglected like the rest of the house, yielded no prize for Frankie. A photograph of Rabbitte, posing with a woman and a small baby girl, stood on top of a locker in what was probably the master bedroom. This was a surprise to Frankie; he had always assumed that Rabbitte was a loner with no interest in the opposite sex but here he was posing with a woman, probably a wife, and a child, probably his daughter. Did this woman live in this house at some stage? Could she have been responsible for introducing the wrought-iron furniture, now rusting in the back garden? Could the child have played on the swing? There was more, it seemed, to Rabbitte's life than he had previously believed.

Only the bathroom remained for inspection. There was little of anything in the narrow room to search except for an elongated cabinet that had a full-length mirror for its door. It contained the usual array of male toiletries. Only when he opened the medicine box, partially hidden on the top shelf, did he find the syringes and drug equipment. It confirmed what Jean-Pierre had already told him: Rabbitte was a drug addict. About to put the medicine box back, Frankie noticed that the plastic tray-like divider did not sit properly inside the box. He eased the tray out and found four wads of twenty-pound notes, each circled with an elastic band, spread along the base of the box. Without counting the bundles, Frankie guessed the amount to be in the region of three thousand pounds.

Underneath one of the wads of notes he spotted an envelope. Inside it he found a single 35-millimetre frame of film. Examining the sprocket-edged negative, he quickly identified the images of a man and woman kissing each other. As a photographer he was used to looking at images reversed black to white and had no difficulty recognising the picture as the one he had shot of McCall and Jacqueline Miller. For several seconds he stared at the small frame, unable to believe he had finally found the evidence he wanted, the evidence that would prove he had not invented the story, the evidence that would, he hoped, lead to the biggest break in his career.

First he must ring Emma and tell her the news. In a moment of hesitation, he thought about not telling her, going alone with the story but dismissed the idea immediately. He knew how necessary it was to have someone with the reputation to exploit the situation . . . and Emma Boylan, he decided, was the perfect choice.

He replaced the money in the medicine box, fixed back the tray and returned it to where he had found it. He had no intention of taking Rabbitte's money but he had no problem at all in taking the piece of film.

Mission accomplished.

Pleased with himself, he moved downstairs to use Rabbitte's telephone. His call was put through to Emma without delay but their conversation had barely begun when the front door of Rabbitte's house came crashing into the hallway.

13

'Blast, I've got company, I'll call you back.' These were
the last words Emma heard before Frankie hung up.
Prior to that she had heard what sounded like a crash
of timber breaking in the background. Frankie had
mentioned something about the front door, mutterings
she couldn't make sense of, but he failed to elaborate.
What had happened? Emma held the mute telephone
in her hand for a full ten seconds, pondering the
dilemma, before replacing it. Frankie was in trouble,
that much she was sure of, but what sort of trouble?
He had company, that's what he had said, but who could
it be? Rabbitte? No, surely not, Frankie had seen
Rabbitte go into the Organ Grinder. But if it wasn't
Rabbitte, who could it be? In the short telephone
conversation before the abrupt cut-off, Frankie had
sounded excited. He had found a negative, he told her,
and insisted that having the negative would prove that
his story was true.

   He had promised to ring her back. Should she wait?
No, only one thing to do: drive to Rabbitte's house
immediately, get to the bottom of whatever was
happening. After a frantic search, she found Rabbitte's
address in the *Post*'s files and prayed he had not moved
house in recent years.

As always, the traffic *en route* to Fairview was slow, traffic lights switching to red as though on cue as she approached each intersection, turning a fifteen-minute journey into half an hour. With evident relief, she pulled up by the kerbside in Barrow Lane, turned the ignition off, got out of the car and looked around. All appeared quiet. She couldn't tell if Frankie had parked his car there because she did not know what sort of car he drove. Slate-grey rain clouds closed in on the narrow street as she quickened her step along a pavement still blackened from a previous shower. As big drops began to fall, she spotted Rabbitte's house. About to reach out and press the bell, she noticed the door already slightly ajar. Closer inspection let her see that the door had been forced open, splinters of timber had broken loose from the jamb where the bolt had been dislodged. Emma's heart took a sudden lurch.

Gingerly, she pushed the damaged door open and stepped into the hallway. 'Frankie, Frankie, hello! Are you here?' she shouted.

No answer.

'Anyone home?' she asked, making her way along the narrow hallway and into the kitchen. Someone had pulled the place apart and the smell was enough to induce gagging. There was no sign of Frankie.

The living room yielded nothing either but it was obvious that, like the kitchen, it had been thoroughly done over. Chairs and tables were tossed on their sides among piles of scattered books, papers and magazines. A computer and printer with leads, unplugged and twisted into knots, sat on top of the mess. A reporter's tape recorder lay smashed to pieces on the floor, piles of cassettes scattered in every direction. Somebody in an awful hurry and with no respect for property had done a thorough job of trashing the place. Was it wanton destruction or the result of an indiscriminate search. If it were the latter, had the searchers found what they were looking for? Emma was about to leave the room when she noticed the telephone among the debris. Bloody streaks were visible on the instrument. Already nervous, Emma experienced the first stirrings of panic setting in. 'Frankie, Frankie, where are you?' she shouted, her voice taking on a new urgency.

No answer.

She backed out of the room, headed up the stairs, taking two steps at a time, before pushing the bedroom doors open. No sign of Frankie in either room. Both rooms had been turned upside down, sheets, blankets, pillows and mattresses removed from bed frames, wardrobes, lamps, chairs and pictures thrown into piles.

She moved back on to the landing and opened the bathroom door.

She screamed.

Frankie Kelly, naked except for his underpants, lay sprawled on the floor, his head slumped awkwardly on the rim of the toilet seat, his eyes closed and blood streaks dried on his face. The blood had come from an ugly-looking gash in his forehead. After a momentary paralysis, Emma rushed to him, put her face next to his to see if he was alive. Her own breath was coming in such gasps that she had difficulty in telling if he was breathing or not. 'Frankie, please, Frankie, say something; tell me you're all right . . . you're not . . . Frankie, it's me, Emma.'

No response.

He was breathing. She could tell now. He was alive. His breath was coming in faint little gasps, uneven and painful. The relief she experienced at seeing him breathe was short-lived. With a start, she noticed a syringe sticking into his arm. The needle remained inserted into a swollen vein on his right arm, the plunger pressed all the way home. For a brief second, Emma froze. 'What can I do? I need help,' she said aloud, urging herself into action. Thankful that she had brought her cellular phone with her, she punched the numbers that would connect her with the emergency services. As she gave instructions for the ambulance, she heard Frankie moan. She shouted into the phone, 'Hurry, hurry, for Christ's sake,' before returning her attention to Frankie. 'I've got help coming,' she said to the lifeless face. 'Hang on in there, help is on its way . . . Jesus, who did this to you?'

His eyes flickered open and shut several times in rapid succession. Somewhere down in his throat, a low moan emerged. Emma put her hand to his forehead and pressed gently, 'It's me, Frankie,' she said, trying to hide the fear in her voice. 'You're going to be all right.'

But Emma did not believe her own words; she knew that Frankie was far from being all right. Saliva drooled from his mouth; his eyes, when they opened, revealed irises rolled upwards; his body was convulsed and his moans were growing weaker. His left hand, she noticed, seemed particularly agitated, the fingers tapping erratically on his cigarette case. Emma attached no particular significance to this action, thinking it a symptom of the distress and pain he was in. The cigarette case, like his clothes, had been thrown on the floor of the small bathroom. The pockets of his shirt, jacket and trousers were all turned inside out. The inference was obvious to Emma, or at least she thought it was. They – whoever *they* were – had searched him for the film negatives. But had they been successful in their quest? It was a question that did not bother her right now; her immediate concern was Frankie's welfare. *What is keeping the ambulance?* Impatiently waiting, she looked at the items scattered on the floor. The contents of a cabinet lay strewn about the floor: soaps, shaving foams, gels and blades; other male toiletries were dumped in the bath tub.

Beside Frankie's bare feet, she noticed an upturned medicine chest, its contents emptied on the floor along with several syringes and containers. Emma knew enough about drugs to recognise the accoutrements that went hand-in-hand with drug addiction. Rabbitte's cache? Yes, of course. This was where Rabbitte took his fixes. Had someone gone to a lot of trouble to make it look like Frankie Kelly was a junkie? Was that what this was about? If that were the case, Emma could not see the logic behind it.

Growing increasingly impatient for the ambulance to arrive, Emma punched the familiar *Post* numbers into the pad of her mobile phone and had Bob Crosby on the line within seconds. Amazed at how calm she had managed to sound, she told him what had happened and asked him to send a photographer and inform the gardaí. Finishing the call, she noticed that Frankie's fingers were still trying to touch his cigarette box. In a flash of inspiration she understood that Frankie was trying to tell her something: he wanted her to get rid of the joints. With a syringe lodged in his arm, the irony of not wanting to be found in possession of a few marijuana joints would have amused Emma were the situation not so serious. She picked up the case and placed it in her coat pocket; its removal would, she expected, give the gardaí less reason to suspect Frankie of being responsible for what happened.

Hearing the wailing siren brought a sigh of relief to Emma. She moved to the top of the stairs as the ambulance braked to a stop outside the house. The siren's deafening crescendo abruptly stopped and two paramedics came running through the front door. 'Up here,' Emma yelled. 'He's up here; he needs help, quickly, quickly.' She watched as the two white-clad men pounded their way up the stairs, carrying with them a stretcher, a small oxygen tank and a face mask. Working together in a well-practised drill, they moved Frankie on to the portable stretcher, covered his nakedness with a blanket and hauled him downstairs with maximum speed.

As they slid the stretcher into the back of the ambulance, one of the men, the driver as it turned out, asked Emma if she wished to accompany them to the hospital. Yes, she did. She scrambled into the back of the ambulance and moved to Frankie's side as the driver slammed the door shut and dashed around to the cab.

Muted by the ambulance walls, the siren began its wail as the vehicle shot forward. garda squad cars, blue lights flashing, screeched to a halt outside Rabbitte's house as she sped away. She would have to give a statement to the gardaí later and was glad to be spared that ordeal, if only for a few hours. Dismissing the world outside the speeding ambulance, she gazed at Frankie, his face white as chalk, his body perfectly still, and wondered if he would survive.

Outside the Mater Hospital's emergency bay, the back doors of the ambulance were thrown open. Emma looked on helplessly as the orderlies helped remove the stretcher bearing Frankie, placed it on a gurney and wheeled it through the swinging perspex doors that led to the emergency wards. Emma was allowed to follow the stretcher inside but was prevented from entering the intensive care unit. 'You can wait in the visitors' lounge down the corridor if you'd like,' a young man in a green coat told her, pointing her in the right direction.

'When will I know how . . . '

'We'll keep you informed of his progress.'

'Fine, that's fine,' Emma said, defeated.

'Are you his wife . . . his girlfriend?' the man asked.

'No, no, just a friend . . . a close friend.'

'It's hard to take,' the man said, 'when they decide to overdose . . . he's the third one this week.'

'No, no, you're wrong,' Emma snapped, sounding sharper than she had meant to. 'He did not overdose; this was done to him . . . someone tried to kill him.'

The orderly gave her a knowing look but said no more as Emma turned on her heels and walked down the corridor towards the visitors' lounge.

Jimmy Rabbitte enjoyed his third brandy-and-ginger ale and was in the mood for more. This was unusual for Rabbitte. Most days he preferred to drink pints of Guinness and invariably his moods swung from dark and sombre to bad-tempered. But not today. Today he felt like celebrating. He insisted on buying extra rounds for his two regular drinking companions, another unusual departure from tradition. 'Did ya win deh lohhery or wha?' the barman asked as he pushed Rabbitte's glass under the upturned Hennessy dispenser.

'No, my friend, no such luck,' Rabbitte replied, cocking his head to one side, giving the barman the benefit of what he believed was a conspiratorial wink, 'but I did manage to pull off something of a master stroke in the line of my investigative work. You know what, ould son, I'm still the best damn journalist in the business.'

'Yeah, sure y'are,' the barman said, smiling, aware of Rabbitte's dependency on drugs and his liking for alcohol.

Rabbitte returned his attention to his two drinking

pals who, on the strength of his new-found generosity, had switched from ale to large whiskeys. The three men were deep in discussion, arguing the pros and cons of government policies, when a middle-aged, blonde woman, wearing stylish designer clothes and looking for all the world like a corporate executive, picked her way through the pub's revellers and gestured that Rabbitte should join her. It was obvious from the look Rabbitte gave the woman that they knew each other. Sloshing the brandy in its glass, he gestured to his drinking companions and nudged them before speaking. 'I've got to talk to this ould one . . . to do with undercover work, you understand . . . I'll be back in two shakes of a lamb's tail.' In spite of his outward bravado, Rabbitte failed to mask his agitation, his impatience, a fact not lost on his drinking companions.

Outside the front door of the Organ Grinder, the woman, whose name was Mary-Jane Grace, stood waiting to talk to Rabbitte. Rabbitte had used her as his supplier for almost a year but until today he had never known her to contact him in such an open fashion. It was a development he viewed with growing alarm. He hoped the look on his face conveyed the displeasure he felt at having her turn up at his favourite watering hole. 'What the hell's the matter with you?' he asked, 'I've paid you all the money I owed so I don't . . . '

'It's nothing like that. I came to warn you about your house . . . '

'My house? Warn me? What the fuck are you talking about?'

'I have a contact who monitors police radio traffic. I've just got word that the cops are taking your house apart.'

'What? What sort of shit is this . . . my house . . . ?'

'An ambulance called to your house about an hour ago, took away some fellow to the Mater Hospital, someone who, from all accounts, had taken an overdose. At first we thought you were the one taken to the hospital, but obviously that part of the report was wrong.'

'Of course it's wrong; the whole idea is a load of nonsense. It's wrong, I tell you; the whole fuckin' thing is wrong.'

'Believe me, it's not wrong.'

The authority her words carried convinced Rabbitte that she was speaking the truth. He wished now he had not drunk that last glass of brandy. 'Jesus Christ, what the hell is going on? I don't understand any of this.'

'What concerns me . . . what concerns my boss,' the blonde woman said, 'is what they might find in your house. I just hope you do not have any contact names – you know the sort of thing I mean – left lying around.

Rabbitte thrust his hands into his trousers pockets, cleared his throat by spitting a glob of phlegm on to the pavement. He took a moment to think before answering. 'No, of course not; I'm not bloody stupid. But Jesus, I do have stuff . . . and I have money . . . bloody hell . . . '

'Well, Jimmy, if I were you, I'd make myself scarce for the next few days. Take my advice: drop out of circulation for a while. Keep the head down till this blows over.'

Rabbitte stared at the woman with an unsteady tilt to his head, finding it difficult to come to terms with what she was saying. He opened his mouth to say something but before he could utter a word, she turned away from him and headed towards a chauffeur-driven Mercedes that had approached and slowed down to a crawl alongside the footpath.

Visibly shaken by what he had heard, Rabbitte stood watching her get into the big black car and pull away into the traffic, trying to understand how his plans had so suddenly come apart. Who could be responsible? Francis Xavier Donnelly was supposed to meet with him at the house the next day at noon. Had Donnelly decided to move the schedule forward by a day? Had Donnelly decided to look for the negative himself and then tip off the cops? Rabbitte did not think so; Francis Xavier could be a ruthless bastard but this was not his style. No, something more sinister was afoot, something far more sinister.

The evening had closed in, winter darkness casting its gloomy pall over the land. But nowhere was that gloom more evident than in the visitors' lounge down the long corridor from the intensive care unit. Emma sat uneasily on her chair, her thoughts swamped with re-enactments of the events that had led to Frankie Kelly being rushed to the Mater Hospital. While waiting, she had picked up the various magazines scattered on a glass-topped coffee table and flicked through them without registering their contents. Nothing could ease the turmoil in her head. She had been only half an hour in the room but it felt like an eternity. Through huge glass doors she watched absent-mindedly as a stream of people – doctors, nurses, nuns, patients in dressing-gowns, visitors and orderlies – passed by in what appeared to be an endless procession. Other people sat quietly in the steel-framed chairs placed around the walls of the visitor's lounge, lost in their own private worlds, occasionally glancing in her direction but always keeping their distance. In the corner of the room, a television set showing teletext remained mute and ignored.

Emma decided to leave the room, stretch her legs, maybe get a cup of coffee from the vending machine down the corridor, when her name, announced over the intercom speaker, startled her. The disembodied voice requested that she proceed to Station B outside the intensive care unit.

On arrival there, Emma sensed bad news immediately. The doctor didn't need to say a word; the bad tidings were etched on his face all too transparently. 'I'm terribly sorry,' he said, 'we tried . . . we tried everything but we lost him.'

Emma stared at the doctor, a pleasant looking man in his mid-forties with a high domed forehead and huge bushy eyebrows, unable to say anything in reply. A single teardrop ran down her cheek. The doctor put his hand on her shoulder and pressed reassuringly. 'He never really had a chance,' she heard him say in a low voice barely more than a whisper, yet with every word perfectly modulated, 'the concoction injected into his blood stream was lethal – a cocktail of rogue heroine and washing-up liquid – we'll know more when we do tests.'

Emma wiped the tears forming in her eyes, still unable to bring herself to speak.

'Can I get you a taxi or something,' the doctor asked, 'or is there someone I can call for you?'

'No, thank you, doctor,' Emma replied, her voice cracking under the strain, 'I'm all right . . . just let me sit here for a while please.'

'If you're sure you are all right, I'll have to go . . . I'm needed back in surgery. If you need anything, one of the nurses will look after you.'

Alone now in Station B, Emma cried. Tears that had welled up fell freely. Her throat had dried up and hurt as she tried to swallow. She wanted to scream, pound the walls of the small room with her fists, kick out at a world capable of inflicting such cruelty, but instead she sat there crying, trying to control her emotions, trying to bear the unshakeable sadness threatening to crush her.

She failed to notice the big detective enter the room and only registered his presence when he stood right in front of her. 'Well, well, what have we here?' Lawlor said, easing his weight into the seat beside her, 'Emma Boylan, hard-nosed reporter and super sleuth upset by the death of a junkie.'

Emma glared at him but made no reply.

'Oh, come on now, Emma, what the hell's the matter with you – where's your professionalism gone . . . that detached, clinical non-involvement shit you're so full of, huh? I thought the first rule of journalism was to maintain a distance?' A pause. 'Is there something that you know about the two-bit photographer that we don't . . . ? Is that it?'

Emma still refused to talk.

'Okay, have it your way, Emma, but I'm going to need a statement from you one way or another. We can have a nice little cosy chat here or you can come down to the station; which is it going to be?'

'I'll tell you what I know,' Emma said reluctantly.

'Good, now we're getting somewhere. Suppose you start by telling me how you, of all people, happened to find Frankie Kelly . . . and in the house owned by Jimmy Rabbitte.'

Emma gave Lawlor an abridged version of events leading up to her discovery of Frankie. She was careful to avoid all mention of missing negatives or that she and Kelly were helping each other with enquiries into the death of Alan McCall. When she finished relating her minimalist account of events, Lawlor furrowed his brow, nodded and leaned forward in his chair. He remained silent for several seconds before speaking. 'I think there's a lot more you're not telling me, Emma, but it doesn't matter much at this point – we can get a fuller statement later – besides, one junkie more or less is of little consequence one way or th'other.'

'He's not a junkie; he's . . . ' Emma started to say before stopping suddenly, annoyed with herself for having allowed Lawlor goad her into making unnecessary comments.

'Ah ha, so there *is* more to this than meets the eye . . . you *do* know more than you're letting on.'

'I only know that Frankie Kelly was murdered.'

'Murder? Murder, you say? Oh, I hardly think so. I think he was making a fix. He just got careless about what he was injecting into himself.'

'That's not true.'

'No? Well then, there's always the possibility that he deliberately decided to put his lights out, who knows . . . who knows what goes on inside the head of these fruitcakes. One way or the other, we can be fairly certain Frankie Kelly caused his own demise.'

Emma refused to be drawn any further by the detective's deliberate provocation. Lawlor, she knew from past experiences, was playing a familiar game but it was a game she had no interest in playing – not now, not with Frankie lying dead in the next room.

'If you're finished with me, I would like to go,' she said, rising from her chair.

'No, I'm not finished with you – more's the pity – but you can go . . . for now that is.' In what was meant to sound like an afterthought, he said, 'Of course, if this did turn out to be murder, you would automatically become the number one suspect.'

'Go rot in hell,' Emma said, walking away from him.

14

She woke crying, lying crossways on the bed, her head tilted over the side, her eyes matted with tears. In that twilight world, floating halfway between sleep and wakefulness, she remembered details, fragmented and half-formed, of the nightmare not yet fully expunged from her brain. She had seen Frankie Kelly's naked body being thrown into an open grave. A grotesquely fat priest in full regalia – chasuble, alb, cassock, maniple and stole – wearing sunglasses and a bright red party hat, explained to her that this was unconsecrated ground – a place where the damned were cast into the everlasting black mist of Satan's evil-filled abyss. Emma moved closer to the gaping pit in an attempt to catch a glimpse of its interior but the obese priest butted her with his huge belly, managing to knock her to the ground in the unexpected move.

From this vantage point she watched as several men, all wearing brown desert shoes, shiny black bin liners and multicoloured waistcoats, shovelled earth into the hole. On hands and knees, Emma crawled to the edge of the grave and peered into the depths. Inexplicably, the clay being thrown into the recess had turned to rubbish – old torn magazines and papers, beer cans, dirty encrusted take-away food containers – all the contents from Rabbitte's house complete with suffocating smell, all of it covering the body of Frankie Kelly.

'No, no, no,' she heard herself say as several pairs of hands grabbed at her. The last thing she saw before being wrenched away from the grave was the sight of Frankie's hands pushing through the rubbish, the fingers opening and closing, blood running down his arms. She continued to scream but she knew no sound accompanied the terror cries.

This was the point at which she crossed into consciousness again. Her heart pounding, her mind disorientated, she realised that what she had experienced had been only a nightmare. But thinking of Frankie Kelly now, in full wakefulness, she realised it was a nightmare likely to recur for a long time to come.

Orange juice, black coffee and a slice of toast with marmalade helped ease her into the reality of the day. Getting into her office, she hoped, would dull the pain and awfulness she felt; having Bob Crosby demand copy from her would, for once, be a welcome diversion from the dark thoughts swirling about inside her head. She looked at the cigarette case she had taken from Frankie Kelly once more before dressing for work. Opening the lid, she removed the three joints from its interior, walked to the bathroom and flushed them down the toilet. Watching them disappear, her eyes misted. A part of what she had shared with Frankie washed away in a gurgle of water. Like some prized talisman, she pressed the cold metal case to her chest and closed her eyes. Seeing his smiling face again, she thought about what had passed between them. For one giddy moment, she had allowed her heart to overrule her head, ignoring common sense. She wished she'd given in to her desires and, at the same time, was glad she hadn't.

Placing the cigarette case back on her dressing table she wondered what she ought do to with it. Should she make an effort to return it to Frankie's relatives? No, probably not. But it reminded her of the horrific scene she had discovered in the bathroom of Rabbitte's house. She would make up her mind later what to do with it, meanwhile she had better get dressed and think about getting to work. In an effort to fight off depressive thoughts, she consciously picked bright clothes to wear; kelly-green silk scarf, tailored white blouse, double-breasted ivory suit, the skirt's hemline above the knee to emphasise legs clad in sheer glossy champagne-coloured tights, an outward expression of elegance to fool the outside world but mostly to fool herself. She added a final layer of lip gloss, brushed her hair, stood back to look at the completed picture in the mirror and nodded wearily. All things considered, she didn't look too bad. She nodded for a second time and spoke to the image. 'You're as ready as ever you're going to be, my girl.'

Pulling the door closed behind her, she heard the telephone in her apartment ring. Should she go back inside and answer it? Should she ignore it? Curiosity won the uneven battle. She re-entered the apartment and picked up the receiver. 'Hello, can I help you?' she asked.

'Is that Emma Boylan?' a male voice asked.

Emma recognised the voice but couldn't place it.

'Yes, this is Emma Boylan. Who am I speaking to?'

'Oh, I'm glad I caught you. This is Damien Conway here; you might remember we talked at my aunt's house in Leeson Crescent a week or so ago.'

'Yes of course, of course. I knew I recognised the voice. You're Jacqueline Miller's nephew. Do you have any news on her?'

'Yes, that's why I'm calling you. I just wanted to let you know she has made contact with me and that she is fine. False alarm on my part earlier I'm afraid. I was worrying about nothing at all. She left a note for me. I just didn't see it. You must think I'm really stupid. Anyway, all's well now; Aunt Jac is staying with my mum for a week before going abroad for a holiday.'

'And she's definitely all right then?'

'Yes, yes, she is indeed ... well, no actually, to tell you the truth she's been working a bit too hard, that's all. She has had a little recurrence of a problem stemming from her accident all those years ago ... nothing that a little rest and care won't sort out.'

'You mentioned to her that I wanted to talk with her?'

'Yes, I did, Ms Boylan, but she told me she has no recollection of making an appointment with you. Aunt Jac is not denying it ... she just can't remember, and that's not like her at all, you'll agree. She asked me to apologise to you and to tell you she'll get in touch with you later on when she's feeling better. I hope you don't mind?'

'No, not at all. I appreciate you taking the trouble to contact me, Damien. You say she's staying with your mother at the moment. Can you tell me where exactly that is?'

After a moment's hesitation, Damien answered. 'I'd prefer not to say if you don't mind. I really don't want anyone to bother her.'

'Fine, that's OK. I can understand your concern,' Emma said, resisting the urge to probe further. 'Thanks again for your help and tell your aunt that I look forward to hearing from her as soon as she is feeling any way better.'

'I'll tell her. Bye.'

Emma put the telephone down, unconsciously puckering her lips in a display of concentration. She thought about what Damien Conway had told her, to see if it told her anything new. It didn't. But there was something in Conway's voice that tugged at her curiosity, a nervousness that let her know all was not well with the young man. Her professional instincts told her that Damien was not being truthful or honest with her. But why should he want to keep whatever it was from her? More than ever, Emma felt the need to know more about Damien Conway and his elusive aunt, Jacqueline Miller.

Francis Xavier Donnelly, Tom Pettit and Shay Dunphy sat in conversation around a table in the darkened end section of Doheny & Nesbitt's, one of the Baggot Street bars most frequented by politicians and media people. The clock on the smoke-stained wall behind the counter showed the time as being five minutes shy of midday, a quiet time for business, a lull before the lunch-hour rush. Drinking coffee, all three men looked ill-at-ease, each glancing furtively around the premises between sips.

Francis Xavier had summoned his two fellow members of the PCCC to discuss what he described as alarming developments. It had been less than twenty-four hours since the three of them had faced the wrath of Fionnuala Stafford. By the end of that bruising encounter an agreement of sorts had been reached and they were not scheduled to meet again until after the proposed noon rendezvous between Francis Xavier and Jimmy Rabbitte.

'I'm afraid, gentlemen,' Francis Xavier said, after a tentative sip of coffee, 'things have gone from bad to worse since yesterday's bout of bitching in the war office with our beloved Taoiseach.'

Dunphy and Pettit groaned in unison. 'I didn't think it was possible for things to get any worse than they already are,' Pettit remarked.

'Neither did I,' Francis Xavier agreed, 'but they have.'

'Right, let's have it,' Pettit said impatiently, 'what's happened?'

'Early this morning, about four o'clock, I had a telephone call from Jimmy Rabbitte.'

'That man's a bloody nutter and no mistake,' Dunphy said. 'I suppose he wanted to cancel your meeting today, eh? That'd explain why you're here and not with him, right?'

'Right,' Francis Xavier, agreed, 'but it's a damn sight more serious than either of you might imagine. Rabbitte was in a terrible state of agitation on the phone. I couldn't make head nor tail of what he was going on about at first but gradually, in spite of the ranting and raving, I managed to make sense of his diatribe.

According to him, Frankie Kelly was found in *his* house yesterday. He had apparently taken a drug overdose and had to be rushed to hospital by ambulance.'

Total shock showed on Dunphy's face. 'You're not serious! That could mean that someone has connected the photographer to Alan McCall's murder and to Jacqueline Miller. We're really up shit creek if Kelly opens his trap about those photographs he shot outside Miller's house.'

'Kelly won't be talking to anyone,' Francis Xavier said, 'because he's dead. I checked with the hospital. They confirmed Rabbitte's story. Frankie Kelly died from a drug overdose.'

No one spoke. It was as though the three men had been suddenly struck dumb. The muffled sound of traffic from Baggot Street, the clinking of glasses and bottles in the bar and the good-natured banter of the bar staff failed to impinge on their thoughts. Francis Xavier broke the spell. 'You could be right about one thing, Shay: the person who found Kelly in Rabbitte's house could make a connection between the photographer and McCall's death.'

'Who?' Do we know who it was?' Dunphy asked.

'Yes. It was Emma Boylan.'

'Oh, shit,' Dunphy exclaimed, 'I don't fucking-well believe this.'

'Well, you'd better believe it,' Francis Xavier replied. 'It's just what we don't need right now. Emma Boylan of all people – muck-raker extraordinaire with the *Post*. Apparently, she was the one who found the unconscious Kelly and called the ambulance.'

Dunphy continued to shake his head in disbelief. 'But what the hell was Emma Boylan, or Frankie Kelly for that matter, doing in Rabbitte's house in the first place?'

'I'd have thought the answer to that was simple enough,' Francis Xavier said, an ironic twist on his lips. 'They were looking for the piece of negative, the frame showing McCall and Jacqueline Miller kissing each other outside her door, the selfsame negative that I should be collecting from Rabbitte this very moment.'

Pettit, who had been shocked into silence by these revelations, found his voice. 'So *who* has the negative now?'

'I wish I knew,' Francis Xavier answered gravely. 'I have to assume that Kelly went to Rabbitte's house to retrieve it. Obviously someone else had the same intention. That someone else, whoever he or she might be, discovered Kelly already there, set it up to look like Kelly was a junkie, and ran off with the negative.'

Pettit looked wan and exhausted, the bags under his eyes dark as bruises against the chalk-white face and his voice, when he spoke, little more than a rasping whisper. 'Someone else?' he said, looking at the two men opposite him. 'But apart from Rabbitte himself and the photographer – who is dead – and the three of us, who else knew about the negative?'

Pettit's question hung in the air for a moment before Francis Xavier put in words what all three of them were thinking. 'Fionnuala Stafford knew about the proposed meeting – I told her about it myself.'

Dunphy wrinkled his brow and pulled a puzzled

face. 'You're not seriously suggesting that the Taoiseach went to Rabbitte's house . . . and that she . . . '

'No of course not,' Donnelly snapped, 'but *someone* knows . . . and that someone killed the photographer.'

Dunphy remained less than convinced. 'Who says the photographer wasn't a junkie? We're allowing our imaginations to run away with us. What happened could have been simple. Kelly could have overdosed *himself*. Maybe he was already stoned when Emma Boylan found him. She might have discovered the negative before calling the ambulance.'

'No, I don't agree.' Francis Xavier said. 'We know from the photographs that my man, Joe Stones, took from his van in the street outside Miller's house, that Boylan and Kelly were working together. I'd say she found Kelly after someone had got to him and after that *someone* had relieved him of the negative.'

'Hm, it could have happened that way, I suppose,' Dunphy conceded, 'but somehow I don't think so. No, I'll tell you what I think: I'd say our mystery caller might have mistaken Kelly for Rabbitte. After all, it *was* Rabbitte's house.'

'We're going around in circles,' Francis Xavier said, attempting to bring the discussion to a conclusion. 'The truth is, we don't know what happened; we can speculate until we're blue in the face but none of this tells us who has the blasted negative.'

Tom Pettit held his two hands up in exasperation. 'This whole farce has gone far enough . . . it's got completely out of hand. For christsake, here we are discussing a shitty little negative when we know for certain that at least one murder has been committed, a murder that we, by our actions, might have helped the culprit to get away with scot-free, and now, as if that were not enough, it looks as if we might have a second murder on our hands.' He paused, inviting the others to respond, but continued when they remained mute. 'I mean, for christsake, where is it all going to end? Can someone answer me that, huh?' Another pause. 'Well, let me tell you, I for one want nothing more to do with the whole stinking mess.'

'It's a bit late for that,' Francis Xavier said, a sour grin on his lips.

Dunphy nodded in agreement. 'A bit like locking the stable door after the horse has bolted, I'd say. A bit late to get squeamish now, my friend. We're in too deep to back out now.'

'I don't agree, dammit,' Pettit insisted. 'I've always believed that when you find yourself in a hole, the only way out is to stop digging. Well, we're in one godawful hole at this minute, gentlemen, up to our goolies, if the truth be told, and we're digging ourselves deeper in by the minute. It's time we stopped.'

'What do you suggest we should do,' Dunphy asked.

'We go to the police, make a clean breast of things, tell them . . . '

' . . . tell them?' Dunphy interrupted. 'Tell them what? Tell them that we, elected representatives of the people, attempted to pervert the course of justice, that we compromised a murder inquiry by our actions. Is that what you want? Can you imagine the scandal? Shit will hit the fan by the bucketful. Jesus, man, just think about what you're saying; it'd be political suicide. Hari-fucking-kari. Worse, we'd be lucky if we didn't end up being charged for McCall's murder ourselves.'

'Shay's right,' Francis Xavier insisted, we must hold our nerve, Tom. Stick to our plans, tough it out. This thing will eventually blow over . . . it always does.'

'I wish I could believe that,' Pettit said, dejectedly, 'I just want to know where in hell's blazes it all ends. It'd help a lot even if we knew who has the negative?'

'I imagine,' Francis Xavier said, 'that we'll know the answer to that soon enough.'

'Emma Boylan? Do you think she has it?' Pettit asked.

'No, Tom, as a matter of fact I don't. All things considered, I do *not* believe Emma Boylan has it.'

'And how do you make that out?'

'Simple enough Tom, If she had it we would have heard from the *Post* by now.'

Dunphy drained the dregs from his coffee cup and looked at the other two men through half closed eyelids. 'Until we know who exactly has the negative we're more vulnerable than a backyard shithouse door in a gale.' Francis Xavier cringed at Dunphy's overuse of colourful expressions; the young politician, it seemed to him, had nothing original or even sensible to say. For once, however, he did not bother to offer a rejoinder. Considering the jitters his two fellow committee members were displaying, he decided not to tell them the other piece of bad news he had received the previous night. Better that they should not be aware that he no longer knew the whereabouts of Jacqueline Miller. As far as Francis Xavier was concerned, Jacqueline Miller represented a huge threat that could, at any moment, destroy them, should she decide to talk. There seemed little point in adding this extra factor to Dunphy's and Pettit's anxieties right now; besides, what could they do about it even if they did know?

The pub was beginning to fill up with lunchtime trade so Francis Xavier decided it might be best to end the discussion for the moment. Uneasily, the three men began their exit from the pub, saying hello to a few regulars they knew, and applying their professional smiles. Stepping through the pub's front door and on to the Baggott Street footpath, they were confronted by Jimmy Hiney, who along with a few of his colleagues from the opposition benches, was on his way into the pub. 'What's this then?' Hiney asked, 'Fionnuala Stafford's three wise men mixing it with the common folk; there must be something big in the air.'

'Just getting out before the riff-raff get in,' Francis Xavier answered through a forced smile, walking away from Hiney and his friends, determined not to get caught up in conversation. Dunphy and Pettit were equally anxious to escape. When they were a safe distance from the pub, Dunphy remarked, 'Did you hear what that gobshite Hiney called us: the three wise men; no fear of him ever being mistaken for one of the wise men.'

'No,' Pettit said with heavy irony, 'if he was wise and perceptive like you, he might have referred to us more accurately as the three blind mice.'

15

Widowhood did not sit well with Sarah McCall, a fact she readily conceded. How could it? It was not something she had ever envisaged, not once, not for a single moment. But without warning that became her state. In an instant, the lifestyle she had come to know and accept was over. To her, the prospect of rearing twins without a father was almost impossible to come to terms with.

In the three weeks since Alan's murder, Sarah's mother had taken charge. With minimum fuss and bother, she managed the day-to-day running of the household; everything from setting the breakfast table to getting John and Stephen to and from school. Sarah had allowed this to happen without protest but more recently, the past few days in particular, she had found herself wanting to pick up the threads of her life again. This change came upon her because of the way the two boys looked at her in the past week. They had been remarkably brave about their father's death, their resilience a beacon of hope in the vacuum his death had left. But now they wanted their mother back with them. She could tell it from the sideways glances; it was as though they were saying: we've lost our dad, please don't let us lose Mum as well. Their unspoken words provided the jolt she required. And they were right, she concluded: it was time to break away from the self-absorption that had swamped her, and let some light back into her life.

Some aspects of the daily routine, however, took a little longer to return to normal: the telephone for example. Sarah did not wish to speak to anyone on the telephone. She had told her mother as much a thousand times. The callers invariably wanted to talk about Alan, a subject she found unable to discuss over the telephone with any degree of confidence. She could hear the dreaded instrument ringing now and was glad when her mother stilled its clamorous call. Until the past three weeks she had never truly appreciated her mother's competence. Back in the days before she had married Alan, back when she had lived with her parents, she had not recognised the strong, resourceful side to her mother's personality. Not that she ever thought of her mother as being weak; it was more a case of not seeing her as a person at all; Mum was just Mum, taken for granted, always there when she was needed.

Her mother interrupted her thoughts. 'I *do* think you ought to take this call, Sarah.'

'Please, Mum, I really would prefer not . . . '

'I think you should, Sarah. It's a man who says he wants to talk about your pregnancy.'

'What? My . . . ? Oh, you mean it's Dr McCormick.'

'No, Sarah, it's not your doctor.'

'Not Dr McCormick, but that's . . . but, nobody knows I'm . . . '

'I think you'd better find out. I have him on hold.'

Reluctantly, Sarah moved to the telephone and pressed the instrument to her ear.

'Hello, Sarah McCall here, can I help you?'

'Ah, Mrs McCall, how good of you to take my call. I know how upset you must be since the tragic loss of your husband but I feel what I have to say to you warrants this intrusion.'

'My mother says you mentioned my pregnancy. I want to know why something so private should be known to . . . to a stranger. How did you come by such information? Who exactly are you?'

'Forgive my bluntness, Mrs McCall. This is a bad time for you but I knew you would not come to the phone unless I said something, shall we say, dramatic, to grab your attention.'

'Okay, you've grabbed my attention; now will you kindly answer my questions.'

'Fine, no problem, I'll tell you what I know. Let me start by telling you that I knew your husband. I knew him quite well.'

'Who are you?'

'Christie, that's Christie spelled with an *ie*. My name is John Christie.'

'Can't say I ever heard Alan mention your name, Mr Christie. Now, can you please explain what this is about.'

'I've called to let you in on a little secret.'

'Look, Mister-whatever-your-name-is, I'm not in the mood to play games. Goodbye.'

'No, no, don't hang up! Please don't hang up. Listen.

I'm on your side. OK? It's just that I think you should be acquainted with certain information about your husband, information he kept from you.'

'There were no secrets between myself and Alan.'

'I'm afraid I must take issue with you there, Mrs McCall. You see, your husband was having an affair at the time of his death.'

It took a second for the words to fully register with Sarah. She stood there, as though frozen, telephone to her ear, saying nothing, stunned. The man's words – *having an affair* – echoed inside her head, making her feel dizzy. *Having an affair*, just three words, but deadly as a bullet to the nervous system. She wanted to slam the telephone back in its cradle, but stopped herself. No, she couldn't leave it like this; some instinct made her pause, made her want to hear what else this madman had to say. 'If this is your idea of a joke, Mr . . . it's a pretty sick one.' Sarah felt the tears run down her cheek, her words faltered, distorted by the sudden tightness in her throat. 'Alan McCall is . . . *was* a good man, do you hear? A good man, a faithful and loving husband. He loved his family, his children. How dare you insinuate that he . . . that he . . . ' Unable to continue, Sarah slammed down the telephone.

The suddenness of the garda press conference caught most of the media people, including Emma Boylan, by surprise. Like her colleagues gathered in the cold briefing-room of the Phoenix Park headquarters, she wondered what lay behind the unexpected call. An excited buzz went about the room before the platform party arrived at their designated seats behind a blue baize-covered table, bedecked with bottles of mineral water and microphones. As the gathering media people shuffled into rows of steel-framed chairs, conversation became animated, all of them indulging in the game of second-guessing what would be announced. On one question a measure of agreement emerged: the briefing would have something to do with the McCall murder.

Flanked by Commissioner Horgan and Press Secretary Parkinson, Detective Inspector Lawlor addressed the assembled press corps. A preamble, citing the forces as winners in the battle against crime, which was greeted with barely concealed yawns by his audience, was followed by a résumé of known facts in the McCall murder investigation. 'There's been a development,' Lawlor announced with obvious satis-faction. 'We can now say with certainty that Alan McCall was not murdered in his own apartment. Our forensic findings enable us to state without fear of contradiction that McCall met his death somewhere other than in Clyde Road. Exhaustive investigation by garda personnel have come up with two witnesses who confirm that McCall was absent from his apartment at the time the state pathologist estimates his death took place. Furthermore, we have succeeded in gathering comprehensive evidence that will point us to where exactly the murder took place. Forensics have collected fingerprints, bloodstains, tissue samples, fabrics and certain organic matter on, and around, the body, the sort of evidence that will help our investigations come to a speedy conclusion. I am not at liberty to give you more details at this stage – for fear of tipping off the perpetrator – but I can confirm that we are following a definite line of investigation.'

A barrage of questions from the floor assailed Lawlor but nothing of further significance emerged from the exchange. Of all the assembled media personnel in the room, Emma alone, made no attempt to glean further information from Lawlor. As the detective inspector's eye caught her's in a fleeting glance, she recognised the challenge he flashed in her direction but her mind rejected the probe, pursuing instead its own line of inquiry. Lawlor's announcement that McCall had not been murdered in his own apartment was no surprise. It meant, too, that she was one step ahead of the law: she *knew* where McCall had met his end. Frankie Kelly had been right from the start; McCall *had* visited Jacqueline Miller and he had captured the event on his camera. Poor Frankie, she thought, what a pity he wasn't around to enjoy this posthumous vindication. Even the reports of his death in the press were unsympathetic, pointing to drug abuse as the cause. Emma's report in the *Post* was little better. Forced to take the official line, subjected to Bob Crosby's evaluation of Frankie's death, she made little mention of suspected foul play. She could have and should have insisted on putting her own point of view across but she didn't. Why? Her single column piece was not something she could be proud of. What a pity she could not tell Frankie how sorry she was for having ever doubted his story. What a pity . . . but no, no, no, she forced herself to blank his image from her mind. She had to be tough, remain professional, objective, focused, and get on with her job, if for no other reason except to follow the leads he had given her. It was the least she could do for him.

Slipping away from the press conference, Emma drove her Volvo out of the garda car park, nosed it into the busy midday traffic on Constitution Hill and headed for the city centre. Traffic was congested, and drivers were bad-tempered. Crawling, bumper-to-bumper, along the Liffey's quays, her journey back to the *Post's* building seemed to take forever but it did at least have one benefit: it gave her time to sort out her thoughts. She experienced intermittent flashes of euphoria doused by darker thoughts of failure and frustration. A spectacular scoop beckoned to her, tantalisingly close. She alone, among the media personnel, knew the murder location. She alone could point the finger and name the names of those who visited the house in question at the time of the murder. But she needed more to run with the story; she had no evidence at all.

It was frustrating that her one and only eyewitness, Frankie Kelly, was dead. The photograph he had taken of Alan McCall entering Jacqueline Miller's house had gone missing. Sure, she had a photograph of the country's youngest elected politician, Shay Dunphy, leaving the house, but it had been artificially enhanced and would count for nothing without corroborating evidence. And what of Jacqueline Miller herself? So far, the woman had proved to be most elusive, all efforts to trace her coming to naught.

Emma continued to evaluate the scraps of information she had already accumulated. Her thoughts centred on Jacqueline Miller's nephew Damien Conway. The young man had been seen leaving the house on the evening of the murder. There was something about his relationship with his aunt that she found odd but she couldn't put her finger on exactly what it was. He certainly did not look like a killer to her but then, as she had learned from past experience, killers rarely look like killers. All she had were questions, questions, questions – and no answers. She banged her fist on the steering wheel and cursed. A motorist in the lane next to her, thinking her reaction a result of pent-up frustration brought on by the snail-pace traffic, smiled knowingly in her direction. She attempted a reciprocating smile, failed miserably, then returned to her thoughts. The greatest scoop of her career might be within her grasp, but to make it work she still required quite a few key pieces of the jigsaw to fall into place.

Stuck at a red light at the Ha'penny Bridge, watching pedestrians emerge from it and pour across the road in front of her car, she came to a decision: she would talk to her editor Bob Crosby, lay all the facts, as she knew them, before him and let him decide whether or not to run with the story.

The room was uncomfortably warm, the central heating on full blast, but she refused to open the window, refused to allow winter's chill penetrate her refuge. Lying fully clothed on the bed, face cushioned softly in the pillow, Jacqueline Miller forced back tears and tried not to think. A hiccuping shudder ran through the length of her body. *Somebody walking over my grave.* She could hear her sister moving about downstairs, cups being washed and put away, cupboard doors opening and closing, the barely audible sound of a radio, and wondered how long she could stand being cooped up as a guest in Regina's house. She felt restless; God, she felt so restless, but where could she go? Who else could she turn to?

It was an hour since Regina had gently knocked on her door and offered to bring some soup and a light lunch to her room. She had refused, explaining that she had a headache, but promised to go downstairs later. Jacqueline Miller did not really have a headache, at least not in the conventional sense, but she did find it hard to get used to the idea of sharing a house with other people, even when those people were her older sister Regina and her husband Ed Conway. The house itself, a spacious, semi-detached redbrick, 1940s vintage, situated on the outskirts of Celbridge village, was spacious and comfortable. Ed, a tall active man of forty-seven, commuted twelve miles daily to the city, where he worked as a solicitor. With two partners and a staff of five, he ran the practice from a Georgian building in Fitzwilliam Square. Regina, younger than Ed by eight years, had given up full-time work several years earlier but continued to give classes in speech and drama on Saturday mornings. It wasn't that she needed the money – Ed's thriving business saw to that

– but it got her out of the house and she welcomed the break from domesticity.

Since moving in with Regina, Jacqueline had spent most of her time in her bedroom. Imperfections on the walls and hairline cracks on the ceiling had all become depressingly familiar to her. Occasionally, out of sheer frustration, she forced herself to take long walks outside the house but the room's sanctuary provided the measure of solace she craved right now. Anything was better than having to talk to her sister about recent events. She could not avoid the subject forever, but how could she explain what had happened? Turning up, dishevelled, wearing clothes that were obviously not her own, looking as though she were at death's door, was bound to raise questions. She had steadfastly refused to elucidate, promising instead that all would be explained in due course. Besides, even if she did succeed in putting recent events in chronological order, would Regina understand? No, of course not! How could she, when the whole episode with Alan McCall remained beyond her own comprehension! And what of strait-laced Ed? What would he make of the story? The prospect did not bear thinking about.

Damien Conway provided the only respite from the oppressive atmosphere she found herself cooped up in. Initially he had demanded an explanation for her abrupt disappearance. It perplexed him that she would not confide in him. She attempted to reassure him by stressing that what had happened had been unavoidable. Her answers, though failing to fully satisfy him, mollified him enough to let go of the subject. Any topic was welcome as long as it moved away from the reason behind her flight from Leeson Crescent. She had listened as he talked enthusiastically about his plans for developing his business. He had brought up the subject of finance, telling her he could do with the money she had promised him. He showed her his projected profit figures and plans for expansion but emphasised the urgency of an immediate cash injection to kick-start the project. She was about to say yes, caught up in the fire of his enthusiasm, when reason doused the spirit of her unquestioning largesse. The disappointment in his face was all too evident when she insisted that he wait until his feasibility plan got the nod from her bank manager. His expression usually had the effect of melting her resolve but not on this occasion. She would gladly give him the money but she felt it important that he should get used to the discipline of good practice.

Handling Damien had been easy, but coming to terms with her sister, his mother, was most tiresome. Regina meant well, Jacqueline could not deny that, but in trying to show sympathy and understanding, her sister managed instead to annoy and irritate her. Regina's conversations invariably raked over episodes from the past, unearthing painful reminders of a time when both of them lived with their parents and their brother Sean. At pains to understand the reasons behind the long-standing feud that existed between Jacqueline and her parents, Regina returned to the subject of that strained relationship at every opportunity. 'How can you remain so bitter towards your father,' she would ask, 'and Mum; what could she have ever done to you that you should treat her so badly?' Jacqueline made no attempt to give an answer, steadfastly refusing to react to her sister's probing into the dark side of her past.

She had almost drifted off to sleep when she heard the gentle knocking on her door. 'Jac,' she heard Regina say. 'Jac, is it all right if I come in? I've a nice cup of tea for you and a freshly baked scone.'

'Yes, come in,' Jacqueline answered, moving her legs off the bed and sitting on its side, 'I'd love a cup of tea, thanks.'

'It's stifling in here,' Regina said as soon as she entered the room. 'Why don't I open the window . . . let a little air in? What do you say. OK?

'Yes, yes, you're right, I hadn't noticed, thanks.'

Regina placed the tray she had been carrying on the bedside table and moved to open the window. Conversation concentrated on trivial matters, with Regina doing most of the talking. She chatted about her speech and drama classes, relating funny anecdotes about pushy mothers who insisted that their precious offspring were destined to go into films, television or the stage. Inevitably, the conversation reverted to the familiar subject of their family history. 'I think it would do you good to pop down the country and visit Mum; we could go this weekend. Damien can do the driving. What do you say? You always enjoy his company and it'll give him a chance to expound on his latest business ventures?'

'No, Regina, I've no desire to go down the country.'

'It'd do you a world of good, Jac, honest it would. Mum is not getting any younger . . . we both know that. Living on her own in that big house can't be much fun for her. I know you put money into her bank account on a regular basis and help to pay for the upkeep of the house, but you know what she'd like better than all that? More than anything else she would like to see you. It's not fair the way you refuse to meet her. Whatever difference there is between the two of you should be forgotten. It's been too long since you've been home, far too long. You haven't set foot in our house since the day poor Sean died. You didn't even attend his funeral. At the time we put it down to your grief. I know how close the two of you were but you never went back – not once, not even after your terrible accident. Why Jac, why?'

'I don't wish to discuss that period of my life. I wish to God you would drop it. You know how much it upsets me . . . just let it be. OK?'

'Fine,' Regina snapped, hurt by her sister's reprimand, 'I just want things to be the way they once were – our family, I mean – together, happy, like families ought to be.' When no further response came from Jacqueline, Regina walked out of the room and shut the door with more force than was necessary. Jacqueline put her cup of tea to one side and placed her head in her hands. *Dear God, will it never end*, she mouthed silently into her hands. In spite of her earlier resolve not to visit the past, she found herself transported back to the 'happy times' her sister had spoken about.

Happy, yes; she felt so happy. Jim and Mary Miller, her parents had taken her to the Shelbourne Hotel for her eleventh birthday. Her older brother Sean had been brought along to join them for the meal. Born with Down's syndrome, Sean had been taken home from the residential centre he attended during the week, so that he could be part of his sister's celebrations. As an additional complication to his already curtailed lifestyle, Sean suffered from asthma. Subjected to a daily diet high in magnesium – all the things he hated, things like fresh green vegetables, unmilled wheat germ, soybeans and the like – he was, on this occasion, allowed to eat what the others were having. His awkwardness at table, a feature Jacqueline had only become aware of as she grew older, usually embarrassed her but she tried not to let it bother her on this occasion. She could see the simple joy in his face as he stuffed his mouth with total abandonment. A smiling waiter brought a special birthday cake to their table and encouraged her to blow out the cake's eleven candles. She had begun to take a big breath in readiness for the task when her mother suggested that Sean be allowed to help her blow out the candles. She had agreed but felt it was unfair. This was her birthday after all, not his, but rather than cause a scene, she smiled and invited her brother to join in the exercise. Between them, they extinguished all the tiny flickering lights with one big huge breath each. Proud mother and father, along with other diners seated at nearby tables clapped their hands and sang the happy birthday song. The waiter shook Sean's hand and praised him, while their mother leaned over and kissed him on the cheek. Her dad, seeing the look of disappointment in her face, rescued the situation by making a little speech. He stood up, called for attention and told everyone what a wonderful girl she was and how proud he was of her on this her eleventh birthday. Everyone in the hotel's dining room joined in a round of applause. She had never felt so pleased in her life. Being eleven was certainly a good feeling.

Only Regina, her older sister, missed the celebration. As a final-year student in St Catherine's secondary boarding school, Regina had to swot hard for her Leaving Certificate. Jacqueline insisted that a piece of the cake be kept for Regina. 'What a nice idea, Jac,' her mother said, surprised and delighted with her youngest daughter's thoughtfulness. 'We can send her a portion tomorrow.'

A ringing telephone greeted them within seconds of their return home from the hotel; Regina had taken the trouble to call her sister and wish her a happy birthday. Experiencing a giddy pleasure, Jacqueline chatted on the phone, proclaiming herself the happiest girl in the whole wide world. As a further treat, her parents had allowed her to stay up late and watch one of her favourite films on the television. She had seen *The Railway Children* three times already but it still retained a special magic for her.

It was past midnight when she finally went upstairs to her bedroom. The whole evening had been a wonderful success and she did not feel the least bit sleepy. Yes, eleven was a good age and she felt all grown up, no longer a child. Undressing, her hands gently cupped the contours of her budding breasts as she moved in front of the mirror. Although still small, she considered her developing breasts proof that she was becoming an adult. She welcomed the prospect. Taking one last look at her slim body before reaching for her nightdress, she was shocked to see the reflection of her brother Sean in the mirror. 'What are you doing in my room,' she asked, not hiding her annoyance. 'Get out and go back to your own room.'

Sean stood inside the door, dressed only in his pyjamas, smiling at her, his mouth open, his tongue protruding, but saying nothing.

'Did you hear what I said?' Jacqueline asked.

'Happy birthday,' Sean blurted out, having difficulty forming the words, 'Sean loves Jac. Happy birthday.'

'Thank you, Sean, and Jac loves Sean but Jac wants you to go back to your own room. OK?' This time Jacqueline tried to hide her annoyance. Because of her brother's disabilities she had to make allowances. For most of his fifteen years he had attended specialist clinics but his mother liked to have him home to the house as often as possible. It sometimes annoyed Jacqueline to see the lengths her mother was prepared to go in order to facilitate Sean. Because of his asthma, carpets had been removed from his room in order to eliminate the risk of house mites, a contributing factor to asthma attacks, or so the experts assured her mother. In addition, Mother would aerate his bedroom twice daily, early in the morning and again in the evening. Nothing was too much for her if it helped make life easier for Sean.

For as long as Jacqueline could remember, her mother had told her that Sean was special. 'He's one of God's special children,' she would say, 'so you must always, always treat him with love and understanding.' It was only in recent years, ever since she turned nine, that she noticed how Sean's face and general appearance looked different from all of the other boys she knew. On a few occasions recently when she had gone to the local shop with her brother, her friends had crowded around him and chatted happily with him, listening to his funny way of talking, not in the slightest way embarrassed. At first she felt they were only trying to humour him but as she watched them laugh and joke with him it became obvious that they genuinely enjoyed his company.

Seeing Sean's eyes fixed on her bare breasts, she quickly pulled on her nightdress and rushed towards him in order to push him out of the room. It was then that she noticed he had exposed himself, his hand clutching his penis. With an intake of breath, she froze, unable to take her eyes off the object. At school, in the relationships and sex education classes, she had seen outline drawings of the male reproductive organ but this was her first time to see one in real life. Her first reaction was one of disgust; *uuuugh*, it was ugly, made more repulsive by the way Sean's hand moved up and down its length. In the brief moment it took her to absorb the sight before her, Sean's free hand reached to touch her breasts through her nightdress. With a swiftness that surprised both of them, she drew out with her hand and hit him a stinging slap across the face.

'Out of my room you ugly, ugly thing,' she said, pushing him out the door. 'Don't you ever, ever dare come into my room again, you hear me, I hate you . . . hate you . . . you disgust me.'

Back in her room she thought about what had just taken place. As the shock wore off, she could not dismiss the sight of Sean's display from her mind. Although she considered it ugly – a horrid red-headed snake was the image that came to mind – she could not deny it held a certain curiosity value for her. It was the size of the thing that astounded her most; she had no idea men's 'thingies' could be so big. She knew the proper term was *penis* but her friends at school always referred to it as a 'thingy' or 'willy'. She thought about Sean and wondered why he had come into her room. Had he been spying on her through the keyhole? Had the sight of her undressing made him do what he had done? Yes, she decided, that might have been what had brought him into her room. Some of the fault lay with herself in that case, she told herself; she should have locked her door. Thinking about the words she had used, she realised how cruel they must have sounded to him. Equally, to have slapped him across the face had been the wrong thing to do. Sean was not like other boys, a fact her mother had drummed into her often enough. The phrases '*one of God's special people*' and '*not always responsible for the things he does*' sprang immediately to mind. As she thought about her brother's disability she began to feel guilty for what she had done and for the hurtful things she had said.

She could not sleep. Jumbled images in her mind refused to go away. Sean's aroused thingy, his hand reaching to touch her breasts, the slap she had given him; each scene played over and over again inside her head. But it was the slap that bothered her most, and with good reason. Because of Sean's acute asthmatic condition, she feared her actions might trigger an attack. If that happened there would be hell to pay. The conclusion that she had been at fault became inescapable. After some time, tossing and turning, she decided she would never get any sleep unless she went to his room and apologised. That way, she hoped he would understand how sorry she was and forgive her.

Back in her bedroom in Regina's house, Jacqueline dismissed the reverie. The childhood memories were too painful to relive. She did not want to think about what happened next, best to blot it from her mind entirely. But she knew that was wishful thinking; she could never erase the events, no matter how hard she tried. Staying with Regina only helped stir such memories. One thing was certain, she would have to find somewhere else to live. She would leave this very day, get away, try to get her head back together. But before that happened she knew her mind would force her to revisit the scenes that had followed on from the night of her eleventh birthday.

Already, she felt herself revert to the age of eleven.

16

Tiptoeing barefoot along the landing in the darkness, holding on to the banister, remembering not to step on the one loose floorboard she knew existed there, afraid to make a sound in case she should wake her parents, Jacqueline made it to Sean's door. Birthday or no birthday, she knew how upset Mum and Dad would be if they discovered her out of bed, especially after midnight. She paused for a second outside her brother's door, as an odd thought struck her: she was now eleven years of age plus one day. The realisation brought a smile to her face.

No one can call me a child any more.

Turning the handle, she pushed the door open and eased herself on to the bare boards of his room. As always, a soft glow illuminated the room; the 15-watt bulb, a constant feature ever since Sean's childhood days, remained in operation at the insistence of their mother. Sean was still awake. He beamed his best smile at her as she approached his bedside. Jacqueline held a finger to her lips. 'Shsssh,' she whispered, 'I came in to say I'm sorry.' Sean smiled and indicated that she should sit on the side of his bed. Looking at his rounded innocent face, Jacqueline could tell that the earlier incident had already been forgotten. 'Sean,' she whispered into his ear, 'I'm really sorry for saying those horrid things I said to you earlier. I didn't mean any of that stuff, honest. And I shouldn't have slapped you. I thought that you . . . anyway, it doesn't matter, I was wrong and I'm sorry. OK?'

'Sorry, Jac, I'm sorry too . . . love Jac.'

'Good, Sean, I'm glad. I thought you'd never speak to me again,' she said, leaning over to kiss his cheek before departing. 'We're friends; that's all that matters. Mum would have a fit if she knew I hit . . . f you told her . . . told her that . . . you know.'

'Secret,' Sean said, as his hand shot out to touch her breast.

'No,' Jacqueline said, pulling back, but stopping when she saw the fright in his eyes. 'Look, look, it's all right, Sean; calm down. I'm not going to clout you, but well, you can't just touch, I mean, you're not supposed to touch me . . . to touch a *woman* like that . . . but it's all right.' Her struggle to find the right words to pacify him were having little or no effect. His head pressed back in the pillow, his breathing coming in short little bursts. Jacqueline, now in panic, fearing an imminent asthmatic spasm from Sean, grabbed the inhaler from the top of the bedside locker and offered it to him. He pushed it away, shaking his head from side to side, fear in his eyes.

'Don't do this to me, Sean,' she said, desperately trying to find a way to show him she meant him no harm. She took his hand and placed it on her breast. 'There, there, look it's all right, I don't mind . . . please, Sean, I won't slap you . . . I know you mean no harm.' The smile was back on Sean's face. He tried to say something but the words would not come. Jacqueline allowed his hand to remain on her breast for a few moments before attempting to remove it. For the briefest of seconds he resisted her effort but then in a move that caught her by surprise, he grabbed her hand and pulled it beneath the sheets and on to his crotch. The shock of having her hand touch the hardness there brought a shout from her. 'No, no, Sean,' she began but her protestation was cut short as the main light in the room flashed on and her mother came rushing over to the bedside.

'What's this?' she yelled. 'What in God's name is going on here?'

Jacqueline jumped with fright, quickly withdrew her hand from beneath the sheets and turned red-faced to face her mother. Before she could utter a word, her mother's hand caught the side of her face with a forceful blow, hard enough to knock her sideways. 'You dirty filthy little bitch,' her mother screamed, hitting her with the other hand. 'Jim, Jim, come here this instant,' she shouted to her husband. 'Get in here this instant. See what this little trollop has been up to.'

'I wasn't up to anything,' Jacqueline managed to say through tears before another stinging blow landed on her face. 'Don't you dare open your mouth to your mother, you dirty, filthy little tramp.'

Jim Miller came rushing into the room, still adjusting the bottoms of his pyjamas, a look of dismay on his face. 'What on earth is going on? Will someone tell me what the fuss is about?'

'I found this little trollop in here with Sean, she

was . . . she was, Jesus Christ, Jim, she was *at* him, she was . . . At a loss to find words to describe what she thought her daughter had been up to, Mary Miller resorted to her hands again. 'I'll kill you, you little rip, you hear me, so help me God, I'll kill you.'

Jim Miller pushed himself between mother and daughter.

'Stop it. I said stop it! No one is going to kill anyone, all right. We're all going to calm down and find out what's going on.'

'What's going on? Jesus, Jim, any fool with an eye in his head can see what's going on.'

The look that Jim shot his wife was severe and uncompromising. 'Okay, all right, fine, that's enough. I said calm down and I mean it. Jacqueline can go to her bed now and you and I will discuss this. OK?'

'No, it's not bloody OK, Jim. I want the little rip out of the house immediately, this minute.'

'Jac is going back to her bed now. I'll talk to her tomorrow after you and I have had a chance to discuss this matter. Jac, go to bed.'

'She's not going anywhere until she explains to me . . .'

'I said enough,' Jim insisted, gently taking his daughter by the shoulder and ushering her out the door. 'I'll talk to you tomorrow Jac. Sort this out. OK? Goodnight . . .'

The sound of Sean's respiratory system struggling for air brought everyone's attention back to the bed. Wheezing, gulping for breath like a fish on a river bank, Sean's face was turning blue. Mary Miller grabbed the inhaler and held it in place over his mouth, telling Sean when to breathe. In a matter of seconds, Sean's breathing eased considerably. Looking over her shoulder, she shot a withering glance at her husband. 'Get her out of here immediately, d'you hear me. Just get the little bitch out of here.'

Jacqueline ran to her bedroom, got between the sheets and covered her head with blankets. She was shaking all over, too traumatised to cry. Somewhere in the distance she could here the raised voices of her parents. *Please let me die God, please let me die now.* Death seemed like an attractive alternative to her present position. Her favourite teacher, Miss McGuire, whom she regarded as the wisest person in the whole world, announced in Christian doctrine class that when a person dies, whether that person suffered from hunger, ravages of war, injustice, illness or any number of other unpleasant afflictions, God and his angels made sure they were happy in their new home in Heaven. To Jacqueline, this magical place and the all-caring God that Miss McGuire spoke about represented exactly what she needed right now.

Her entreaty to the Almighty seemed to work because for the first time in her life she found a mechanism to shut out the real world and replace it with a blank.

As Emma outlined her views to Bob Crosby in regard to the McCall murder, she noticed that the news editor only looked at his watch twice. Considering it had taken her the best part of half an hour to place the facts in a chronological order before him, that wasn't at all bad. In Bob Crosby's busy world, time, or lack of time, represented the real enemy. Overweight, balding, the wrong side of fifty and suffering from a stomach ulcer, he struggled daily with the impossible deadlines demanded by the *Post* but always managed to get there. Getting his attention for ten minutes was considered quite an achievement but getting his undivided attention for half an hour was unheard of. Apart from the two glances at his watch, Emma could tell he was impressed with the investigative work she had done and the wealth of background information she had unearthed.

'This could be big,' he said, without excitement, 'but we haven't got enough to run with.'

'Not enough?'

'No, Emma, not enough at this point. What we have here is the bones of a great story. There's no doubt we are looking at a conspiracy, a conspiracy that possibly reaches all the way into the government, the gardaí and God knows who else but – there's always an unfortunate *but* – we can't go to print without cast-iron proof that McCall met his death in Jacqueline Miller's house or, at the very least, being able to place him at her house around the time of death. You're going to have to dig deeper, Emma: find Jacqueline Miller, talk to her, go back to some of the people who knew her in the past, talk to her nephew, Damien Conway, find out what makes him tick, talk to McCall's wife, find Jimmy Rabbitte, ask him about the tip-off he received on the phone about McCall – you should follow up on that. Find out who made that call and you've probably found the person who murdered Alan McCall. Jeez, Emma, I don't need to tell you your job but I will say this: find me one piece of solid evidence, just one piece, and we've got the scoop of the year.'

Emma puckered her mouth and punched her fist into the palm of her other hand unable to hide her frustration. 'D'you know what really bugs me? I almost had that piece. Frankie's picture of McCall entering the house would have blown the whole case wide open.'

'Yes, it would, but unfortunately you don't have it so let's forget about it. Find Jimmy Rabbitte, talk to the people involved; get the wind up a few of the other key players – someone is bound to let slip something – rattle all the cages and something's bound to emerge. A word of advice: move quickly but be damn careful; remember there's a murderer on the loose out there. The sooner he's discovered, the better. The problem is that this isn't going to remain hot forever. If you don't crack it soon, someone else will. I'd be most aggrieved if that were to happen.'

'Don't worry, Bob, I still have one or two angles I want to try.

'Good, just remember, time is of the essence.'

'Cheers, Bob, I'm already on my way.'

One day into her eleventh year on planet Earth, Jacqueline Miller lay in her bed and watched as June's morning sunlight streamed in through her window. It was Saturday morning; that meant not getting up for school.

It was her favourite day, the one day in the week when she could lie on in the morning. Sunday she had to get up and go to Mass with her parents but Saturday was free.

Familiar noise from downstairs: the radio, her father and mother and Sean, muffled sounds drifting up to her room. She thought about her birthday celebrations the previous evening, reliving the joy she had experienced at the hotel. It had been a wonderful evening, truly wonderful. Afterwards when she came home ... no, she did not want to recall what happened after she came home. Something unpleasant, yes, a vague impression lingered in her head, something ugly, something she could dredge up if she wanted to ... but she did not want to dredge it up.

Sean opened the door and waved to her in his usual energetic way. 'Going back, Jac, goodbye.'

'I thought you were staying for the whole weekend, going back on Sunday night like you usually do.'

'No, Jac, Mum says no. Going back early. Mum's driving. Bye.' Smiling, still waving at her, Sean backed out of the room and closed the door. Jac could not remember a time before when Sean had not kissed her cheek when saying goodbye. She had always hated it when he did that but now, now that he had failed to kiss her, she felt like something was wrong. Uneasy thoughts entered her head – something to do with Sean, something unpleasant, but the sound of a car door opening and closing banished the threatening thoughts from her head.

She got out of her bed, crossed to the window of her room and saw her mother and Sean fasten their safety belts inside their car. She watched as the car backed out of the driveway with Sean bouncing his head backwards and forward, smiling happily, in the passenger's seat. Two black and blue holdalls sat on the back seat; one, a large Adidas canvas bag, the other a smaller version with the same logo. It was a familiar sight, one she had come to expect every time Sean left the house to return to his special school. The big holdall contained clothes and footwear; the smaller one contained Sean's increasing array of medicines and items that were supposed to help control his asthma, items such as tablets, syrups, inhalers and a peak flow meter – a device for quickly measuring breathing capacity – which only his mother knew how to use.

As she watched the car turn the corner of the street in front of their house and disappear, a feeling of guilt put a damper on her spirits. Although it was Saturday morning, and later in the day she would line out with her school chums for a game of camogie, an event that always made her feel happy, something was bothering her. Sean had gone back to his special school and she was relieved. It wasn't right, she knew that, but it was what she was feeling. Tomorrow, Sunday, her two best school pals, Jane and Natasha, were coming to her house and it had always annoyed her to see them make such a fuss over Sean. The two girls appeared to be totally smitten by his ever-present smile and the comical faces he never tired of pulling. At least now, with him out of the way, she would not have to watch as her friends fawned over him. Perhaps that was why she felt so bad about it.

Jacqueline had nearly dozed off when her father came into her room. It was his voice that woke her up.

'Wake up, sleepy head, I've brought you a cup of tea and one of your favourite biscuits; time to rise and shine and meet the day.' Jim Miller held the tray in his hands while his daughter moved into a sitting-up position, then, when she was ready, allowed her to take it. A slight man with spiked grey hair and a pleasant face, Jim Miller worked as a schools inspector, or to give him his proper Gaelic title – *cigire*. But his real interest in life revolved around the theatre and his love of acting. Jacqueline had become familiar with the sight of her father pacing up and down the sitting-room floor, script in hand, reciting lines and sometimes putting on strange accents. Nobody was allowed to interrupt his concentration at such times but Jac had listened quietly on many occasions. She never understood the lines he spoke but she still liked to listen. When she was younger, about six or seven, she remembered being frightened when she saw her father dressed up in a bright red military uniform and speaking in a voice she did not recognise. It was not until he changed back into his own clothes and spoke with his familiar voice that she stopped crying and accepted him as Dad. After that she had learned to distinguish the difference between what were characters and what was Dad. It was during those years that Jim Miller's talent as an actor became widely acclaimed in the amateur world.

'I wanted to talk to you about what happened last night,' he said as he sat on the side of her bed. Getting no reaction from his daughter, he gently touched her cheeks with the back of his fingers and smiled. 'You're at an awkward age, Jac; still a child but all grown up at the same time. It's an age where natural curiosity about the developments taking place in your body is bound to cause you some confusion. I understand that, Jac, and I think I can understand why you did what you did to Sean last night.'

Jacqueline wanted to answer her father, tell him that she had done nothing to Sean but, unwilling to think about the ugly events, she remained silent.

'Your need to find out about such things is the most natural thing in the world so you are not alone in thinking such thoughts; you mustn't think that what you did was bad ... you are not a bad person, Jac, hundreds of girls your age have done what you have done ... explore the differences between man and woman ... between boy and girl. But what you did with Sean was not the right way to go about discovering such differences. What you did only managed to upset your mother and confuse poor Sean. Do you know what I'm saying?'

Again, Jacqueline struggled to find words but could not bring herself to utter a single word.

'As your dad, someone who loves you more than anyone in the world, I'd like to be the one who explains these things in a way you can understand, all right?'

No, it wasn't all right.

That morning, Jacqueline was raped by her father. The event marked the beginning of a horror that would be repeated over and over again.

17

'Look, I'm sorry, but I cannot allow you to see Mrs McCall. She has enough to contend with without talking to reporters.'

The woman speaking to Emma stood sentinel on the doorstep, arms folded defiantly in front of her generous breasts, daring anyone to defy her. Emma had other ideas; she did not give up so easily. She had travelled that morning to Rathkenny, a village set snugly in the heart of rural Ireland, situated halfway between Carlow and Kilkenny and did not relish the thought of returning to Dublin empty-handed.

She pleaded. 'I know you want to protect Mrs McCall from unnecessary intrusion into her grief – I can appreciate that – but I think I might be able to help her. I am investigating the death of her husband. My only brief is to track down whoever it was that killed him. It would help me enormously if I could speak with her . . . please.'

'The answer is still no, young woman. Now, please respect our right to privacy and leave us alone; leave us in peace here.'

Emma gathered her thoughts and was about to have another shot when she heard a voice call out from inside the hallway. 'It's all right, Mum, I'll have a word with her; I'd like to hear what she has to say for herself.'

'Do you think you're being wise, my dear?' the woman asked as she made way for Sarah McCall on the doorstep.

'Yes, thank you, Mum. I'll handle this now.'

The mother frowned at Emma for a moment before withdrawing inside the house. 'Dear Mum,' Sarah said, giving Emma a tight little smile, 'she's been so good to me these last few weeks I don't know what I'd have done without her.' She sighed before continuing. 'But, I've got to learn to face the world again and stand on my own two feet. You know my name of course but I don't know yours.'

'I'm sorry, I should have introduced myself; I'm Emma Boylan, investigative journalist.'

'With which paper?'

'I'm with the *Post*. I have been working on this . . . '

'Do come inside. We'll talk there. I see no reason why we should stand here in the cold talking on the doorstep.'

Sarah McCall ushered Emma into a comfortable reception room and asked her if she would prefer a cup of tea or coffee. Emma opted for coffee. Sarah went to organise the refreshments, leaving Emma a few moments to take in her surroundings. The room, she could see, like the rest of the spacious two-storey house, reflected good taste and understated affluence. Some instinct told her that the decor owed more to Sarah McCall than to her late husband. None of the men she had ever known would have ever chosen the delicate pastels that adorned the room. And the furniture too, so elegant, each item perfectly conforming to its surroundings. The room said a lot to Emma about Sarah McCall's personality. Until now, Emma had only seen photographs of Sarah – photographs taken at the time of her husband's funeral. She noted that in real life Sarah McCall looked much better than the newspaper pictures might have suggested. Taller than Emma by a few inches, her figure was well proportioned; she had good legs, a long neck and a pretty face framed with ash-blond hair. Emma put her age at somewhere in the early thirties, probably a year or two younger than herself.

Sarah McCall returned to the room and sat in an armchair opposite Emma. 'Mum will bring us some coffee in a few minutes,' she said, sizing up Emma. 'So tell me what exactly it is you want to talk to me about?'

Sarah's direct approach impressed Emma. It was obvious to her that Sarah was not the sort of person to put up with idle chit-chat or evasions.

'You know, I presume,' Emma said, 'that the gardaí no longer believe your husband met his death in his apartment?'

'Yes, I read the reports in the press and I've also had a detective down here briefing me, but I knew all that before it appeared in the press. I knew from the start.'

'You did? But . . . '

'Yes, you see, I had this friend of mine – a friend of Alan's really – go to his apartment on the night of the murder. His name is Greg Mooney; you've heard of him?'

'Yes, I have; he's the member for the Dublin–North constituency, been in the Dáil for quite a while.'

'Exactly; I see you know your politics, Emma. That being the case you'll also know that he is a respectable and reliable source.'

Emma listened as Sarah McCall recalled the night of her husband's murder, giving a lucid description of all the events surrounding the dreadful occasion. Stopping only to allow her mother serve coffee and a plate of biscuits, Sarah explained how she had made several efforts to contact Alan that night, how she had discovered a discrepancy in his story about staying in Greg Mooney's house and how she had persuaded Mooney to drive across the City to Alan's apartment before midnight. Emma remained silent, impressed with how well Sarah had endured such torment and loss, and was still able to talk about it so freely.

'Have you told anybody else this story?' Emma asked.

'Yes, I told Inspector Lawlor; he's the detective in charge of the investigation. Do you know him?'

'Yes, I know him.'

'I gather from the way you say that, you are not too impressed with Lawlor.'

Emma smiled. 'How perceptive of you, Mrs McCall.'

'Please call me Sarah. I'm glad someone else shares my misgivings about the man; I think Lawlor is useless. When I told him about Greg Mooney, do you know what the clown did?'

'No, tell me,' Emma coaxed, having some difficulty in picturing Lawlor as a clown but in total agreement with Sarah's sentiments. 'There's nothing that would surprise me when it comes to Detective Lawlor.'

'He immediately put Greg down as a suspect. Can you credit that? It was only when he interviewed Greg and checked the telephone records that he knew his suspicions were cockeyed. As it turned out, it was Greg Mooney who helped Lawlor establish the facts.'

'So, if Alan was not in his apartment, where do you suspect he might have been?'

'That's the bit that beats me. I've no idea, none whatsoever, but then, I'm beginning to discover there's a whole lot of things I know very little about.'

'What do you mean by that, Sarah?'

'Well, something has happened in the past few days that really frightened me; something that I can't make head or tail of.'

'Can you tell me about it; perhaps I might be able to help.'

'God help me, I do need to talk to someone – someone other than that clown Lawlor – but I'm not sure talking to a newspaper journalist is such a bright idea.'

Emma closed her notepad, put her pen back in its case and looked Sarah McCall straight in the eye. 'Why don't you forget I'm a journalist for the moment. Anything you want to remain private, I'll treat in the strictest confidence – off the record. If I can help in any way, I will. That's a promise.'

Sarah was silent for a moment, as though evaluating Emma's words, then gave her that tight little smile again before nodding her head in assent.

'Maybe you're right. Maybe I do need to talk to someone. Tell me, Emma, do you have children?'

'No, I'm not married . . . I am engaged though . . . and I love children.'

'I have two boys, John and Stephen; they're twins. Nine years of age. Two days before the awful events we have talked about, I discovered I was . . . I *am*, pregnant. It came as a bit of a surprise for both of us; nothing we had consciously planned, if you know what I mean, but Alan was thrilled with the news. We were both thrilled. As I said already, this news came just two days before . . . '

Sarah stopped to dry her eyes with a tissue before continuing.

'With the exception of Dr Goodbody, no one except myself and Alan knew . . . or at least that's what I believed until the day before yesterday. I had a telephone call from a man, a complete stranger, who talked about my pregnancy.'

'A stranger telephoned you to say he knew you were pregnant?'

'Yes, I know, it doesn't make sense – no sense at all – but that's what happened. He used my pregnancy as an excuse to talk to me on the phone.'

'And, what exactly did he want with you?'

'He was a nutter – a weirdo. Spoke with an educated accent, sounded British or maybe someone putting on a British accent. He went on about knowing Alan, knowing Alan better than I know him, knowing his secrets . . . I hung up on him.'

'Did he say what those secrets were?'

'It was all nonsense of course, but yes, he did say some awful things before I hung up.'

'Can you tell me what they were?'

'You've promised that what I'm telling you is confidential?'

'Yes, I promised . . . and I mean it. What did this mysterious caller have to say?'

'According to the caller, Alan was having an affair.'

'Did you believe him?'

'No, of course not. If you knew Alan you would never ask such a question. Alan and I had a happy marriage; we loved each other; we lived for each other. I have become pregnant. Doesn't that tell it all?'

'Have you any idea, any idea at all, who it was that called you?'

'I have never heard his voice before in my life but . . . but here's an even stranger bit . . . he gave me his name.'

'What?'

'I know, it's bizarre; he gave me his name. John Christie he said. Christie with an *ie*.'

'And you've never heard of anyone with that name before?'

'No, it's been going round and round in my head ever since, driving me up the wall. I've looked up all Alan's contacts; his name appears nowhere.'

'And yet, this man knows you are pregnant?'

'That's the bit that's driving me crazy altogether . . . makes no sense . . . how could he know that?'

'Could your doctor have told someone, let it slip to . . . '

'No, not a chance. Old Dr Goodbody is in his seventies, an absolute gentleman. I'd depend my life on him.'

Emma thought about what she had heard, trying hard to see how this new information might fit in with what she already knew. Nothing came readily to mind. There remained one further item she wished to discuss with Sarah McCall. It was an awkward question and there was no easy way to put it. 'Does the name Jacqueline Miller mean anything to you?'

'No,' Sarah answered without hesitation, 'should it?'

'I don't know, to tell you the truth. I was wondering if you or Alan might have had any connection with her?'

'Who is she?'

'She writes educational books, school books. I've seen her with your husband in a picture taken at a press reception for one of her book launches.'

'In the line of business, Alan attended hundreds of receptions and launches of all sort, and no doubt had his picture taken with hundreds of people. It happened all the time. Why have you picked on this woman in particular?'

'I'm grasping at straws,' Emma said, trying to sound casual. 'It's just that a photographer I know claims to have seen Alan visit her house.'

'What photographer? Who is he? Have the gardaí spoken to him?'

'His name is . . . *was* Frankie Kelly. He's dead. Officially he died from a drug overdose last week.'

'What do you mean, *officially*?

Emma told her about the strange circumstances surrounding Kelly's death, careful not to give details about his part in taking photographs outside 32 Leeson Crescent.

Sarah McCall put forward several reasons that Alan could have had a meeting with Jacqueline Miller, all of them innocent. But it was obvious that Emma had sown a seed of doubt in her mind. Their conversation came to an end when the twins barged into the room, unaware that their mother was wi th someone. After introductions and the usual small talk, Emma made moves to leave. She promised to let Sarah know if she made any further discoveries. Sarah, in turn, took Emma's business card and promised to get in touch with her if she received any further calls from the man calling himself John Christie.

Less than two hours later, Emma was back in the *Post* building, sitting behind her desk. Her first task was to make a telephone call to Larry Carroll at his stud farm in County Kildare. She got through to Muriel who informed her that Larry was unavailable at the moment. She promised to give him the message and that he would contact her as soon as possible. Twenty minutes later he was on the line to her. After the usual preliminaries and good humoured banter on the subject of her recent experience in the covering yard, he asked what she wanted from him.

'The last time we spoke,' Emma said, 'you told me about a series of telephone calls you received at the time of your break-up with Jacqueline Miller, do you remember?'

'Oh yes, I remember telling you. What about it?'

'Can you tell me a little more about him?'

'What's there to say; he was an absolute nutcase. He warned me not to marry Jac, claimed, amongst other things, that she was damaged goods. What about him?

'What did you tell me his name was?'

'Christy.'

'Was that Christy a Christian name or a surname?'

'Whew, I don't know, never thought about it really. I always assumed Christy was his first name but I suppose it could have been Christie as in Julie Christie, the actress. Yes, I suppose it could have been his surname.'

'You told me that you had some of his calls on your answering machine. I know this is a long shot but do you by any chance still have those tapes?'

'No, not a chance. They were daft rants. I erased them straightaway. Sorry.'

'One last question. What sort of accent did he speak with?'

'Let me see now. Yes, I remember! He had a strange way of talking, sort of posh but it might have been put on. Could have been an English accent of course.'

Emma thanked him for his help and hung up. All of a sudden, the name John Christie had taken on a new significance. Who the hell was he? How did he fit into the murder of Alan McCall. What connection had he with Jacqueline Miller? Emma thought about all the facts she knew in regard to the case. It had all started with a telephone call to the *Dublin Dispatch*, a call that told Jimmy Rabbitte that Alan McCall would visit 32 Leeson Crescent. Emma would wager a bet that the person who talked to Jimmy Rabbitte was the same person who had telephoned Sarah McCall. He was also the same person who, six years earlier had telephoned Larry Carroll. Bob Crosby was right when he said the person who tipped off Rabbitte will be the murderer. Well, she hadn't exactly found that caller yet but she had his name, and that at least was some progress.

It was important now to track down Jimmy Rabbitte. She remembered the strange look on his face the day he spoke to her outside Alan McCall's apartment in Clyde Road. Rabbitte knew something that she did not. What could it be? And how did Frankie Kelly come to meet his death in Rabbitte's house? Suddenly, the most important thing in the world from her point of view was to find Jimmy Rabbitte.

18

Analyst and patient sat in high-backed, leather-covered armchairs across from one another. Dr Tim Belcher liked to conduct his psychoanalysis sessions this way and had little time for the old-fashioned notion that a psychiatrist should remain upright while patient lay recumbent. If there were advantages to the old Freudian style – a contention he doubted – then those advantages were outweighed by the more positive interaction achieved from reading the facial expressions and body language that accompanied a patient's spoken word while in an upright position.

John Christie, sitting opposite him now, did not oblige him in this respect. Although the patient did sit upright, little was given away. Body rigid, knees together, shoulders pressed against the armchair's buttoned back, Christie represented a study in stillness. Dressed in a tailored pinstripe suit with satin-lined waistcoat, designer shirt and tie, Christie also wore a black hat with a wide flat brim – the sort a Spanish dancer might wear – with hair tied in a knot at the nape of the neck. Asked by Dr Belcher to remove the hat, Christie's refusal was direct and curt. 'I feel more comfortable with it on, if you don't mind.'

In contrast, the psychiatrist's idea of comfort meant

wearing woollen cardigans, open-neck shirts, casual slacks and Hush Puppy shoes. But he did accept readily that people had the right to decide for themselves what made them comfortable. Over long years of experience he had grown used to the peculiarities of his patients; discovering that one of them preferred to remain hatted seemed a pretty innocuous matter to him. He was less tolerant on the question of eyes. It had been a long-standing habit of his to look a patient straight in the eye, to journey behind what he liked to term the gateway to the soul. Christie's eyes were partially hidden behind a pair of tinted shades. As with the hat, Christie declined to remove the spectacles when requested. Belcher's first instinct was to insist but in this patient's case he changed his mind. He reasoned that if Christie's eyes were set in the same mode as the rest of his body, little if anything would be revealed. The patient's stillness had a disquieting effect on him.

Now sixty-one years of age, Belcher had treated hundreds of patients, listened to countless problems – everything from drug and alcohol abuse to a wide variety of phobias and neuroses with a plethora of sexual perplexities thrown in for good measure – but Christie's case was surely one of the strangest he had encountered. He had first met him six years previously. Back then, consultation had lasted for two years; the outcome had proved inconclusive. The strategy for the psychotherapy had been straightforward enough: break down the patient's self-imposed structures and attempt to rebuild from scratch. But working in those obscure regions of the psyche had proved to be a difficult and wearisome process. The outcome had been impossible to accurately access.

What had happened in the intervening years? Why had the patient come back? Perhaps he was about to find out. With someone like Christie, you asked few questions and listened a lot, more akin to confession than psychotherapy; a case of penitent and priest rather than patient and analyst.

The psychiatrist's attention now focused on the slow stream of words coming from Christie. The voice was precise, controlled, the words pronounced with the hint of an English accent.

'I protected her then, you know, back five or six years ago, perhaps more, but time is of no consequence. I protected Jac when she was unable to protect herself. Now, I find I must come to her rescue once more. She, poor girl, does not understand that I'm on her side – quite the reverse I'm afraid – but someday she'll have the strength to fight her own battles. First, though, she'll have to learn not to allow her heart to rule her head. Until that day comes I must go to her aid, protect her.'

The patient fell silent for a long time, barely moving a muscle before speaking again.

'She, Jacqueline, that is, she still sees me as evil you know. That is the part I find most difficult to take ... most difficult. She has never forgiven me for Sean's death. Yes, that's right; she blames me for her brother's death. I never laid a hand on the wretched boy but I did nothing to prevent his death . . . a mercy really . . . for everyone, including Sean himself. It was what Jac wanted, not that she would ever admit as much. But I knew what she thought of him. Randy little bugger, always feeling himself, disgusting habit. I must not blame Jac in any way . . . no, no, that would be entirely wrong. Jac wanted to love him as a brother, used to pray to God, ask how she could love her brother, but she never could. All her friends loved him to bits, loved his quirky little smile, loved his bright-eyed personality, his trusting nature. They wanted to be with him . . . but not her. She could never get used to his face. She saw him in a completely different light. When she saw those eyes – and the way they looked at her – she imagined him undressing her in his mind, sizing up her breasts, lingering on her crotch, unnerving for a young girl. It made her feel violated.'

Unusually for Dr Belcher, he took advantage of a pause to put a question to Christie: 'You said you did nothing to prevent the boy's death. Does that mean you could have saved him? Tell me more about that.'

'The boy? Ah yes, the boy. You mean Sean, of course. Wretch. On top of all his other problems the boy suffered from a chronic disorder of the respiratory organs.'

'He was asthmatic?'

'Yes, yes, the boy was an asthmatic, another problem that bothered Jac. She could never tell when he would suffer an attack, always worried in case his inhaler was not to hand. Hell to pay when that happened. It was the sort of thing that could not be allowed to go on.'

A pause, longer than usual, followed. This time Belcher remained mute, allowing his thumb and index finger to smooth his clipped moustache, his hooded eyes never once straying from his patient's face. It was a full minute before Christie continued.

'It happened at the annual community sports day of all places. Sean loved football, followed the English League, knew all the player's names and the positions they played in. He even knew their transfer fees. He didn't play himself. No, no – couldn't of course – no co-ordination, but he watched it on the television. Anyway, on this particular day he was wearing his Leeds United colours, becoming quite excited, cheering on the local soccer team as they went ahead one-nil, his enlarged tongue making unintelligible sounds. After the half-time break he suffered a seizure. His mother, by his side as always, immediately went for the aerosol inhaler and held it over his mouth. But it was no use. This time Sean did not recover his breath. Panic ensued. They rushed him off to hospital but it was all to no avail. He was dead on arrival. Jac and her older sister Regina shed tears. His mother . . . inconsolable. What had happened was straightforward enough; an accident they called it later. The aerosol inhaler in his mother's bag had been switched with one that had been used up. It represented the perfect solution to an impossible situation.'

A long silence followed. Dr Belcher listened to Christie's even breathing and tried to detect eye movement behind the tinted shades. As far as he could tell there was none. After what seemed like an eternity but was in fact no longer than a minute or two, Christie produced a pocket watch, checked the time and spoke to Belcher. 'I would like to come back, Doctor, as soon as you can schedule another appointment for me.'

'Fine. How about next Monday, same time. Will that suit you?'

'Thank you, Doctor, that will suit me fine.'

'Where in God's name has everyone gone?' Emma shouted into her phone as she slapped it back on to its cradle, her frustration at boiling point. Having spent a full hour on the telephone and come up with nothing, she was not happy. It's a conspiracy, she decided. All the people she needed to contact had decided to be unavailable at the same time. Swearing vengeance on the person who invented 'voice-mail' she tried to calm herself. No, of course it wasn't a conspiracy, she acknowledged, but it was very annoying all the same. Jimmy Rabbitte, the first name on her hit list had, it appeared, vanished from the face of the earth. She had made contact with several former colleagues of his but none of them had any idea where he had gone . . . or if they had, they had no intention of telling her.

Jacqueline Miller's mother had the dubious honour of ranking second on Emma's 'most-wanted' list. The chance of getting in touch with her had looked promising initially. A call to Sr Michele in Tullamore appeared to bring results. The nun confirmed that she had an old telephone number that Jacqueline had given her back when she worked at the school. Emma thanked the nun and tried to reach the number she had been given. The connection no longer existed. *Great, just great.* Maybe Larry Carroll could help; he might have the number to the Miller household. Her call to Carroll – not appreciated by him on this occasion – brought her the same useless number that Sr Michele had already given her. Emma admitted defeat.

Failure number three concerned Shay Dunphy. Emma had a plan of action ready to tackle the young politician when he talked to her . . . *if* he talked to her. She would inform him that she had a photograph, a splendid black and white study that showed him leaving 32 Leeson Crescent. That, she hoped, would throw him off balance for a few minutes. She would play it by ear after that. She would probably threaten to publish the picture in the *Post* unless he agreed to meet her face-to-face. It didn't happen of course. Her best efforts to get Dunphy at the end of a telephone line failed. Schemes involving him would have to be put on hold for the moment. And maybe that was just as well, she thought. In all probability, Dunphy would have called her bluff, maybe threatened to take an injunction against the *Post.* One way or another she would have been taking a risk because her boss, Bob Crosby, had no intention of running with the picture in the first place. At least not until he saw something more concrete by way of evidence.

Dialling once again, she hoped her run of bad luck

would change. The telephone rang in Leeson Crescent. No answer. *Damn.* She had not expected Jacqueline Miller to answer but she had hoped that the nephew, Damien Conway, might be there. No such luck. She would have to try something else. Remembering that Damien had told her about his graphic design business, she looked up the Golden Pages directory and found his business address. Having had her fill of telephones for one day, she decided to drive to see him.

Damien Conway's studio building greatly impressed Emma. Situated in one of twenty Regency-style buildings set around a tree-lined square called Joyce Park, its parking-lot had been cleverly placed below ground level so as not to spoil the overall appearance of the place. On the coast road leading to Sandycove, tucked behind electronically controlled gates, the purpose-built offices had all the marks of elegance and exclusivity. As Emma entered Graphique, the company owned by Conway, and approached the reception area, she couldn't help but wonder how someone so young could afford to occupy such opulent premises. If she had to guess Damien's age, she would have said he was twenty, maybe twenty-one, and certainly no older. The computer graphics business, she knew, had its share of entrepreneurial whizz-kids: young Turks capable of making huge amounts of money. A recent television documentary she had seen showed how Steve Jobs, at the age of nineteen, had developed Apple computers, earning him millions in the process. And everyone knew how Bill Gates, with his Microsoft empire, had become the world's richest man. Usually, as far as she could tell, such successes were based on talent and flair in the fast moving hi-tech communications industry. Her one meeting with Damien Conway had not led her to believe he belonged to that special league.

The receptionist, with an appearance that put Emma in mind of a contemporary skinny supermodel, seemed friendly enough when she spoke. Emma informed her that she wanted to speak to Damien Conway. The supermodel smiled, then quickly sighed. 'You and half the country,' she said, 'I've got three calls holding for him and he's got some people with him already. Are you sure you want to wait . . . might be better if you made an appointment and came back later.'

'I think I'll wait.'

'Fair enough, but don't say I didn't warn you.' The receptionist gave a little nervous giggle before showing Emma to a waiting area to one side of the reception area. 'I'll let you know when Mr Conway is available.'

Prepared for a long wait, Emma sat down, picked up a copy of a glossy catalogue that had been produced to go with a recent high-profile fashion show in aid of the children of Chernobyl and began flicking through the pages. Almost immediately, she heard the sound of raised voices and the sound of people entering the reception area from the interior of the building. Although Emma could not see who the people were, she recognised the voice of Damien Conway. He was remonstrating with two men. She tried to make sense of what was being said, but without the benefit of seeing the speakers, found it difficult to follow. It sounded to her as though the two men had come to repossess some computer equipment. Much mention was made of lease payments not being met, of final notices having been sent and ignored and of commitments entered into but not adhered to. Damien Conway whined and acted as though he were the injured party, claiming it was not his fault and insisting he had made all payments required of him. This contention was strongly challenged by the men from the leasing company but with great reluctance, they agreed to check things out. In a parting shot, they warned they would be back the next day to collect their equipment if the paperwork was not in order.

As soon as the two men made their exit, Emma got up from her seat and approached the receptionist's desk. The receptionist was in the process of informing Conway about his calls on hold and was telling him about the lady waiting to see him when Emma interrupted. 'Hello, Damien,' she said.

Surprised, Damien turned on his heel and faced her. Before he could open his mouth to speak, Emma reached out to shake his hand. 'I hope I've not caught you at a bad time but I was hoping you could spare me a few moments.' It was obvious from the expression on his face that he was less than pleased to see her but from somewhere he dredged up a faint-hearted smile. Wearing a fashionably baggy black suit with a charcoal shirt buttoned to the neck and no tie, he reminded Emma of a trendy young cleric.

'How are you, Emma? he said with forced enthusiasm, then turned to the receptionist and asked her to inform the callers on hold that he would get back to them later. Leading Emma to his office, he offered her a coffee and invited her to sit down.

'Nice place you got here,' Emma said, easing herself into a comfortable settee chair as she admired the framed posters and *objets d'art* in the plush room. An ironic smirk flickered across Damien's lips. 'It's called putting up a front,' he said. 'It's supposed to work wonders for the business.'

'Well, I'm certainly impressed . . . so it must be true.'

'You think so? I wish I could say the same for my suppliers; but enough about that. What did you want to see me about?'

'Your aunt, Jacqueline Miller.'

'Of course. What about her?'

'Is she still staying with your mother?'

'No, she's not. Yesterday, she upped and left without any warning.'

'She's gone?'

'Yes. It quite upset Mum . . . she felt Jac was not well enough to be on her own.'

'Any idea where she might have gone? Back to Leeson Crescent perhaps?'

'No, I don't know where the hell she has . . . look I'm sorry. I'm having a bit of a bad day. The truth is, I don't know where she is. She told Mum she intended staying out of circulation for a few weeks and left instructions for me to keep an eye on her house.'

'I see; that sounds like she's going to be away for some time. That's a bit awkward. I need to speak to her; it's really important.

'Don't we all. Nothing we can do about it though. Sorry, I wish I could help you. Tell you what though; why don't you contact my mother – talk to her – tell her *why* you want to talk to Jac. I'm not saying she'll be able to help you but it can't do any harm. I'll give her a shout if you like?'

'Yes, thanks, that would be a great help.'

Damien dialled his mother's number and told her that he was sending a friend to talk to her. It was obvious to Emma as she listened to the one-sided telephone conversation, punctuated by long pauses, that Damien was being subjected to a series of questions. It soon became apparent that Damien's answers were satisfactory; Regina agreed to meet Emma. After putting the telephone down, Damien gave instructions on how to get to his mother's house and Emma made notes in her pad. She would have to go back through the city again before heading out to where the woman lived. If she was lucky enough to avoid traffic snarl-ups she should get there in less than an hour. Damien showed her to the door, smiling goodbye, but it was plain that he was relieved to be shut of her.

On the road to Celbridge, Emma thought about Damien and his nervous temperament and wondered what lay behind his relationship with his aunt. Could it be that Jacqueline Miller was bankrolling her nephew's business? It would explain the lavish office. But if that were the case, why was he having trouble with the leasing company? The more she thought about him, the more she realised how little she knew about Damien Conway. Meeting his mother, she hoped, might shed some light on the young man.

Regina Conway's handshake was perfunctory, her movements jerky. There could be no doubting the similarities between mother and son. Emma also detected a vague resemblance between Regina and the photographic images she had seen of Jacqueline. Less attractive and not as striking as her younger sister, she had sandy-grey hair that looked tired and colourless and her eyes seemed sorrowful and weary at the same time. Wearing no make-up and dressed in clothes that owed more to comfort than fashion, she fell into the 'put-upon' category.

She brought Emma into her kitchen where, it was obvious, she had been busy scrubbing oranges. She sounded out of breath when she spoke and her voice had the huskiness one associates with heavy smokers. 'I hope you don't mind if I carry on with my marmalade while we talk?'

'No, of course not. You carry on with what you're doing; it smells delicious.'

Cutting the oranges in half and squeezing out juice as she talked, what Regina had to say was already known to Emma but the extra details did help create a more complete picture. On the important question of where Jac might have got to, Regina could shed no light. Tying the orange pips in a muslin bag, she spoke as though her activity and conversation might ward off whatever fears she felt for her sister. In the course of the conversation, Regina made several references to her father. Emma encouraged her on the subject and discovered that Jim Miller had been in touch with Regina recently to enquire about Jac. 'Dad and our Jac have not spoken to each other for years, not since Jac was in her teens,' she said, slicing the orange skins and putting them into a large preserving pan.

'Why don't they speak?'

Regina stopped work on the marmalade, cleaned her hands, sat down and lit up a cigarette. 'I wish I knew. I really do, but like so many things in our family, I seem to be the only one who knows nothing about them. Huh, it's as if I lived on a different planet for a while . . . or they did.' She stopped talking for a second, blew a plume of smoke, tipped the ash off her cigarette with her index finger and observed Emma through narrowing eyes. 'I do know that all this venom and ugliness stems back to the time before my parents split up. I was the last one to know about that as well. It came as a complete surprise to me. I thought they hadn't a bother in the world. I have begged Jac to tell me what happened. She won't even talk about it, gets mad when I bring up the subject. I've beseeched Mum. She refuses to say a word either. I'd love to know what the hell it is they are protecting me from.'

'You said your father got in touch with you recently. Surely he can tell you what happened?'

'Yes, you would think so, wouldn't you, but no, he

says he won't open his mouth until Mother decides to say what happened . . . a real catch-22 situation. It's hopeless.'

'And have you asked your mother?'

'She's worse than Father – refuses to say a word. She's become bitter in recent years, blames all the evils of the world on him but refuses to say what exactly he did that was so terrible.'

'What does your father do? I mean, for a living?'

'He works as a schools inspector, a job he hates. Unhappy man. His real love is the theatre. I can remember as a schoolchild going to see him in plays put on by the local drama group. It gave me a lifelong interest in theatre. He was good. Handsome too. Talented. It's my belief that he could've made a living as a professional actor. Unfortunately, Father lacked the courage to give up his safe pensionable job. He's still at it you know.'

'What? Oh, the acting.'

'Yes, isn't that great? One of the evening papers had a review of a play he took part in recently. He was singled out for special mention. They even had a picture of him. I have the cutting if you'd like to see it.' Without waiting for an answer, Regina left the kitchen and returned seconds later with the cutting and handed it to Emma. For the first time since Emma had arrived in the house, Regina appeared to relax a little. A stream of smoke curled out of her nostrils as she observed Emma's reaction to the cutting. Emma scanned the piece and could see it was a good review. The play in question was *Hedda Gabler.* The author of the review, in overblown prose, claimed that the production had succeeded in capturing Ibsen's powerful portrayal of the isolation of the individual. Jim Miller, in the critic's opinion, never put a foot wrong. In the role of Judge Brack, Miller effectively captured the complexity of the character in a dazzling performance that was truly a *coup de théatre.* Lavish praise indeed. A black and white picture showed Jim Miller, as Brack, wearing stylish period clothes and *pince-nez* glasses, attached to a string, kissing the hand of the actress in the title role. Even allowing for period costume and make-up, Emma was struck by the resemblance between Jim Miller and his daughter Jacqueline.

'I'd love to have seen that performance,' Regina said, 'but I didn't even know the play was on.' She ground out her cigarette butt in an ashtray, took the cutting back from Emma and pointed at her father's picture. 'Do you know: I truly believe Dad is only content when he's playing a part on stage.' Regina folded the cutting and put it away, allowing Emma to steer the conversation back to the subject of Jacqueline's accident. She asked questions about the break-up of her engagement and the depression that Larry Carroll had spoken to her about. Regina had little to add. 'I was married at the time. Damien was at secondary school and I was trying to hold down my job as a teacher, so you can understand, I had no time to get involved in my family's problems. I do remember Jac suffering from depression – she had had such a bad run of luck. I should have done something at the time, I know that now. I still feel guilty. Eventually she got over whatever it was that bothered her and got on with her life. It's only now . . . now after all the success she has enjoyed with her educational books these past few years that the depression seems to have returned. I do not understand it. I've tried to reach out to her, listen to her, but it's as if she has erected a wall around herself. I can't break through it – and she doesn't want to let me through. All of a sudden I feel I no longer know my sister. I don't know what to do.'

'Do you know if she has a romantic interest at the moment?'

Regina showed surprise at being asked this question but after a little hesitation replied. 'As far as I know Jac has had no what you call romantic interest since her engagement with Larry Carroll ended. In other words, since her accident. But, then . . . '

'Yes?'

'Well, it's something Damien said to me. On a recent visit to her house he was surprised to discover she had a caller. Nothing unusual in that of course and he wouldn't have given it a second thought – he had met some of her friends before – but on that particular occasion he was sure Jac did not want him to meet the caller. Damien thought perhaps she might be entertaining a man friend.'

'Damien is very close to his aunt, isn't he? He seems very concerned for her well-being.'

'Yes, Damien and Jacqueline are very close. She

helped him set up his own business – financially, that is. My sister is very well off – much more money than my husband or I could ever hope to have. It's great that she has been so generous to Damien – and he has put her money to good use. I worry about him because of his young age and lack of experience in business but I think he has a good head on his shoulders, least I hope so.'

'On the question of the caller, did Damien get a look at whoever it was?'

'No, not as far as I know. Why do you ask?'

'Oh, it's just one of those human interest things I'm always looking out for. If she did have a boyfriend, it could account for the strange behaviour you talked about. You know what they say about love never running smooth.'

'I'd like to believe it was something as simple as that, but I doubt it, I really do.'

As the conversation came to an end, an idea formed in Emma's head. Considering all that Regina had to say, Emma believed she had some idea of what might have happened in Leeson Crescent on the night of Alan McCall's murder. If she was right, then Jacqueline Miller could be in grave danger.

19

Vinny Bailey could scarcely believe his eyes. Shock would best describe his feelings. What confronted him did not tie in with the homecoming he had so eagerly looked forward to for the past three weeks; indeed, it was not remotely like he had visualised. Someone had rewritten the script. The scene where he was supposed to take Emma in his arms, smother her with kisses, tell her how much he missed her and make passionate love to her, had been cut completely. What greeted him instead could not be further from the imagined scenario.

The apartment had been trashed, a complete mess. A lampstand lay across an upturned chair, its shade bent out of shape, glass splinters from the smashed bulb glistening on the floor. The living-room carpet had been cut into jagged strips and heaped into an ill-defined pile in the centre of the room. Shelves, brackets, tables, chairs, television set, hi-fi, CDs and magazines lay strewn across the floor. Pictures had been stripped off the walls, frames broken, glass cracked, the backs ripped off.

Vinny cursed. Detective Inspector Lawlor frowned, shook his head, then smiled. He remained silent as Vinny rushed into the main bedroom. There was no one there but the place had also been ransacked. In panic, he darted into the smaller guest bedroom. Same story. Ditto, the rest of the apartment. Emma was not there – the uppermost fear in his head – *Thank God, oh, thank God, I thought she might*... Relieved that his worst fears were unfounded, he faced Lawlor.

'I didn't know they sent plain-clothes detectives to investigate house break-ins?' Vinny said. His sarcasm did not bother Lawlor.

The garda's self-satisfied smirk worked overtime as he removed his overcoat, placed it on an upturned chair and looked at Vinny askance. 'When I was told that the apartment where my friend – hot-shot investigative journalist Emma Boylan lives – was broken into, I thought it only right and proper to take a personal interest. As a favour to her, you understand.

Determined not to rise to Lawlor's facetious prodding, Vinny righted a high stool and placed it beside the service counter that divided the dining area from the kitchen. Before sitting on it, he cleared away the smashed cups, saucers, plates and assorted cutlery at the base of the stool with his foot. His mind, all the time was working furiously to understand what had happened. There was something going on here that he could not fathom; first the break-in – that in itself was not the main problem. Break-ins were a fact of life in Dublin – but linked with the presence of Lawlor, this took on a more menacing dimension. 'Who reported the break-in?' Vinny asked.

'One of your neighbours, a Mrs Harrison... lives

one floor below you. Came home from work about five-thirty this evening and heard a racket going on in your apartment. Curiosity got the better of her so she came up to your door to investigate. The ould biddy got the fright of her life. A man wearing a balaclava over his head opened the door and told her to get to fuck out of his face, threatened to blow her eff'n head off. She scurried back down to her own apartment, scared shitless, had a glass of water and rang the gardaí. My friends down at the shop told me about it . . . so here I am.

'Does that mean Emma is not aware . . . ?'

'She wasn't; she is now. I got her on the mobile about five minutes before you turned up, told her I was here . . . and that a nice surprise awaited her. She should be here any minute.'

'I'd like to know why you are taking such an interest in this. There must be a hundred more serious crimes in the city. So what's going on?'

'Well now, Vinny, I thought you'd be able to tell me. Now that you are shacking up with Boylan, I'm sure she keeps you up to speed with all the sleuthing she does for that comic she works for.'

Stung by Lawlor's jibe, Vinny struggled for a strong rejoinder. 'Emma and I are engaged to be married,' he said, knowing how weak it sounded, 'but that doesn't mean we live in each other's pockets; she does her job, I do mine.'

'You call what you do a job? Wheeling and dealing in glorified second-hand junk, flogging furniture that's half eaten away with woodworm and buying a lot of old paintings covered in soot and smoke. Jesus, what way is that for a grown man to earn a living?'

'I wouldn't expect you to appreciate art or antiques.'

'A load of shite, that's what it is . . . just like the mess here. Can you tell me if anything is missing?'

'Not straightaway, no. On first glance nothing appears to be missing but it's hard to say. I've been out of the country for the past three and a half weeks.'

'Oh, I see, Lawlor said, a new glint in his eye. 'Then you won't have heard about your fiancée's involvement in the death of the photographer Frankie Kelly.'

'No, as I said, I've been away.'

'Well then, allow me to bring you up to date, Mr Bailey. A week is a long time in the life of an investigative journalist but three and a half weeks is . . . Frankie Kelly, photographer, was found dying from a drug overdose. By his side, the woman who raised the alarm; yes, none other than your own beloved Emma Boylan. The house had been turned over – just like here – a complete mess. Bit of a coincidence that, don't you think? Anyway, the ambulance took Kelly to the hospital . . . a distraught Emma Boylan by his side. How d'you like that? She remained by his side in the hospital until he croaked. Touching, don't you think? Such devotion. I was there, Vinny boy; saw it with my own eyes. She cried her eyes out . . . most pitiful thing I ever saw. I couldn't understand it myself. I mean, if you saw this photographer fellow, scruffy, long-legged fucker, you know the type – hippie hair, roguish looks, denims, boots, all smiles and shit, about ten years younger than yourself. But you know what they say, Vinny?'

'No, tell me; what *do* they say?'

'Well now, I'm no expert in that particular field of human relations but they say women go wild for that sort of thing; even the hoity-toity tight-arsed ones fancy a bit of rough now and again.'

Vinny listened, knowing from past experience how Lawlor liked to enrage when trying to elicit a particular response but he was determined not to allow himself to walk into the detective's trap. He would wait until Emma returned; she would have a perfectly reasonable explanation that would contradict Lawlor's insinuations. And he would believe her.

Vinny had good reason to dislike Lawlor. Their paths had crossed on several occasions in the past, each experience an unpleasant one, with Lawlor ever willing to employ dirty tricks to achieve his ends. The question of right or wrong never seemed to bother him in the slightest. The bad blood between the two men first came to the surface just after Vinny had left college, when he actively participated in most of the city's protest marches. Being idealistic and more than a little naive at the time, he took to the placard like a duck to water. The causes he espoused were wide and varied. Back then, the destruction of the city's architectural heritage had greatly exercised his mind – and his feet. On top of that, he decided to fight on the side of Joe Citizen who, he believed, was getting a raw deal from the state. This particular crusade involved everything from taxes that were too high, housing waiting-lists, mean and degrading social-welfare allowances, low wages, to more frivolous causes like the ever increasing cost of the working-man's pint. But it was his support for the Republican cause in Northern Ireland that brought him into conflict with the law and to the attention of Lawlor.

Even though his sympathies for that same cause had diminished over the years to the point of inertia, the gardaí insisted on linking his name with the more subversive elements of that movement. He had been hauled in a few times for questioning but apart from the nuisance this presented, it did not bother him. He had long since cut all ties with the movement. If the law enforcers of the land wanted to believe otherwise, there was not a lot he could do about it. More recently, since meeting up with Emma Boylan, he had come to the attention of Lawlor through his involvement in one of her investigative pieces. Emma had scored a win over Lawlor, something the detective would not easily forget, or forgive for that matter. Vinny realised that since forming a relationship with Emma, he too represented fair game as far as Lawlor was concerned.

Vinny knew he had to make some reply to Lawlor's thinly veiled insinuation that Emma's grief for the dead photographer was in some way open to question.

'The difference between you, Lawlor, and Emma, is that she's a human being. The death of a fellow human makes her sad. I've seen her cry at funerals. Whereas you are a cold-blooded, unfeeling, insensitive excuse of a man, devoid of all feelings, pity or decency.'

'Sticks and stones may break my bones but names can never hurt me,' Lawlor said, his words contradicting the faltering smile on his face. Vinny, seeing he had scored a direct hit, was about to follow through with more of the same but stopped when Emma burst into the room.

'What the hell . . . ?' she shrieked, momentarily stunned, before taking in the mess all around her. She glared at Lawlor for a second before switching her gaze to Vinny.

'Vinny, Vinny you're here,' she said going over to him, 'I didn't expect you until tomorrow.' Ignoring Lawlor, ignoring the mess, they hugged each other and kissed.'

For once, Lawlor felt, and looked, uncomfortable. 'When you're both quite finished pawing each other and swapping spits, there's a little matter of a break-in to be discussed.'

Letting go of Vinny, Emma turned and faced Lawlor with a look guaranteed to wound lesser mortals. 'What's to discuss?' she asked. 'We've been broken into, something the law should prevent, but doesn't. It's up to the gardaí to find the culprits. That *is* your job after all; it's what we taxpayers pay you to do.'

'Always the bitter word, Emma! That's the trouble with you sisters today, all full of fight, ready to bite the head off any man who bids you the time of day. All I want to do is ask you a few questions about what's happened here. Do you think I could do that?'

'Fine, fine, Detective Inspector, fire away; ask your questions.'

'I've reason to believe there's a connection between the break-in here and the break-in at Jimmy Rabbitte's house.'

Vinny shot a quizzical glance at Emma.

'Who is Jimmy Rabbitte?' he asked.

'You really don't know what's been going on, do you,' Lawlor said to Vinny, before Emma could answer, the words 'going on' heavily laced with innuendo.

Emma, quick to spike this line of conversation, replied 'The only thing that's *going on* is taking place in that overactive cesspool you call your mind.' Before Lawlor could reply, she turned to Vinny and explained. 'Jimmy Rabbitte once worked at the *Post;* more recently, he worked for the *Dublin Dispatch*. The photographer, Frankie Kelly, also worked with the *Dublin Dispatch* before his death. He came to my office one day and offered to share some information he had. In return, I was to help get him a job with the *Post* – he hated the *Dispatch*. I agreed to help him. Together we worked on the information he gave me. On the day he met his death, I arranged to meet him in Rabbitte's house – he said he had something of vital importance to give me, something that would crack open the case we were working on. When I got there, Frankie was close to death – the victim of a drug overdose. I believe the overdose was forcefully administered, not self-induced.'

'Are you suggesting that this photographer fellow was murdered?' Vinny asked.

'Yes, I believe he was. Of course our friend Lawlor here refuses to believe that. He'd rather...'

Lawlor intervened impatiently. 'That's bullshit Emma and you know it. Your own paper, for Christ's sake, made no suggestion of foul play in a piece written by yourself – and *you* were there.'

'That means nothing; my editor insisted on sticking to the official line.'

'More bullshit, Emma. If you really believed . . . but look, tell me, did you get this piece of vitally important information you mentioned from Kelly when you found him?'

'As I've already told you, he was in no condition to give me anything by the time I got there.'

'Yes, but he could have *left* something for you.'

'Well, he didn't. I believe that whoever got there before I did, got what Frankie wanted to give me.'

'That's not the way I read it,' Lawlor said. 'I think that whoever tore the place apart failed to find what Kelly had to offer. I think the same 'whoever' is responsible for this mess in your apartment.'

'And what leads you to that conclusion? Vinny asked.

'How else would you explain the fact that nothing has been taken?'

Emma, for once, conceded that Lawlor's point was a good one. She had been having thoughts along similar lines but she was not going to admit as much to him.

'Your theory is fine, up to a point; only problem with it is this: I don't have whatever it is they are looking for.'

'I see,' Lawlor said, in a voice that clearly indicated he did not believe her. 'Well, in that case let me give you a little piece of friendly advice. If you find you have information or are attempting to withhold evidence of some crime, I'll have no hesitation in charging you with obstructing the course of justice.'

'A crime, you say? What crime would that be?

'Don't play smart ass with me, Emma. You're too clever for your own good but I'm watching your every move. Put a foot wrong and I swear I'll have your guts for garters!'

'Charming, Detective Inspector, just charming. Are you quite finished?'

'For now, yes, but watch it, I will . . . '

'I know, I know! Goodbye, Detective.'

Lawlor retrieved his overcoat from the upturned chair, folded it neatly over his arm, took a last knowing look at Emma and moved towards the door. 'I should fix that broken lock on your door straightaway; you'd never know when your visitors might want to make a return visit.'

Vinny and Emma held on to each other after Lawlor had left. Vinny, glad to be shot of the detective, allowed his mind to shift gears and engage in thoughts of romance. Emma's mind, however, remained firmly locked in the slipstream of Lawlor's words. She was in no doubt that he knew about Frankie Kelly's negative film. If he knew that, then it was fair to assume he had made the connection between the negative and the murder of Alan McCall. What she couldn't figure out was how he had made the connection.

It was after midnight by the time Vinny and Emma finally made it to the bedroom. After Lawlor's exit, and a little playful romance, Vinny managed to repair the lock on the door, a temporary job that would have to do until a locksmith arrived to attend to it the next day. They had invested far too much time and finance in the property to neglect any aspect of its security. Six months earlier they had bought the apartment as an engagement present to each other. One of four similar units on the third floor of a modern redbrick, steel and chrome-embellished building, set on the banks of the Grand Canal, it overlooked the lock gate at Hubband Bridge and offered a vista that stretched between Mount Street and Baggott Street bridges. It was this picture-postcard view of the waterway that appealed to them on their very first inspection of the property. So far, they were pleased with their purchase. The break-in, they could happily have done without.

As Vinny tested his culinary expertise in the kitchen, Emma attempted to restore some order to the apartment. Vinny's scope for producing one of his 'special' meals did not look too promising. On inspection of the fridge he discovered that Emma had allowed its contents to run low during his absence. Undaunted, he attempted to rustle something up. Using the most basic ingredients – eggs, onions and potatoes – he created tasty Spanish omelettes. They washed the food down with a reasonable Chablis.

Vinny talked about his trip to the Continent, enthusing about the paintings and artefacts he had purchased and the export orders he had landed. In particular, he was excited about a series of maps by John Ogilby he had discovered and bought. They were the original prints dating back to the 1600s. His attempt to describe the high artistic merit of these early examples of cartography failed dismally to ignite any kind of response from her. She, in turn, recounted the events that had taken place while he was away. Because of what Lawlor had said, she felt it prudent to include details of her investigative liaison with Frankie Kelly, being careful, however, to avoid all mention of the photographer's meeting in their apartment. Her brief outline of events satisfied Vinny, prompting him, in the aftermath of the meal to put his arms around her and kiss her. Usually, this would have led to a bout of lovemaking but on this occasion Emma extracted herself from the embrace. 'You randy devil,' she said, pushing him away. 'Let's clean this place up first; I can't stand to look at it this way. We'll hold the fireworks for the bedroom. OK?'

Eventually it was time for bed. The room had been tidied a little but it was easy to see that everything was not as it should be. Getting it back into shape would have to wait; they were both too tired to tackle it straightaway and, besides, they had more pleasurable pursuits on their minds. As Vinny undressed and prepared to get into bed, he could hear Emma in the bathroom, washing her teeth and gargling with mouthwash. Slipping beneath the duvet, his eye caught a gleam of light coming from beneath the vanity unit on the other side of the room. It looked gold and shiny. Probably one of Emma's cosmetic items, he thought, most likely something the intruders had knocked to the floor. He got out of bed, crossed to the vanity unit and got on his hands and knees to investigate. He stretched a hand beneath the unit in an attempt to retrieve the object. It was while Vinny was in this undignified position that Emma emerged from the bathroom. 'What's this,' she laughed, seeing Vinny's rear end poking out from beneath the vanity unit, 'I think we're both too knackered to play piggyback tonight.'

Vinny extracted himself, holding a gold-coloured cigarette case in his hand. 'Look what I found,' he said, examining the case. 'This does not belong to either of us, does it?'

'No, it does not.'

Vinny noticed an odd look on Emma's face as she stared at the case. He opened it and saw it was empty.

'Any idea how it got there?' he asked.

There was a moment's silence before Emma answered, her eyes fixed on the cigarette case.

'Yes, I do. It belongs to the photographer, Frankie Kelly.'

'What? But . . . but how did it get into our bedroom?'

Emma recounted how she had found Kelly dying in Jimmy Rabbitte's house. Leaving nothing out, she told Vinny about Frankie's marijuana habit and how, not wanting to get caught in possession, he pushed the case at her as he lay close to death. She described how she had taken it home and thrown the three joints she found inside it down the toilet. 'I wasn't sure whether I should send it to his family or not. I certainly did not want to give it to Lawlor, so I just held on to it.'

Vinny agreed that she had done the right thing and was about to put it aside when he noticed something odd sticking out from the bottom of the case. At its base, a separate metal plate, held in position by four elaborate corner bolts, left an almost invisible space between it and the main body of the case. Using the tips of his finger nails, he gently prised free a small frame of film from its lodging. Emma gasped when she saw it.

'Jesus Christ, Vinny, that's the negative! That's the negative that Frankie Kelly was killed for. This small frame of film is the reason why they ransacked Jimmy Rabbitte's house – the same piece of film they were looking for when they took this place apart this evening.

'What do you intend doing with it?'

'I intend to prove where Alan McCall was on the night he was murdered – and I intend to have the biggest scoop of my career.'

20

February ended with the land covered in a blanket of snow. The whitening of the country continued for three days without let up. After the first day the novelty of the situation had diminished for everyone except school children. Commuters complained about the delays in getting to and from their workplaces and farmers complained about their inability to get feed to their livestock. By the end of the third day the clamour of complaints had grown in volume as more and more people became impatient with the conditions. Dublin Airport cancelled all flights for a time. Traffic snarled up and road conditions became hazardous. Children loved the snow, of course: snow to play with, schools closed, double bliss. But the white virginal world, with its strange kind of beauty, was background to a political storm of far greater significance than anything nature could conjure up. On the last day of February – the third day of the snow – newspaper headlines and television news bulletins swept stories about the weather and its effects from the top spot.

Emma Boylan's front-page story with its fifty-point headline: 'Government Linked to Murder Cover-up', sparked the biggest political upheaval since the fall of Reynolds's government in 1994. Then a scandal involving a paedophile priest had caused the furore; this time murder took centre stage. Boylan's exclusive revelations were accompanied by a series of photographs. The main picture showed murder victim Alan McCall. It depicted him standing at the basement door of 32 Leeson Crescent as he kissed Jacqueline Miller. Two versions of this photograph appeared side by side. One was dark, badly lit and showed McCall wearing glasses, a scarf and a hat. The second version – computer enhanced – showed him without the trimmings. Another set of before and after prints showed the country's youngest elected representative Shay Dunphy with, and without, disguise as he made his exit from 32 Leeson Crescent.

Emma's story continued on the inside pages of the *Post* where a photograph of Frankie Kelly appeared underneath a sub-head:

PHOTOGRAPHER'S MYSTERIOUS DEATH: DRUG OVERDOSE OR MURDER?

In the article that followed, Emma credited Kelly for his photographic evidence and outlined in some detail how his perseverance ended so tragically for him. With complete approval from her editor, Bob Crosby, she detailed the facts as she knew them. Crosby knew he was playing a dangerous game by allowing her to go into print and name names but he trusted her instincts and fully believed the story would hold up. 'Let them sue our asses off,' he said defiantly. 'We've got enough evidence here to sink the lot of them.'

As expected, legal reactions came fast and furious. The government sought to have an injunction imposed on the paper's edition but their move came too late – two editions had already hit the streets. Separate legal challenges came from Francis Xavier Donnelly, Tom Pettit and Shay Dunphy, all three men dismayed by the fact that they were mentioned in Emma's revelations about the government's secret PCCC Committee.

But the force of the legal backlash paled when compared to the media madness that followed. Bob Crosby was forced to hold a press conference. The newspaper's switchboard jammed. Interest in the breaking story grew to fever pitch. Television, press and radio journalists, local and international, packed into the *Post's* conference room. Emma, facing microphones, tape machines, TV cameras, flash guns, sat on the platform alongside Crosby. Bombarded by rapid-fire questions, she answered succinctly, never giving more information than asked for. Questions were, in general, unsympathetic to her point of view. Several reporters attacked Emma's methods of obtaining information. 'Your article implies that Shay Dunphy murdered Alan McCall,' one hack shouted. 'Isn't that an example of the worst kind of trial by the media?'

'Wrong,' Emma replied. 'I haven't accused Dunphy of anything. I've merely put him at the scene of the crime on the morning after McCall's body was found.'

'If you're not accusing him of murder, why drag him into this mess in the first place, especially before all the facts are known?'

'I believe Shay Dunphy has some explaining to do.'

'This woman Jacqueline Miller; how does she feel about this invasion of her privacy? Have you even bothered to talk to her?'

'I've talked to members of her family and have made indirect contact with her. She has had every opportunity to talk to me.'

Questions continued in this vein for half an hour with Emma steadily being put on the defensive, having to deny she was peddling an anti-government agenda. Bob Crosby, fearing the questions might get out of hand, brought the conference to an abrupt end. Through cries of 'Shame, shame' and boos, he promised further revelations in the *Post* in the coming days. Emma felt exhausted after the ordeal but agreed, nevertheless, to give individual interviews to a number of important news reporters.

It was midday by the time she finally got back to her office. Switching on the portable television that sat in the corner of her bookshelves, the first image to greet her was a close-up of her own face. Seeing herself as others did, on the screen, never failed to take her aback, not least because she noticed how the bright lights exposed the tiny lines that had began to encroach around her eyes, and how her bottom teeth appeared too prominent when stressing a point. Her replies to the reporters, she was glad to note, had come across well and sounded self-assured, though she would never get used to the sound of her own voice on television.

After her piece finished on the screen, the cameras

went live to Kildare Street, where, according to the continuity announcer, a statement was expected from the Taoiseach. At first, little activity appeared on the screen except for a series of picturesque scenes reminiscent of those associated with miniature snow globes. Weightless crystals, like tiny feathers, drifted lazily down on Leinster House, home to Dáil Eireann. The camera slowly panned along the façade of the three-storey, granite building, lingering for a moment on the front door. The building, flanked by the National Library and the National Museum, originally built for the Earl of Kildare in 1745, was bought by the Irish government in 1924. In that long history it can seldom have seen a more dramatic development behind its stately exterior than the events unfolding on this day.

Reporters huddled outside the huge wrought-iron gates in front of the building, waiting impatiently, hugging themselves and stamping their feet to keep warm. A sudden flurry of activity at the doorway caught everyone's attention. Spellbound, Emma watched the screen as Fionnuala Stafford, accompanied by her handlers, made her way through the snow and faced the assembled press. After some slightly forced banter on the subject of the weather she launched into an attack on the *Post* newspaper. Expressing abhorrence for what she described as scurrilous journalism, she took the opportunity to deny strenuously that her government had any hand, act or part in a cover up. 'Not my style,' she said, dismissing such a notion with a wave of her hand. 'Never was, never will be.' She went on to pay tribute to Alan McCall and insisted that she and her government colleagues were anxious to establish how he had died and would fully cooperate with the garda investigation. Jim Carberry, a well-known television reporter, interrupted her in full flow and asked if she could explain the presence of Shay Dunphy at Leeson Crescent. Without blinking an eyelid, she faced Carberry and answered. 'At this point in time it is impossible to say what, if anything, happened at the address you mentioned. As to the photographs which purport to show Shay Dunphy and the late Alan McCall there, I question their authenticity. There is something very odd about the appearance of these pictures. The *Post* admits that two of the photographs have been computer enhanced, altered beyond recognition, in other words *tampered with.* The question I ask is this: if they can mess around with two photographs, why should we accept the others at face value? For an answer I need only look to where the pictures originated from; the *Dublin Dispatch*, for God's sake. Has our country come to a stage where decent, law-abiding people, where the government itself, a government freely elected by the good people of this country, can be held up to ridicule by the low-life vermin who inhabit the gutter press?'

Emma watched as the Taoiseach continued to rubbish the press and her article in particular. She had expected opposition to her story but the virulence that accompanied the attacks took her by surprise. In quick succession, interviews with Shay Dunphy and Francis

Xavier Donnelly flashed on the screen. Donnelly, accosted by a hoard of reporters, attempted to make his way up the snow-covered steps of his Mount Street office. Standing at the door, he faced the cameras and poured scorn on the revelations in the *Post*. 'Anyone who believes the garbage in that paper needs to have his, or her, head examined. I ask you, is the *Post* really serious? Do they actually expect people to believe that this government above all governments would have anything to do with the movement of a body from one place to another . . . as some sort of elaborate cover-up. It's preposterous.' Donnelly answered a few other questions in similar bullish fashion, giving the impression of a man full of confidence, a man with nothing to hide.

Next, the face of Shay Dunphy filled the screen. Unlike Donnelly, he looked anxious and frustrated, and had about him the air of a man who wished to be anywhere else but where he was. In reply to a scattering of questions put to him, he refused to be drawn except to say he had been in touch with his solicitors and had instructed them to issue a writ for libel against the *Post*.

In the streets of Dublin, Galway, Cork and Limerick, a series of televised vox-pop interviews gave Emma some respite from the criticism coming from the politicians. Against a backdrop of snow-decked shops, people confronted by microphones reacted to the story of the government's alleged cover-up by expressing the opinion that politicians were capable of every deceit imaginable.

As Emma continued to measure the fallout from her story, Bob Crosby's portly figure appeared in her office. He plonked his ample buttocks on the edge of her desk. 'Well, what do you think?' he asked.

'It's more or less as I expected – more, actually: politicians going ape-shit, the public on our side.'

'Yes, that's about the size of it,' Crosby agreed, 'but we're taking real heat from the legal people. Our esteemed chairman is pissed off with me for not clearing your story with him.'

'Don't tell me the politicians have got to him.'

'No, he takes no crap from that lot, but he is concerned with the legal implications should this story backfire.'

'Well, he has no need to worry on that score. I can substantiate everything I've written. I'll stand over every line, every word. I can prove that the photographs are authentic. Bloody hell, Bob, I'm a responsible journalist, you know . . . '

'Yes, I know all that. Nevertheless, we're going to have to do more digging, make sure our facts are one hundred per cent airtight. If we slip up on this one, both of us could be looking for a job.'

'Bob, have I ever let you down?'

'No, Emma . . . not yet.'

'Well, I've no intention of letting you or anyone else down so you can go back and reassure our beloved chairman that we are professionals; we know what we are doing. And as far as that digging you mentioned goes, well I'm off to the midlands again. Within the next few hours I hope to be face-to-face with Jacqueline Miller's mother.'

Francis Xavier Donnelly sat behind the desk in the study of his house, his elbows on the polished walnut top, his hands balled and pressed against his temples. Earlier, he had watched himself on the television, impressed by his own performance, pleased that he had been able to present such a positive response to the reporters. It was just as well, he thought, that those same reporters could not see inside his head. Alone in his private study he could at least give vent to his real feelings. It had been a long time since he had felt so low. His worst nightmare was being played out in the press, on the radio and on every television channel. The lifestyle he had enjoyed as a mover and shaker in government circles could, if he was not careful, come crashing down about his ears.

Beset by doubts and questions, he wondered why fate had singled him out for such cruel treatment. Why did life continue to deal him such a bad hand? Must disappointment always be his bedfellow? A feeling of helplessness descended on him. He thought about his other great misfortune in life, thirty years earlier; leaving St Ignatius's Seminary in County Galway before taking his final vows for the priesthood.

The blow, back then, had been a devastating one. As a young seminarian, he had been greatly impressed by Fr James Grant, Professor of Ecclesiastical History. With a thirst for learning, his young impressionable mind opened like a water lily in sunlight to the professor's vast repository of knowledge. There was little the great man did not know; everything from the Carolingian period and the Inquisition to the Reformation and Counter-Reformation movements and everything since, up to, and including, the Second Vatican Council. From the start, the professor took a paternal interest in Donnelly's quest for scholarship and spent many hours after class discussing the many theological issues of the day. Over the space of four years, a strong bond of friendship had grown between student and professor but a month before the day of ordination something happened to change the course of young Donnelly's career. Late one evening he had gone to Fr Grant's room to return books he had borrowed some days earlier – something he did on a regular basis – but on this occasion he found the professor with another lecturer, Fr Jack O'Brien, rolling about on the floor, naked, touching each other's private parts. A recording of Gregorian chant played on a small turntable, drowning out the sound of Donnelly's arrival. What he saw disgusted him. He turned on his heels, ran to the nearest bathroom and was physically sick. The next day he left the seminary.

He was reminded of that sad event today; the feelings of loss, pain and disillusionment were the same. A shudder ran through him as he sat behind his desk, head in hands, wallowing in self-pity. It was while in this state of introspection that Mrs McNamee interrupted his thoughts to announce the arrival of Shay Dunphy.

Dunphy stormed into the small study. Barely waiting for the housekeeper to close the door, he pressed his hands on the desktop and leaned his body forward until mere inches separated his face from Donnelly's. 'We are fucked,' he said, his voice verging on the hysterical. 'We are up shit creek without a paddle.'

Francis Xavier, his painful reverie now vanished, resumed the external shell he normally showed to the world.

'Sit down, Dunphy, and pull yourself together,' he said firmly. 'If we are to get out of this mess we'll need to keep cool heads. If we watch what we say, measure our words, get our stories in sync, deny everything, we might just pull it off.'

'Like fuck we will. I don't think . . .'

'You don't think, period! That's your problem. From now on, you're going to have to engage your brain before you open your mouth. Did you hear how well the Taoiseach handled the press this morning? As a person, I can't stand the woman but as a politician she was masterly, denied everything, rubbished the Emma Boylan story.'

Dunphy sat down and sighed. 'I don't know,' he repeated. 'I've seen pictures of gardaí going into Leeson Crescent. They are bound to figure out exactly what happened.'

'Yes, they will discover what they have already surmised. They'll establish the fact that McCall was there and that he was moved but they'll find no evidence to link us to what took place there that night.'

'What about my photograph? It's plastered on every newspaper in the country, on every television screen. Jesus, they have practically accused me of killing McCall.'

'We both know you didn't, so let's not bother worrying about that. Without proof, they have nothing; just remember that. I've a few photographs myself: pictures of Emma Boylan, Frankie Kelly and Damien Conway, all coming and going from that house.'

'Oh! You mean the ones you had your ex-cop friend take.'

'Yes.'

'But how can you use them without tipping off the whole world that you knew about the address all along?'

'Easy. I can let them slip into the hands of the media without anyone knowing where they came from. The pictures will make no difference in the long run but they will help muddy the water for now, give us a breather, space to get our act together. I'm hoping our intrepid plodders in the gardaí find whoever really killed McCall. That would take the spotlight off us and on to the killer.'

'Yes, you could be right,' Dunphy conceded. 'It's just a pity that we compromised the gardaís' chance of that happening by what we did that night.'

'Well, you know what they say about twenty-twenty hindsight. There are a lot of things we should have done . . . but it's too late now. Let's hope our friends in blue get lucky. Meanwhile it's important that you, Pettit and myself remain hidden away from all reporters, and if we do have to speak to them, that we each tell the same story.'

'Where is Pettit now?' Dunphy asked.

'I don't know; keeping his head below the parapet if he has any sense. I've attempted to locate him but all I get is his voice-mail. I'll keep trying until I make contact. My worry is that he might break . . . come out with his hands up. He can be such a silly old bugger.'

'He's an ould bollix all right,' Dunphy agreed, 'but I can't see him putting his job, his career, in jeopardy, not now . . . no, he'll do the right thing.'

'I hope you're right. In the meantime I suggest all three of us get together tomorrow, Saturday, here in my house – say three o'clock. We can put a script together, rehearse a few answers, go on the offensive. Until then, I suggest you do a vanishing act.'

21

Mary Miller stood inside the partially opened door, determined not to let Emma into her house. 'I have nothing I wish to discuss with you,' she said, each word laced with a weary resignation. 'Goodbye to you.'

Before the door fully closed, Emma made a further attempt to engage the woman in conversation. 'Please, Mrs Miller; it's important we talk. I think your daughter Jacqueline could be in danger. I've travelled from Dublin to see you, so please.' Silence followed this request but the door did open a fraction further. To Emma, the situation felt a little bizarre; she found herself standing on the doorstep of a house in the town of Cloughan in County Offaly, attempting to hold an interview with someone who clearly did not wish to talk to her. The first strands of darkness had begun to encroach but enough light remained for Emma to study the face staring back at her. Even though Mary Miller remained partially hidden by the door, Emma could tell that she had once been a beauty and that even now, in her mid-to-late fifties, she retained the kind of high cheekbones and refined looks associated with Sophia Loren. However, Emma doubted that Sophia Loren had ever displayed the degree of disillusionment etched in Mary Miller's expression at this moment. Taking advantage of the hiatus, Emma made a last appeal. 'I promise I only want to ask a few questions; won't take more than a few minutes.'

'You say Jacqueline might be in danger?'

'Yes, but it's a complicated business; you see, she has . . . '

'I don't want to know anything about her. She left this house when it suited her . . . hasn't darkened the door since.'

'And why is that?' Emma asked, realising immediately she had asked the wrong question, approached the subject too abruptly.

'None of your business, young lady,' Mary Miller said. 'What happened in this house is nobody's business . . . *nobody's*, and certainly not something I'm likely to discuss with the first person who turns up, uninvited, on my doorstep.

'I promise you, Mrs Miller, I only want to help; I want to know . . . '

'You want to know too much, that's what you want. Well, let me tell you something; Jacqueline Miller is responsible for tearing this family apart . . . she is the cause of all the bad and ugly things that have happened here.'

'I'm not sure that's true,' Emma said, in what she hoped was a calming voice. 'I talked to your daughter Regina and she told me . . . '

'You talked to Regina, did you?' she asked, not expecting an answer, 'Regina, my oldest girl; the only one to escape the Miller curse, left the house before

Jacqueline began to cast her evil spells. She was the lucky one. The rest of us all became victims. Not that her son Damien has been so lucky. Jacqueline has her claws into him now, using her money to inveigle him into her poisonous web. The young man does not have the wit or wisdom to see through her, more's the pity. She'll destroy him as she has destroyed the rest of us: like my poor boy Sean, sweet innocent, loveable Sean, a beautiful boy. She ruined him, the greatest gift God ever gave me . . . destroyed. She ensnared her father too. Jim, my foolish husband, who had the weakness of all men; she corrupted him too. I can forgive her everything except for Sean. For what she did to him, I can't find it in my heart to forgive. May God have mercy on me. Jacqueline is no longer my daughter – hasn't been for a long, long time. She tries, with encouragement from Regina, to worm her way back to me by sending money, paying for the upkeep of this house and so forth but she hasn't got the nerve to show her face to her mother. She knows what she's done to my family; she knows she has broken my heart.'

'Can you tell me about the accident?'

Mary Miller's face distorted into a mask of outrage. 'Accident? Accident, did you say. It was no accident . . . no, I tell you, as God is my judge, it was a deliberate vile act.'

'But I thought the lorry driver was convicted. I thought he had been asleep at the wheel when he crashed into Jacqueline's car?'

The expression on Mary Miller's face changed from

outrage to one of shock. 'Oh, I'm sorry,' she said, putting her hand to her mouth, 'I wasn't talking about Jacqueline's accident. No, no, I mean yes, of course *that* was an accident.'

'Are you saying there was another accident?'

'I'm not saying another word. I've already said far more than I ought to have said. Please go away.'

The door closed in Emma's face before she could say another word. She stood there, staring at the door, glued to the spot for several seconds before accepting that the interview was over.

On her sixty-mile journey back to Dublin, she ran Mary Miller's lines over and over in her mind. What had she meant when she declared it was no accident? Try as she might, Emma could not figure it out. Feeling frustrated, she decided to file it away in her head in the hope that eventually, when she had more inform-ation to hand, it might make sense.

Sunday morning, she was not feeling too good. Jacqueline had lost count of the days but she could see Mass being celebrated on the mute television, so unless the world had turned upside down or the Church had taken over the television channel, it had to be Sunday. She glanced at the screen from time to time, waiting for the news to come on, and returned to the recent days' newspapers in front of her.

Jacqueline Miller's two-roomed flat, situated like thousands of other flats in the Phibsborough area of the city, was warm, comfortable and had the anonymity she required right now. And if everything she had read in the papers turned out to be true she would need this space for a while to come. She noted that the main report in the *Post* had been written by Emma Boylan, the woman Damien Conway told her had called to her house. With all the events of recent weeks, she was glad she had not met Boylan. According to another newspaper, the gardaí had put out an appeal for her. The article had put it rather delicately, saying the gardaí wished to speak to her in order to eliminate her from their enquiries. She smiled to herself, a nervous smile. They would have to wait, she decided, they would have to wait until she was good and ready. She needed space. She needed time. That was why she had found it necessary to disappear out of circulation. Being lost in the middle of nowhere suited her just fine. She decided to remain in the flat on Cabra Road, safe in the sprawling suburbs of Phibsborough, until she knew exactly what she wanted to do.

She felt tired, dog-tired, tired of the relentless intrusion into her life. A good night's sleep would help, but that simple requirement eluded her. The previous night was no different than the ones before; she had tossed and turned for hours, wanting desperately to sleep, trying without success to cleanse her mind of activity. Sleep, when it did finally arrive, brought joy at first. She felt herself melt into the arms of Alan McCall. They were making love, their bodies rising and falling in an ever-increasing flow of pleasure. She could feel him inside her, hear his breath quicken, hear him whisper their secret words of love. But just as the explosion of delirium approached, everything changed. She felt a burning pain, something tearing her apart. The body clinging to her became coarse and hurtful, the guttural moans ugly. Her eyes shot open. She gasped in horror. The face above her was that of Jim Miller. 'No, Father,' she screamed. It took several seconds before she realised she had been dreaming, the same dream that had haunted her for so long. She had cried after that. The crying continued until fitful sleep had once more overtaken her.

Sitting in front of the television now, fragments of the dream returned. She could see her father's handsome face and the demon that lay behind it. Did he, she wondered, have nightmares too. Did the awful deeds of the past, the terrible things he did to her, remain with him? Did he sleep at night? Did the events from her childhood still haunt him? She hoped with every fibre in her being that he lived in the same hell he had created for her.

Mass concluded on the television. She turned the volume up, ignored a clutter of advertisements and waited for the news to come on. The first item on the bulletin was about her. A picture of 32 Leeson Crescent with an encampment of photographers outside its front railings appeared on the screen. A cut to a picture of the late Alan McCall followed, providing a backdrop for the news-reader's résumé of known facts in the case. Jacqueline felt her breathing shorten to little intakes and puffs.

'Gardaí now suspect that Alan McCall met his death

in this house,' the newsreader said.

'Well, bully for them,' she said aloud, the nervous smile back on her face. Connecting herself to the events being outlined on the news item remained a problem for her. Oh, she was there all right, no point in denying that but the episode remained confused. Talking to the gardaí and helping them with their enquiries was not something she wanted to face ... not yet. Sure, she could tell them who killed Alan McCall. She had seen the face, the same face that had haunted her for so many years, but how could she explain all the other stuff. To do so would mean exposing her own family to infamy. Hadn't they all suffered enough already? How could she bring more misery and pain on their heads? And yet, that was what she would have to do sooner or later. It would be later if she could help it. First she had to put certain affairs in order. After that ... after that whatever happened would be in the lap of the gods.

Detective Inspector Lawlor, his face something like that of a bulldog looking for a scrap, pushed back his chair and made to leave the commissioner's office.

'Sit down, Lawlor,' Commissioner Horgan said, his modulated tones, as always, under control. 'All I'm saying is that a little discretion is called for when dealing with the sort of high-profile people involved in this case.'

Lawlor shrugged his shoulders and made a quizzical grimace. 'Discretion my arse. We're still dealing with a murder here, remember.'

'Yes, of course we are; all the more reason to be discreet. If you bring two elected members of the Dáil and the party general secretary in for questioning, you had better be one hundred per cent sure you know what you're doing. You can just imagine how their spin-doctors will play this out in the media – even if we get it right. No matter which way we turn they will attempt to portray us as a bunch of incompetent, flatfoot plodders. So, I'll ask you once again, how sure are you?'

'I'm as sure as it is possible for anyone to be, that's the point I've been trying to make. Look, *I* know; *you* know; the dogs in the street know that Dunphy visited the scene of the crime on the night of the murder. I say we start with him. Bring him in. Question him. Fingerprint him. Confront him with the evidence.'

'What evidence?'

'The photographs.'

'You would never prove the photographs are genuine.'

'But they are.'

'Perhaps. All I'm saying is we can't prove they are genuine.'

'So what do you suggest, Commissioner?'

'Subtlety, Lawlor; that's the name of the game at this stage. Softly, softly. I suggest you find a way of getting Dunphy's fingerprints without letting him know you are doing it. Find a glass, an ashtray, a cup, anything he might have touched, take a set of prints and compare them to the prints you found at Leeson Crescent and McCall's place in Clyde Road. If they match, we go in with the hobnailed boots: nail his arse; tip off the press. Then, in the full glare of flashing bulbs and television cameras, drag him in.'

'And what about Emma Boylan?' Lawlor asked. 'We could have her for withholding evidence, withholding evidence in a murder case and obstructing the course of justice; that's a serious offence.'

'Be your age, Lawlor. Emma Boylan is the flavour of the month; she has managed to discover more than all of us put together on this case so far. How do you think it will look if we drag her in?'

'Sounds to me like I'm blocked no matter which way I turn.'

'Well, there is one thing you might consider.'

'And what might that be?'

'You could bring in Damien Conway. What's the update on him?'

'He's up to his neck in debt. Overdrawn on two bank accounts, outstanding bills all over the place but a clean sheet otherwise.'

'Bring him in. Let the public see we are doing something. He's been identified going into Number 32 on the evening of the murder. Who knows what he might tell us. Make a public show of bringing him in for questioning. It might force Jacqueline Miller out of hiding. She's a woman after all; there's no telling how she might react. She could decide to defend her nephew. If she does, we've got her. It is imperative that we question her. She's probably the only person who can tell us exactly what happened. Your first priority is to find her. I don't care how you do it. Just find her.'

Lawlor left the room, closed the door and spoke to the commissioner's nameplate, tipping his forelock in mock obedience as he did so. 'Right boss, whatever you say boss.'

Emma Boylan did not have to work hard to find Jimmy Rabbitte. He had contacted her instead. He wanted to meet her urgently, he said, had things to tell her that, in his words, would knock her socks off. After much humming and hawing they had agreed to meet in the Fiddler's Elbow bar in the old village of Blanchardstown. Curious to know what Rabbitte had to tell her, she headed out through the Phoenix Park, where the snow of the past few days had melted and turned into slush, drove through Castleknock Village and, following Rabbitte's instructions, found the Fiddler's Elbow in a narrow side alley off Blanchardstown's main street. She had no difficulty finding a parking space; it was four o'clock, Monday evening, the graveyard hour in pub-land. Unlike the other pubs in the village, all of which had been renovated and tarted-up to look like picture postcard establishments, the Fiddler's Elbow had been neglected over a long period and was in urgent need of a little love and affection. A briquette fire that had almost burned itself out in an open grate failed to give any heat. Except for two drunks sprawled on bar stools at the counter, and a barman looking at an American chat-show on the television, the place appeared empty. Emma glanced around the drab lounge. Where was

Rabbitte? She was about to order a mineral water when she spotted an arrow sign pointing the way to the public bar.

Jimmy Rabbitte, his gauntness more pronounced than ever, sat uneasily on a seat in the darkest corner of the bar, with a half empty glass of Guinness on the wrought-iron table in front of him. He acknowledged Emma with a slight nod of the head. 'Sit down, Emma. Thank you for coming.'

'You look shit,' Emma said, unable to refrain from commenting on his appearance.

'Thanks. I needed that,' Rabbitte replied, managing a brief smile. 'Can I get you a jar?'

'I'll have a mineral water. Ballygowan if they have it, thanks.'

A plump, middle-aged woman, dressed in a sheep-skin coat, black slacks and wellingtons brought the mineral water to their table. Noticing the questioning glance coming from Emma, the woman decided her appearance needed some explanation. 'I've been out in the backyard trying my best to get a few logs for the fire. 'Tis a bit cold in here after all the atrocious weather we've had. Winter in the middle of spring! What's the world coming to, I ask you? That fecker behind the bar in the lounge is too lazy to scratch himself. More interested in looking at Oprah Winfrey than doing anything around here to help a body.' Getting nothing more than sympathetic nods from Rabbitte and Emma she returned to the other side of the counter and disappeared through a door that led to the back of the pub.

Alone now, Rabbitte wagged his index finger at Emma's face. 'You stole my story,' he accused her. 'Took my piece of film, stole it from my house.'

'You brought me here to tell me that?'

'No, I am pissed off with you but that's not why I dragged you to this dump. I want to talk to you. I have something to sell . . . something you will want to buy.'

'Oh . . . like what?'

'I can give you a story so explosive that it will probably bring the government down.'

'Oh yeah?'

'Yes I can. I can give you names, details, times, a catalogue of misdeeds in high places that will rock the state to it's foundations.'

'Seems like I've heard that line somewhere before. What exactly do you have, and more to the point, what do you want from me?'

'I can prove that this government paid me to give them Frankie Kelly's pictures. I can also prove that the person I negotiated with talked to the Taoiseach about the matter. I'm not codding you, I have it all.'

Emma could tell by the expression on his face that he was deadly serious. She tried to play down her own rising interest.

'OK, let's suppose for a moment that what you're telling me pans out. Why are you telling me? What do you want?'

'What do I want? A good question. I want my life back, that's what I want. I can give you and the *Post* the biggest story of the year . . . shit, the biggest story of the decade. What I want is a just reward.'

'You know very well that the *Post* will have nothing to do with chequebook journalism.'

'Bollix to that, Emma. You forget that I used to work for the *Post*. They'll do what they have to do, just like everyone else, especially if they get an exclusive scoop like the one I'm offering you now.'

'They might have done it back in your day but not any more. Correct me if I'm wrong but I believe the reason you got the chop from the *Post* had to do with illegal payments.'

'Yes, the bastards hung me out to dry. They pushed me to get the stories, were delighted when the circulation went up, basked in my glory when I won awards but turned their backs on me when the heat turned up on the payment for stories scandal.'

'Let me see if I've got this straight,' Emma said, trying to read the enigmatic expression on Rabbitte's wasted face. 'You stole Frankie Kelly's film and after realising what was on it, you decided not to play it straight with your employers, the Du*blin Dispatch*. Instead you got the bright idea that you could blackmail the government. How am I doing so far?'

'Not bad.'

'Right! So you sell the negatives to a certain person in the government for a sizeable amount of cash. But this didn't satisfy you; you got greedy. You held on to a single frame of film and decided to go back to the table for a second helping. This is where things began to unravel. Your house was broken into. Someone took the place apart. They didn't find anything . . . except poor Frankie Kelly and your stash of illegal drugs. Later, these same people broke into my place, thinking that I might have the negative. As it turns out, I did have it but I didn't know it at the time.'

Rabbitte took a sip from his Guinness and nodded several times before speaking. 'That's more or less what happened all right. I was double-crossed. I ended up with nothing. The cops want to bust me for possession of drugs. The *Dublin Dispatch* is taking legal action against me. I owe a bundle to my supplier. On top of that I've got a few loan sharks on my tail. Well, enough is enough. I want out, Emma. I'm willing to do whatever it takes. I want to tell my story, expose the people who played me for a sucker. I'm willing to give you the whole ball of wax – but not for nothing.'

'Do you have anything in mind?'

Rabbitte sighed, shook his head and bit his bottom lip. For a moment it seemed to Emma that he was about to cry. What was it she saw behind the glazed eyes? A glimmer of the person Rabbitte used to be? She watched his Adam's apple doing flip-flops in his scrawny neck as he tried with some difficulty to find the words he wanted to say. When he finally spoke, every syllable seemed to take an effort. 'I want to get back to being what I once was: a good reporter. I want to rejoin the human race. I feel really bad about Frankie Kelly – in a way I feel responsible for his death.'

'You are responsible for his death.'

'OK. Have it your way. I am responsible for his death.

How do you think that makes me feel! Jesus, I worked with him, had the odd jar with him. I liked him. He was a good guy, a damn good photographer, a bit of a lad with the ladies but all right for all that. Such a waste of life, a terrible waste, and all because I was stupid, strapped for cash, needing extra money to feed my habit. His death, more than anything else, has made me take stock of my life. I need help, Emma.'

'How do you think I can help?'

'I had a hard look in the mirror this morning. I forced myself to see what had become of me. I cried, Emma. I sat in front of the mirror and cried. I couldn't stop. I remembered what I once was. I remembered Mary, Mary, my wife, and little Jenny. I remembered the great plans I had for the three of us. How could I have let it all slip away? For the first time in a long time I faced up to the truth. I fucked up big time. I got all my priorities arse-about-face. I took Mary and Jenny for granted, neglected them. I thought my work was more important. I thought I was more important than anything else. Mary and little Jenny would always support me, or so I thought. But of course they got fed up coming second to my job, to my ego – and then – then the drugs.' Rabbitte stopped for a moment, moistened his lips, shook his head and blinked his eyes like someone attempting to gather his thoughts together. 'Seems to me like my whole world has been swallowed up in that hole in my arm. I need to get off the stuff. I need help to do that. I need to get my life back together. I'm not sure exactly how to go about it but I think, maybe, the *Post* could help me. If they could look after my mortgage ... It's eighteen months since my last payment; the building society is threatening to evict. I need a good solicitor to deal with the action the *Dublin Dispatch* is taking against me. I'm also going to have to fight the blackmail charge – more legal expenses – but most of all, I need treatment for my drug habit. If the *Post* can look after that – and my other problems, you get my story.'

'I could talk to Bob Crosby, see what he thinks. I think some arrangement along the lines you suggest might be possible.'

'There's one other thing.'

'I thought there might be. What is it?'

'When I've resolved my drug problem; when I'm clean ... when I'm healthy again, I'd like to get my old job back at the *Post*.'

'Jeez, I don't know.'

'I can see how that might be difficult but look: I'll even work without payment for a few weeks to show how serious I am, prove to the *Post,* prove to Crosby, maybe even prove to myself that I can cut it again.'

'And if I agree to that, you give me everything you've got on the McCall murder?'

'Every sausage. Like I said, I can give you the name of the person who offered me money for the photographs.'

'Yes, but can you *prove* it? I mean, do you have hard evidence?'

'I don't blame you for thinking I'm stupid, Emma, after all the things I've told you. Even I think I'm stupid, but I'm not dumb. I recorded the person who came to my house to offer me money. I always use cassette recorders when doing interviews. I've become a master of secretly hitting the record button. With all the rubbish thrown about in my house, it was easy to conceal what I was doing.' Rabbitte stopped talking, reached into his inside pocket and produced a cassette. 'The full conversation is recorded on this. No fear of anyone mistaking who the speakers are.'

'Just tell me one thing, Jimmy. On the day you got the tip-off about Alan McCall visiting Jacqueline Miller's house, can you recall how the caller sounded?'

Rabbitte thought for a minute before speaking. 'Let me see. The person ringing me sounded a bit toffee-nosed. Could have been a poofter – or someone educated at an English public school. But there was something odd about the voice.'

'Odd? In what way?'

'It was as though he was putting on a voice, distorting his true accent.

'I see. Can you tell me his exact words?'

'I can . . . but I won't. I will give you nothing else until I find out if we have a deal or not.'

'Well, I'm going to have to talk to Bob Crosby first but I think you can take it from me: we've got a deal.'

22

'You see, I had no choice in the matter,' Christie said without a flicker of emotion, 'I had no power to stop what happened. I watched as he died.'

'You mean the politician? Are you talking about Alan McCall?' Belcher enquired.

'Yes, of course. The knave in the pack; the politician – McCall – I watched as the blood drained from his body. Justice was served. McCall lied, cheated, abused a trust, took advantage, used people . . . he deserved to die.'

A silence followed. The person with the assumed name John Christie sat opposite Dr Belcher, eyes hidden behind designer shades, making it difficult for the psychiatrist to gauge what was going on inside the perfectly chiselled head facing him. Belcher embraced the silence. Until today he had never felt anything so intense as the cold chill of evil now emanating from the patient sitting opposite him. He experienced a feeling of dread so palpable that it might have been physical. Apart from his own breathing – a little wheezy because of his bad chest – and the soft patter of raindrops on the window-panes, the room had gone quiet as a morgue.

In common with most people in the country, Dr Tim Belcher had been exposed to the media's unrelenting coverage of the politician's murder and the controversy surrounding it, but to have someone sit in front of him and admit to an intimate knowledge of the deed was a little unnerving. This new knowledge forced him to re-evaluate what he knew already about the patient.

It had been six years since their first encounter. In those early months he had established that the patient suffered from what used to be called Multiple Personality Disorder and has since become recognised as Dissociative Identity Disorder (DID). At the time, the disorder had been viewed with some scepticism in much the same way that ME had its doubters. Little had changed in the intervening half-dozen years to alter that view among medical practitioners and the psychiatric fraternity. With DID, the dominant belief among the more respectable psychiatric practitioners was that the syndrome is merely a con-job enacted by hypnotisable patients with the overt encouragement of the therapists. Dr Belcher had been a little sceptical himself on the question of multiple personalities, but the patient now sitting in front of him convinced him otherwise. After their initial half-dozen therapy sessions, he was left in no doubt of its validity. On a number of dates, the patient had arrived in his clinic as a separate and distinct personality. Each of these personalities had its own pattern of perceiving and thinking, its own emotions, attitudes, tastes, talents, behaviour, speech, body language and dress code. He had witnessed first-hand how the different person-alities took full control of the patient's behaviour at different times. The manifestation known as John Christie first appeared in one of those early sessions. At other times, the alternating selves took other names, ages and genders. These experiences, along with his research into the phenomenon, led him to believe that each personality represented exaggerated parts of a 'self' that had been fragmented by severe and repeated bouts of stress and guilt. Each personality helped in some way to mask actions which were too difficult for the 'self' to face.

That one of these alternating selves – the one known as John Christie – should be sitting in front of him now meant that he had failed to alleviate the problem; that Christie should admit to being present while a person was killed only helped to underscore the extent of his failure.

Jim Belcher's thoughts were interrupted by a sudden movement from his patient. 'I do not wish to talk any more today,' Christie said, glancing at the dial of an expensive pocket watch that was attached to his waistcoat by a gold-plated chain.

'But we still have almost half an hour in hand,' Dr Belcher said, 'don't you want to tell me anything further about your association with Alan McCall?'

'No, not today, Doctor; not today. There is still a cancer, a malignant cancer to be cut out – one more necessary task that I must supervise.'

Belcher resisted the temptation to probe further. He remained in his chair as Christie stood up and moved towards the door. Before leaving, Christie turned and spoke to Belcher.

'I'm not sure when I will be back but be assured, Doctor, we shall get together soon enough.' The door closed.

Dr Belcher thought about what he had just heard. In the free time available to him before his next patient arrived, he decided to re-examine the file in front of him. It was certainly a strange case. The same feeling of unease that he had experienced six years earlier was surfacing again. Except now, with Christie's admitted involvement in a murder to contend with, he had more reason than ever for a sinking feeling in his stomach. The knowledge placed certain responsibilities on his shoulders and brought the whole area of ethics into question. Because of the issue of diagnosis and criminal responsibility, the question of DID had become particularly relevant in the forensic field. He needed to be sure of what moves, if any, he should make. Did his patient participate in the killing of Alan McCall or had his patient been the murderer? If, as he suspected, his patient had murdered another human being, he was duty-bound to inform the proper authorities. But was suspicion, however strongly felt, enough to break confidentiality? It was a question that placed him in a serous dilemma.

He looked out the window and noted that the rain had become heavier, and across Dublin Bay, the sky had darkened considerably. Within seconds the rain developed into a heavy downpour with raindrops drumming loudly against the window panes. In a strange sort of way he welcomed the sound. It reflected the dark thoughts churning about in his head. He thought about cancelling the remaining three clients waiting to see him but decided against it. Such a measure would not help matters. This problem, he acknowledged, was not about to go away. Reluctantly, he tidied the file in front of him and replaced it in the corner cabinet.

Dim lights, an open fireplace filled with blazing logs, and a night-time crowd improved the ambience of the Fiddler's Elbow. The down-at-heel daytime look had been miraculously replaced by a warm welcoming glow. With one hour remaining before closing time, Jimmy Rabbitte would under normal circumstances be drunk by this stage of the night but on this occasion he was only slightly inebriated. Along with his boozing pal Snotser Moran, he had been propping up the bar since nine o'clock that evening. Rabbitte had started on pints of Guinness but had switched to brandy for the past two rounds. Yet, when he spoke, his voice showed little evidence of alcohol indulgence. Years of abuse had given him a high tolerance level. 'Right,' he said to Snotser, 'we'll have one more for the road, then I'm off.'

'Hah? Wha's dat? Am I hearin' ya righ'?' Snotser asked, a look of incredulity on his face, his slurred speech in marked contrast to Rabbitte's. 'Off is it? Jay-zuss, Jim-bo, da night's just beginning so 'tis. Wha-da . . . wha-da fuck's got into ya a-t'all?'

'Got to stay sober for a while longer, me ould pal.

Got to ring someone and tell them the game's up.'

Jimmy Rabbitte surprised himself and shocked Snotser Moran by sticking to his word. He left the Fiddler's Elbow after downing his drink-for-the-road, and returned to the digs he had been staying at while his house remained under garda surveillance. In preparation for his trip to England the next day, he stripped to his skin, wrapped a towel around himself and headed for the small bathroom off the landing. He pushed a pound coin into the slot on the bath's boiler meter and turned on the taps. He placed a towel on the side of the old bathtub while the gushing water filled the room with steam as it inched its way up the tub's stained enamel. He lowered his bony body on to the towel and thought about what lay ahead of him. He thought about the decision he had taken to change his way of life.

It had been an eventful day and he felt bone-weary. In the company of Emma Boylan, he had met Bob Crosby in the Good Food Kitchen, an upmarket café in Rathmines. Crosby had insisted that they eat while they talked, said he was starving. Emma ordered a chicken dish, Crosby tackled a minute steak and he, after much consideration of the menu, decided on a mixed grill. While endeavouring to consume the food on his plate he presented his demands to Crosby, the same demands he had earlier outlined to Emma. Crosby had agreed readily enough. In return, he had told Emma and Crosby all he knew about Francis Xavier Donnelly's attempt to buy Frankie Kelly's negatives from him.

Crosby had taken the cassette recording from him, played it on the personal stereo Emma had brought along, listened to its contents on earphones and nodded with satisfaction. After coffee – he declined dessert – he shook hands with Crosby and Emma on the deal. Crosby insisted that nothing be consigned to paper, preferring instead to rely on, what he termed, a gentleman's agreement.

Only five minutes after parting, the food in his stomach began to churn and rebel. He felt nauseous. His system, more used to a diet of drugs and drinks, rejected the food, forcing him to throw the lot up.

Stepping into the water, he sighed deeply. Involuntarily, he was forced to take stock of his thin body. Not a pretty sight, was the thought that occurred to him as he wondered how he could have let himself get into such a state. Seeing his wizened manhood brought a sad smile to his face. There was a time, he remembered, back when he first discovered the ecstasy of orgasm, that he truly believed he could pole-vault with the damn thing if he had a mind to. Look at it now – a physical metaphor for what his life had become. He thought of the woman he had loved and married, the baby they had been blessed with; he thought about the life he had once enjoyed, the life he had thrown away. He knew he would never have it back but he was determined to reclaim what was possible. Tears were forming in his eyes, merging with the steam from the bath.

Back in his room, towelling himself dry, he looked

at the airline ticket and checked his departure time again. At 8.15 am, he would board a plane at Dublin Airport that would take him to Heathrow, London. Emma had given him the ticket along with literature for the Dimbarry Clinic. She had booked him into the clinic for five weeks. His treatment there would start the following day. Dimberry, according to her, had earned itself a reputation for dealing successfully with high-profile alcoholics and drug addicts and prided itself on its discretion. It was the sort of place that Rabbitte would never be admitted to if the *Post* were not picking up the tab. He still could not believe how readily Crosby had agreed to help him out in all the areas where he was in trouble. But most rewarding of all for him, was the promise from Crosby to give him a trial period as a journalist with the paper when he came back from England. With that prospect in mind, he felt confident that he would come through the ordeal. It would be hell on earth but he was determined to meet the challenge head on. His last drink-for-the-road with Snotser Moran really was, he truly believed, his last alcoholic drink – ever. Getting off the drugs would be a lot harder. His experience in dealing with people who had attempted to kick the habit had forewarned him of the struggle ahead.

Only one thing remained to be done before he turned in for the night, something that would not wait until after his stint in London. He needed to tell Francis Xavier Donnelly that he had got even with him; it wouldn't do to let that bastard think he had got one over on Jimmy Rabbitte.

Jimmy Rabbitte had arrived in Heathrow by the time Emma left the morning meeting between Crosby and the paper's legal team – Tommy Reilly and Clive Webster. She was on her way to the Glebe Theatre in Baggot Place to see if it were possible to get a lead on Jim Miller. It was for his performance in *Hedda Gabler* at the Glebe that Jim had got such glowing reviews. Going there now was probably a waste of time, a forlorn hope, but she needed to get away from the office.

Back at the office, Crosby had lost his cool, thrown one of his rare tantrums, before finally sitting down and allowing his legal experts get a word in edgeways. His annoyance was brought about by the non-appearance of the Francis Xavier Donnelly exposé in the *Post*. Along with Emma, he had stayed late the previous evening, turning what Rabbitte had given them into a front-page story. At 3.30 p.m., his legal team forced him to scrub the entire story. But, what really shot his blood pressure to boiling point was the series of photographs on the front pages of rival newspapers, showing Emma Boylan, Frankie Kelly and Damien Conway, entering and leaving 32 Leeson Crescent.

The reason for the non-appearance of the Francis Xavier Donnelly exposé had come about simply enough. Donnelly had obtained an injunction in the early hours of the morning, preventing the *Post* from printing a transcript of the cassette recording between himself and Jimmy Rabbitte. A High Court hearing had already been planned for the following day. This was not an altogether unusual event in the newspaper business.

Actions of a similar sort happened on a regular basis and had come to be accepted as a normal occurrence but what got Crosby so fired up on this occasion was the speed with which Donnelly had discovered the *Post* had secured the cassette. It did not surprise him that Donnelly, given his political connections, could secure the service of a judge at such short notice, but how, he wondered had the party general secretary found out in the first place. After assurances from Reilly and Webster that the *Post* would have no difficulty having the injunction set aside at the High Court hearing, he calmed down a little. 'We're still going to lose two days pissing around, sitting on the hottest scoop of the year. What if someone else gets hold of the story?'

'That's not going to happen, Bob,' Emma assured him, '*we* have the cassette locked in the safe. No one else can get near it.'

'I don't know, Emma, I really don't. We have to assume Jimmy Rabbitte rang Francis Xavier Donnelly after our meeting yesterday evening. The knucklehead couldn't resist having one last dig at Donnelly, shouting his mouth off, gloating over how he would ruin him, telling him, most likely, to buy the *Post* today; I wouldn't be at all surprised if he told him we have the cassette.'

'It could have happened something like that,' Emma admitted.

'Talk about biting off the hand that feeds you! But I'll tell you what really worries me: did Rabbitte make a copy of the cassette, give it to anyone else? It's like something he'd do.'

'No, Bob, he'd never do that. I think he's serious about drying out and getting back to work. He knows you can pull the plug at any time so he won't do anything stupid.'

'Stupid? What about ringing F. X. Donnelly? On a scale of one to ten, I'd say that rates as pretty damn stupid.'

'If he did ring him, and it looks like he did, I doubt if he realised Donnelly could have the story pulled at such short notice.'

'Ah well, what's done is done.' Crosby said, 'With a bit of luck we should be able to run with the story on Thursday. Who knows, with the extra publicity from this injunction business, the whole affair might gain legs, turn out to be an even bigger story.'

Somewhat mollified by his own reassurances, Crosby went on to question how the other papers had secured photographs of Emma and others outside the door of 32 Leeson Crescent. Emma opined that Donnelly or Detective Inspector Lawlor must have hired a photographer to keep watch on Jacqueline Miller's house. It was plain to see that there was no substance to the text that ran alongside the photographs. After Crosby had calmed down completely, he accepted that the photographs were innocuous and served no purpose other than to muddy the waters for a day or so.

By the time Emma made it to Baggot Place, a dull morning haze had settled over the city, obliterating the sky. The twenty-minute walk from her office to the theatre failed to clear her head of the many conflicts vying for attention there. Two thoughts, in particular, continued to occupy her. Who killed Alan McCall? Who killed Frankie Kelly? In Alan McCall's case, she had no doubt that the politicians had moved the body from one location to another in the mistaken belief that they could avoid a scandal, but she doubted if they had anything to do with the killing itself. She felt sure his death had much more to do with domestic issues. If that were the case, how had Frankie Kelly become a victim? She had no answer for that – yet. Talking to Jim Miller, she felt, might shed some light on the situation.

Finding the Glebe Theatre closed confirmed her belief that she was going to have one of those days. Theatre people, she reminded herself, were creatures of the night, not given to early morning activity. Not that she considered 10 a.m. early but she supposed the thespian world considered it an unearthly hour. She rapped with her knuckles on the timber door a second time in the vain hope that someone might be inside. No response.

A framed poster, attached to the wall beside the door announced the forthcoming attraction as *Conversations on a Homecoming* by Thomas Murphy. Emma, whose visits to the theatre were few and far between, had a vague recollection of seeing this play years earlier. She wasn't sure but she thought she might have gone to see it in the Peacock Theatre with a boyfriend before she had ever met Vinny. She had little recollection of either the play or the boyfriend.

She was about to turn away from the door when she thought she heard a sound coming from inside the theatre. She stopped and listened. Yes, there was a sound coming from behind the door. She could hear a bolt being pulled back. A gaunt looking man, dressed in a black tracksuit and trainers, opened the door. Emma put his age at thirty or thereabouts. With a shaved head and a ring in his nose, he appeared languid and spoke with a rich deep voice that seemed at odds with his slender frame. 'You looking for someone?' he asked.

'Well, yes, I suppose I am. What I mean is: I was hoping to get some information.'

'Oh, you want tickets for *Homecoming* is that it?'

'No, no, I don't. I was wondering if . . . '

'Wait a minute; don't I know you? I've seen you somewhere. I just can't place you. You are an actor, yes?'

'No, I'm not an actor,' she replied, copying his pronunciation of the word actor, with the emphasis placed firmly on the second syllable. My name is Emma Boylan, I am a journalist with the *Post.'*

'Yes, that's it. I was absolutely positive I had seen you before. What brings you to the Glebe? I thought you were more involved in the current affairs area . . . had no idea you covered theatre as well.'

'Well no, I don't usually cover theatre but on this occasion I'm trying to track down Jim Miller; I believe he played here recently.'

'Ah, Jim. Why on earth didn't you say so; come on

in,' he said, his face transformed into a broad smile as he ushered her into a dimly lit auditorium. 'My name is George Ennis, actor-in-waiting, ha, ha, and, as it so happens, I share a house with Jim Miller.'

'Are you serious; that's great. Is he involved in the current show?'

'You mean *Conversations*? Yes, absolutely, he is. The show is still in rehearsal; dress tomorrow night followed by two preview nights – they are the absolute pits – and then curtain-up Saturday. Jim is Michael. Born to play the part, he was, absolutely superb in rehearsals. The man's gifted.

'Will he be here this morning?'

'Absolutely not. Gosh no. Only Muggins here is daft enough to be here at this godawful hour of the morning. I had to get a few props ready for this evening's rehearsal. It's looking good don't you think?'

'Sorry?

'The set. It's looking good don't you think.'

'Oh, I see. Yes, yes it is,' she agreed, trying to sound enthusiastic, but not convincing enough to cloak her lack of interest. All she could see was a drab stage that represented the interior of a sixties-style pub, complete with counter and bar stools. Stained mirrors with advertisements in gold leaf and an assortment of bottles on shelves formed a backdrop. A dusty picture of John F. Kennedy appeared under a sign that read, 'The White House.'

Sensing Emma's lack of enthusiasm, George attempted to justify his own approval. 'When the actors come on and the lights come up, the whole thing is transformed. It's like a page of time torn from the past in rural Ireland. Absolutely unbelievable. Jim is the star of the show; he is absolutely magic. He does not play the part of Michael, he lives it; always gets totally into the part. He's a complete Stan-o-freak.'

'A what?'

'He is a student of the Stanislavsky school of acting. You've heard of method acting?'

'Yes, it's what people like Daniel Day-Lewis and what-d'you-call-him, De Niro do. They try to become the characters they play.'

'You're absolutely right. Well, back in the 1890s, Stanislavsky, the founder with the Moscow Art Theatre, brought the method to world attention. I'd say that no one has had a greater influence on stagecraft. The little I know, I've learned from Jim Miller. He's worshipped at the Stanislavsky shrine for years. He's even attended workshops in Russia to learn the skills of acting from today's masters over there.'

Emma allowed George to talk for several minutes on the subject of Stanislavsky before bringing him back to the subject of Jim Miller. 'Will Jim be here today?'

'Yes, absolutely. He'll be here tonight but if you like, I could take you to the house right now. You could talk to him straightaway. I'm finished here for the moment and am going back anyway. If we hurry we can catch him before he leaves for the day.'

'You sure? I'm not putting you out of your way?'

'No, not at all. I promised Viv – that's my good lady's

name – I'd be back about now, so she is expecting me. We can have a cup of coffee and a chat. I think it's great that you should want to do an interview with Jim. No one deserves the recognition more than he does.'

Emma nodded, managed a little smile and brushed aside the twinge of conscience she felt. Not putting George wise to her real intentions was a small price to pay for getting the opportunity to meet Jim Miller.

23

Walking along Baggot Street Lower, George Ennis kept up a non-stop commentary on various productions that had played in the Glebe Theatre. Leading Emma into Pembroke Street, he admitted that he himself would never amount to more than a mere 'journeyman actor'. 'The sort of acclaim reserved for the Jim Millers of the world will never be mine,' he told her, pausing before continuing in a philosophical vein. 'It's a fact of life; some people are born to be stars, others – like myself, for example – are mere acolytes; there to give definition to the star.'

'And that's enough to satisfy you?' Emma asked.

'Yes, part of the secret of life is to accept our place in the great scheme of things. My love of the theatre and the many actors I like to call friend is enough to keep me motivated. I've long since accepted the fact that we can't all play the leading role.'

Just as Emma began to wonder how much further they had to walk, George took a left turn into a cul-de-sac off Pembroke Lane. 'This is where I live,' he informed Emma and proceeded to give her a potted history of the area. 'This lane was once used as the back entrance to the Georgian houses on Fitzwilliam Square North. All these small stone-cut buildings you see in front of you were originally built as coach houses or groom's quarters for the big houses on the square.'

'What happened to change all that?'

'Time and tide, as they say, wait for no man. By the fifties the privileged families had moved out and the property developers moved in. With an eye to profits they cannibalised the houses, turned them into office accommodation. At the time in question, the smaller outhouses at the rear were of no interest to anybody. For years they had lain there, dilapidated for the most part or turned into garages. Of course all that has changed now; the lane has been transformed from being a row of eyesores into trendy mews buildings. In the space of two decades I've seen these properties jump in value and prestige to such an extent that only someone with a very healthy bank balance could afford to live here today.'

Emma, who had not imagined George to be in this upwardly mobile bracket, looked at him quizzically. 'I didn't think actors were that well paid?'

'You're absolutely right there,' he said with a sad-eyed smile, 'I could never afford to live here if it weren't for my good lady; she's the one with the dosh.'

George took a key from his pocket and opened the door to a recently renovated mews. 'Home sweet home,' he said, ushering Emma into a sun-filled lounge.

'It's lovely,' she said, genuinely impressed by what she saw.

The open-plan room with its white marble fireplace and polished pine floor had flair and style. French doors opened on to a paved patio garden. Furniture had been chosen with care and taste, but above all with an eye to comfort. It was obvious to Emma that whoever bought the furniture and fittings had not been fettered in the least by lack of finances.

'Jim's room is upstairs,' George said. 'Let's pop up and see if he's still there.' George moved up a spiral timber staircase that led to a brightly lit landing, its walls decorated by a series of hand-washed batiks. He knocked on a rosewood door to one side of the landing. 'Jim! Are you there, Jim?' he asked, gently pushing the door open. There was no one in the room. 'Damn it; we've missed him.' The disappointment in his voice sounded almost comical to Emma's ear. The room, she could see, a bedroom-cum-study was spotlessly clean and tidy, lit by a gentle beam filtering in through a porthole window.

A yellow Post-It note, weighed down by a multi-coloured marble cube, sat on the top of a Davenport writing desk. George removed the marble and examined the note. His face ran through a series of expressions, childlike in their animation, as he read the note. 'Bugger it!' he said, as much to himself as to Emma, 'He wants me to read-in his part at this afternoon's rehearsal . . . some unavoidable business has come up, he says here.'

'Jim Miller is not a full-time actor?'

'No. He continues to hold on to his job as a schools inspector. Absolutely daft if you ask me. He receives enough acting offers to give up the day job but for some reason, best known to himself, he refuses to entertain the idea.'

'So, in essence, he's an amateur actor? Yes?'

'Absolutely not. Good God, no. He's a part-time professional actor; the word amateur is not a description Jim Miller would recognise.'

Before Emma could pursue the question further, a woman wearing nothing more than a slip and bedroom slippers entered the room. 'Who is this woman?' she asked George while glaring at Emma. George spun around to face her. 'Oh, Viv, I didn't hear you come in behind me. This is Emma Boylan, journalist with the *Post;* she's here to do a story on Jim Miller.' Turning to Emma, he said, 'Emma, this is Viv Norton, my partner. You probably know her as the lead singer with her group Glass Tool.'

'I'm pleased to meet you,' Emma said, shaking her hand. 'I've seen you on the television, heard your hits on the radio . . . they are great.'

'Great,' George echoed, 'an understatement if ever I heard one. Viv's debut album stayed ten weeks in the British charts; her last two singles have made the top ten and Sony have signed her for a three-album deal.'

As George recited Viv's achievements, Emma's eyes appraised the singer. She had indeed seen Viv on television and had been impressed by her honey-sweet vocals. It struck her as extraordinary that the emotional firepower she exuded could possibly come from such a diminutive frame. Looking at her now, without make-up or glitter, seeing the steel-hard look in her eyes, she no longer looked the paragon of sweetness so carefully projected through the television camera lens. For such a young person – she couldn't have been more than twenty-two or three – there was a worldly wise air about her. Although her voice retained a childlike quality, Emma detected a more threatening timbre barely concealed beneath the surface. It was the sort of voice that exuded an unquestionable authority.

'Miss Boylan,' she said, with studied politeness, 'I do hope you will excuse me if I talk to George on a private matter for a moment?'

'Yes, of course. I was just about to go anyway. Jim Miller isn't here; it was him I wanted to see. I expect I'll catch up with him again. Thank you very much, George, for your . . . '

George, who seemed impervious to Viv's anger, gestured with his hands to Emma, 'You stay here; I'll be back in a minute after I've heard what Viv wants to say. You stay here. OK?'

Before Emma could reply, Viv had taken George by the elbow, in much the same way a mother might guide an errant child and ushered him out of the room. Emma was left standing there, attempting to regain her equilibrium after her exposure to hurricane Viv. As she wondered how somebody like George could have become Viv's lover in the first place, she took stock of Jim Miller's neatly compartmentalised study and bedroom. The impression created convinced her that he must be a control freak. Like a well constructed stage set, everything appeared to have its own area with nothing out of place. One set of shelves contained books devoted to drama and theatre, most of the them unfamiliar to Emma. Glancing at the titles, she saw names only vaguely familiar to her: Brecht, Beckett, Pinter, Pinero, Ionesco and Strindberg. Stanislavsky's *An Actor Prepares* had pride of place. Another section contained works by Irish playwrights. Emma was on safer ground here, being familiar with the names of Synge, O'Casey, Shaw, Behan and Friel. A separate cabinet of books contained academic studies, school textbooks, volumes on the subject of education and the role of examinations, grading procedures and the third-level education points system.

As Emma observed Jim Miller's neat environment, the sound of raised voices coming from a room on the opposite side of the landing increased in volume. It was impossible not to overhear Viv, her every word cutting through the air like a surgeon's scalpel. George's bass sounds, never rising to the same heights, were more difficult to make out. Unashamedly, Emma listened.

'I want him out of here by this weekend, do you hear? This weekend,' Viv repeated with a determination not open to question.

'You're not being reasonable,' George replied.

'I've been too bloody reasonable, that's the problem. No woman on earth would put up with the crap I've had to put up with. I've worked my butt off to buy this place. And I continue to work my butt off to provide the money to keep it going. You refuse to get a real job, refuse to grow up. It's time to forget about the theatre and all those spongers who take advantage of you.'

'Now, just hold it a sec, Viv, I . . .'

'No, you hold it a second. I took in your pal Miller as a lodger because of your insistence but now I insist he goes.'

'Jesus, Viv, you are going totally over-the-top on this. All this fuss because Jim had a girlfriend to stay with him last night.'

'Girlfriend, hah. I've no difficulty with him having a girlfriend. He can shag his brains out as far as I'm concerned. This morning after you had gone to the Glebe, I saw him sneak a – a minor out of this house. That scares the shit out of me. Have you any idea what age she was?'

'No, I don't; I didn't see her. But you know what Jim is like; he fancies them young . . . not much harm in that. Best of luck to him if he can still pull them, I say.'

'That's so friggin' typical of you, George. Well, it might interest you to know that on this occasion the girl . . . no, the *child* – that's what she was, a child – could not have been a day over fourteen; a schoolgirl for Christsake. I can turn a blind eye to a lot of things but not that. I will not tolerate it under my roof. Do you hear me? Not in *my* house. Apart from anything else it's illegal; it's statutory rape, that's what it is, statutory-friggin' rape.'

'Okay, all right, Viv, I'll have a word with him; tell him not to . . . '

'No, George, you just tell him to pack his bags . . . get to hell out of here.'

Emma listened as the argument continued, all the time examining the contents of Miller's room. What she was hearing gave her a creepy idea of how he might have fallen out with his daughter Jacqueline. Hoping to find some clue that might help her establish that connection, she continued to scan his room. The knowledge that her time was short and that George and Viv might come back at any moment added urgency to her task. A scrapbook caught her interest. It contained press reviews and photographs from various plays in which he had played leading roles. Black and white studies showed him in various guises; Helmer in *A Doll's House*; Salieri in *Amadeus*; Joxer in *Juno and the Paycock*; Norman in *The Dresser* and dozens of other characters unknown to Emma. Miller's chameleon-like talent for changing appearances in each of the characterisations impressed her greatly.

As George and Viv continued to argue, Emma dared herself to raise the lid of the Davenport. Inside, she discovered a collection of Jacqueline Miller's books along with press cuttings and photographs. There were several sealed letters addressed to Jacqueline Miller. All of them had the words 'Return to Sender' written in black marker across the top. How very interesting, Emma thought. Glancing through the press cuttings, it became obvious that Jim Miller liked to keep track of his daughter's activities. Each cutting referred to an event in her life. One report praised her success with the Abbeygate Babes camogie team; another cutting told of her horrific accident. Several showed pictures of her attending book launch receptions. A series of Polaroid photographs caught her attention next. One print showed Number 32 Leeson Crescent; two other prints showed similar properties. Emma suspected that these represented the other two houses Jacqueline Miller owned. Jim Miller's interest in his daughter, it seemed to her, bordered on the obsessive.

As Emma placed the contents back in the writing desk, a single scrap of paper fell from between two books. She hunkered down to pick it up from the floor and read what was scribbled on it. The name and address written there in neat handwriting meant nothing to her. On an impulse, she decided to put it into her pocket. Viv and George were still shouting at each other – something to do with a car that George crashed – with no sign of a let-up. Emma decided it was time to get out. As quickly and as quietly as possible she headed down the stairs and out the front door. Even though she had not met with Jim Miller, she felt her visit to the mews had not been a waste of time. On the contrary, it had been most informative. The more she thought about it, the more sure she felt she knew what had happened in Leeson Crescent on the night Alan McCall was murdered.

Is it true that the women are worse than the men
They went down to Hell and were thrown back
*   again . . .*

The lines of the old ballad ran through Lawlor's head every time he came face-to-face with the Taoiseach. He did not like Fionnuala Stafford and he knew that the feeling was mutual. It was of little consequence to him; he had always said he would do business with the Devil himself if there was advantage for him in it. Dealing with politicians, in his opinion, was akin to dealing with the powers of darkness; they were wicked and evil but they did have power and influence. Serving them, however unpleasant, had its benefits. For one thing, it could fast-track one's career. Fionnuala Stafford was as worthy an emissary from Hell as he was ever likely to encounter.

Pushing his dislike for the woman to one side, he examined the sheet of newsprint she pushed across her desk at him. He tried to hide the shock he felt at seeing the headline and the text that followed it.

'Where did this come from?' he asked, without taking his eyes off the page.

'That's the article Judge Chadwick slapped an injunction on last night. It would have appeared on page one of the *Post* today but for his action. As you can see, Jimmy Rabbitte has decided to spill his guts ... talk about his deal with Francis Xavier Donnelly. And, as if that were not enough, he claims that I was fully aware of these shenanigans.'

Lawlor continued to read, astounded by the revelations contained in the article in front of him, not least because, as far as he could tell, it was a true and accurate account of what had happened. 'How long can you keep this from hitting the streets?'

'The *Post* will have the decision overturned by tomorrow ... and it will appear on Thursday; that gives us today and tomorrow to try and salvage things.'

'So, what do you plan to do about it?' Lawlor asked

'It's more a question of what *you* must do?'

'Oh, how do you make that out?'

'If you had been more efficient in doing what I asked you to do at our last meeting, we wouldn't be in the mess we are in now.'

'With all due respect, Ma'am, that's a load of horlicks and you know it. No point in blaming me for what's happened. Your general secretary, Donnelly, is the one responsible for what's going down, not me; he's the one who cocked up big-time.'

'Yes, I can't deny that, the man is a fool . . . and a very dangerous fool at that, but you were supposed to take Jimmy Rabbitte out of the picture. That was the one thing I asked of you . . . and you failed.'

'Unfortunately, the heavies I hired were not to know someone else would be in Rabbitte's house at the time.'

'That hardly excuses what happened. They killed the man, for God's sake. I never wanted that.'

'No? Aren't you being a bit disingenuous? You wanted Rabbitte roughed up a little and left as a vegetable; the distinction is a subtle one.'

Stafford dismissed his comment with a backhand flick. 'It's of academic interest now; they got the wrong man and Rabbitte is still at large and singing like a canary.'

'What do you want me to do, Ma'am?'

'Well now, I would have thought the answer to that was fairly obvious. I want you to get Rabbitte.'

'Is that all?'

'No, dammit, Lawlor, that's not all. I want you to find Jacqueline Miller before she too decides to talk to the press. Surely to God, that's not beyond your ingenuity?'

'Easier said than done, Ma'am. If it weren't for that gobshite Donnelly, it would have been a lot easier. He hid her in a private nursing home for a whole week after the event, told no one, and then lost track of her. I mean, can you believe that man?'

'Forget about Donnelly for the moment. Finding Jacqueline Miller is our top priority; she's the one person who can identify Alan McCall's killer. Find her. Find her fast. Get her to talk. Get her to give us a description of the murderer. Get her to co-operate; then at least we'll know which direction to look. Find the murderer and the spotlight will shift away from the amateurish cover-up that Donnelly set in motion. I need action. I need it *fast*. I've less than two days to save the government.'

'I have decided to drag in Damien Conway; hold him for questioning.'

'Remind me: who is Damien Conway?'

'He's Jacqueline Miller's nephew. He is the only suspect we have in sight at the moment.'

'Ah ha, one of the family, how very interesting. Don't statistics show that more than half all murders are domestic in nature. So what's the story with Conway? Did he do it?'

'Hard to be positive at this stage. He could have, I suppose. Yes, he could very well have done it.'

'You don't sound too sure. Does he have a motive?'

'Yes, it's a bit far-fetched but not out of the question. Our investigations have turned up a few odd facts about the lad: he's only twenty-one years of age; he has set up his own business in graphic design but the company has been financed by his aunt. However, from the digging we have done it turns out he has little experience in the big bad world of business; his trading is decidedly dodgy – high overheads, few orders and lousy credit control. The banks are threatening to call in their overdraught facilities. But here's the bit that set off alarm bells. We've managed to discover the contents of Jacqueline Miller's will and it makes for interesting reading. Damien Miller is the sole beneficiary in the event of her death. Could be worth anything up to three and a half million. How about that?'

'How does that tie in with the death of Alan McCall?'

'Well, this is supposition of course but he might have found out that his aunt was having an affair with McCall. He might have feared that the liaison could develop into something serious, something a bit more permanent. What if he believed McCall was about to leave his wife, move in with his aunt.'

Stafford nodded. 'I see what you're getting at; something like that would threaten his inheritance.'

'Exactly,' Lawlor agreed, 'we're talking about a lot of money here. You can imagine how disappointed he would be if he felt it could all disappear. It'd be motive enough to eliminate the possibility from his aunt's life. People have been murdered for a lot less.'

'They have indeed; you could be right, I think you should bring him in; anything that takes the spotlight away from the government is to be welcomed. Make a bit of a song and dance of it while you're at it. With this story about to break, I'll fire F. X. On the question of Shay Dunphy and Tom Pettit, I'll announce the setting up of an enquiry to look into their actions; that should buy me a little time.'

The ironic smirk on Lawlor's face spoke volumes. 'Why not sack the two of them as well while you're at it, Ma'am,' he said. 'No point in having balls if you don't flaunt them.'

'That's exactly what I'd love to do but unfortunately I can't . . . not yet. The opposition will table a motion of no-confidence as soon as this story hits the news-stands. I need the votes of Dunphy and Pettit to stay in power. During the breathing space the vote will give me, I want you to find Rabbitte; find Jacqueline Miller . . . get her to talk. Charge Damien Conway with the murder; we'll worry afterwards about whether he's really guilty or not.

'And for doing all this, I get . . . ?'

'You get to hold on to your job, Detective Inspector. You might even get promotion to deputy commissioner in time . . . as long as I stay in power, that is.'

'And if I fail?'

'If you fail, we all fail. I go to the country in an election I can't win. And you my friend go back to wearing a uniform again.'

'I see.'

'Good! We understand one another.'

24

It was rare enough to see a smile on Bob Crosby's face, but yes, there could be no doubting the joyous expression. The man was definitely happy. In fact, Emma could not remember the last time she had seen Bob in such a good mood. It was Wednesday afternoon, a cold day in March, but the smile on the editor's face, like the newly bloomed daffodils outside the building, gave a lift to the otherwise grey day. 'We got them, we finally got them,' he said. 'If this doesn't bring down the government, nothing will.' Crosby's excitement was a result of the news contained in the fax sheet gripped firmly in his hand. It confirmed that, at last, they could publish the results of their interview with Jimmy Rabbitte. Judge Edward Chadwick had rescinded his injunction stopping the *Post* from running the story.

After Bob Crosby had left her office, Emma thought about the effect the story would have on the country when it made the news-stands the next morning. It would rock the government, of that she had no doubt, but she did not share her editor's enthusiasm for the prospect. Instead she had moved ahead to the story behind the story. Alan McCall's murder and the attempted cover-up would have grave political implications, sure, but what of the human dimension? What of those innocent people outside politics who were unwittingly caught up in the affair? There was McCall's wife and two children. How would Sarah react to seeing her late husband's indiscretions plastered all over the newspapers, talked about on television and whispered about by her neighbours? How was a wife supposed to react when she discovered the man she loved, the man she thought loved her, had been cheating on her? Emma tried to put herself in Sarah's place, tried to imagine what it must be like. It was not a pleasant thought. The emotion most likely to dominate in such a situation would be that of anger.

And the twins – what would they think? At nine years of age they were old enough to understand that adults sometimes behaved badly. But bad behaviour was not something they would ever associate with their dad, not the perfect dad who loved them and always brought home presents for them. The shock to them, when they saw the stories, could only be imagined. Short of sending them to another planet, there was no way they could be shielded from the media coverage. It would be on the television, the radio, everywhere they looked. Reporters would try to badger them for comments. Their classmates would also be exposed to the scandal and would react in the way that children sometimes did. They would call the twins names and give them a hard time. How would they stand up to such a strain?

And what of Jacqueline Miller? How were the revelations going to affect her? Inevitably, she would be painted as the scarlet woman, the politician's mistress, his bit on the side. It never ceased to annoy Emma that women who found themselves in situations such as this inevitably got cast in the role of the slut or whore whereas the man, who probably instigated the affair in the first place, was subjected to no such insults. At worst he might be called a ladies' man or a bit of a lad, names that carried little rebuke and probably added a certain macho street-cred in some cases. What would the media call Jacqueline Miller? Sooner or later she would have to come out of hiding. When she did, the reporters would be waiting, the media interest unrelenting.

Emma's thoughts were interrupted by the sound of her telephone ringing. The switchboard receptionist informed her that George Ennis was in reception and wanted to see her. 'Send him up,' she told the receptionist, wondering what could be so urgent as to drag George Ennis away from his beloved theatre.

As soon as Ennis entered her room, she knew it was not going to be a pleasant meeting. He was flushed, an angry scowl distorting what was normally a pleasant, if nondescript, face and when he spoke his base voice boomed around her office. 'You are some bitch,' he said, 'coming to me, all sweetness and honey, pretending that you wanted to write a story about Jim Miller.'

'George, please sit down,' she requested him, indicating a chair to one side of her desk, 'There's no need to raise your voice. Please sit down and tell me what this is all about.'

'No damn you, I'll stand. What I have to say to you can be said standing. You are a lying, deceitful bitch; you are . . . '

'No, George, you're wrong, Emma replied, determined to control her voice, 'I didn't lie to you. I told you I wanted to *talk* to Jim Miller – I still do – so can you please calm down and tell me what brought all this on?'

'As if you don't already know. You're a cool one and no mistake, I'll say that for you. You conned me into taking you to see Jim under false pretences.

'Not true.'

'Of course it's true. I wouldn't have let you within an ass's roar of my house if I'd known what you were up to. When Jim Miller returned home last night he told me the full story. He told me how you have been harassing his family. You have been writing articles in the press about one of his daughters – I can't remember her name – insinuating all sorts of unpleasant things; all lies according to Jim, a man I've never known to lie. You've also been pestering another one of his daughters – I can't remember her name either – she lives in Celbridge. You pretended friendship to her as well, fooled her the same way you fooled me. And when you've got what you want, you go back to your newspaper, take up your poison pen and write your scurrilous reports. You've been talking to everyone who ever knew his family – driving down to the midlands to talk to his wife. You buttonholed his daughter's former boyfriend and her teaching colleagues; you even tricked your way into his daughter's house in Leeson Crescent – just as you tricked me yesterday.'

'I tricked nobody, I simply . . . '

'Tell me, Miss Boylan, is there no depth to which you will not sink in the pursuance of tittle-tattle? Do you enjoy interfering in other people's lives? Do you ever stop to think of the damage you are inflicting on your victims? Poor Jim Miller; I've never seen a man so distraught. When he discovered you had been in his room – his bedroom, for God's sake – he went absolutely stark raving mad. For a moment I thought he was going to kill me for letting you in. I explained to him how you had fooled me but he still called me the most awful names. It was absolutely terrible. Do you want to know what he did next? I'll tell you: he sat on the side of his bed and wept. It tore me up to look at him like that. I watched him sob for ages, afraid to say a word. Then, like a man in a trance, he began to pack his things. When I protested, he just ignored me, refused to speak to me at all, just went about the task of putting his possessions into boxes. Thanks to you, Miss Boylan, he has gone now . . . where, I don't know. I ask the question: what sort of a bitch can do that to a good man? And believe me, Jim Miller is a good man. He might have his faults – we all do – but underneath he's a good man. You have destroyed him. I hope you are proud of yourself; you have destroyed one of the finest men I've ever known.'

Before Emma could begin to answer, George Ennis stormed out of her office, banging the door behind him with enough force to shake the walls of her room. It took several minutes before she recovered from his verbal lashing. She thought about what he had said, re-ran his words like a tape recorder, attempting to discredit the implications while at the same time trying to justify her own actions. Could what George Ennis had described in such devastating terms be true? Was she the uncaring bitch he so forcefully portrayed? No, she decided, she was not. She was not the monster of George's creation; she was an investigative journalist; it was her job to get at the truth. If that meant sometimes stepping on people's toes. That was too bad but she never intentionally went about trying to destroy anyone – Jim Miller included. She just wanted to unearth the truth. Only those with something to hide had anything to fear from her. Did Jim Miller have some reason to fear her? It sounded that way to her. Why had he reacted so negatively to her visit to the mews? Pondering these questions, she absent-mindedly retrieved a piece of paper from her pocket. She looked at it for a while before recognising it as the paper she had found among Jim Miller's books the previous day. Studying it, she wondered whether she should follow up on the information contained on it.

T. Belcher MD Psychiatrist
Consultant to the College of Psychology Studies
Dublin Municipal University
The Grove, Rock Road, Blackrock, County Dublin.

Odd. Why had Jim Miller got a psychiatrist's name and address hidden away in his books? No point in trying to get an answer from Jim Miller at this point. Even if she could make contact with him, George Ennis's visit to her office let her know that he would have nothing to do with her. She considered the possibility of meeting with this psychiatrist but dismissed the idea. It was a stupid idea, she told herself; no self-respecting psychiatrist would ever consider discussing one of his patient's problems with a third party, especially if that third party happened to be a journalist. Time to come up with plan B, she told herself. But she had a problem with that too; she did not have a plan B.

Fionnuala Stafford had taken special care with her wardrobe this morning. Likewise, she paid particular attention to her make-up and hair. It was important, she felt, to present a well-groomed, confident front to the world; important to show she was on top of her job, in charge and unfazed by the crisis threatening the stability of the government. Inwardly, she did not feel confident but she suppressed such emotions. I'm a fighter, she told herself. Becoming leader of the party had been a tough journey but she had made it. Becoming Taoiseach, making it to the top spot in the country, had taken a supreme effort, courage and determination – all qualities she possessed in abundance. An important lesson she had learned along the way was never to show self-doubt, never to show weakness or vulnerability. Those who exhibited such flaws were stamped upon; she knew that to be a fact because she had done it to others herself. The next few days would require superhuman efforts on her behalf if the government were to stay in power.

Tomorrow, when the Jimmy Rabbitte revelations became public, she would be ready to do battle. Attack the attackers, go on the offensive – always an effective plan of action. Self-preservation was at stake. She had no doubts about her own ability to stand up to the inevitable grilling that lay ahead but she was less sure about one or two of her own deputies. It was important to make sure that no own-goals were scored. With these fears in mind, she had already spoken to Francis Xavier Donnelly and Shay Dunphy.

Donnelly had been his usual self, refusing to recognise his own culpability in the present crisis. While talking to him, she successfully masked the temper and impatience welling up inside her, projecting instead what sounded like a sympathetic ear, speaking to him in terms of how best his talents could be put to use in some other areas of government. It had been a difficult pill for him to swallow but with promises of a top job in Brussels, he had eventually agreed to her demands. He would announce his resignation the next day at a press conference scheduled for an hour before her own.

After he had left the meeting, she felt pleased with herself. He had been difficult to handle but it could have been worse. Offering him the job in the European parliament had been a big price to pay for his compliance but it had only been a promise, and promises could be broken. If he kept his promise to make no waves in the immediate future, accepted blame for the present debacle, exonerated all others, she just might honour her pledge on this occasion. One way or another, it would cause her little concern. What mattered most was getting Donnelly out of the picture and deflecting attention from elected members.

Shay Dunphy had been a bit more difficult to sort out. He had come into her office all bluster and bravado, behaving as if she were one of those gullible hacks from the press. She let him have his way at first, even pretended to be impressed by his performance, but gradually reeled him in like a fisherman playing with a big catch, until, in the end, she had him where she wanted him, willing to do exactly as she directed him.

Tom Pettit, sitting before her now, had taken her by surprise. She had expected him to be docile, reverential, willing to accept her directives without question, but the man had shown a stubborn streak she had never seen him display before. 'I intend to resign tomorrow,' he insisted. 'I can no longer live with all this deceit. I feel I have let down my voters, betrayed their trust in me, failed to uphold the values I so often exhort others to embrace.'

'That's not true,' the Taoiseach responded. 'You, more than anyone else in our party, represent decency and high standards. As one of the longest serving members of the house you have rightly earned the respect of your peers . . . and my respect, as well as that of the voters. You still have what it takes to play your part in government as a frontbencher. It is my intention to promote you in the forthcoming reshuffle. More than ever the country needs strong, reliable people of your calibre.'

'I don't wish to sound ungrateful, Ma'am, but I question your motives in suggesting such a promotion.'

'What? What's that, Tom? Is it that you feel you are not up to it? Don't you believe you have earned it?'

'Yes, Ma'am, I believe I'm up to it and, yes, I believe I have earned it.'

'So, what exactly is the matter then?'

'I'll tell you what's the matter. Before Alan McCall's death you were about to appoint him as minister for agriculture. It's my understanding that you were going to pass me over.'

'My goodness, Tom, where on earth did you get such a notion! That's simply not true.'

'Look, Ma'am, let's cut the bullshit; I've been around the block more than a few times so don't insult my intelligence. I'm not naive and I'm not stupid. It was talked about in the corridors; everyone knew you summoned McCall to your office to give him the good news.'

'God preserve me from wagging tongues. As usual they got it wrong. Look, I don't usually divulge what goes on at my private meetings but in this one case I'll make an exception. It's true I called McCall into my office but it was to tell him about a junior position I thought he might be interested in. I knew he was ambitious; I knew he wanted to make it to full ministerial rank but I felt he wasn't ready for that responsibility yet. I needed to know if he would take the less high-pressured office before I offered it to him in public. I wanted to avoid the possibility of a squabble in front of the media. He argued at first; said he was the right man for the full ministerial job but I told him how age and experience were needed for the Agriculture portfolio. I explained that we required a more mature person to represent the country at the tough negotiations that lay ahead with the eurocrats. He was disappointed of course but realised that what I was saying made sense. So you see; I never had any doubts in my mind. You were the obvious candidate for the job.'

'And do you still feel the same way?'

'Yes, Tom, of course. You are the man I want fighting for the farmers and the whole agricultural sector in Brussels.'

'This is all a bit much for me to take in. It's something I've always felt should have been mine, something I've striven for, something I have dreamed about.'

'Well, it's a dream you're not likely to achieve if you go on with any more silly talk about resigning.'

'You're right of course, Ma'am. Obviously, your offer puts a whole new complexion on things. Yes, I'll be honoured to serve as minister in this administration. Thank you for giving me the opportunity, Taoiseach.'

'Good, good, I knew you would see sense. In the meantime we've got to deal with this unpleasant business about Jimmy Rabbitte. Dreadful business. I'll need you and Dunphy to sit with me at tomorrow morning's press briefing. All you have to say is that you have confidence in me as your Taoiseach and show that you stand firmly behind the government.'

'What do we say when reporters ask about the revelations in the press?'

'I'm glad you asked me that. If any awkward questions are put to you, answer them by saying you have been advised not to speak on the matter at this stage. Tell them you have nothing to hide and that you'll be happy to give full explanations to the enquiry I intend setting up.'

'And if they persist; if they press us to be more forthcoming?'

'Look, Tom, you didn't get where you are today by letting the press dictate your actions. Stand up to them, stick to the same line, look confident, put your hand on your heart, convince them you have nothing to hide . . . do that and together we will win the day.'

25

*I've done it, I've conned the con-artist; I have outwitted her. It was hard to contain the feelings of satisfacti*on going through Tom Pettit's head. As he crossed the glass-enclosed walkway that joined the Taoiseach's department with Leinster House, he felt like jumping in the air, kicking his heels together and punching the air with a clenched fist in the same way that footballers did after scoring a goal, except that at sixty years of age his act of celebration might look a bit foolish to any onlookers who happened to be in the vicinity. No, not quite his style, but the idea appealed to him. Prudently, he confined the gymnastics to the confines of his head but the feeling he experienced had the same uplifting effect. His elation came from having got one over Fionnuala Stafford. He had fooled her into believing he was contemplating resignation – something he had no intention of doing – and had forced her into offering him the job he had always wanted.

From the recent setbacks, some good had come, for him at least. He felt proud of the performance he had put on for her. He had listened attentively as she spun her lies about not wanting Alan McCall for the job. He had pretended to believe her, having the right expressions on his face while feigning acceptance of her assurances that she had always wanted him for the job. He had witnessed the Taoiseach at her most devious, telling lies without any shame, engaged in manipulation that she believed would bring her unqualified support and undying gratitude. She had managed to sound so sincere, even pious, as she pretended affection and loyalty but it was her talk about his age being an advantage that he found most despicable. A few days before Alan McCall's death, a friend of his, working in the Taoiseach's department, had slipped him part of a memo from Stafford's desk in which she had written: 'Age matters – we must promote a younger identity for the voter.' He had known then that she had planned to pass him over.

Watching her operate at such close quarters was a valuable experience. He knew for certain now what he had always suspected: like all the other deputies, he represented nothing more to her than a pawn in a power game, a power game skilfully played by a master. He smiled to himself as he thought about it. How could he have been naive enough ever to have thought otherwise – and yet he had been a believer. He had wanted to play his part in shaping the country he dearly loved; he had wanted to use his role of politician as a platform for effecting change, as a way to bring about improvements for the people who voted for him. He had tried, he really had, blindly following the party leader, answering the whip obediently, always ready to defend government policy. It seemed almost ludicrous to him now that he once actually believed his contributions counted for something.

Well, so be it! He would put his principles on the back burner. Maybe it wasn't too late for the old dog to learn new tricks. He would play the game according to Fionnuala Stafford's rules. Why not? Everyone else, it seemed to him, had adopted her code. Yes, he could live with that as long as he got the position he wanted. He would play the game as good as the next man – or woman. But Fionnuala Stafford would soon discover he was not the lapdog she supposed him to be. He had enough evidence about her shady wheeling and dealing to destroy her. And that was exactly what he intended to do. It was a good feeling, a feeling of security, a feeling of not being beholden to anyone.

For the first time since Alan McCall's death, he believed things could go his way for a change. Once he was conferred as a minister, he would allow himself a few days in the job to savour the feeling. That would be enough to satisfy him – enough to show the world and his voters that he had achieved his goal – and then, just when Fionnuala Stafford thought she had him where she wanted him, he would destroy her. He had made up his mind; he would expose her for the hypocrite that she was really was. His revelations would, he fully realised, most likely topple the government. If that happened he would lose his job but that did not bother him any more. Having had the honour, if only for a day, or a week, was enough; it mattered little to him how long he held the position.

For once in his life he would show that his voice did count for something. Tom Pettit felt good; he expected the next few weeks of his life to be the most exciting time of his life. More than ever, he wished he could jump in the air like a goal-scoring footballer.

The clock on the car's instruments panel said 9.15 a.m. The morning sun struggled to break through ridges of slow moving cloud but it would take more than sunshine to cheer up the man whose fingers drummed uneasily on the steering wheel. Detective Inspector Lawlor sat, unmoving, in his unmarked garda car, observing the high-performance vehicles parked all around him. His own Toyota Camry looked decidedly sedate in comparison. He counted three Porsche Boxsters, numerous four-wheel drives, all with fancy embellishments; a scattering of BMWs and a few TVRs for good measure. Lawlor resented everyone who owned such 'fast-lane' cars. With envious eyes he watched the owners of these extravagant toys – young executives, both male and female, all complete with mobile phones, designer clothes and jaunty gait – as they made their way to and from the elegant offices set around Joyce Park.

According to a sign he had read at the electronically controlled gates guarding the complex, the park represented the country's most advanced technological site. All companies housed in the park, so the legend read, were at the cutting-edge of the computer and communications revolution. Bollix to *that,* had been Lawlor's reaction.

Two car rows away from where he remained parked,

he spotted photographer J. J. Kane sitting in a Ford Fiesta that looked even more out of place than his own car. Kane, looking like an extra from some biblical movie epic, rolled his window down, grinned and acknowledged the detective's presence. Next to Kane, a television camera crew waved to him as they waited in a chrome-enhanced Cherokee Jeep. Like Kane, the television crew had been tipped off by him that something big was going down in Joyce Park this morning. He had asked them to wait for his move, assuring them that it would be worth their while. Both parties continued to glance in his direction anxiously, awaiting some action.

Lawlor, in turn, waited for the arrival of the garda squad car. He had arranged for uniformed officers with central control half an hour earlier. That they should be late did little to dissipate his ugly mood. But he knew he could not make his move until the uniforms arrived. Flexing his fingers impatiently, he forced himself to remain in his car, all the while scanning his surroundings. To one corner of the park, almost directly opposite to where he sat, he picked out the Graphique Communications business sign on Damien Conway's building. This was where he would head as soon as his back-up arrived. In most respects the building looked similar to its neighbours but there appeared to be more activity around its entrance than the others. At one stage Lawlor counted half a dozen people emerging from Conway's building and grouping around the door. At first he thought it might represent a smokers' break but as he watched he could see they were not smoking. Instead they appeared to be engaged in a very animated conversation. Within minutes, they disappeared back into the building, only to be replaced by another small group of people. Lawlor was too far away to hear what was being but he could tell from their actions that tempers were raised.

Lawlor checked his watch, checked the clock on the car's instrument panel and cursed. He had by now waited fifteen minutes in the car park. The non-arrival of the squad car was pushing his patience past boiling point. In an agony of impatience, he shifted uneasily in his seat, wanting desperately to lash out at someone, anyone, everyone. It was obvious to him from the activity at Conway's building that something was not right; all the more reason for wanting to move without delay. He was about to check with central control when the garda car pulled up alongside him. 'About bloody time,' he hissed. The driver, a sullen, middle-aged sergeant named O'Meara looked at Lawlor with weary contempt as he slowly climbed out of the car. O'Meara's partner could not have been more different – a pleasant-faced rookie named Quinn who looked as though he had not yet begun to shave.

Lawlor had already got out of his car before O'Meara killed the engine. 'Follow me,' he shouted to the uniforms, as he made his way towards Conway's building. In quick succession he was followed by O'Meara, Quinn, the photographer and the television crew.

Lawlor and entourage pushed their way into the

reception area, creating a path as groups of people, all talking excitedly, gesticulating and arguing vehemently, parted to clear the way. The babble of conversation came to an abrupt stop. All eyes focused on the new arrivals. Even the receptionist, who had been in verbal battle with someone on the telephone, suddenly slammed the instrument down and looked at Lawlor. 'What can I do for you?' she asked, making no attempt to cloak her irritation.

'I'm Detective Inspector Lawlor,' he replied, in his most officious voice. 'I'm here to see Damien Conway.'

'Well, in that case you're a bit bloody late, Detective; you can join all the other people here looking for him. Damien Conway has done a runner.'

'What?'

'Done a runner,' the receptionist repeated, her irritation turning to anger, 'Damien Conway has disappeared, taken off, vanished, left us all in the shits here.'

'And who are all these people? Why are they here?' Lawlor asked, indicating the people standing around listening to the conversation.

'They all want to get their hands on Damien Conway; they're staff and suppliers looking for money owed to them. Word got out somehow that Damien had made a run for it last night. He left without paying anybody. No money to cover the wages. He never paid our PRSI – deducted it all right but kept it himself. He paid no VAT, paid shag all. We're all mad as hell; no holiday money, no overtime – not a damn penny to pay us anything; we won't even get redundancy payments, how do ya like that?'

A big man with a bushy beard and mien of menace who had been listening to the conversation, pushed his way up to Lawlor and confronted him. 'You the law?' he asked testily.

Unfazed by the big man's aggressive stance, Lawlor squared up to him. 'Yes,' he replied, 'I am the law, do you have a problem with that?'

'Do I have a problem? Shit, do I ever? I would have thought that's fairly obvious; I want you to press charges against Damien Conway. He owes me sixty thousand pounds for software I've supplied. I presume that is why you're here?'

'No, that's not why I'm here.'

'Jesus, isn't that just bloody typical! What is it then that has brought you here? Was he caught dropping litter on the street? Did he forget to pay his dog licence? Something serious like that, was it?'

Lawlor took a deep breath to help keep his temper in check. It was a trick he had learned from an old sergeant he once served under; sometimes it worked, sometimes it didn't. On this occasion it worked. 'I'm here to arrest Damien Conway for the murder of Alan McCall.'

The moment the words were out Lawless regretted them. As though on cue, the babble began again. The photographer began taking random pictures. The television reporter, accompanied by his cameraman, talked to various people about their grievances. Lawlor and his uniformed back-up attempted to make their exit but found their way blocked. In an instant Lawlor found himself staring into the lens of a television camera, a microphone thrust into his face. 'Could it be, Inspector, that someone tipped young Conway off,' the reporter asked. 'Could it be that he knew you were coming? Everyone here appears to have got the word. Can you offer any comfort to these people who have been cheated by Conway?'

Lawlor, aware that the footage they were shooting would probably run as the top item on the six o'clock news that evening, resisted the urge to make a smart-ass reply. Instead he looked straight into the camera lens and spoke with a fake sincerity that only his mother would have thought genuine. 'The people waiting around here willingly sold goods to Conway on credit. They allowed themselves to be taken in by the fancy set-up here. What is their loss compared to the loss of a life? The staff have been inconvenienced, nothing more; they'll all get jobs within days in the computer and communications sector so there's no great loss there. Of far greater importance to any of this is the loss of a person's life. We want to speak to Damien Conway about the murder of Alan McCall. So if you will pardon me...'

26

'Anyone home?' Vinny yelled, closing the apartment door behind him.

Silence.

He moved forward towards the kitchen. The place was empty. If Emma had been somewhere in the apartment, he would have known without her having to make a sound. That was one of the things he loved about her: the power she had to create atmosphere by her mere presence. It was a phenomenon he could not explain; far easier to define the emptiness he experienced when she was not around.

He had seen so little of her since his return from the Continent that he had persuaded her to meet him for lunch. The arrangement had been that he would pick her up in the apartment at 12.30pm. He had already booked a table for one o'clock in Patrick Guilbaud's restaurant in the Merrion Hotel. She had protested of course, said she had a mountain of work to get through, but for once he had been firm. 'You've been working too hard,' he told her. 'It's time you took a break from the Alan McCall case and all that slimy stuff going on in government circles.' Before she had time to demur he had kissed her, a long sensual kiss, the kind to send shock waves through the body, the kind that usually demands further gratification. Emma had other ideas, though. Playfully breaking the embrace, she had smiled and called him a horny devil and accused him of bringing out the worst in her. He had readily agreed, saying her worst was also her best. They had laughed at that and she had agreed to meet him for lunch.

All that had happened five hours earlier, after breakfast.

It was now 12.30pm. and there was no sign of her. Late as usual, he thought; nothing new there. When it came to domestic issues, Emma's adherence to any kind of timetable was impossibly slipshod. It was something he had learned to live with. As if on cue, the telephone rang. Instinctively, he knew it would be Emma on the other end of the line. He was right.

'Vinny, you're there, listen , I'm sorry...'

'You're going to be late, right? he said, cheerfully, finishing her line, 'No problem. I'll tell you what: why don't I go on to the Merrion, meet you there; that way we . . . '

'No, Vinny, I'm really sorry about this but I'm going to have to cancel.'

'What? Ah Christ, Emma, I've booked the table and all. Are you sure you can't ... '

'No, all hell has broken loose here. The reverberations from the Jimmy Rabbitte revelations are greater than any of us expected. The government is fighting for survival, holding press briefings left, right and centre; everyone scurrying for cover. We could be looking at a general election. I don't know for sure but we're all on heightened alert. I've lined up interviews with some of the main players and some of the media want to interview me because I was the one to break the Jimmy Rabbitte story. On top of that there has been a big development in the Alan McCall murder inquiry. A warrant for Damien Conway's arrest has been issued but it seems Conway has gone missing. So you see how it is. Honestly, Vinny, it's hectic here.'

'Dammit, Emma! There's always something, always something more important than the two of us . . . it's always the same.'

'No, Vinny, it's not always the same. Today is exceptional and, as I say, I'm sorry, but it's what my job is all about . . . I really am sorry but I can't get out of this.'

'OK. All right. I understand,' Vinny said, calming down. 'You're right, of course. It's just that I was so looking forward to it. Look, not to worry, I'll ring, cancel the table.'

'Thanks, Vinny, I'll see you this evening . . . and I promise I'll make it up to you. You hear me? That's a promise.'

'Oh, you're a bad, bad person, Emma. D'you know that?'

'Yes I am. You're pretty bad yourself at times.'

'Goodbye.'

'Cheers.'

Vinny replaced the telephone and smiled. The annoyance he had felt a moment earlier now totally evaporated. The unmistakable sexual innuendo in Emma's voice had lifted his spirits; his thoughts catapulting forward to the coming night when more than his spirits would be uplifted. Since his return from the Continent their lovemaking had been different. She clung to him as if her very life depended on it. She cried. After achieving fulfilment, she cried, soft gentle sobs. It was as though she were in another world, another planet, floating on a different level of pleasure, a pleasure he was part of and yet somehow excluded from. When he had attempted to talk to her at such times, she had always pressed her finger tips gently to his lips and made an almost inaudible shushing sound. He did not know what went through her head in those moments of tranquillity and he expected he never would. Women were a mystery unto themselves, he concluded, not for ordinary mortals like him to understand. It was enough that she loved him and that he loved her.

Enjoying the glow that came from thoughts of the love they would make that night, Vinny telephoned the restaurant, cancelled the table, and decided to make himself a coffee. He heaped four spoonfuls of Colombian Special into the coffee maker and set the process of brewing the perfect coffee in motion. Impatiently, he waited the four minutes it took for the brew to settle before depressing the plunger. He filled his favourite mug with the dark nectar and made himself a small snack of Cream Crackers and Cheddar cheese.

It was at this point that the door bell chimed. Bollix,

probably some little gurrier trying to sell me raffle lines. But it wasn't. A suave-looking man, dressed immaculately in a dark suit and waistcoat, stood outside the door. 'Hello. My name is Jim Miller,' the man said, his words perfectly modulated. 'I'm looking for Emma Boylan. Could you tell me if she is here?'

'No, she isn't here at present,' Vinny replied, 'perhaps you'd like to give me a message for her; I'm Vinny Bailey, her fiancé.' Vinny felt the man's eyes, compelling in their intensity, bore into him as they stared out from a handsome face. If he had to guess at the man's age, he would estimate it at somewhere between forty-five and fifty-five; it was one of those faces impossible to get a more accurate fix on.

'Yes, I would like to give you a message for Miss Boylan,' Miller said after a little hesitation, 'Do you think I might come in for a moment?'

'Yeah, sure,' Vinny said, stepping awkwardly to one side and leading him inside. 'Would you like a coffee. I've just made myself a brew?'

'Most kind of you. Yes, that would be fine. As it happens, I missed breakfast this morning.' Miller followed Vinny into the kitchen and pulled a stool from the counter and sat down. After what seemed like a long silence, Vinny placed a mug of coffee, cream crackers and cheese in front of his visitor. 'It's strange that you should call now, Mr Miller, because . . . '

'Please call me Jim.'

'Oh, right you be, Jim. I was about to say, Emma should have been here right now. I just got a call from her before you arrived to say she couldn't make it. Something to do with all the upheaval in government; the political storm over Alan McCall's murder.'

'Yes, I can imagine. I've heard about the warrant for Damien Conway's arrest and his subsequent disappearance act. The boy is innocent of course . . . but why he should run is a mystery to me. It's for that very reason I wished to speak with Emma. You see, I'm the father of Jacqueline Miller, the woman at the centre of the so-called storm.'

'You mean . . . '

'Yes . . . I mean that my daughter was the person with whom Alan McCall was having the affair. It was Emma Boylan who exposed the fact to the world at large. She is the one responsible...'

'Now just a minute. If you've come here to complain about Emma, then our conversation ends right this second.'

'Please do not misunderstand me. I'm not here to complain. I appreciate that Emma Boylan is only doing her job; she's doing what she gets paid to do. I attach no blame to her.'

'So, why do you want to talk to her?'

'I want to warn her.'

'Warn her?'

'Yes, I want to warn her to be careful about how she develops her story. You see, she called to my place of residence a few days ago – uninvited by me, I must hasten to add – and I feel she may have left there with a false impression of my involvement in all that's happened. I want her to be aware of her responsibilities when dealing with people who can't answer back. I want her to think twice before pointing the finger of accusation in certain directions because, unwittingly, she could precipitate a tragedy worse than that which has already happened.'

Vinny put down the mug of coffee he had been drinking from and shook his head. 'I'm sorry if I appear stupid to you, Mr Miller, but you've lost me. I really do not know what you are talking about.'

'Miss Boylan does not tell you about her work?'

'No, certainly not to such an extent that I would know the ins and outs of any particular article she might be working on. She's an investigative journalist; that's her job . . . and she takes it damn seriously; she's a true professional. I work in the antiques and fine art business. I don't tell her everything about my job – she wouldn't be interested in it anyway – and she couldn't be bothered to go into details about what she is working on with me. We have an understanding; it makes for a simple, uncomplicated life.'

'I see. I see. Well, in that case maybe you would be good enough to give her a message.'

'I certainly will.'

'Tell her she could be jumping to the wrong conclusions, getting her facts wrong. Tell her to leave my family be. Tell her to stop prying into matters that shouldn't concern her.'

'This is beginning to sound very like a threat to me.'

'No, Vinny, it is not a threat; my intentions are for

the best. I want you to tell Emma Boylan not to attempt to put pressure on my daughter Jacqueline. If she persists in chasing the poor girl, the consequences could be more terrible than she could ever imagine. Will you give her that message for me, please.'

'Yes, I will. I'm not sure how much notice she will take but, yes, I'll certainly tell her.'

'I appreciate your help in this delicate matter,' Miller said, standing up from his seat, 'and thanks for the coffee and biscuits. I'll see myself out.'

After Jim Miller had left, Vinny tried to make sense of what he had been told, but without knowing the background to the episode in question, he couldn't. No doubt Emma would know what it was all about and would know how to deal with it.

It was three o'clock by the time Emma got back to the *Post* building. She wanted to write her article for the next day's publication, and then get out and do some more footwork. The news that Damien Conway was wanted for the murder of Alan McCall competed for top banner headlines with the government's fight to stay in power. The fact that she had an interest in both stories put her under extra pressure. She was about to call the switch and tell them to hold all calls for an hour when a call from England came through on her line. Her initial irritation melted when it turned out to be Jimmy Rabbitte who wanted to talk to her. 'Hey, Jimmy, how are you doing? You're the last person in the world I expected to hear from.'

'Well, that's very nice, I must say; thanks a bunch!'

'You know that's not what I meant; I'm delighted to hear from you. It's just a bit unexpected, that's all.'

'Hard to get rid of a bad thing.'

'You said it, Jimmy. So tell us, what can I do for you?'

'Well, you could come over and rescue me from this godawful place for a start.'

'That bad?'

'Bad? Ha! Don't make me laugh. It's worse than bad but don't worry, I haven't fallen off the wagon yet.'

'No one said it would be easy. Which reminds me, how come you are able to call me in the first place? I'd have thought that Dimbarry Clinic would prohibit the use of the telephone.'

'And you'd be right. It's a strict regime here. I got hold of a mobile; it's against all the rules but I had to make contact with you.'

'You're still an awful chancer.'

'I know, I know . . . but listen Emma, I contacted you to tell you something I should have mentioned when we were talking with Crosby. Unfortunately, at the time my brain was a little befuddled. It's about the break-in at my house . . . and Frankie Kelly.'

Emma sat bolt upright, her interest suddenly razor-sharp. 'You know something?'

'I do. I'm coming apart at the seams here at the clinic but my brain has begun to function again. I've had many solitary hours to contemplate, get my head straightened out, and I've been stringing a few things together.

Remember how you said I was responsible for Frankie's death?'

'Sorry, Jimmy, I should never have said that.'

'No, you were right Emma. It's a fact that's been plaguing me ever since. I feel really bad about it . . . so I tried to figure out how it happened. As you know, Emma, I got to meet with a lot of low-life on a regular basis, what with the drugs, the loan sharks and all that. The thing is: it was only when I got here, after a few days of having my brains unscrambled, that I recalled a conversation I had with one of my suppliers. She – yes, my main supplier was a woman – named the two people who broke into my house. At the time she was speaking in a sort of coded language but it's only now that I figured out what she was on about. I can't mention their names over the wire for obvious reasons but believe me, Emma, they are two seriously bad dudes. They are ex-cons with a record as long as your arm, but lately they appear to be immune from the law. Word on the street is they're working for certain parties *within* the law. Basically, these two guys hire out 'muscle' and run a debt collecting service. They don't send reminder notes when a payment is late; they break a few fingers instead. In more recent times they have branched into the 'contract' business.'

'Are you saying what I think you're saying?'

'You can put whatever construction you like on it, Emma, but you're a bright girl. I expect you know exactly who availed of their services to do my house. Only trouble is, the bastards got poor Frankie instead of me. You don't need to be Albert Einstein to figure out why someone would want me out of the picture.'

'Right, right, Jesus, Jimmy, if you're right . . . '

'I am right. Trust me on this one, Emma. That's why I wanted to talk to you. When I get out of here, if they don't kill me first, I want to work with you on the story. Between the two of us we can nail our muscled friend, get him kicked out of the force and locked behind bars where he belongs. There's just one condition.'

'I thought there might be; what is it?'

'That Crosby gives me a year's contract and that I share the story by-line credit with you.'

'You're not asking for much, are you? Even I don't have a contract, not that I want one, but I've never had to share a by-line on a story.'

'Look, Emma, I need a start. I don't want to go back to reporting court cases, accidents and dog shows. This way, Crosby will let me on to the front page . . . once he knows you are there as a safety net. I want to prove I can cut it at the top level. I need your help to do that and in return, I'll share what information I have. I swear to you, Emma, I'll work my arse off. Honest! You won't regret it. What do you say?'

'You really do know the names of the heavies that set-up Frankie?

'Yes.'

'And you're sure our mutual friend hired them.'

'Positive, but I'll need your contacts to prove it.'

'Then we've got a deal.'

'Without even running it past Crosby?'

'No, even I must bow to him. What I want you to do is this: put everything you've just told me in writing, adding any extra details you can think of, then send it direct to Bob. You do that and we've got a deal.'

'Thanks, partner.'

Emma hung up and stared at her keyboard. Jimmy Rabbitte's call had got her excited. The thought of proving that Lawlor had set up Frankie Kelly would mean everything to her. Her only problem would be having to wait until Jimmy Rabbitte returned from England before setting the wheels in motion. If Rabbitte was right – and she had every reason to believe he was – then Detective Lawlor was the one who organised the goon squad that had killed Frankie. It explained so much. No wonder Lawlor had not been anxious to follow up on the crime. It meant that the detective was an even bigger bastard than she had previously believed. If working with Jimmy Rabbitte meant she could prove Lawlor was bent, she would do it with pleasure. The idea of the big detective safe behind bars, among the very criminals he had helped to put away, was a pleasant thought. Sadly, Frankie would not be there to see it but it would give her some satisfaction to know she had helped to put his killer away.

She took a deep breath. *Christ what a day.* But she had to force herself to put Jimmy Rabbitte and thoughts of Frankie Kelly out of her head and get back to the workload in front of her. She had been telling the truth when she rang Vinny earlier; the day was turning out to be one of the most hectic days she could remember in a long time. Cancelling her lunch appointment with him represented the least of her upheavals. Her schedules had begun to go awry from the first meeting of the day. The session in government buildings had lasted longer than expected. Her colleague from the *Post,* Tommy O'Keeffe, the paper's chief political correspondent, whose job it was to cover proceedings in the Dáil, had travelled back with her and it would be his piece that made the front-page headlines tomorrow. Her interest in the Dáil proceedings were not political in the strict sense; she was more concerned with following up on any connection that might exist between proceedings in the house and the death of Alan McCall.

First, she had attended the press briefing in Buswell's Hotel on Molesworth Street, across from the Government Buildings. It should have commenced at 9.30 a.m. but did not get under way until after ten o'clock. The wait, however, had been worth it. In a move that caught everyone by surprise, a very chastened Francis Xavier Donnelly announced his resignation as party general secretary. The questions came fast and furious from the floor but he refused to depart from his prepared statement. His words were subdued, so very different from his usual upbeat appraisals of the government's achievements. He took full responsibility for what had happened at 32 Leeson Crescent. 'I now realise,' he told a hushed gathering, 'that I was misguided. I fully believed at the time that I was acting in the best interests of the government. I was wrong. I have apologised to the Taoiseach and have tendered my resignation. She accepted my apology and my resignation. At this point I would like to make it clear to you that at no time did the Taoiseach know about my actions. I took it upon myself to offer the payments to a third party. It seemed to me a trivial matter at the time, not something to bother the Taoiseach with. I never, at any stage, discussed the matter with her; it was my opinion that she had more than enough on her plate with running the country.' For many of the reporters, who had long endured Donnelly's pompous posturing and overbearing arrogance, this was their opportunity to humiliate him; it represented come-uppance time, and they were determined to savour the moment.

The press briefing had ended in a shambles with Francis Xavier storming off the platform, his face red as beetroot, refusing to answer questions or respond to cries of 'Come clean!' It was an ignominious end to a career.

Emma had gone from that press briefing across the road to the Dáil. The atmosphere there was buzzing with rumour and counter-rumour. Television crews vied with each other for position. Apart from the local media, Sky and other international news commentators were there to record what was expected to be an historic day: the fall of a government.

It did not turn out that way. Fionnuala Stafford, flanked by Shay Dunphy and Tom Pettit gave a forceful performance from the moment she faced the cameras and microphones. She did not look like a person about to relinquish power. 'I am here to tell you,' she told the gathering, 'that the unfortunate business that happened in the wake of Alan McCall's death is now behind us as far as this government is concerned. General Secretary Francis Xavier Donnelly,' she said, affecting a sorrowful tone that fooled no one, 'has accepted responsibility for the mistakes made in that respect and has done the honourable thing by handing me his resignation. While on the subject of Alan McCall's murder, I can tell you that I have had communications from the garda commissioner earlier this morning and he informs me that they now know the identity of the killer and that a warrant for his arrest has been issued. This is good news for all of us who want to see justice served and must be a source of comfort to his colleagues, friends and relations.

'In regard to Deputies Dunphy and Pettit, to my left and right, I am satisfied that their involvement in the episode has been well-intentioned, if perhaps a little over-zealous. I have set up an internal inquiry to look into the matter. I expect to be presented with their findings within three weeks. In the meantime the two deputies have my support and that of the government.' On cue, Dunphy and Pettit spoke. Like well-trained parrots, they both trotted out the same line: they had acted in good faith and welcomed the Taoiseach's decision to hold an enquiry. Both believed the enquiry would fully vindicate their actions. They resisted all attempts to be dragged into giving further details on the matter. Throughout the performance, Pettit appeared to be enjoying the occasion, a fact that struck Emma as unusual; under normal circumstances, the politician looked as if he were carrying the woes of the world on his shoulder. Fionnuala Stafford thanked her two deputies and took charge of proceedings again.

Before anyone from the floor could interrupt with questions, she continued to speak, obviously enjoying the effect her words were having on the assembled media. 'The opposition have seen fit to put forward a motion of no-confidence in my government,' she told them. 'I see their move as opportunistic in the extreme. I can assure you all listening to me now that we will win the vote and will come out of this debacle stronger than ever.'

There was an audible sigh of disappointment from her audience; this was not what they had come to hear.

After the non-event press briefing, Emma had returned to the Dáil bar to find out what other government members had thought of the Taoiseach's performance, and more importantly, to gauge the reaction of the opposition. It was generally accepted that she had done well under the circumstances with a consensus of opinion believing that the no-confidence vote would go the government's way. The story of Damien Conway's arrest warrant was on everyone's lips. The elected members on both sides of the house seemed genuinely pleased that Alan McCall's murderer had been caught. Emma listened to the comments but said little, preferring to keep her own counsel on the matter.

Back in her office, Emma had completed writing her article and was attempting to contact Detective Inspector Lawlor to talk to him about Damien Conway. It was her third time to telephone him since returning from Government Buildings. On each occasion she had been told he was not available, but this time he had come to the telephone. 'What can I do for you?' he asked gruffly. Emma's first inclination was to say – not a lot – but she resisted the temptation.

'I hear you tried to arrest Damien Conway this morning out at his office,' she said, all sweetness. 'You don't seriously think he did the murder, do you?'

'What sort of a stupid question is that, Emma? Of course I believe he did it. I don't arrest innocent people.'

'Well now, that makes a change. So where is this fugitive from the law now, this desperado, and what makes you believe he did it?'

'Oh, he did it all right. I wasn't too sure at first but once he made a run for it I knew I had the right man.'

'Any idea where he's hiding out?'

'You'd be the last person I would tell if I did know. But don't you worry, I know what car he is driving and I have an alert out with every garda station in the country. On top of that, we're watching the airports and ferryports. The minute he makes a move, I'll have him.'

'I see, and what if I told you I think you're making a mistake, that you've got the wrong man?'

'I'd tell you to take a running jump for yourself. I'd tell you to leave the detective work to the professionals;

I'd tell you to get back to that fantasy world you call the *Post* and keep churning out the garbage you feed to your unfortunate readers.'

'Yes, Sir, certainly, Sir, I consider myself suitably chastised,' Emma sneered and was about to launch in to a scathing attack on him when she was interrupted by an incoming call. 'I'll talk to you again, Detective.'

'The pleasure will be all yours,' Lawlor replied.

The waiting call was from Vinny. According to the receptionist, it was urgent.

27

Sarah McCall had dropped John and Stephen off at Rathkenny National School and was backing the GTi Golf into her driveway when she noticed the small green An Post van pull up behind her. Checking her watch, she saw it was 9.45 a.m., ten minutes earlier than the post usually arrived. As she got out of the car Dennis Bowen, the town's longest serving postman, came waddling up to her, the perpetual smile that served as his trademark blazoned across his face and a fistful of letters in his hand. Sarah liked Dennis. To her, he represented one of the constants in Rathkenny, always cheerful, always ready with a kind word and always willing to do a good turn. Due for retirement within the year, he would be sadly missed by just about everyone. Having spent his entire adulthood as a postman, he knew everyone in the town and everything about them. But he was not a person to indulge in gossip. Dennis Bowen had developed the habit of listening, offering comment when called for, and could be depended on not to pass on what he had been told. 'And how are you this morning, Mrs McCall?' he beamed, handing her the letters. 'Looks as though the weather might be taking up; t'will be good for the weekend I'd say. 'Bout time, eh?'

'How are you, Dennis? Yes, it's looking good right enough. It's just as well too because I have promised the twins I'll take them down to Waterford tomorrow; we're staying for the weekend with their Nanny.'

'Oh, bedad now that'll do them the world of good; two fine lads God bless them.'

After waving cheerio to Dennis, Sarah went inside the house and put the kettle on. A cup of tea was just what she needed. As she waited for the water to boil, she set about opening the letters. As usual, most of the correspondence was addressed to Alan. It was over two months since his death but the letters continued to come, a daily reminder to her of the terrible event that had shattered her life. Not that she needed the post to remind her of the tragedy; the newspapers were full of articles in which his name cropped up. Equally, programmes on the television and radio constantly referred to his murder, always alluding to the secret love life they believed he indulged in. She had little doubt that her neighbours had also seen and heard what was being said about her late husband. Indeed, she had noticed the strange looks some of the mothers gave her down at the school. What was it she saw in their faces? Pity? Understanding? Perhaps, but it was her belief that what she saw in their faces reflected a sense of relief; relief that it hadn't happened to them.

When the first reports of Alan's infidelities appeared in print, she had been devastated. It couldn't be true, she told herself over and over again; not Alan, he would never do such a thing. But it was true, it was all true.

She accepted that now. With acceptance had come the numbness. How was it possible, she asked herself, to live with someone, to know that person most intimately, and then discover that you hadn't really known the person at all. How could something like that be possible? She had come up with no answers, certainly no answers that made sense. She had experienced feelings of hate and betrayal, moments when she wanted to scream, moments when she wanted Alan back to face her. She wanted to ask him directly: why did you do this to me? How many times did you come home from that woman's house after having sex with her, then get straight into our bed and snuggle up to me? Answer me, Alan. Why in God's name did you do it to me . . . and to the boys? But, of course, there was no one there to answer. After these one-way question sessions she would cry. She would cry until there were no more tears to shed. There were conflicting thoughts too. She would remember how she had loved him, how he had loved her, moments of sheer ecstasy, tender sweet moments, touching each other, delicate intimacies, whispered sweet nothings, smiles, eye contact, so many, many special times. And there were the precious times spent with the boys. In her mind's eye she could see how he lavished his love and affection on the twins. Was that a sham too? Where had it all gone wrong? These were questions destined to remain unanswered.

She poured herself a cup of tea and opened one of the letters addressed to her. The neat handwriting on the envelope did not look familiar but she could tell by the postmark that the letter had been posted in the Dublin area. She had only read a few lines when she realised this was something different . . . this was something she did not want to confront. But she did.

Dear Mrs McCall
I feel I must put pen to paper and tell you a little about myself. I am, what is euphemistically known as, 'the other woman', the woman who shared a bed with your husband, Alan McCall. Strong hints have already been made in the press, so you will not be surprised to know that my name is Jacqueline Miller. How you must hate me, I can only imagine. In my defence, let me say straightaway that it was never my intention to come between husband and wife. But it happened. I had known Alan for several years and our relationship was a platonic one. I never intended it should be anything other than platonic. We met through our involvement in education – he, with the department; me, with my school books.

My experience with men had not been a happy one and I had no desire to inflict further pain on myself in that respect. I never had any designs on Alan, I assure you. All I ever wanted was friendship. However, Alan persuaded me over a long period that his feelings for me ran deeper than mere friendship. During this time, his ob-

vious charm had weakened my resolve and I found myself falling for him. Even still, I declined to give in to the feelings he had awakened in me, knowing he was a married man with children. So, why did we become lovers? How do I answer that without causing you more pain than you have already endured? I don't know, Sarah. I hope you do not mind my familiarity in calling you by your Christian name, but I feel as though I know you – we have so much in common.

I slept with Alan after he had convinced me that his marriage with you was dead. I'm sure I don't have to tell you how convincing Alan can be. I truly believed him. The expression he used when I brought up the subject of his marriage was always the same – we're sleeping single in a double bed – they were his very words. I realise now what a dreadful fool I was to believe him. I continued to believe him until the fateful night when both our worlds came crashing down. I still find it impossible to come to terms with what happened that night. I will never understand it. But I must tell you this. At supper that evening Alan and I watched the nine o'clock news and when his name was mentioned in connection with an expected government reshuffle, he confided in me that the Taoiseach had promised to make him the Minister for Agriculture. I knew how much it meant to him and how hard he had worked to achieve it but instead of expressing delight he became with-

drawn and serious. He told me that things would have to change between us when he became Minister McCall. There was too much danger of being found out, he said – the public wouldn't stand for it. I was speechless. He then gently held my hands and spoke to me as though I were a child: 'There is something else I have to tell you,' he said, all the while holding my hand. 'I discovered today that Sarah is pregnant.'

After that I can't remember a whole lot of what was said or done. But what neither of us knew at the time was that another presence had entered the house. You already know what happened after that. I back away from going into details because of fear. I fear for my future. The presence that entered my house that night is still at large, still capable of destroying lives. I am scared, very scared. I am scared for myself and for you, Sarah. The spectre of Alan McCall remains a potent force, an evil entity that knows no bounds. My purpose in writing is to warn you to be careful and not to take anything for granted. For me it is too late. I am already damned. I have no refuge. I am lost, irrevocably lost. But you must be strong. You must survive. I want you to survive.

In sorrow, I say goodbye to you.
Jacqueline Miller

After reading the letter twice, Sarah replaced it in the envelope. She began to shake. She rested her head on the table and began to sob, her whole body trembling.

'Alan!' she said. 'Oh Jesus, Alan! Why are you doing this to me!'

For as long back as he could remember, from foggiest childhood recollections, Damien Conway had been fond of his grandfather. It was a closeness that continued through his teenage years, right up to the present time. If pushed to declare a preference between his father, Ed Conway, and Jim Miller, he would have picked his grandfather without hesitation. Not that Jim Miller ever looked anything like a grandfather, certainly not the stereotypical grandfather one so often sees depicted – the old codger with wrinkled skin, stiff joints, buttoned cardigan and walking stick. Nature had blessed him with a fine bone structure, clear skin and the sort of handsome looks that challenge time itself. Jim Miller, fully aware of his nonconformity to the perceived norm, went to great lengths to make sure it stayed that way. Diet and exercise came high on his list of priorities. He learned early in his drama studies the importance of having a healthy body. When performing a demanding role on stage, peak physical fitness is of paramount importance and he carried this acting ethic into his everyday life. Working as a schools inspector and part-time professional actor meant he had to make do with a modest income. His lifestyle was simple enough and he had managed to make his money stretch to cover his needs. Clothes were his only extravagance. Jim Miller put the same sort of effort into his everyday appearance as he did when going on stage. To him, life was a performance.

He encouraged the boy to call him Jim. Damien usually complied but on the odd occasion, especially when being lectured, he would use the dreaded grandfather tag. Since his school days, Damien's mother, Regina, had always brought him with her when visiting her father. In those days, Damien had never fully understood why his grandparents lived apart. Even to this day, he still did not know the facts. He had brought the subject up with his mother a few times but she never seemed inclined to talk about the subject. Over the years he had got used to the situation to such an extent that he no longer thought about it.

Until this morning.

Sitting next to Jim Miller, watching him eat a breakfast of yoghurt, muesli and brown bread, in a house he had never been to before, forced Damien Conway to think about his enigmatic grandfather. On the previous evening he had contacted him, although he had been difficult enough to locate. After several false trails he succeeded in contacting the actor, George Ennis. It took some persuading to convinced Ennis that he was who he said he was, but eventually he managed to prise a mobile phone number out of the actor. At first Jim was cautious, but after listening to Damien's tale about having been accused of Alan McCall's murder and having to go into hiding, Jim agreed to take him into the house where he was in temporary residence. The house was owned by a teacher friend of Jim's who had gone to work in Brussels for a year.

'Did you have a good night's sleep?' Jim Miller asked.

'Not really,' Damien answered, spreading butter on his toast. 'I tossed and turned all night. I just can't seem to figure out how to get out of the mess I'm in. I'm not that bothered about the Alan McCall business. As I told you last night, I did not kill the man. Given time I will be able to prove it. It's my busin   ess interests that bother me.'

'You mean the financial mess: all that money you owe people?'

'Yes. If I could make contact with Aunt Jac, I know she would lend me the money to rescue the situation, but I can't make contact. She appears to have disappeared off the face of the earth.'

Damien stopped talking for a second and poured himself a second cup of coffee. Before putting the cup to his lips, he looked directly into Jim's eyes. 'You *do* believe that I had nothing to do with McCall's murder, don't you?'

'Yes, of course, dear boy; of course you had nothing to do with such an awful deed.'

'Please, don't patronise me . . . and don't call me *boy*,! OK?'

'Right, Damien, I have no intention of patronising you and I'm sorry for calling you boy. Just getting you back for all the times you called me grandfather. Could be worse; I could call you *lovey*.'

'It's not funny, Jim. I really am in a bit of a bind. What I can't understand is this: why would they suspect me of killing Alan McCall? I never even met the man . . . and even if I had, why would I want to kill him for Christsake?'

'I don't believe they really think you did it – unless

they are even dumber than I thought. No, the truth is: they want to take the heat off the government – the scandal about moving Alan McCall's body – they want someone else in the frame; you just happen to be the most convenient scapegoat to hand.'

'But why me?'

'Because you were there the night of the murder. They'll try to make out that you resented the fact that a married man was making a fool of your rich Aunt Jac.'

'Well, they would be right about her making a fool of herself with Alan McCall. I still can't believe she was taken in by the man. What the hell did she think she was doing?'

'My daughter Jacqueline has always been a strange one. As you know, she and I have not seen eye-to-eye for many years but in spite of that I have kept a watching brief on her. I knew for some time that she was having an affair with the politician.'

'You did? But how? I mean, I visited her all the time but I never had any suspicion . . . not until...'

'I made it my business to know what Jac was up to. I take my role as a father very seriously. I was outraged when I discovered Alan McCall had become her lover. I could understand her finding a man, wanting a man. She is a very attractive woman, but I couldn't understand how she could have allowed herself to be hoodwinked by a sleazeball like McCall. I read all about him in the papers, watched him make fine speeches on television, listened as he spoke about family values, saw him pose for pictures with his respectable family, loving wife, adorable brats. It was enough to make anyone puke. I had decided to do something about the affair, to expose McCall. I telephoned . . . '

'You telephoned who . . . ?'

'Nobody, nobody at all. It's of no consequence now. Fate intervened as it usually does. I, for one, cried no tears when the politician met his maker. He got exactly what he deserved.'

Taken aback by the deep resentment in Jim Miller's voice and the fleeting look of hatred on his face, a frightening thought occurred to Damien. He held back from giving expression to these thoughts, commenting instead, 'I'm surprised the cops are not after you as a suspect.'

'The same thoughts have crossed my mind several times in the past few weeks, but no, the long arm of the law has not bothered with me . . . not yet at any rate.'

'Do you have any idea who did kill Alan McCall?'

'Yes, Damien, as a matter of fact I do know who killed him.'

'You do?'

'Yes, I do.'

'Who? For God's sake tell me who?'

'No, Damien, I'm not at liberty to impart such information . . . not even to you.'

'But why?'

'I can't say anything until certain developments are in train. I have to confront Jac first.'

'What? Does that mean you know where to find her?'

'Certainly, I do.'

27

One hour after Jim Miller and Damien Conway had finished their breakfast, about the same time that Sarah McCall's body went through spasms of shock and despair, Emma Boylan inched her way through the heavy traffic in the Ballsbridge area of the city and headed for the coast road that would bring her to Blackrock. She hoped to meet Dr Tim Belcher and persuade him to talk to her about Jim Miller. Since Vinny's telephone call to her office on the previous day, she had tried, unsuccessfully as it turned out, to follow up on Miller. Politics got in the way. Reverberations from the Taoiseach's miraculous escape from the jaws of defeat had echoed through the media. Her proposal that Tom Pettit would be her new Minister for Agriculture caught everyone by surprise. The opposition demanded answers: how could Pettit, the subject of an enquiry, be given such a job? In reply Stafford pointed out that a warrant for the arrest of McCall's murderer had been issued. On this basis, she explained, the government and Pettit were exonerated from any wrongdoings whatsoever. She knew this was not true but hoped her positive affirmation would convince all of its validity. She was wrong; the opposition were quick to pounce upon the weakness of her argument. Nonetheless her government still managed to scrape through by the narrowest of margins when a division was demanded.

A copy of the early morning edition of the *Post* lay spread across the passenger seat as Emma battled with the bumper-to-bumper traffic on the Rock Road. She couldn't help but steal glances at its front page every time traffic lights and hold-ups brought her to a standstill. 'Government Survives,' the banner headline proclaimed. A picture of the Taoiseach shaking hands with her new Minister for Agriculture, Tom Pettit, appeared beside a photograph of Damien Conway. The text beneath Conway's photograph told how the young company director was wanted for the murder of Alan McCall – his aunt's lover. Emma had her own views about Damien Conway's guilt or innocence but she had, in the past few days, ruled him out as the prime suspect. It was her contention that the gardaí were looking for the wrong man. Meeting Dr Tim Belcher, she hoped, would help her to establish the identity of the real killer. Her course of action, she realised, was unorthodox; a long shot at best but she was frightened enough by what Miller had said to Vinny to persuade her to visit the psychiatrist. It was difficult to see where else she could turn. Talking to Jim Miller would have been the best course of action but she had no idea how to contact him. That left her with little option. The question was: would the psychiatrist see her? There was only one way to find out and she was now in the process of doing just that.

Emma found Belcher's house with little difficulty.

It was part of a well-maintained streetscape that catered for well-to-do residents and private businesses. Climbing the granite steps to the front door, it was impossible not to be impressed by the view. A picture-postcard view of Dublin Bay stretched in front of her, with Howth Head clearly visible in the distance. The discreet, matte-grey nameplate spelled out the psychiatrist's name, his qualifications and the clinic hours.

A middle-aged woman with a pleasant face let her in and asked her if she had an appointment. Emma said, no, she did not and apologised for coming unannounced but stressed that it was urgent she talk to Dr Belcher. The woman smiled kindly and asked Emma to wait in the drawing room, saying she would see what could be done. Ten minutes later the woman returned and informed her that Dr Belcher would see her now.

Emma shook hands with Belcher and apologised once again for not having made an appointment. Without any further preamble, she explained who she was and told how she had been investigating the murder of Alan McCall. Belcher nodded and gestured that she should continue talking. She told him what she had learned about Jacqueline Miller and how her inquiries had brought her to the mews where Jim Miller was staying. 'That was where I got your address,' she said, showing him the piece of paper she had found in Jim Miller's books. 'It wasn't until yesterday, not until he contacted my fiancé, that I decided to see you. I couldn't think what else to do. Can you help me?'

'Perhaps, perhaps I can. Tell me this: what exactly did Jim Miller say to your fiancé?'

Emma told him everything that Vinny had related to her. When she had finished, the psychiatrist nodded and with a questioning grimace asked, 'What is it exactly you think I can do for you, Miss Boylan?'

'I realise that you cannot talk to me about your patients,' Emma said, 'but I believe that on this occasion there are grounds for dispensing with the rules.'

'Rules? What rules would they be, Miss Boylan?'

'Well, I assume that someone like you Dr Belcher, as a psychiatrist, is a bit like a priest in the confession box – not allowed to divulge anything you hear in confidence – even if the person talking to you has confessed to some horrendous deed.'

'Well now, young lady, you're wrong in that respect. I, for one, am nothing whatsoever like the priest in his confession box. I'm not in the business of moral judgements, however, I am duty-bound to report any evidence concerning a patient who admits to an act we believe to be a danger to others or himself. You see, Miss Boylan, in our profession the prevention of death comes way ahead of confidentiality or canon law.'

'Does that mean you might be able to help me? You've heard what I have to say. Can you add anything to what I already know that might prevent something awful from happening?'

'Yes, as a matter of fact I can. You see, I've had good reason to follow the news reports in relation to Alan McCall's murder. I'm familiar with the articles you've written on the subject. When my housekeeper, Mrs Daly, told me you were here, I knew straightaway what this was all about. Under normal circumstances I would never talk to someone who just came in off the street – so to speak – but I'm pleased you have come. I think there's a possibility we might be able to help each other.'

'In what way exactly?' Emma asked.

'For a few weeks now I've had a strong suspicion that a patient of mine has been responsible for the politician's death. I must stress here that I use the word suspicion. I haven't had enough to go on – hard evidence, if you like – to warrant me contacting the proper authorities. But your arrival here now is timely. Twenty minutes before you arrived, my patient, the one we are both talking about, left this house. What transpired between the two of us in that conversation convinced me it was time I contacted the gardaí. I was considering doing that when you showed up.'

'Can you tell me what was said to persuade you to report the matter?'

'It wasn't as simple as that, it never is. You see, it wasn't the spoken words alone that concerned me – though it has to be said they were chilling enough – it was the patient's mental attitude: aggressive, disturbed, displaying feelings of extreme righteousness. I saw and heard enough to make me believe my patient could be the killer and . . . this is what's really bothering me: I think something terrible is being planned.'

'Please tell me what was said. Tell the gardaí of

course, but please tell me now. I think I may be able to prevent it. Jacqueline Miller could be in danger; her life could be at risk.'

'No, I wouldn't say that ... not Jacqueline Miller. I do agree she is central to what's happening but I believe you are jumping to the wrong conclusions.'

'But you said it yourself: you told me you heard enough to convince you that...'

'Yes I did, but you are wrong to assume ... '

'Okay, all right, just tell what precisely was said?'

'I'm not sure it will make a lot of sense to you.'

'I'd still like to hear what was said.'

'Very well, I'll tell you the exact words; maybe you can figure it out:

> I am going to cut the cancer out; the seed must not be allowed to grow. It must be plucked out and destroyed, lest it, too, contaminates all who come in contact with it.

Tell me, Miss Boylan, what do you make of that?' Emma thought for a minute before jumping from her chair. 'Oh, sweet Jesus, Sarah McCall is the one in danger. Sarah is pregnant – Alan McCall's baby – the baby, yes the baby, that's the connection. Of course, why the hell didn't I see it sooner. Sarah is the one in danger; it has been Sarah and her baby all along. I've got to go, Dr Belcher. I've got to go to warn her. I hope I'm not too late.'

Dr Belcher looked at Emma, both his eyebrows raised, a look of enlightenment on his face. 'McCall's wife? Pregnant?' he said, 'I didn't know that. She's expecting Alan McCall's baby. Yes, that would explain so much. I believe you could be right. We must take action straightaway. I'll cancel my other appointments and go with you.'

'No, Dr Belcher, that won't be necessary.'

'That's where you're wrong again. You don't have sufficient grasp of the complicated psychiatric aspects involved in this case. Without such knowledge, it's possible you could do more harm than good.'

'I hardly think so. I know . . .'

'You know nothing, Miss Boylan, when it comes to psychiatry and you certainly know nothing about my patient. I don't wish to appear rude but I can't allow you to go rushing into something that's outside your field of expertise. I need to acquaint you with the facts behind this case; I can fill you in on the journey.'

The driver's face remained hidden as he sat behind the wheel of the car parked opposite Dr Tim Belcher's private clinic. The eyes remained alert, watching every move as Emma Boylan and Dr Belcher descended the steps and got into Emma's car. The merest hint of a smile broke on the shaded face observing them. As Emma and the psychiatrist moved into the traffic, they were completely unaware of the silver coupé pulling away from the kerb opposite them.

29

The telephone's continuous ringing roused Sarah
McCall out of her stupor. Jacqueline Miller's letter
remained gripped in her hand. She raised her head from
the table top, one eye wearily opening to check her
surroundings. A desire to still the telephone forced her
to move. A little out of breath, she held the instrument
to her ear, listened but said nothing. She recognised
the voice immediately. It was Dennis Bowen, the
postman. 'Are you all right, Sarah?' he asked, concern
evident in his voice.

It took a second to realise she should answer the
man. 'Yes, Dennis, I'm fine, thanks,' she said finally,
clearing her throat and hoping she sounded better than
she felt. 'What can I do for you?'

'I'm sorry to bother you at all,' the postman said,
'but I was worried about you. Probably means nothing
at all but I thought I should check with you.'

'Sorry, Dennis, what are you talking about?'

'I had this strange-looking fellow stop me down near
the post office about half an hour ago. In a big car he
was. Rolled down the window and asked if I could tell
him the way to Alan McCall's house. Well, there's
nothing new in that; ever since Alan became part of the
government, there have always been people looking for

him . . . brought more visitors to the town than the tourist board ever did, but this fellow I met today looked a bit shifty, if you know what I mean. I explained to him that Alan McCall no longer . . . aaah, what I mean is . . . explained what had happened, told him that you and the children still lived in the house. He said he would like to pay his respects to you so I gave him the directions. He drove off and I thought no more about it until about five minutes ago. I was driving down River Street when I saw his car parked in the Dew Drop Inn car park. No sign of yer man to be seen. Now, you know me, Sarah, always curious about strangers, so I took a look inside the bar. They were not long opened and there was no one in the place except that new barman, Dan Kane. Neither sight nor sound of yer man anywhere. That struck me as a bit strange, so I just wanted to make sure you were all right. You can't be too careful these day . . . after what happened to poor Alan and all that.'

'Well, he hasn't been here but thanks for your concern. I'm fine.'

'Good, that's a relief. But listen, Sarah, I know you might think I'm a pain in the rear-end the way I poke my nose into everything, but I couldn't help but notice when I was handing you the post this morning that your garage door was slightly open. I meant to say it to you at the time but it went completely out of my head when we got chatting. Anyway, with all the go-boys that are around nowadays, you can't be too careful.'

'You're right, Dennis. I'll check it and make sure it's

closed. The hasp is broken anyway – I meant to have it fixed weeks ago but what with all that's been happening lately, I never got around to it – but, you're right, there's no point in advertising the fact that it doesn't close properly. By the way, Dennis, can you tell me what this person looked like?'

'Well, I'll tell you the God's honest truth, I didn't get a great good look at him. He only rolled the window a little bit down but I'd say he could have been one of them Jehovah's Witnesses or Mormons or one of them born-again merchants, I don't know. Wore dark glasses, he did, and had longish hair as far as I could tell . . . spoke with an educated accent though, looked respectable enough but you never know.'

'Thanks for the warning, Dennis. I'll check the garage door and make sure it's pushed all the way down. I don't know what we'd do in Rathkenny without you to keep an eye on us.'

'Well, bedad now, Ma'am, you'll find out soon enough when they put me out to pasture next year.' With a hearty laugh, he hung up. Sarah went to the front of the house and checked the garage door. To her surprise, she found it closed. Odd, she thought; it was not like Dennis to be wrong about something like that but he must have been mistaken. The door was definitely closed all the way down. Looking at the lock, she made a resolution to do something about it in the next few days.

She had barely got back inside the house when she thought she heard a noise. A sort of scraping sound appeared to come from the utility room. She decided to check it out. The utility room, to the back of the kitchen, was where she kept the washing machine, baskets of laundry and the deep freezer chest. It was connected to the garage by a sliding door. This entrance to the house was seldom used, though it did come in handy enough on the occasional weekend when the twins returned from their football games with muddy boots.

She stepped into the small room, looked around, saw nothing unusual and was about to return to the kitchen when she sensed, rather than saw, a movement behind her. Before she had time to turn around, something crashed down on the back of her head.

Emma drove while Dr Belcher sat in the passenger seat. Heavy city traffic slowed progress to barely more than a crawl. It was not until they made it to the Naas Road, heading in a southeasterly direction down the N9, that they began to pick up a little speed. When Emma suggested that they contact Sarah McCall on the mobile to let her know they were on their way, Dr Belcher advised against it. 'It could be a mistake,' he warned. 'We don't know if she is danger or not. No point in upsetting her unduly. Let's wait until we get there. If there is any hint of trouble we will call in the cavalry.'

Emma kept her eyes on the road as she skirted the town of Naas on the bypass, but her mind was desperately trying to understand what Dr Belcher was telling her. He talked to her about DID and how separate personalities, living in the one body could lead independent lives. John Christie, he informed her, was one such personality. When Emma queried this concept, he explained that the host-body could experience periods of blankness and could be said not to exist except in a void during these periods when John Christie took over. He likened it to the blackouts common in alcoholism, but of a more extreme, and dangerous, nature. Emma, vocal in her scepticism, received a strong rebuke from Belcher. 'You can believe what you like,' he said irritably, 'but I can assure you that what I am telling you is indisputable fact. Psychiatrists have found increasing presentations of such disorders in the aftermath of sexual abuse. So whether you believe me or not, I'm only saying what has already been recognised and accepted by medical science for years.'

Emma wanted to pursue the subject further; she wanted Belcher to get down to more specific details, to tease out the John Christie phenomenon but her thoughts were distracted when something odd caught her attention in the rear-view mirror. For some time now she had had a vague feeling of being followed. Driving slightly above the speed limit, she had overtaken some of the slower cars and had allowed one or two faster cars to overtake her but she had a feeling that one car in particular, a silver coupé, remained at a constant distance to her rear. Whenever she increased or reduced speed, the silver car remained at a similar distance, just visible. Dr Belcher, unaware that he no longer had Emma's undivided attention, continued to expound on the subject of DID.

At 11.25 a.m. precisely, Lawlor got word of the first reported sighting of Damien Conway's car. Garda Pete Dooley, stationed in the town of Timolin, spotted a silver Mercedes coupé with the registration number he had been told to watch out for and got in touch with central command immediately. The car, according to Dooley, was travelling south along the N9, heading in the Carlow direction. Lawlor checked the map on his office wall and picked out Timolin. He traced the N9 through the village with his finger and followed the route all the way to Rosslare Harbour. It seemed probable to him that Conway was making a break for the ferry. He had barely formed this conclusion when another report came in; this time the car was spotted going through the village of Moone. It confirmed his opinion.

The sergeant in Moone garda station wanted to know if he should have the reported vehicle stopped by one of his patrol cars or not. Lawlor sent back a message advising the sergeant not to impede the vehicle's progress but to alert all stations along the route and to report each sighting. Lawlor could feel the adrenalin surge in his body. The prospect of a full-blooded murder hunt never failed to excite him. As far as he was concerned, Damien Conway was on the run, fleeing from justice, attempting to hop on a ferry and abscond to England. It was the sort of incident that made his job seem almost worthwhile. He allowed himself a rare smile of satisfaction. Conway would not make it, he decided; he would see to it that the car was stopped before he even got near Rosslare Harbour.

Lawlor's request to the Garda Air Support Unit for the use of the force's one helicopter met with initial resistance but after explaining the urgency of apprehending Alan McCall's murderer, he received immediate cooperation and the necessary clearance. Time was of the essence. Flashing lights and screaming sirens sent motorists and pedestrians scrambling to get out of the way as his car weaved an erratic path through the city's traffic lanes. The journey from Phoenix Park to Baldonnel aerodrome, which normally took over half an hour, had been cut to fifteen minutes. Within seconds he had crossed the tarmac, ducked beneath the whirling rotors and hauled himself into the helicopter. Almost instantly he was airborne. Although Lawlor had used the AS 355 N Squirrel once before – accompanying the commissioner to Templemore for a graduation ceremony – this was his first time to use the chopper in active duty. Like most members of the Garda Síochána, Lawlor resented the fact that the aircraft was piloted by Air Corps pilots instead of someone from his own organisation. He had great sympathy with his colleagues who had undertaken flying lessons at their own expense only to be deprived of having a shot at being the force's answer to 'Top Gun'. But none of that mattered to Lawlor now; the helicopter's two Turbomeca Arrius 1A turboshafts lifted him high into the skies above Dublin and headed southeast.

The back of her head hurt like hell. Her body ached when she tried to move. Stubbornly, her eyes remained closed but after a supreme effort she managed to open them. What she saw made little sense. The kitchen ceiling appeared to hang above her, the top kitchen cupboards edged into her peripheral vision. For a second she thought she must be dreaming, seeing the world upside down. Full consciousness dawned. No, it was not a dream; she was lying on the flat of her back and the kitchen ceiling really was suspended above her. Memory kicked in. She recalled the flash of pain, the tumble into darkness, the nothingness. What had happened since? How long had she been unconscious? She tried to move. Something stopped her. Only her head was capable of any animation. Attempting to swivel it from left to right brought searing pain. Now she could see a little more of her immediate surroundings. Forcing her eyes to focus, she saw the upturned legs of the kitchen table to each side of her. Her mind struggled to establish what had happened. Her arms and legs were secured to the four legs of the upturned kitchen table. In spite of this realisation, and the fear welling up inside her, she continued her attempt to rationalise the situation.

It was then she heard the voice. It came from a position behind her head, the speaker unseen. 'I'm glad you decided to come back to us again,' the voice said. 'I was beginning to fear that the smack across the head might have done permanent damage but thank goodness you're all right. You stayed out long enough for me to achieve what I require.'

The voice had brought with it the chill of the danger. Her mind raced back to Dennis Bowen's telephone call – the garage door and her visit to the utility room. Attempting to look back to see who stood behind her only succeeded in inflicting pain in her neck and head. It was only now that she became aware of her nakedness. Her legs were stretched apart and secured by the ankles to two table legs. In similar fashion, her arms were secured by their wrists to the table's other two legs. From somewhere, she found the strength to speak. 'Who are you? What are you doing with me?'

'Ah good, you really are back with us. I'm so glad you decided not to scream. I'd hate to have to stuff your mouth before I had to. Who am I, you ask? I thought you would have guessed by now Mrs Mc. We had such a stimulating conversation on the telephone just recently.'

Sarah remembered. She remembered the phone call and the voice. 'You are the person who claimed to know all about my husband's secrets, right? You are John Christie?'

'You're correct Mrs McCall. I am John Christie and I have looked forward so very much to our little get-together.'

'Why are you doing this to me? I've never done anything to you. My clothes . . . why have you . . . '

'Oh don't go fretting about your clothes; you can have them back when I'm finished with you.'

'You're not going to . . . going to rape me . . . ?'

'Good God, woman, no. Whatever must you think of me? Rape, sex, huh, why the very idea. No of course not. I am no pervert.

'Then please untie me. Tell me what this is about?'

'I'm afraid I can't do that – not just yet. I apologise for any discomfort caused. You see, I've come to take something from you, something that Alan McCall gave you.'

'What? I don't follow, what are you talking about?'

'You're pregnant, Mrs McCall. You are pregnant by Alan McCall's seed. I'm here to take it away from you.'

Sarah McCall screamed.

Although the cabin in the Squirrel was spacious and uncluttered, Lawlor still felt a degree of claustrophobia. Helicopters were all very fine and dandy but he would restrict his use of them to emergencies like this present one. There was something unsettling about being strapped into a glass bubble, hurtling into the sky, with nothing but fresh air between him and the earth below. He looked down on the sprawling city of Dublin as it began to give way to green fields and farmhouses but he did not find the aerial view in the least bit exhilarating. Brushing aside the slight fear he always experienced when airborne, he listened on his headphones to the latest reports on the progress of Damien Conway's Mercedes. Keeping his road map to hand, he plotted the car's route with a series of 'x's. 'How long before we catch sight of him?' he asked the pilot showing him the latest position.

'It'll take us another twenty minutes,' the pilot replied, not bothering to glance at Lawlor, 'so we'll need to keep the information coming to us from your ground units if we're to make visual contact.'

'No fear of losing this car; I'm pretty certain I know where the little bollix is heading,' Lawlor said, allowing himself a little yelp of satisfaction.

They were approaching the town of Carlow from the air when the first unexpected report came in. Lawlor had fully expected Conway's car to take the N80 out of Carlow and pass through Enniscorthy, Wexford and continue *en route* to Rosslare. But according to ground reports, Conway's car did not take that route. Instead the car headed in a more westerly direction, taking the N10. Stretching the map across his knees, Lawlor identified the N10. He could see that if Conway were to continued travelling the N10 it would take him to Kilkenny. Why Kilkenny? He could not figure out what Conway was up to but he gave instructions to his pilot to change course.

For once the pilot looked at him. 'I thought you knew where 'the little bollix' was headed,' he said, a sardonic smile on his face.

Lawlor was about to leap in with a caustic rejoinder but decided to ignore the remark instead. In his opinion, the pilot was a proper shithead but right now he needed his cooperation and decided there was little point in antagonising the Air Corps man any more than necessary.

Five minutes later, after receiving further reported sightings from ground patrol cars, Lawlor made visual contact with the car near the village of Royaloak. 'Yes, yes, yes,' he shouted excitedly, indicating the silver car for the pilot's benefit. 'There it is; let's sit on the fucker.'

'You're sure that's the one we're after,' the pilot asked in his 'preserve-me-from-fools' voice.

'Of course I'm bloody well sure. Just don't lose it. OK?'

'Well, my friend, we're going to lose visual contact for a while when it goes through the forested area you see ahead of us.'

Lawlor cursed and pounded a fist into his palm. He could see the large area of forest as it spread out below him, the trees forming a natural canopy above the road, effectively cloaking the traffic from his view.

'No sweat,' the pilot said, enjoying Lawlor's discomfort, 'we'll pick him up as soon as he breaks cover again . . . about five miles further on.'

But when they got to the spot where the road exited the tall pines there was no sign of the silver Mercedes.

The clock on the dashboard read twelve noon as Emma motored through the town of Rathkenny. Her constant glances in the rear-view mirror had not caught sight of the silver car since emerging out from the forest road, some ten miles back. With obvious relief she dismissed the notion that there ever had been anyone following her in the first place; she put it down to a figment of her overwrought imagination.

It was her second time in a month to drive through the small picturesque town and this time she knew exactly where to find Sarah McCall's house. Unlike the previous occasion, when the weather had been indifferent, today's bright sunlight added warmth to the shopfronts and houses. The small town looked like a haven of peace and tranquillity. Even the people walking on the footpaths seemed happier, more content, their steps a little jauntier than before. It was enough to counter the dark thoughts circulating in the back of her mind. She approached the house in a slightly more positive frame of mind.

The Golf sitting in the driveway was an encouraging sight; it meant Sarah was probably at home. With Dr Belcher by her side, Emma walked up to the door, pressed the bell and waited. 'Shsssh, I think I hear someone moving about inside,' Emma said angling her ear towards the door.

'Well, God bless your hearing,' Belcher said, 'I didn't hear a thing.'

Although no one came to the door Emma insisted she had been right about the sound from inside. They had waited a full minute when a post van came up the street towards the house and stopped at the front gate. The driver, a man in his sixties wearing An Post livery, got out of the van and approached them. 'Can I help yis?' he asked abruptly.

Emma bestowed him with a smile. 'Hello, yes, we

were hoping to see Mrs McCall but there doesn't appear to be an answer.'

'Would yis be connected to the other fellow that was looking for her earlier?' the man probed cautiously.

'What other fellow would that be?' Emma asked.

'Dark glasses . . . parked his car in the Dew Drop Inn . . . haven't seen hide nor hair of him since.' He paused. A worried look appeared on his face. 'I rang Sarah – that's Mrs McCall – but she said she was all right. Jayzus, I don't know, she didn't sound too good. I rang again a few minutes ago and the blasted line was dead. I thought to meself, that's quare. So I drove up here. Do either of yis know what's up?'

Emma decided there was nothing to be gained by holding back. 'I'm Emma Boylan and my friend here is Dr Belcher. We are concerned that Mrs McCall might be exposed to danger.'

'What's that? Danger, did you say? What sort of danger?'

Dr Belcher spoke up, the urgency in his voice unmistakable. 'I don't wish to alarm you unduly but I'm treating a patient who could possible pose a threat to Mrs McCall. From what you've said, the person in dark glasses could be that patient, in which case we might possibly have a problem on our hands.' Belcher held out his hand to the postman. 'I'm a psychiatrist, my name is Tim Belcher, and your name . . . ?'

'The name's Dennis Bowen, pleased to meet yis both,' he said shaking Belcher's hand and Emma's in turn, 'About this problem . . . ?'

'We need to see if everything is all right inside the house. Perhaps if you were to knock on the window or back door she'd recognise your voice.'

'Aye, that's a good idea. I'll nip around to the back door. You can follow me if you like.' Emma and Belcher did as invited and watched as he knocked on the door and tried the handle. There was no response. Dennis Bowen moved to a large window beside the door and pointed to the pulled blinds. 'Jayzus, something wrong all right; Sarah would never pull the kitchen blinds fully down in the middle of the day.'

'Can we get into the house?' Emma asked.

'Yis could get in all right,' the postman said, 'but mebbe we should call the guards first.'

Dr Belcher's frustration began to show. 'Yes, yes, yes. I agree, dammit. Call the gardaí by all means but let's get a move on here first. If someone is in with Mrs McCall, she needs our help immediately.'

Bowen, stung by the doctor's words, grimaced and began moving to the front of the house. 'Jayzus, if Sarah McCall is in trouble I'll not be found wantin'. Come on, follow me. We can get in through the garage.'

Emma and Belcher followed the postman as he waddled through the garage and into Sarah McCall's utility room. 'We can get to the rest of the house through the kitchen,' Bowen said, opening the utility room door. In the act of taking his first step into the kitchen he stopped and howled like a wounded animal. Emma and Belcher pushed past him.

Both of them gasped in horror.

30

By now Lawlor had got used to the whine of the helicopter's engines and the metallic chopping motion of the rotors but still did not feel any more comfortable with his situation. On the contrary, his feelings of cooped-up frustration were becoming intolerable. His voice had taken on an ugly edge. 'Jesus Christ, he can't have just vanished; how could we have lost him! How the fuck is that possible!'

The pilot, no longer making any attempt to mask his dislike for the big detective, allowed his mood to veer from surly indifference to one of belligerent disapproval. 'You're the smartass who knew e*xactly* where the car was headed. You're the genius who wouldn't let the local forces on the ground stop the car. The whole escapade is bonkers, stupid . . . all arranged just so you could appear on tonight's news bulletins claiming credit for having single-handedly captured McCall's killer.'

'OK, OK! Spare me the sermon,' Lawlor snapped. 'You're supposed to be the eye-in-the-sky, so where has our silver car gone? You tell me.'

'I can only tell you what both of us saw – the car entering the forest belt. We lost visual contact because of the trees; it should have reappeared five miles further on but it failed to do so. Conclusion: he must still be down there somewhere.'

'What? You mean he might have stopped for a piss or something . . . maybe had a crap while he was at it? Some crap! We've been hovering for about ten minutes. I don't know . . . the fucker could have taken a kip in the time he's been down there.'

Irritated by Lawlor's querulous comments, the pilot manoeuvred the helicopter into a steep banking movement and headed back in the direction he had come from. 'I suggest you take a close look at your map,' he said to Lawlor, 'because on the first pass-over I thought I saw a minor road branching off from the N10. I couldn't see all that well with the density of trees but I think it might be worth your while to investigate it.'

Lawlor grabbed the map and ran his finger over the area in question. Discovering that the pilot was right infuriated him. 'Shit, shit, shit,' he hissed, there is a road, shit, yes, there is a road. It's almost a quarter of a mile into the forest. Why the hell couldn't you have mentioned it to me when we were passing over it?'

'I didn't mention it because you gave me to understand that you *knew* where Conway was going.'

Lawlor ignored the jibe. Studying the map, he suddenly slapped the much-creased paper with his hand. 'Oh, no, I don't believe this; the road goes to the town of Rathkenny – that's where Alan McCall lived, it's where his family still live. How could I have missed it! Jesus, I've even been to the house; I should have worked it out . . . should have known that

Conway was headed there.'

'Seems to me like you should have figured out an awful lot of things, Detective Inspector, before you started this wild-goose chase. This baby we're flying costs the guts of a thousand pounds an hour to keep in the air. It really would be most helpful if we had some idea about exactly what we're supposed to be doing. Know what I mean?'

'Shut the fuck up and get this whirligig to Rathkenny.

The jagged circle, cut into the exposed flesh of Sarah McCall's lower abdomen and delineated by rivulets of blood, caught their attention immediately. Sarah, struggling against the cords that bound her to the table legs, had her mouth stuffed with a wad of cloth, her terror-filled eyes darting about madly in her head. Standing above the naked body, his back to the intruders, John Christie held a knife in one hand and surveyed the tracery he had created. Dennis Bowen's howl and the gasps from Emma and Dr Belcher failed to register with him. Emma opened her mouth to speak but Belcher made a gesture with his hands to indicate silence; he wished to handle the situation. His voice, when he spoke, sounded calm, even sympathetic. 'Hello, John, this is Tim Belcher here. I think we need to have a few words, what do you say?'

John Christie responded immediately by darting around to face the doctor. For the first time, Emma saw the person known as John Christie. Whatever she had been expecting, this was not it. She could not see the eyes because of the dark glasses but the finely sculpted features looked refined, smooth . . . not the face of a madman. An abundance of hair had been pulled back, clearing the ears, and tied in a ponytail at the neck. Dressed in a three-piece charcoal grey pinstripe suit, shirt and tie, John Christie's slight figure stood motionless for a second before speaking. 'Why have you come here?' Christie asked, addressing Dr Belcher. 'Our next appointment is not for another week.'

To Emma, the voice sounded clipped, the articulation strained and artificial.

'Listen to me,' Belcher said, his voice smooth and friendly in contrast. 'You come to me because you have personality difficulties. Isn't that so? You trust me don't you? Of course you do. You've told me your role is to protect Jacqueline Miller. I know because you've told me. OK? You're angry because of the hurt that has been heaped upon Jacqueline and I can understand that. But what you are doing now will not help her. What you are doing now will only add to her grief.'

'I don't want to hear this. I've a job to do. The wrongdoers must not go unpunished. Jacqueline is weak; she'll never stand up for herself. If it were not for me, the whole world would walk all over her. I have to look out for her.'

'You want what is best for her; that is commendable but you're going about it the wrong way. Let me help. You've listened to me in the past. You know I'm on your side. Please listen to me now.'

'No, you want to destroy her.'

'That's not true, but if you will not listen to me I will be forced to appeal over your head.'

'Go ahead, it won't change anything.'

'Jacqueline Miller, I know you are there,' Belcher said, staring into Christie's face. 'I want you to hear me. I know you can hear me. Do not fight me any longer.'

Belcher's words shocked Emma. 'What are you saying? she asked him, her voice almost a croak.

Belcher shot her a furious glance and indicated that she should remain silent. He turned back to his patient. 'Jacqueline, please, Jacqueline, you must insist that John Christie allow you to speak to me. He shares your body but only because you once invited him to do so; you have the power to make him go away again. That is what I want you to do now. John Christie is making you a prisoner in your own body; he is doing things in your name that you would never never condone – not in your own mind. Please Jacqueline, down deep I know you can hear me. Come on, push John Christie away and listen to me. You know; we *both* know that what is happening here – in your name – is wrong, very wrong. Please, Jacqueline, you must do what is right.'

Immediately, a transformation took place. Emma watched as the personality known as John Christie dropped the knife and clasped both hands across his chest. The knife's bloodstained blade had barely hit the floor when the face began to shake and quiver. A series of hiccuping movements dislodged the dark glasses. A woman's scream filled the air.

It was Jacqueline Miller.

Emma felt like joining in the scream. Shocked beyond belief, she stared wide-eyed as Jacqueline Miller emerged from the persona that had been John Christie. Dr Belcher caught Jacqueline as her knees buckled, saving her from hitting the floor.

Belcher held her in his arms and shot a glance to the others. 'She's in deep shock but she'll be all right. We had best attend to Mrs McCall quickly. Emma, will you untie her and get her out of that contraption. Dennis, can you fetch the gardaí; call the local doctor and see if you can get an ambulance. Use Emma's mobile phone.'

Emma, still trying to take in all that had happened, rushed to Sarah McCall. 'Sarah, it's me, Emma Boylan. you remember? You're going to be all right now.' But Emma knew as she removed the wads of cloth from Sarah's mouth and began the task of untying the cords from her hands and legs that it would be a long time before Sarah would be all right. It was obvious that Sarah was only semi-conscious, her eyes moving rapidly, too fast to focus on anything. She tried to speak, her mouth opened and closed, but no words materialised.

'Please, Sarah, don't try to talk; the doctor is on his way. You're going to be all right. The cuts are superficial. I know it looks bad, all that blood, but no real damage has been done.' Emma found a box of Kleenex tissues and dabbed at the blood circle. As she thought, the incision had not been deep, just the top layer of skin, but she could imagine the terrible pain

Sarah had suffered. She found Sarah's clothes on the back of a kitchen chair and helped cover her nakedness. As she tried to comfort the stricken woman, she noticed that Dr Belcher had moved Jacqueline Miller to an easy chair and was speaking to her in little more than whispers. The psychiatrist had taken off his coat and had placed it around Jacqueline's shoulders but still her body continued to shake as though from cold. Emma recognised the eyes she had only seen before in photographs. It was impossible to guess what thoughts, if any, went through Jacqueline's head. She looked haggard and worn and her breathing came in short, uneven heaves. It was hard to believe that the pathetic figure being comforted by Dr Belcher had, only minutes earlier, been about to cut open Sarah McCall's stomach and remove a living foetus. As Emma gazed into Jacqueline Miller's face, she was shocked to see the features change and take on odd distorting shapes. It was as though the face had suddenly became soft and pliable. Jacqueline spoke, but the voice coming from her mouth was that of a child. 'Can't play today girls, sorry.' The words and the strange delivery caught everyone by surprise. Emma was about to say something but stopped when the child's words began again. 'Have to stay in the house . . . not allowed to play . . . Daddy's girl, always Daddy's girl. Must do what Daddy says 'cause Daddy loves his special girl.'

She had assumed the lok of a frightened eleven-year-old. Her fractured words reflected an ever-increasing dread. 'I do, I do, I do love you, Daddy. I'm not telling lies but . . . but I do not like this game . . . don't want to do that. No, no, no, please don't! No, it hurts. It hurts me down there . . . No, Daddy, no ,aaah, no. I don't like. My mouth? No, no please! Please, no! It makes me sick . . . ugh. Can't swallow, choking me, must spit out.'

The talking stopped abruptly and a series of body-wrenching sobs ensued. 'What's happening?' Emma asked Belcher, but he signalled her to be quiet. Jacqueline Miller's whole body began to convulse. Suddenly she pushed Belcher to one side and stood upright. When she spoke again it was John Christie's voice that emerged.

'You listen to me, Alan McCall,' the distinctly male voice began. 'You are not fit to live among decent people. You have made a fool of Jacqueline and that is not right. You pretend love and affection. Lies, lies and more lies. Why do you tell her such lies? You come to her, have your way with her, take advantage of her, spill your seed into her, then boast that your wife is pregnant. You tell Jacqueline you no longer need her. You cannot do that. No one can do that to Jacqueline. She believed you, she gave you love, her heart, her bed, her body. Death is too good for you.'

The torrent of words stopped. Jacqueline's arms began to wave wildly about before her body slumped to the floor. Dr Belcher attempted to help her back on to the chair and had begun to gently lift her when she screamed. Her own voice had returned. 'Where am I?' she asked, looking around the kitchen, trying to focus but not settling on any one or any thing. 'What am I doing here? Who are you?' She rose to her feet and gazed in the direction of Sarah and Emma. Her eyes passed over Emma but it was obvious she recognised Sarah. She screamed again. Belcher, fearing the worst, moved quickly to her side and placed his arms around her. She became calm instantly and allowed the doctor to press her head to his chest.

A momentarily quietness, eerie in its intensity, followed. No one spoke or moved.

The silence shattered without warning.

The door to the utility room burst open. Emma, Dennis and Belcher spun around to see what was happening. Someone kicked at it forcefully. It flew to the wall and slammed against it. Jim Miller, followed by Damien Conway, stormed into the kitchen. Miller stopped, stood rigid in front of Belcher and Jacqueline, his demeanour theatrical in its absurdity. Conway took in the whole scene, seemingly unable to comprehend what was going on. He looked to Jim Miller for an answer. Miller appeared oblivious to all but his daughter Jacqueline. Dressed formally, like someone about to have dinner in a posh restaurant, he spoke to her as though he were reading from some unseen script. 'I have come for you, Jac. I have come to take you away from here,' he said, each word, each syllable articulated with dramatic precision. Jacqueline turned her head to face him. Her eyes, though glazed, peered out at him, her expression betraying no emotion of any kind. Dr Belcher continued to hold on to her as he addressed Miller.

'My God, man, don't you think you've done enough

damage already? Can't you see the woman needs help right now? You have some nerve coming here to . . .'

'Be silent, quack. Do you suppose for one second that some psyched-out-psychiatrist is going to tell me what is best for my daughter? Jacqueline is mine, do you hear me? Mine. She is my special girl, the one who loves me like any good girl should love her father. I will take care of her . . . I have done so in the past, and will do so again.' Miller paused for a second, held out his arms and spoke directly to his daughter. 'Jacqueline, come to me, come to your daddy.' Silence. For one highly charged moment nothing happened; no one moved, no one dared speak. Then, with a sudden movement of her shoulders, Jacqueline shook herself free from Dr Belcher. With a jerk of the head, she responded to Miller. Before Dr Belcher could stop her, she had moved into the open arms in front of her. A triumphant smile settled on Jim Miller's face. He embraced her. 'You see,' he said, throwing a quick glance to Belcher and Emma, 'my little girl still loves her daddy.'

By the time Emma spotted the knife in Jacqueline's hand, the weapon had already began its lightening fast upward trajectory. The triumphant sneer on Jim Miller's smiling face shattered. A look of terror took its place. The knife's blade, propelled by Jacqueline, rammed into his crotch. Blood dripped from the blade as Jacqueline withdrew it.

Miller screamed.

His hands shot to the area where the knife had left its mark. He began to stagger backwards. Blood oozed from between his fingers. His eyes opened wide in disbelief. Unable to remain upright, he collapsed on to his back. Jacqueline leaped like some wild animal on top of him. In a mad frenzy, she drove the knife repeatedly into his stomach and chest, all the time screaming unintelligibly. Dr Belcher, first to react to the carnage, hauled Jacqueline off Miller's bloodied body. The struggle ended as abruptly as it had begun. Jacqueline lay on the floor, her hands, face and clothes splattered in blood. She remained silent, her eyes closed, her body rising and falling with great gasping breaths. Beside her, Jim Miller lay still, blood flowing freely from a body that had already ceased to breathe. Damien Conway, ashen-faced, shaking violently, turned to get out of the room but vomited on the kitchen floor before he made it to the door.

A thunderous roar filled the air.

At first it sounded like the house was about to crash down about them but Emma recognised the sound of a helicopter. The unmistakable clatter of rotor blades sounded as though they were about to slice through the walls of the house when, after several seconds, the numbing noise began slowly to ease in volume. Dennis Bowen, who had remained immobile and open-mouthed during the terrible altercation between Miller and his daughter, snapped back into life. 'Sounds like help has arrived,' he said as the reverberation continued to pierce the air. He opened the door into the living room and looked out the front window. Emma moved to his side. She watched as the helicopter, with its great rotors still spinning, sat on the open space across the road from the house. The machine was mostly white and had the word Garda printed on a yellow strip that ran horizontally along the body work. With a shudder, the engines stopped. Only the sound of blades slicing through the air at ever decreasing revolutions remained. Emma was surprised when she recognised the bulky body that opened the cabin door. She turned to Dennis Bowen.

'It's Detective Inspector Lawlor,' she said, concern in her voice. 'Could you keep an eye on Mrs McCall while I talk to him . . . I'll fill him in on what's happened here.' Without saying a word, Dennis moved back into the kitchen, apparently glad to let Emma handle the detective.

Lawlor leaped from the helicopter's cabin, ducked beneath the slowing rotors and headed towards the house. After what had just taken place inside the house, Emma was numbed to further shocks but she did wonder how it was that Lawlor managed to arrive in Rathkenny at such an opportune time. She moved into the hallway and had the front door opened in time to see Lawlor cut between the Post van and the Conway's Mercedes coupé before he pounded his way up the garden path, kicking the gate open in the process. He stopped abruptly when he caught sight of her. 'Holy shit,' he cursed, 'I don't need this. I should have guessed you'd be here. Wherever there's trouble, I'm bound to find Emma Boylan.'

'For once in my life I'm actually glad to see you,' Emma said, blocking his entry to the house. 'We've a very delicate situation inside the house. Let me tell you what the story is before you go rushing in there; it might save a lot of confusion.'

'Get out of my way, Emma,' he said brushing her to one side. 'Conway's car is still here, that's all I need to know; I've got him.'

'What are you talking about? You don't seriously believe Damien Conway had anything to do with what happened to Alan McCall?'

Ignoring Emma's protestations, making no attempt to answer her question, Lawlor pushed his way through the hallway and into the kitchen. What he saw stopped him in his tracks. For a moment he stood there, saying nothing, amazed by the scene in front of him. He looked at the blood-soaked body of Jim Miller, then at Jacqueline Miller. She had crumpled into a foetal position, lying comatose at the feet of Dr Belcher. In the centre of the kitchen, positioned beside an upturned table, Dennis Bowen held a blanket around the shoulders of Sarah McCall. Lawlor stared at Damien Conway, the object of his helicopter chase – as the young man propped himself against a wall, his head bent over a pool of vomit. A sickly drool continued to dribble from Conway's mouth.

For several seconds, no one said anything as Lawlor tried to take in the almost surreal tableau in front of him. For once, he seemed genuinely stunned by what confronted him. 'I'm calling for back-up,' he said, punching numbers on his mobile phone, 'in the meantime, will someone tell me what the fuck has happened here?'

31

Never before had Rathkenny experienced anything like it. It was as though the sleepy little town had been whacked by a thunderbolt and knocked into another dimension. First there had been the spectacle of the silver Mercedes screeching through the narrow streets, frightening the wits out of the townsfolk as it streaked past them. This had been followed ten minutes later by the sight of a helicopter landing, a first for Rathkenny, and then, just as speculation in the town reached its zenith, three garda cars came speeding through the town, blue lights flashing, followed swiftly by an ambulance, its siren blaring. But the thing that really got the tongues wagging was the parish priest, Father McCormick, a man never known to push his Ford Fiesta past the thirty miles per hour mark, doing at least forty-five on his way to the McCall household. And, as if that were not enough, both of the town's physicians – Dr Alan Parkinson and Dr Avril Brady – were seen, within seconds of each other, heading in the same directions.

Some of the more inquisitive residents, unable to contain their curiosity any longer, decided to investigate the unprecedented activity and made their way to the scene. By the time they arrived, two members of the Garda Síochána were already in the process of placing a cordon around the house. Everyone had questions on their lips. Had there been a robber, a murder maybe? Was Sarah McCall in trouble? Premature birth perhaps? Had her two boys been kidnapped? The two garda officers were no help; they said they were as much in the dark as everyone else. The residents found this hard to swallow but it was the truth; the two gardaí had not been allowed inside the house.

Lawlor had been there only three or four minutes when the ambulance arrived to take Sarah McCall to Kilkenny hospital. As soon as the distraught woman had been carried out the door, Emma explained to Lawlor what had happened in the house. Lawlor had been furious at finding Emma in the house but, in spite of all the misgivings he had about her, he trusted her enough to believe her account of what had happened. What she had to tell him made him most uncomfortable. Jacqueline Miller, in the guise of John Christie, she informed him, had murdered both Alan McCall and Jim Miller. At first he did not fully comprehend what she was saying and thought she might be suffering from shock but eventually she convinced him that something totally out of the ordinary had happened. Eventually, she got through to him that Jacqueline Miller and John Christie were one and the same person and that she had killed Alan McCall and Jim Miller. Lawlor remained sceptical and seemed genuinely aggrieved that he would not now be taking Damien Conway into custody. With the body of Jim Miller lying dead on the floor and

Jacqueline Miller being attended by Tim Belcher and Dr Avril Brady, Lawlor had set about taking charge of proceedings. Miller's body could not be moved until the state pathologist arrived from Dublin; so he started taking steps to preserve the scene from interference or undue intrusions.

It was at this point that Rathkenny's local sergeant, a burly, ginger-haired man in his fifties named Bill O'Sullivan, barged his way into the house. Gesticulating wildly with two huge hands, he informed Lawlor that he, as local sergeant, had jurisdiction in Rathkenny and no jumped-up Johnny from Dublin, irrespective of rank, race or religion had the power to encroach on his patch. Emma, who had been witness to this little verbal spat, expected Lawlor to throw a tantrum and was surprised when the Detective Inspector gave the appearance of complying with the sergeant's wishes. Moving aside, without protest, Lawlor began punching a series of numbers on his mobile phone and waited to get through to garda headquarters in Phoenix Park. While waiting to be connected to his superiors, he watched O'Sullivan's amateurish attempts to preserve the crime scene. Lawlor shuddered; the whole operation was degenerating into a shambles. By now the local doctor and the parish priest had arrived. O'Sullivan afforded both men the status of dignitaries and allowed them to move unhindered around the kitchen, unintentionally destroying evidence, sometimes stepping over the dead body of Jim Miller in the process, with little or no regard for adhering to proper crime-scene procedures.

For the sergeant, the murder of Jim Miller represented the most momentous event in his career and he was, it seemed to Emma, treating the occasion with unseemly enthusiasm. Looking at the flush of anticipation in the sergeant's face, she could visualise his thought process in action, conjuring up images of himself as the focus of national attention. He was, she suspected, already imagining the hoards of media personnel that would soon swamp the town with their cameras, microphones and notebooks, all wanting to interview him. O'Sullivan could not disguise his innermost feelings of importance any more than he could conceal the tingle of excitement running through his body.

His anticipated notion of glory received its first setback when Lawlor, sporting his ever-present egregious sneer, handed him the mobile phone. 'The commissioner would like a word with you, Sergeant O'Sullivan,' Lawlor said. O'Sullivan sighed, a sigh of irritation, took the phone in his spade-like hand and pressed it to his ear. The look of disappointment on his face spoke more effectively than any words ever could.

'Looks like I must hand over command to you, Detective Inspector,' he said to Lawlor after he had finished the call, 'I'm to take my orders from you.'

'Good, I'm glad that little bit of business is sorted out,' Lawlor said, enjoying his new authority. 'Now here's what I want you and your boys to do.'

Emma slipped away from the two men as Lawlor began to issue orders; she wanted to talk to Dr Tim Belcher alone. But she would have to wait a while longer.

Belcher was talking to Dr Avril Brady beside the couch where they had placed Jacqueline Miller. Earlier, Emma had listened as Belcher advised the local doctor on Jacqueline's condition. Both doctors had agreed that she should be sedated as a temporary measure until the special ambulance arrived to take her back to Dublin. While waiting to talk to Belcher, Emma took the opportunity to file a report to the *Post* on what happened in Rathkenny. Even as she gave details of the events, non-stop activity continued all around her.

Sergeant O'Sullivan, she could see, had put the disappointment of being consigned to second place in the investigation to one side and adopted a positive role in helping to sort matters out. He detailed one of his men to accompany Dennis Bowen to the school where Sarah McCall's two boys attended. The sergeant, aware that the twins would require special attention, knew they would feel less frightened if the news of their mother's hospitalisation came from Bowen, their friendly postman, rather than a uniformed member of the gardaí. Bowen waved goodbye to Emma, obviously relieved to get away from the house. He had agreed with O'Sullivan that the best thing he could do would be to drive Stephen and John to their grandmother's house in Waterford, get them as far away as possible from the media circus that would inevitably descend on their home.

Using the telephone in the hallway to the *Post*, Emma could see that Damien Conway had locked himself inside the small bathroom situated on the half-landing above her head. She could hear him flush the toilet on regular basis. This gushing and gurgling of water was accompanied by another more human activity; the sound of Damien puking into the toilet bowl. He had been there for over twenty minutes already and showed no sign of emerging. She could sympathise with him. Watching his Aunt Jac stab Jim Miller was bound to have a most profound effect on the young man. She had seen him stand immobile, as though turned to stone, while the horror lasted, his mouth agape, his eyes wide open, seeing and not seeing at the same time, until the dreadful deed had concluded. It was at that point that he had fallen to his knees, opened his mouth in order to scream but only succeeded in retching instead. Damien Conway, it was clear to her, was in a state of deep shock and in need of help.

After filing her report to the *Post,* Emma finally managed to get Belcher's attention and had persuaded him to join her in what used to be Alan McCall's 'constituents' clinic'. The room, in marked contrast to the rest of the house, lacked warmth and character. With an oversized teak desk, several office chairs, a glass-top coffee table set on a chrome frame, and floor to ceiling shelves filled with ledgers and dull-looking reports, it was obvious that this was one area where Sarah McCall had little input. Emma ignored the austere surroundings as she took a seat and faced the psychiatrist. She wanted answers from Belcher; she needed to know much more about Jacqueline Miller's disorder; she required explanations for the bizarre behaviour she had witnessed before the brutal stabbing to death of Jim Miller.

Firstly, she explained to him about her mistaken belief in thinking that Jim Miller, and not his daughter Jacqueline, had been his patient. Belcher gave her a little smile that said he understood. 'I did try to point out that you were jumping to the wrong conclusions but I had to be absolutely sure myself about my patient before I could speak.'

'What I don't understand is this: since Jacqueline is your patient, how was it that I found your name among Jim Miller's possessions?'

'From what you have told me earlier, it seems that Jim Miller kept close tabs on his daughter, hoarding press cuttings, photographs and the like. He probably followed her to my clinic on one of her visits and simply wrote down the name and address.'

'I still don't know how I could have got it so wrong. I never – not for a single moment – thought Jacqueline Miller was the one who posed a threat to Sarah McCall.'

'You might have got your Millers mixed up but if it hadn't been for you, Sarah McCall would probably be dead by now. Be grateful you saved her life and the life of her unborn baby.'

'Yes, I can see that . . . and I am. Of course, I'm grateful. But how could I have been so wrong about Jacqueline?'

'Look, let me try to explain. To understand you need to know where all this started. I've been treating Jacqueline Miller for the past six years, but the trouble began a long time before that. As a young girl, Jacqueline Miller was subjected to the most appalling treatment: she was raped.'

'Raped? Jacqueline Miller was raped?'

'Yes, I regret to say, but worse still, the person who raped her was her own father, Jim Miller.'

'Bloody hell!'

'Yes, a real nightmare for the child. He continued to rape her for a period of years. To survive the intolerable traumas, Jacqueline developed defences.'

'What do you mean defences?'

'She developed the ability to slip into another consciousness, into what we call a state of personality dissociation. In effect she brought about an amnesia which allowed her to blank out what her father was doing to her. During these blank periods, new invented personalities inhabited the vacuum. These were different identities; they were the ones that carried the terrible burden that Jacqueline refused to face.'

'Are you saying that these personalities, although living in her body, could lead their own independent lives?

'Yes, in a manner of speaking; you see, when these separate personalities take charge, Jacqueline Miller, as we know her, experiences periods of blankness and could be said to disappear. Today, for instance, before her frenzied attack on her father, what you saw was a manifestation of two of her alternating selves.'

'You've seen these changes before?'

'Yes, Emma, on many occasions. The child's voice

we heard coming from her is a regular. That child – her name is Jenny Swan – is forever eleven years of age, trapped in a timewarp, forever absorbing horrors that were inflicted on her – horrors that Jacqueline Miller is unable to face up to as herself.' Dr Belcher looked at Emma as though trying to ascertain if he should tell her more. After a short pause he spoke again. 'Jacqueline's most frequent dissociative manifestation of late has been male.'

'You mean John Christie?'

'Yes, I do, Emma. Jacqueline Miller has found the means of dealing with recent upheavals in her life by dissociating into John Christie. In Christie, she has found an aggressor to fight her corner in a world that has dealt her one cruel blow after another. I first met the John Christie personality six years ago. It was after Jacqueline's motoring accident. I didn't know it then but in the intervening years I've concluded that the stress of the crash and the impending marriage was what triggered his appearance at the time. Christie represents the very darkest thoughts in her mind, the kind of thoughts that she would never believe she harboured there. You must understand, Emma, that the mind is a strange entity and none of us know what kind of abnormalities might remain hidden in its multi-layered recesses. People like Jacqueline, people who are subject to DID, allow us to get a glimpse of what's hidden inside all of us. Luckily, most of us do not have to go through what she is experiencing.'

'But John Christie . . . John Christie is male, talks like

a man, even dresses like a man . . . '

'Whenever an alternative personality takes charge, he or she dresses to suit it. In that respect they have nothing to do with Jacqueline Miller's own taste.'

'And the voice?'

'Same thing. We all have the power to create many contortions with our vocal cords – we just don't bother all that much to do so. With DID, voices, diction and vocabulary present themselves in different ways, ways appropriate to the different selves. Even their ages, as well as their sex, can be different.'

'How did you discover that Jacqueline Miller was subject to the disorder?'

'She was referred to me by an eminent doctor who had helped patch her up after the dreadful road accident. Jacqueline Miller commenced a series of intensive therapy sessions with me then. Those visits continued for two years uninterrupted. I believed then that I had alleviated her problems.'

'Well, it's fairly clear from what we both witnessed here today that you did not, wouldn't you say?' Emma remarked.

'True, I'm afraid, you're right. Since the death of Alan McCall, I've had a number of visits from Jacqueline, as herself, as Jenny, but mostly as John Christie. It seems obvious now that this time Christie was triggered into existence when Jacqueline discovered that McCall's wife was pregnant.'

'Why do you say that?'

'It represents yet another betrayal for her. She just

couldn't accept that the man who swore he loved her could at the same time make his wife pregnant.'

'So, Jacqueline Miller killed Alan McCall.'

'No, you're wrong again; you don't understand what I'm telling you. Jacqueline Miller is no more capable of killing another human being than you or I am.'

'But I saw Jacqueline Miller kill . . .'

'No, what you saw was John Christie. You saw John Christie, acting as her protector, kill Jim Miller. And we can now say with certainty, it was Christie who killed Alan McCall. Jacqueline Miller would never be capable of carrying out such a deed but Christie would have had no such qualms.'

'I'd call that splitting hairs,' Emma said. Before she had a chance to voice further doubts on the subject, Lawlor entered the room. 'And I'd also call that splitting hairs,' he said, for once, agreeing with Emma. 'We're not going to be fooled by all this nonsense about another personality being responsible for the deed.'

'Nobody is trying to fool anyone,' Belcher said curtly. 'Whether you want to believe it or not Dissociative Identity Disorder is an accepted disorder.'

'We'll soon find out all about that,' Lawlor said. 'Dr Lee Bracken, our own criminal psychiatrist, is on his way here as we speak. He works with us on all that new criminal-profiling stuff. He has access to worldwide databases storing details of thousands of murder cases; knows all the scams. He'll soon cut through the crap here and tell us what's what.'

'He'll agree with me,' Belcher said, defiantly. 'I know

of Dr Bracken's reputation and I've read all of his papers on the subject of profiling and DNA. He knows criminal science and he'll understand, as I do, how DID has become relevant in the forensic field, how it plays a significant part in a case such as this because of the issue of criminal responsibilities. I'll give him Jacqueline Miller's files and he'll have all the evidence he needs to see that the woman is not mentally fit to stand trial. He'll confirm that she is in need of psychiatric care for a long time to come.'

Abruptly, their conversation halted. The ear-splitting clamour of a helicopter landing outside the house drowned out all other sounds. Because the garda helicopter was already in Rathkenny, at the behest of Lawlor, the forensic team had used one of the Air-Corps' five hi-tech Dauphins to airlift them to the scene. For the people in the village of Rathkenny, this day would be long remembered as the day two helicopters had landed in their town. Dr Tara O'Reilly, the assistant state pathologist, along with Dr Lee Bracken, the garda criminal psychiatrist, and a four-man forensic team had arrived. No sooner had the aircraft made its noisy landing than an ambulance, complete with wailing siren, screeched to a halt outside the house. It was in this vehicle that Jacqueline Miller would be consigned to whatever mental institution the two psychiatrists deemed fit to send her, provided that Lawlor did not have his way and have her transferred to some jail cell instead.

Lawlor escorted the pathologist to where Miller's

body lay and then introduced Dr Lee Bracken, the garda criminal psychiatrist to Tim Belcher. He instructed both men to report to him within ten minutes. 'I'll feel a lot happier,' he told them, 'when Jacqueline Miller is secure under lock and key.' He paused for a moment, pointedly ignored Belcher, then turned to the garda psychiatrist 'I'm fed-up pussy-footing around here, listening to a lot of mumbo-jumbo, so I need your professional opinion, Dr Bracken, as to whether I bring this murderer into custody, charge her and have her locked up or let you take her to the loony farm.' Not waiting for a response from either of the two psychiatrists, he turned to Emma and pointed her in the direction of the door. 'I want you out of here now.'

'But I need to see, that is, I need to talk . . .'

'I don't give a twopenny fuck what you need! I want you out of my hair, out of my way, out of my sight, away from the crime scene, on your bike . . . now.'

'But Dr Belcher came here with me in my car. He . . .'

'I'll arrange to get Dr Belcher back to Dublin. I want you out of here now or do I have to throw you out?'

'OK! OK! No need to get rough, I'm going . . . I'm going.'

32

Haunted by reflections of the dreadful events she had witnessed in Rathkenny, Emma headed north for Dublin. Fragmented scenes, horror images bathed in a crimson whirlpool of blood, remained locked inside her head. In the vivid after-images, Jim Miller's eyes, wide open but dead, stared at her from his position on Sarah McCall's kitchen floor. The lifeless eyes challenged her. She blinked, shook her head, shattered the image, and attempted to concentrate instead on the traffic all around her. The road back to Dublin was a particularly dangerous stretch, accounting for weekly fatalities, so she would need her wits about her if she were to preserve her own chances of mortality. It wasn't easy. Even now, hours after the events, she found it next to impossible to come to terms with what she had witnessed. Incredible as it seemed, she had watched Jacqueline kill Jim Miller, watched a distraught daughter kill her father. Never had she seen anything so violent. She winced involuntarily. Observing the murder, seeing blood spout from multiple stab wounds was something she never wanted to see again. And yet, in spite of the appalling way Jim Miller met his death, she could not find it in her heart to feel sorry for the man. So much for her Christian upbringing, she thought, so much for the central tenet of forgiveness, but the truth was, her sympathy and sorrow went more to the person who had carried out the terrible deed than to the so-called victim. What had driven Jacqueline Miller to do such a thing? Alan McCall? Yes, he must share in the blame, but she had no doubt that the real author of Jacqueline's destruction was her father. The more she thought about it, the more she wanted answers to her questions. What sort of a man subjected his daughter to the horrors he had inflicted on her? What sort of monster had Jim Miller been?

Only this morning she had believed Jim Miller was the murderer. She had been positive he was the one posing as John Christie. She had been wrong on both counts. But she had been right in believing that he was thoroughly evil. Although he had not personally murdered Alan McCall, his crimes against his daughter when she was a child had surely precipitated the killing. Did that make him a murderer? Yes, Emma decided. She thought of Jim Miller as a coward, a man who liked to assert his manhood and power over children and young impressionable girls.

Forced to break hard when a speeding motorist swerved on to her lane to avoid colliding with on-coming traffic she cursed and honked her horn. For her trouble, the offending driver gave her the two-finger salute as he continued to pass out several cars ahead of her, lane-jumping with impunity. Emma dismissed the erratic driver and his infantile gesture from her thoughts and resumed her amateur psychoanalysis of

Jim Miller. One thing she felt certain of: Miller had never shown respect for anyone and probably despised himself. It was only as stage characters that he could feel confident and accept praise and adulation. How many other shattered lives, apart from Jacqueline's, had he left behind in his wake! It was not a question she could answer; she could not even hazard a guess but she was sure that his legacy would remain one of pain, suffering and misery. A dreadful thought occurred to her, not a Christian thought, but she could not help thinking that society was better off without Jim Miller.

Her thoughts shifted to Damien Conway. For him the tragedy would probably hit hardest. He had watched his aunt kill his grandfather and learned that she was also responsible for the murder of Alan McCall. It was no wonder that his world had shattered. Emma found it hard not to feel sorry for the young man; as far as she could tell he had been an innocent victim in the whole affair. He would, Emma hoped, when things calmed down, prove some comfort to Jacqueline in the dark days that undoubtedly lay ahead.

One other question bothered Emma: Frankie Kelly's death. It was the photographer's bad luck to be the one to discover the link between Jacqueline Miller and Alan McCall. And for that, he had paid the ultimate price. Yet, it was equally clear to Emma that Jacqueline Miller had no hand in his death. Emma took what comfort she could from knowing that the culprit would not get away with the crime. Jimmy Rabbitte knew the identity of the two hired killers who had smashed up his house and injected the lethal drug concoction into Frankie's arm. The fact that they had mistaken Frankie for Rabbitte made no difference to the end result. But it was the identity of the person who hired Lawlor that intrigued Emma. Rabbitte, when he spoke to her on the telephone, had pointed the finger in the government's direction.

Rabbitte was right, Emma decided. It had to be the government. Who else? Only the government had something to lose if Rabbitte talked. Only the government would benefit if he were taken out of the picture. And if she accepted the hypothesis that the government was responsible, however far-fetched it might appear, it followed, as surely as night follows day, that Fionnuala Stafford had to be the guilty person.

Emma had given the subject plenty of thought since the dreadful day when she had found Frankie Kelly with the syringe in his arm. Another image to return to her time and time again was the picture of Lawlor and Fionnuala Stafford talking together in Government Buildings. That in itself proved nothing but it was interesting that Frankie Kelly was dead twenty-four hours later. Getting real proof of such a conspiracy would not be easy – it never was – but it would not deter her; the opposite was true, it would spur her on. She had won against what seemed like impossible odds before.

Her thoughts were suddenly derailed. The ringing of her mobile phone demanded her attention. Bob Crosby was on the line but his words were breaking up. She asked him to hang up and told him she would call him back as soon as she pulled her car to the side of the road. The stretch of road she was travelling on, half way between Carlow and Naas was particularly heavy with traffic, her small Volvo finding itself wedged between a huge oil lorry and an even bigger truck pulling a Guinness container. Passing out was not an option – the oncoming traffic was equally heavy – so she decided to pull off the road when she got a chance. She would have to wait until she got to the next village or town to make contact with her editor. From the few brief words she had managed to unscramble from his call, it seemed to her that Bob Crosby was in an unusually good mood. That made a pleasant change, she thought, attributing praise to herself for having been the one responsible for putting her boss in that good mood. Earlier, back in McCall's house, she had a brief word with him when she contacted the *Post* to file her report. He had been shocked by the news but unable to hide his delight at what the story would do for the paper's circulation. She assumed that Crosby's reason for wanting to talk to her now was in relation to that report; he was probably looking for some additional details or clarification on some point or other.

Ten miles south of the Nass bypass, on the N9, Emma guided her car to a stop in front of Monaghan's Liquor Emporium, a modern pub of unclear architectural intent, and punched the numbers that would connect her to Bob Crosby's direct line. Almost immediately, Crosby's voice resonated clearly through the tiny earpiece on her mobile. 'Emma, can you hear me?'

'Yes, Bob, loud and clear this time. What's up?'

'Well, for a start we've hit the streets with your story. The public are lapping it up, huge reaction, great headline. 'McCall's mistress is murder suspect'. How do you like that? It has all the right ingredients: sex, politics, lies, unsuspecting wife, murder, the lot. We're selling newspapers like hot cakes . . . but it gets better, Emma.'

'What do you mean?'

'Finding McCall's killer is not the end of the story; it's just the beginning.'

'You've lost me, Bob.'

'Two things have happened that'll give the story legs and make it run and run. First thing: our friend Jimmy Rabbitte has come up trumps, big time. I've just got his report on the Frankie Kelly killing and I can tell you, Emma, it's pure gold. He has given us times, dates, places and names. If even half of it checks out, it puts Lawlor in the frame. We've got him Emma, we've got Lawlor! Can you believe it?'

'Yes, Bob, I do believe it. Lawlor is going down; myself and Jimmy Rabbitte will see to it. I've never been more sure of anything in my life. But even after we've nailed him, there is the person who hired him to think about. I won't rest happy until I've exposed the person who put Lawlor up to it.'

'Well, now Emma, that might happen sooner than

you think. I told you I had two things to tell you . . . and the second item could be even more dramatic than the first. It could also tie in neatly with Frankie Kelly's death.'

'Come on, Bob, what are you going on about?'

'Tom Pettit, that's what I'm talking about. Word has it that Tom Pettit is coming apart at the seams. We've got a strong indication, from a usually reliable source, that Pettit is about to go public on Fionnuala Stafford's role in the attempt to coverup the whole Alan McCall affair.'

'I find that hard to believe, Bob. Fionnuala Stafford is the one who just appointed him Minister for Agriculture. He's less than a week in the job for God's sake. Why would he want to rock the boat now, especially now that we all know who killed Alan McCall?'

'Oh, you're right, Emma, it makes no sense, no sense at all; political suicide if you ask me but that's the story. Word has it that he's really pissed at Fionnuala Stafford . . . has taken exception to the way she handled the whole scandal.'

'So why did he accept the promotion? Why did he wait until now to discover his conscience bothered him?'

'Pettit knows that his appointment was one of expediency, given to him to smooth out current difficulties. He knows that Stafford had the job earmarked for Alan McCall originally. Getting the job by default has hurt his pride; he feels he should have been given the position in the first place on the basis of merit.

You know what they say, Emma – a politician scorned can be a very dangerous animal.'

'So he's doing this for spite, willing to sacrifice his job because of wounded pride? It's hard to credit.'

'I'll tell you what I think, Emma. I think there's more going on here than meets the eye; that's why I want you here as fast as your legs can carry you. I want you to start digging. If Pettit is coming apart, we could see a whole new can of worms open. We know there is something dodgy about the way Francis Xavier Donnelly was drummed out of his job in disgrace. Only Pettit can tell us the background to what really happened.'

'You could be right, Bob,' Emma said, affected by his enthusiasm. 'If Pettit talks, then Francis Xavier Donnelly's part in the attempted cover up is bound to be exposed – and we all know where that'll lead to: Stafford herself.'

'Damn right,' Crosby said, 'Pettit will probably make the link between Lawlor, Fionnuala Stafford and the murder of Frankie Kelly.'

'Coupled with what myself and Rabbitte can dig up, Fionnuala Stafford will be exposed once and for all. She'll be finished.'

'She's already finished, Emma, all that remains is that we bury her. We are about to witness a great scandal unfold before us. Pettit knows that the government's time is up and rather than wait for the inevitable, rather than go down with the ship, he wants to be seen as the one who blew the whistle and get out with some degree of honour.'

As Emma sat in her car listening to her boss, an ambulance passed by, going in the direction of the city. She had no doubt it was the ambulance ferrying Jacqueline Miller to whatever institution she was bound for. Emma found herself making an involuntary sigh. It was impossible not to speculate on what the future held for the unfortunate woman. Emma's thoughts were interrupted by the sound of Crosby's voice on her mobile. 'Emma, you still there?'

'Yes, Bob, I'm still here.'

'Well, you'd better get a move on. Come straight to the office when you get back to the city. This Tom Pettit thing is going to be big; I've a list of items I want you to follow up on.'

'Yes, Bob, I'm on my way.'

Emma put the mobile down and waited for a break in the stream of traffic before edging her way on to the road again. The evening sky had darkened considerably, drops of rain spat on the windscreen, a prelude to the oncoming downpour she could see mustering its forces in the looming clouds in the distance. She switched the wipers to 'intermittent' mode. It was only now she realised how exhausted she felt. The last few days had taken a lot out of her; the events in Rathkenny had drained her, but just when she thought she had earned a respite from it all, just when she thought she could relax a little, spend some time with Vinny, do some of the things normal engaged couples were supposed to do, a whole new set of problems had presented themslves. Well, that was fine as far as she was concerned, that was what made her job exciting. But exciting or not, she did not intend to go directly to her office as Bob Crosby had demanded. She had a far better idea in mind. She decided she would go home, take a nice long bath, share a meal with Vinny and make love for one whole night without interruption. Adjusting the windscreen wipers to 'fast' mode, she began to smile as she thought about the prospect. For once, there was something refreshing about the pouring rain. She watched the silver arrowheads strike the windscreen and experienced a strange cleansing process take place. It was as though the downpour effectively washed away the dreadful deeds of the past few days. Like a watercolour painting exposed to rain, the images merged, the colours and shapes overlapped each other before evaporating, leaving nothing but the faintest trace of what had been there. For one beautiful mad moment, the thought crossed her mind that it would be nice, liberating even, to stop the car, strip naked and run through the rain with her arms outstretched, purify her soul, wash away the residue of the awfulness that clung to her, but the impulse passed quickly. More than anything else, she needed to get home to Vinny. Yes, she told herself, it was time to let the man she loved know just how much she loved him.

After a prolonged bout of lovemaking, Vinny lay with his arms around Emma and listened as she recounted what had happened in Sarah McCall's house. Vinny would have prefered to go to sleep but Emma was determined not to let him. After a longer than usual pause, she gently nudged Vinny to make sure he was still awake. 'It's extraordinary all the same,' she said, 'to think that two women could be made to suffer so much at the hands of men who should have known better.'

'That's right, Emma, blame it all on the men. Isn't it enough that the two men are dead?'

'They're dead, yes. For them it has ended. But for the two women it goes on and on; for Sarah McCall and for Jacqueline Miller the agony goes on.'

'Would you prefer they were dead too?'

Emma elbowed him playfully in the side. 'No, of course not, don't be stupid. But it's not fair; they're supposed to pick up the pieces and go on living. Tell me, Vinny, why are men such shits?'

'Ah, come on now, Emma, ease up. Not all men are bad – and not all women are angels.'

'Maybe not but I'm just saying how it looks to me right now. Jim Miller started the trouble and Alan McCall finished it. I don't know which of them I attach the greater blame to.'

Vinny thought about that for a moment before replying. 'I think Jim Miller was a sick bastard, and I agree with you that society is better off without him. In that respect, Jacqueline Miller did us all a favour.'

'And what blame do you attach to Alan McCall?'

'I think that what Alan McCall did was cruel. He cheated on two good women and ruined both of their lives, and all in the pursuit of selfish pleasure.'

'You're right, Vinny. McCall was willing to risk everything, without regard for anyone else . . . and all for his own self-centred needs. To him, Jacqueline represented nothing more than a bit on the side.'

'I've never seen it any other way. You know what they say: a standing dick has no conscience. But what amazes me in the case of Alan McCall is that neither of the two women had any suspicion that he was cheating.'

'I suppose the man was a very convincing liar.'

'Yes, but even so, you'd expect a woman to know if the man she is making love to is, at the same time, sexually active with another woman.'

Emma gave a little chuckle. 'You think so, eh?'

'Yes, I do. A man would certainly know. I'd know in an instant if you were unfaithful to me.'

'You would?'

'Yes, remember that evening in this apartment when your friend Lawlor tried to insinuate that you and that photographer, Frankie Kelly, might have been up to something.'

'Yes, I remember,' Emma said, wondering where this conversation was going.

'Well, if you really had any romantic leanings towards Kelly, I'd have known immediately.'

'You'd have known? How?'

'Instinct, my dear. It's a man thing. It's something us males are born with.'

'Um; goodnight, Vinny.'